The Truthful Lie

The Unwritten Words III

ALSO BY CHRISTOPHER G. NUTTALL

The Mind's Eye

Bookworm series
Bookworm
Bookworm II: The Very Ugly Duckling
Bookworm III: The Best Laid Plans
Bookworm IV: Full Circle

Unwritten Words series
I: The Promised Lie
II: The Ancient Lie

DIZZY SPELLS SERIES
A LIFE LESS ORDINARY

Royal Sorceress series
The Royal Sorceress
The Great Game
Necropolis
Sons of Liberty

INVERSE SHADOWS UNIVERSE
SUFFICIENTLY ADVANCED TECHNOLOGY

The Truthful Lie

The Unwritten Words III

Christopher G. Nuttall

Elsewhen Press

Prologue I

Imagine ... imagine two worlds.

One of them is human, as common and comprehensible to us as our own. People are born, grow up, marry, have children and die ... a pattern we understand, even if we do not slavishly follow it. The rules are universal, binding everyone; they are relatively simple, understandable and have few loopholes. The rules themselves are unbreakable.

The other world – realm, really – is so inhuman as to be beyond our comprehension. It is a single point that is both infinitely large and impossibly tiny at the same time. It does not, in fact, have time, not in any sense that humans would understand. The inhabitants of the alien realm are eternal, bounded within their universe and yet unbounded by cause and effect, by the harsh and unsentimental rules of the human world. They are, in effect, patterns of energy shaped by ideas ... ideas that are so inhuman, we literally do not have words to describe them. They are – they were – so different from us that their world and ours were never intended to meet.

But they did.

Historical records from that time have been lost in a haze of pain, horror and simple incomprehension, but certain things are clear. The direct contact between humans and the idea entities was utterly devastating. Human minds shattered under pressure from entities so powerful as to defy understanding, human society bent and broke as the laws of the known universe twisted and warped through the presence of the entities. The entities themselves were exposed to cause and effect for the first time in eternity, to the loves and lusts and hates they found utterly incomprehensible. Both sides recoiled, tearing at themselves in a fruitless bid to save themselves from madness. The universe screamed in pain as the Old Gods took form. They ruled for an eternity.

And then the New Gods arrived. Born of contact with

human minds, shaped by human thought and belief, they united the power of both races. They turned on their parents, sealing them back into the realm of ideas. They sought to rule as the God-Kings of Eternity, to command both races in a quest for glory everlasting. Everyone would bow and praise their names. Their rule, it seemed, would never end.

But the New Gods had underestimated their human allies. Determined to free themselves, the humans united their world and turned on their former masters, using powers and knowledge they'd gleaned from the New Gods to lock them out of the human realm. The New Gods howled in frustration as they fell back into the realm of ideas, the Godly Realm, and watched helplessly as all knowledge of them was erased from the world. What could not be destroyed was sealed off, left to rot until time and tide removed it from living memory. The purge was terrifyingly complete. Little knowledge of the entities lingered for the Bookworm, many thousands of years later, to absorb when she triggered an ancient trap and started the chain of events that brought the Empire down.

All that time, the New Gods were waiting. Timeless, they could wait for eternity. Humans being humans, they didn't have to. The Fall of the Empire shattered the barriers keeping the New Gods from returning to the human realm. They could only advance slowly, at least at first, but smaller creatures – shadows that had haunted humanity's nightmares since the New Gods were driven out – went ahead. The New Gods made contracts, offering power and prominence and everything else the humans wanted … in exchange for worship and unthinking servitude. And, on the Summer Isle, they made their first beachhead. The death of the former monarch ensured their tool, Lord Havant the Usurper and his sister, Queen Emetine, were in position to take control. It looked as though they could not be stopped.

They couldn't have known that Crown Prince Reginald of Andalusia would mount a bid for the Summer Isle himself. Claiming that the former king had left his kingdom to King Romulus XIII of Andalusia, Reginald and his ally, Isabella the Sorceress, led an army to the Summer Isle. There, they encountered the entities and their pawns in open battle, winning through a combination of luck, guile and exploiting rules they did not – yet – understand. Their victory, however, came at a price. The entities – and Queen Emetine – made the jump to Andalusia and took control. Thinking themselves safe, they reached into the heart and souls of everyone in the kingdom … and began to secure their power.

Reginald returned, to discover his father a broken shell of a man and his sister in servitude to the entities. Forced to fight for his kingdom, Reginald drove the entities back to one of their old haunts in a final, desperate bid to stop them. There, the entities performed a ritual to bring one of the most dangerous New Gods back into the world. They succeeded …

… And now, the entire world is in dreadful danger.

This is, of course, the truth.

But … it is also a lie.

Prologue II

Kings didn't shake.

King Forsyth of Zycrest sat in the tower and shook. It was undignified, to say the least, for an absolute monarch to shake, but he couldn't help himself. The fear – the fear of *everything* – had pervaded his mind for years, well before his father had died in glorious battle and Forsyth had inherited the throne. He'd been cursed, perhaps. His father had been a brave man, a man who'd been easy to follow if not to like, but Forsyth was a coward. He could barely get out of bed each morning, let alone make the hard decisions. He was so afraid of everything that he'd shut himself up in the tower and hidden from the world.

He knew, intellectually, that there was no reason to be scared. He'd inherited a powerful kingdom, with a council and bureaucracy that existed to make his every whim law, but he was too scared to use it. The fear was just too strong. He wished his father had had more children, a younger son who could take the throne instead of a crippled king. He wondered, sometimes, if he really had been cursed. It was possible. The fear seemed to have no focus. He wasn't scared of the dark, or spiders, or assassins ... he was scared of everything.

Tears prickled at the corner of his eyes. The councillors were already plotting. He knew, although he couldn't have said *how* he knew. They were trying to find a way to legally remove him, to put a distant relative on the throne. Forsyth feared the council, as much as he feared everything else. It was just a matter of time before they declared him incapable of ruling and packed him off to a country estate. Why not? He was too scared to stand up to them, let alone rally the people and lead them in war against the usurpers. The worst of it – he admitted to himself, if no one else – was that he'd be *relieved* if he was removed from power. Who wanted a king who was afraid of the dark?

Bitter resentment welled within him. It wasn't fair. It just wasn't fair. He had male cousins who were strong and manly and performed great feats of daring … all, no doubt, with one eye on the throne. He had female cousins, so cunning that their guile far exceeded the councillors themselves, nudging their husbands towards the throne. A strong king would have no hesitation in slapping them down, in reminding them who was boss, but Forsyth couldn't so much as bring himself to issue a mild reprimand. His weakness shamed him. His weakness humiliated him. And he was too afraid to do anything about it. There was no doubt, in his mind, that he would be removed. It was just a matter of time.

His hands shook, again. He willed them into stillness. Maybe he *had* been cursed. The fear was so strong that nothing, not even alcohol or potions, could quench it. Drunkenness only made the fear worse. The potions … he shuddered, recalling the one time he'd tried to use magic to overcome the fear. The results had been horrific. He'd shamed himself in front of the entire court …

… And something was behind him.

Forsyth knew, beyond a shadow of a doubt, that something was there. He could *feel* it pressing against his personal space. A strange sense of calm washed over him as he stood and turned, one hand dropping to the sword he didn't know how to use. The air seemed … twisted somehow, as if whatever was there wasn't *truly* there. Forsyth eyed it as it took on shape and form, a humanoid figure that looked as if it couldn't decide if it were male or female. He knew he should be scared, he knew he should run, but … for once, he stood his ground. The feeling was so wonderful he wouldn't have cared if the figure had come for him, if he could take the feeling of being *brave* into eternity.

"I greet you." The words seemed to appear in Forsyth's mind without ever passing through his ears. "I greet you, Chosen of the Gods."

Forsyth felt the fear start to return. He'd heard tales of the chosen ones, of men and women honoured by the gods and sent on quests … quests he knew, all too well, he could never handle. His old nursemaid had told him tales until his mother had overheard and told the woman never to speak of such matters again. She'd been dismissed shortly afterwards, without a single bronze coin to her name. It was funny how he'd forgotten her, until now.

"I greet you," he managed. He was king, yet … a god or a god's messenger was so far above him he might as well be scrabbling in the dirt. It never occurred to him to doubt the entity. It was just so *real*. "I … what do you want from me?"

The entity seemed to come closer, without actually moving. "Lead your troops," it said, the words hanging leaden in Forsyth's mind. "Restore us to the world."

The fear grew stronger. "I cannot," Forsyth admitted. The shame overwhelmed him as he sank to his knees, crying like a child. He hated the fear, hated himself … hated himself with a self-loathing too powerful to be ignored. He wanted to stumble to the window and throw himself out, but he was scared of death as well as everything else. "I'm … I'm scared."

"You do not have to be scared," the entity said. It loomed over him, millions of miles tall even though cold logic told him it couldn't possibly fit into the chamber. "Accept me into your heart, King of Kings, and all will be well."

Forsyth swallowed. He was suddenly aware, very aware, that the council had made its decision. He was to be removed from power and … removed. Killed, he knew. They were going to murder him. The new monarch could hardly keep the old one around, just in case he decided to retake his throne. He felt a sudden surge of pure rage, overpowering in its intensity. He was sick, so *sick*, of being scared. He wanted to be free! He wanted to rule as he pleased, to exert his power, to do whatever he wanted. He wanted to be the man his father had been, the man everyone had served …

He looked up. "I accept."

The entity moved forward. There was a flash of insight as it flowed into him, a sudden awareness that he might have made a terrible mistake, then nothing.

***

Xhafer, High Chancellor of Zycrest, made his way up the steps towards the king's chambers, feeling oddly unsure of himself. The council had debated for days and weeks over precisely *what* they were going to do with a monarch who started at shadows, a coward who was too afraid to do anything ... even protect himself. They would never have dared to even *consider* the issue when the last king had been alive – he'd had a temper that had cowed even brave men – but the current monarch was a nightmare. The kingdom had too many problems to risk leaving a coward on the throne. Xhafer regretted having to turn against a man he'd known since childhood, but there was no choice. Better for everyone, including the king himself, if he was quickly removed from power and banished. He was no threat.

The air seemed to shift around him, a faint air of unreality brushing against his awareness as he reached the top of the stairs and stopped for breath. The king's ancestors had designed the tower for defence, ensuring that anyone who climbed the stairs would be exhausted by the time they reached the top. A brave man with a sword could hold the landing indefinitely, as long as his courage and stamina held out. There was no way to escape, as far as Xhafer knew, but who cared? A king who fled, back in those days, would be king no more.

He told himself he was seeing things as he straightened. He was too old, really, for such malarkey. It was why the council had chosen him to bear the message. If he was arrested for high treason – as if the coward-king could muster the will to do it – he would be dead well before the torturers started their work. Or so they'd said ... Xhafer snorted at the sheer absurdity of the thought. The poor king would go into a gilded cage without a fight. There was nothing to be gained by killing him. It wasn't as if he posed a threat.

The antechamber stood empty. Xhafer frowned. Where were the guards? The king needed to be protected at all times, but the guards were gone. His eyes narrowed, then he shrugged as he walked into the bedchamber. He had a flicker of unease as he passed through the doors, a sense that something was wrong ... he dismissed it, effortlessly. The king was a coward and a fool and ...

His thoughts seemed to slam to a halt. His mind was assailed by a series of disjointed impressions. The throne, looming large ... impossibly large. The guards, standing beside the throne, their faces so cold and hard that it was no longer possible to believe them human. And, sitting on the throne, a king … a true king. Xhafer felt his knees buckle as he met the king's eyes. They were so … so *certain* that he found himself dropping to his knees well before his conscious mind caught up. The man in front of him was no coward. Fear washed through him as he remembered the council's debates, remembered how the king's father had treated traitors. And now … resistance was inconceivable. They'd plotted against a true king and his wrath would be terrible.

"Look at me," the king said.

Xhafer looked up. It was like staring into the sun. The king was Forsyth … and yet it wasn't. He had a presence so strong that Xhafer quailed, unable to muster the will to do more than follow orders. The king's eyes bored into his, leaving him feeling naked and helpless. He thought the shadows were closing in, reaching out for him … he couldn't look away. The king had him in his thrall.

"You will serve us," the king said. "And this kingdom will be the core of a whole new empire."

"Yes, Your Majesty," Xhafer managed. His mouth was dry. He stumbled over the words. "I am your loyal servant."

"Indeed." The king's voice was amused, vastly amused. He knew what they'd been planning. "Summon the remainder of the council. It is time they pledged themselves to me."

Xhafer stayed on his knees as he inched backwards. The king … the king had suddenly become a true king. He couldn't rise, let alone turn his back … the door slammed the moment he passed through, but he couldn't so much as consider any thought of defiance or resistance. He'd been the king's man from the moment he'd entered his presence, all thoughts of a palace coup melting like snowflakes in the fireplace. The king was a true king who'd lead the kingdom to glory, who'd reunite the empire under his banner …

… And nothing, Xhafer knew with a certainty that could not be denied, would ever be the same again.

Chapter One

He was bored.

Sergeant Theodore Ashworth stood outside the door and tried to look eager, even though the boredom was killing him. He was used to action and adventure, to marching with the army and fighting with the foe, not standing on guard outside a simple iron door. The Queen Sorceress had given him his orders personally, and he was ruefully aware she could turn him into a frog – or worse – if he disobeyed, but … he was bored. He peered up and down the corridor, wondering if anyone would so much as dare to enter the dungeons. The Queen had taken them for herself, when she'd married King Reginald and moved into the castle. She'd issued orders to keep everyone out of the very lowest levels, unless they had her permission.

Theodore snorted. The castle had only been reoccupied and cleansed six months ago. The prisoners who'd been held at the king's pleasure had been dead well before the Crown Prince had reclaimed his throne. There was no reason for a queen, even a sorceress, to secure the dungeons for herself. It was just a matter of time before the king started filling the cells with new prisoners, with men who'd defied his will or … Theodore snorted, again. King Reginald was out fighting a war with men who'd defied his will. Theodore doubted any of the aristo bastards would last long enough to grace a prison cell. The king wouldn't leave any of them alive, no matter how much they grovelled. They were just too dangerous.

I should be out there, Theodore thought. He wasn't blind to the trust the king – and his family – had placed in the guards, but he wasn't a fancy-pants palace guardsman. The uniform felt itchy and unpleasant, as if whoever had designed it hadn't wanted the guards to move freely. *I shouldn't be here.*

He allowed his eyes to roam the stone walls, silently

counting the bricks and stones. The queen was in residence, as were both surviving princesses, but ... they were in no danger. It would take a brave or foolish man to challenge a sorceress, particularly one in her place of power. Theodore knew the advantages and disadvantages of magic as much as anyone else. He knew what would happen to anyone who tried. It would take time and effort to break the wards, time the sorceress could use to best advantage. Theodore shivered, despite himself. He was a brave man, but magic still made him weak at the knees. The entities who'd infested the kingdom were worse. He'd sensed enough of their power to fear it.

And they're still out there somewhere, he reminded himself, sharply. *They could be anywhere ...*

He forced himself to stand up straighter. There might be an inspection at any moment, although he doubted it. The officer commanding was an experienced man, smart enough to put competence ahead of appearance. He wouldn't punish Theodore for having a button out of place, but if Theodore happened to fall asleep on duty ... the beating would be savage, and the demotion would be worse. Theodore sighed as he returned to counting bricks. He would be relieved shortly, allowing him to get back to the barracks and catch some sleep. Or go into the city for some fun. The city was slowly returning to normal. The local sellers were happy to open their wares to the king's personal guard.

Help me ...

Theodore blinked. He'd heard ... he'd heard someone calling for help. His hand dropped to his sword as he listened intently, wondering if he'd just imagined the cry. It could be another maid, being harassed by an aristocratic buffoon. Or an innocent village girl ... Theodore smirked, coldly. The Crown Prince had issued strict orders against harassing the villagers and given his guardsmen permission to do whatever they had to do to stop it. Theodore had enjoyed those days. It wasn't often he got permission to manhandle aristos, and he'd made the most of it. And he'd been careful not to let himself be identified. The vengeful assholes hadn't known who to punish.

Help me ...

The sound echoed, brushing against Theodore's mind. He

tensed, turning his head from side to side, as the call came again. It seemed to come from a great distance, yet he was hearing it … it was coming from behind him. He turned to look at the iron door. He'd been given strict orders not to open the door without permission, let alone permit anyone to enter or leave the chambers beyond, but … someone was crying for help. His orders warred with the increasing desperation in the voice, with the certainty of punishment competing with the desire to help the person on the other side. The world itself seemed to dim as his fingers moved of their own accord, grabbing and twisting the iron knob. The door clicked open. He practically fell into the chamber.

He stared. The giant chamber had been turned into a workshop. Two wooden tables were placed against the walls – a third wall was covered with half-full bookcases and potions supplies – but they didn't catch his eye. His gaze was locked on the iron cage in the centre of the room. A young girl sat in the centre of the cage, wearing a simple white shift. Her eyes were modestly downcast. Theodore felt a sudden surge of protectiveness, even though he was aware – at some level – that something was wrong. The girl … the girl looked strange, almost inhuman. She was his ideal bride given shape and form. He knew she couldn't be real, yet he refused to believe it. He didn't *want* to believe it.

She looked up. His resistance melted away. She was a prisoner … it was outrageous she was a prisoner. Whoever she was, whatever she was, she could *not* be held prisoner. Theodore stumbled forward, his eyes searching for the lock. He'd open the cage, free her and … he wasn't sure what he'd do then, but it didn't matter. All that mattered was letting her out of the cage. His hands touched the iron padlock and pulled at it, trying to get it free. It was useless. Desperation overwhelmed him at the thought of failing her. He wanted to die … he tried to tell himself not to be silly as he looked around for tools. He'd pick the lock and free her and let her go, and all would be well.

Blue sparks flashed. He found himself flying across the room, slamming into the far wall without any clear memory of what had happened. His fingers hurt, as if he'd burnt them on a hot stove or picked up a superheated rock without thinking. The pain was so intense he was completely unmanned, screaming so loudly he was sure the entire castle could hear him. He thought he saw, just for a moment, something utterly alien within the cage, something so alien his mind couldn't even begin to grasp what he was seeing. And then it was gone and the girl was looking at him with despondent eyes and …

Something blocked his gaze. He looked up into the queen's eyes. "I …"

The queen stared back at him. "Why did you enter the room?"

Theodore hesitated. He wasn't sure himself. There'd been a voice calling to him and … his memories were a jumbled mess. He'd disobeyed orders and he wasn't even sure *why*. He cursed himself under his breath, as thoroughly as he knew how. The very least he could expect was being summarily demoted and sent off on a suicide mission. King Reginald was known and respected for being fair, but … there was no way he could let the matter pass. No one would blame him for ordering Theodore's execution.

"I … I heard a voice," he said, finally. "It needed help."

"I see," the Queen said. "And you listened to it?"

Theodore forced himself to look up, into her eyes. Queen Isabella was … odd, by the standards of the princesses and aristocratic ladies and even the maids who'd once swanned around the court. Her dark hair was cut short, defying fashion; she wore a simple leather shirt, a jerkin and a pair of trousers rather than the dresses the other ladies wore. Theodore knew she'd been a mercenary as well as a sorceress, hired when Crown Prince Reginald had invaded the Summer Isle to claim his patrimony. He felt a flash of admiration that had nothing to do with her stern face, muscular arms and magic. She had the position and power not to have to care what the ladies of the court had to say. She didn't follow fashions. She set them. The next summer was going to be interesting …

He put the thought aside. He was wool-gathering.

"I had to," he managed. The voice was a fading memory. He felt an urge to look past the queen, to look at the girl in the cage … he suppressed it, ruthlessly. "It called to me."

The queen studied him for a long cold moment. "Go outside and wait," she ordered, curtly. "And don't come back inside, whatever you see or hear."

Theodore stood and bowed. "Yes, Your Majesty."

***

Isabella watched the sergeant go, closing the door behind him. It had been sheer goddamned luck – her lips quirked at the thought – that Sergeant Ashworth been unable to open the cage and release the entity. He was a good man, with a splendid record of loyalty and devotion to his monarch, but he'd nearly been seduced into disobeying orders and doing something incredibly dangerous. No, he *had* been seduced. Isabella had worked as many protective hexes and charms into the chamber as she could, designing them to make it difficult for *her* to operate without being aware of the entity's every movement, yet they'd nearly failed. The entity had called the sergeant into the chamber, manipulating him effortlessly. And, somehow, it had bypassed most of the protective spells.

She turned, already knowing what she would see. A young woman knelt in the cage, looking innocent and helpless and frighteningly pure. She looked like Isabella herself, but a version of Isabella that had been washed clean of all taint and corruption and the scars of a troubled childhood, a magical education and years as a mercenary. Isabella wondered, idly, what the sergeant had seen. The entities were shaped by human thoughts, emotions and desires. It was, in some sense, what they *were*. The sergeant would have merely been the first to die – or be warped beyond recognition – if he'd opened the cage.

Maiden Lembu looked up. Her eyes were utterly inhuman. Isabella forced herself to stand her ground, even though finely-honed instincts were screaming at her to run. The entity was no longer pretending to be anything other than a monster. Isabella shivered, remembering her first meeting with the three-in-one. She'd tutored Isabella, showing her how the new rules worked. And she'd offered more, for a price.

"I have eternity," Maiden Lembu said. "It's just a matter of time."

Isabella said nothing. The entities were bound by strange rules, governed by logic so alien that she could barely comprehend it. And yet, some of those rules were clear. As long as the cage remained locked and sealed, as long as there was no way out, the entity was caught like a rat in a trap. The other entities couldn't try to free her either, not directly. But if they did something that *accidentally* damaged the cage or opened a path for the entity to leave …

"I offer what you most desire," Maiden Lembu added. "It's just a matter of time."

"So you keep saying," Isabella said, curtly. She knew the entity was right. Lembu – Mother, Maiden or Crone – was timeless, effectively immortal. It *was* just a matter of time before she seduced someone long enough to compel her victim to free her, or for something – anything – to happen that might let her go free. "And yet, right now, you're my prisoner."

"A prisoner you cannot contain for long," Maiden Lembu said. She stood, her dress spilling around her as if it were made of shimmering light. Perhaps it was. "You have only the barest fraction of understanding."

She stepped up to the iron bars. "And I will teach you, if you pledge yourself to me."

Isabella shook her head. She understood, now, how the entities really worked. They traded power – miracles, really – for worship. They demanded servitude and respect and, in exchange, they promised to grant wishes and … everything. And, the more they manifested on the human plane, the more damage they did. She didn't think they were malicious, not in any sense a human might understand, but it didn't matter. Their motives didn't matter. The results were horrific and *that* was all that mattered.

"Your husband may stray," Maiden Lembu said. "Do you not wish to bind him to you?"

"I know a hundred love spells," Isabella said, tartly. "And they are all banned, with good reason. Do you think I would gain anything by crushing his free will?"

"You wouldn't be breaking his will," Maiden Lembu said. "He would just never stray from you."

Isabella snorted. "One cannot remain faithful and have it mean something if one doesn't have the option *not* to be faithful."

Maiden Lembu smiled. "And you don't want to fit in here?

I could make it happen ..."

"Really?" Isabella snorted, again. "You promise the world, but the price is too high."

She waved her hand, dismissively. She had no doubt the entity could – and would – keep whatever promise she made. It was one of the rules. The entities *had* to make a good-faith effort to keep their side of the bargain. But the price was just too high. Isabella had to admit, at least to herself, that she didn't enjoy being regent in Reginald's absence. She didn't like having to alternately cajole and threaten the king's councillors to make them follow orders, even though the princesses were both in her corner. And she didn't *like* the sneers the women of the court aimed at her back ... she rolled her eyes in disgust. If sneering was the worst they could do, she could endure. She would even feel sorry for them.

"You can't keep me here forever," Maiden Lembu said, again. "And you may come to regret not pledging yourself to me."

"We shall see," Isabella said. "You'll be trapped here until long after I'm dead and gone."

She allowed her eyes to wander over the entity. The human seeming was starting to collapse into something many-angled and *dangerous*. Her head hurt just *looking* at it, as if the entity existed in realms and dimensions the human mind was not designed to comprehend. The appearance of a harmless maiden was just the smile on the face of the tiger, the hints of knowledge and the promise of something more a lure to draw her into pledging herself. She'd worked out some of the rules, through trial and error and observation. She'd work out the rest for herself, given time. And she wasn't alone.

"Your husband will return changed," Maiden Lembu informed her. "And you will regret it."

Isabella said nothing as she turned away. The entities claimed to be able to predict the future, and to offer their insights to their human servants, but she'd never been convinced that the future was fixed. And the insights could be twisted, until they were neutralised. Princess Sofia's prediction might have promised trouble, but Isabella had outthought it. There'd been a price to pay ...

"We shall see," she said, again. There was no point in debating with the creature. She couldn't afford to let herself forget, now or ever, that she had a dragon by the tail and that the slightest mistake might get her killed. Or worse. "Goodbye."

She glanced at the workbench, where she was brewing a mind-expanding potion, then turned and walked through the door, replacing the damaged or destroyed charms as she moved. The chamber was surrounded by cold iron, the one metal the entities couldn't bend to their will, but Maiden Lembu had clearly managed to get a message through the gap. Isabella scowled as she closed the door firmly, muttering another charm in hopes of keeping the metal in place. She'd thought the design was airtight – it wasn't as though the entity needed to breathe – but there had to be a gap somewhere. She would have to find it, sooner rather than later. The maiden had been right. It was just a matter of time until she found a way to break free.

"Your Majesty." Sergeant Ashworth knelt, clumsily. "I offer my life, and ..."

"Don't worry about it," Isabella said. It wasn't the queenly thing to do, she was sure, but it was *practical*. Sergeant Ashworth was a good man. It was how the entity had crawled into his mind. Besides, she'd felt Maiden Lembu's power for herself. She'd been tempted with knowledge. It had been sheer luck she'd pulled back before pledging herself to the entity for evermore. "Just ... be careful."

She turned and headed down the corridor, wondering if she'd done the right thing. She couldn't serve as Queen Regent *and* guard the prisoner, not indefinitely. She wasn't even sure *she* was safe, when alone with the entity. Maiden Lembu was the least of the three-in-one. The mother and the crone were far more dangerous.

And we still don't know what happened to Emetine, Isabella thought. She still had bad dreams about the ritual, when Sofia and her father had both met their deaths. She knew Reginald had them too. *Or the entity she called into the world.*

Chapter Two

"Fire," Reginald ordered.

He stood by the catapults and watched as they hurled giant projectiles towards the enemy castle. Baron Braddock had sent King Romulus his formal defiance well before Reginald had returned to claim the throne, but refused to stand down, submit and pledge himself to the new king. Reginald hated to do it – he was painfully aware he was wasting time he needed for other projects – yet he had no choice. He *had* to squash the baron before his defiance turned into a general uprising and outright civil war.

Sofia weakened the ties binding us to the aristocrats, he thought, morbidly. *But it wasn't as if those ties were very strong to begin with.*

The projectiles smashed against the castle walls. Pieces of debris rained down, splashing into the moat. Reginald smiled, coldly, as fountains of water rose up and fell to the ground. The castle was tough enough to stand off a horde of angry peasants, but nowhere near strong enough to deter a large and experienced army. Reginald could have laid siege to the castle and waited, patiently, for the defenders to starve. They simply *couldn't* have crammed enough food into the fortress to hold out long enough for Reginald's army to weaken and eventually melt away. But he knew he had to win quickly.

And besides, there's no way to know what is really inside the castle, he reminded himself, grimly. The army had passed – and destroyed – a dozen shrines to the old gods, to the entities that had come far too close to overshadowing the entire kingdom. There was no way the baron would *not* call on their help, if he thought he could. *We might run into anything.*

He allowed his heart to harden as the next round of projectiles smashed into the castle battlements. He disliked the thought of killing the baron's wife, mistresses and children, but they'd had their chance to surrender. Baron Braddock hadn't even taken the precaution of sending his wife and children to her parents, even though it would have been relatively straightforward before the army arrived and blocked the roads. Reginald knew what *that* could mean, although he didn't want to think about it. The baron might have ambitions that ranged far beyond merely defying his monarch.

A shout rang out as a handful of defenders appeared on what remained of the walls. Reginald's archers opened fire at once, arrows striking home with terrifying force and sending the defenders tumbling to their doom. Reginald grimaced, feeling a flicker of sympathy no matter how much he tried to remain composed. The poor bastards hadn't stood a chance. They'd probably been forced out by their master in a desperate bid for ... for what? The whole sally had been worse than useless. They hadn't even bought the castle a few short minutes of life.

The archers cheered, then hastily prepared to fire another salvo as they argued over who had killed whom. Reginald listened with half an ear, knowing that it was already impossible to tell who'd struck the fatal blow. It didn't matter, he told himself. The archers would be feted when the castle finally fell, as would the rest of the men. Reginald prided himself on the common touch. No matter how baseborn, a man could rise high in his army. He knew from bitter experience that loyalty had to be rewarded or soldiers stopped being loyal. And a disloyal army was only one bad campaign – or battle – away from disintegration.

"Your Majesty." Captain-General Gars hurried up, looking eager. "The walls are about to topple."

Reginald nodded as a dull rumble echoed through the air. The bombardment was reaching its final stage. There was little hope of the walls lasting much longer. The moat wouldn't prove a barrier any longer, not now the debris provided all the footing his men could possibly want. It wasn't quite the flying men of legend, the soldiers who'd scaled an impossible height to bring death to their enemies, but it would do. The baron was running out of time. Reginald wondered, idly, if one of his men would put a knife in his back. The turncoat might *just* think he could get away with it ...

"Send the ironmen forward as soon as the walls collapse," he ordered, stiffly. "I'll be accompanying them."

Captain-General Gars frowned, then nodded. Reginald understood – the king should not put himself in personal danger, not until he had an adult son and heir – but there was no choice. Not really. The men had to see their leader sharing the danger. It did wonders for morale ... as long as the leader remained alive. Reginald smiled, drawing his sword as the walls and castle started to collapse. The crumbling building looked like a honeycomb. He saw a handful of people running, looking for cover that no longer existed. The archers shot them down before they had a chance to escape.

Reginald raised his sword. "Attack!"

The ironmen ran forward, the archers covering them with practiced ease. Their weapons and armour looked primitive, and were dangerously weak in places, but cold iron was the only weapon they'd found that weakened and killed the entities. And their servants. Reginald shivered, despite himself, as he moved forward. The baron might be an idiot – he'd certainly *acted* like an idiot – or he might have something up his sleeve. He had to have had *some* reason to think his little revolt would succeed. Men like Baron Braddock didn't have the nerve to throw their lives away for nothing.

A handful of bodyguards fanned out around him as he ran towards the remains of the moat. The ironmen were ahead of him, scrambling over the debris and securing the pile of rubble that had once been a gatehouse. It would have been impregnable in happier times, but now ... Reginald shook his head. The next baron, whoever won enough of his favour to earn the position, would have to rebuild. It wouldn't do to have the castle vulnerable to commoners and peasants. The kingdom had quite enough problems.

He landed in the courtyard, trying to ignore the sound of crashing debris as his men plunged into the castle. The scene was a madhouse, a handful of defenders making a desperate last stand that could only end in their deaths. And yet, they kept fighting. They made no attempt to surrender. Reginald frowned as he raised his sword, watching the figures as they died one by one. They were acting oddly and that bothered him. Smart men – particularly mercenaries – would be trying to surrender by now. Reginald intended to make an example out of their master, but he had no particular dislike for the bastard's followers. They'd sworn an oath to follow the baron long ago.

The ground shook. Reginald felt the world *twist*, as if the rules had suddenly changed. Green shoots appeared between the cobblestones, growing with impossible speed. The ironmen shouted, jumping back as plants threatened to wrap around their legs and bring them to their knees. A couple of men were immobilised long enough for the creepers to tighten and crush them, their blood staining the cobbles and feeding the mutant plants. Reginald cursed under his breath, then snapped orders. There was an entity – or at least one of their servants – within the castle. And time was no longer on his side.

"Slice it down," he shouted. The iron swords would cut the roots free, breaking the bond between the plants and their eerie mastermind. "And set fire to the roots!"

He leaned forward, even as the creepers grew stronger. It was a nightmare given shape and form, the ground shaking so badly it was just a matter of time before the remainder of the castle collapsed into rubble. He wondered, as his men splashed fuel on the creepers and tossed torches into the morass, if the baron knew what was going to happen. The fool didn't realise that he and his followers were little more than food for the entity, nothing more than cattle or sheep or …

The creepers seemed to recoil, a strange howl echoing through the air as the flames spread rapidly. Reginald gritted his teeth, trying not to show how badly the sound affected him.   It threatened to unman him, despite his having encountered the entities before. The air grew hot, then cold, then hot again. The entity was trying to ward off the flames, he guessed. It was time to take the fight to the enemy.

Isabella's going to kill me, he thought. *And so will my sisters.*

He put the thought out of his mind as he shouted for his men, then led the charge into the smoke and flames. The air stank of burning creeper, but it was surprisingly easy to breathe as they raced into the remnants of the castle. The entity was bending the rules, again. A handful of bodies lay on the ground, seemingly dead. He beheaded them anyway, just in case. He'd seen the entities at work. Reanimating the dead – even bringing them back to life – was not beyond their power. A shiver ran down his spine as he led his men towards the centre of the castle, the baron's throne room. It was all too easy to understand how so many had fallen under their spell. Reginald himself would give everything he had to have his father back, and he *knew* the price.

The stone walls darkened, becoming weirdly… translucent. Hooded figures stepped out of the walls, as if they were nothing more than … Reginald refused to think about it, refused to even allow the entity the tiniest grip on his mind. He cut the lead figure down, then threw himself at the next. An inhuman sound echoed through the air, once again, as it died. The third raised a sword, striking at him with a savage fury that belied an apparent lack of training. Reginald smiled to himself and took the offensive, battering his sword against his enemy's defences. His old swordmaster would have beaten him for such folly. He supposed it made a certain kind of sense. The Red Monks and their counterparts were largely immune to conventional weapons. And yet, they had to know that his swords were cold iron.

He stabbed forward, cutting off his opponent's arm. The creature stumbled and collapsed to the ground. Reginald had a dizzying sense of impressions, of strange shimmering *things* moving in all directions, as the body crumbled to dust. A human wouldn't have died so quickly … he shook his head as he forced himself to press onwards, his bodyguards bringing up the rear. The baron couldn't be allowed to escape. If he did, everything Reginald had done would be for nothing.

The doorway opened up in front of him. The baron – or one of his ancestors – had clearly had a high opinion of himself. The hall looked disturbingly regal, the sort of thing that tended to upset kings and emperors. Reginald glanced around, noting the strange banners decorating the walls and the oversized chair – it hinted at being a throne – placed at one end of the chamber. The entity lounging on the chair was very far from human.

Reginald shuddered. The baron, if it was the baron, had

given himself completely to the entities. They pervaded him, to the point it was hard to *look* at him. Reginald found his gaze constantly slipping *past* the baron, as if the baron were not truly there. And yet, he was. There was something sickeningly *wrong* about him. Reginald felt his stomach churn as he stepped forward, his bodyguards fanning out behind him. The baron was beyond salvation.

Sofia could have wound up like that, he thought, numbly. His sister had betrayed the family to the entities ... it was still a raw wound, even though he'd tried to tell himself – time and time again – that it wasn't truly her fault. *She's lucky she died before they* really *got their hooks in her*.

His feet touched liquid. He looked down. The stone floor was covered in blood. Reginald glanced up, sharply. He wasn't squeamish – he'd seen men wounded and killed from the day he'd first taken up the sword – but the sight horrified him on a very primal level. People hadn't just been *killed*, he thought. They'd been drained of blood ... he shuddered, helplessly, as the baron looked at him. Who'd been sacrificed to cover the floor in blood?

"Little King." Baron Braddock's voice was cold and hard and *alien*. He spoke in words of burning ash. "Bow before me. Open your heart to me."

Reginald forced himself to straighten. The entities were powerful beyond imagination, but there were rules. They couldn't *force* him to open his heart to them. Sure, they could twist things to the point he'd feel he had no choice ... but they couldn't cross that line. Or so he'd been told. He smiled, remembering Isabella's warnings. His wife knew the entities better than anyone. She'd prepared him and his men for the war.

"Leave that body," he ordered. There was no hope of trapping the entity, not here. There'd been no time to prepare the ritual. They didn't even know the creature's *name*. "Leave this world."

The entity gestured. Reginald glanced down – again – as he felt blood lapping against his boot. The stench was suddenly intolerable. He forced himself to breathe through his mouth as the liquid bubbled, then rose into a roughly humanoid form. Reginald recoiled as the shambling mass lashed out at him, blood splattering against his armour. He cut out with his sword, to no effect. The cold iron passed through the blood as if it was nothing more than … blood. It didn't seem to slow the entity's power. Reginald had no time to think about it before a tidal wave of blood slammed into him, picking him up and throwing him back against the wall. His sword was torn free and tossed away. He couldn't even see where it had fallen. One of his bodyguards yelped, then fell silent.

Reginald cursed as warm liquid washed through his armour, soaking his undergarments and pressing against his mouth. It was suddenly very hard to breathe. He didn't dare open his mouth, not when the blood would cascade into his body. He wasn't sure what that would do, but he didn't want to find out. The entity was cheating. It was trying to drown him …

"Open your heart to me," the entity said. "Open your heart and the pain will stop."

No, Reginald thought. He could hear the creature perfectly, despite the roaring in his ears. *No, you …*

He gritted his teeth and stumbled forward. His eyes were tightly closed, but he could still see – or sense – the entity lounging on the throne. It was weirdly more comprehensible on the throne, although he had the sense that he was looking at the tip of a giant iceberg. The entity itself was still resting firmly within the godly realm, having extruded a tiny protuberance into the human world. Isabella would have understood what he was seeing, he was sure. She had the sorcerous education to make sense of it. Reginald himself didn't particularly care. All that mattered to him was killing the entity before it did any more damage.

His fingers found the dagger on his belt. He drew it. The entity snickered as Reginald stumbled forward. The dagger was no threat, or so it seemed. It made no move to defend itself as Reginald raised the blade and plunged it into the entity's chest. A howl rent the air as the dagger returned to its natural form, an iron blade. The entity seemed to freeze, then snapped out of existence. Blood splashed to the floor. Reginald opened his eyes, blinking away the remnants of the liquid. The baron's body slipped off the throne and landed in a crumbled heap at his feet. For a moment, Reginald wasn't sure he'd killed the right man. Baron Braddock had only been a decade or so older than Reginald. The dead body looked old enough to be his grandfather.

The entity probably drained his life as well as everything else, Reginald thought, as he recovered the dagger and sword and returned them to his belt. Isabella's gift had more than proved its value. The entities seemed to drain mundane magic from the world, undoing merely human spells. They hadn't realised – yet – that their very nature could be turned against them. Not yet. *Poor bastard.*

Sergeant Yodel stumbled into the room. "Your Majesty!"

"Secure the castle," Reginald ordered. The blood on the floor was draining rapidly, but his clothes were still drenched. His bodyguards didn't look any better. "If there's anyone left alive, male or female, offer them the chance to surrender. If they do" – his eyes narrowed – "make sure you bind them with cold iron."

"Aye, Your Majesty," Sergeant Yodel said. "It shall be done."

"And then send a message to Havelock," Reginald added. "Inform them the castle is ours."

The sergeant saluted, then hurried off. Reginald nodded and turned away from the throne, leaving the body behind. The castle wasn't safe any longer, even though the entity was gone. Better to have it pulled down completely, rather than risk leaving traces of the entity's power. He'd seen too much to feel comfortable repairing the castle. The forbidden zones still influenced the unwary, centuries after the entities had been banished from the world.

He rubbed his forehead as they headed for the door. *And that was a relatively small and weak entity*, he thought, morbidly. He'd seen nastier and more powerful creatures on the Summer Isle. *Who knows what'll happen when we run into one of the bigger ones?*

Chapter Three

You can't go around turning people into frogs, Isabella told herself, sternly. *And you can't shut them up by threatening to blast them either.*

She kept her face under tight control as she surveyed the Royal Council. It wasn't *her* council. She might be Regent, in the absence of her husband, but every man at the table knew her powers were very limited. Her *formal* powers, at any rate. And her position was a little anomalous. She might be a sorceress, and thus was the social equal of each and every one of them, but she was also the queen and subordinate to her husband. She had no doubt the councillors were already planning to appeal her decisions to the king. It would have been considerably less annoying if they'd had a good *reason* to appeal.

Lord Epos kept talking, babbling on about trade between the neighbouring kingdoms in a manner that suggested he was putting the point off for as long as possible. Isabella tried to follow the argument, but found herself losing track as he moved from topic to topic without ever getting to the meat of the matter. The nobles were complaining, it seemed, because international merchants weren't paying enough taxes. Isabella found it hard to blame the merchants. It wasn't as if they were getting much for their money. The aristocracy lacked even the basic decency to stay bought. It was easy to understand why the merchants were concealing their profits as much as possible.

"And all trade with Zycrest has ceased," Lord Epos continued. "The last merchants to visit reported that the borders and seaports have closed."

Isabella's eyes narrowed. "All trade?"

"Yes, Your Majesty," Lord Epos said. "The merchants were turned away at the border. They were unable to find a way to slip into the kingdom."

"Really?" Isabella found it hard to believe. "They actually

closed the *entire* border?"

She shook her head. It was *impossible* to believe. Borders were long. Building a wall to keep foreigners out was difficult, to say the least. Hell, the borders themselves were more than a little vague. The local townspeople didn't give much of a damn about legal formalities. The unlucky ones wound up paying taxes to both nations. And if Zycrest had literally closed its borders …

"Yes, Your Majesty," Lord Epos said. "They had guards on all of the roads."

"Interesting," Isabella said. She'd *visited* Zycrest, back before the company – her old company – had signed up with Crown Prince Reginald and followed him to the Summer Isle. There'd been hints of a civil war, but nothing too solid. The new king had been something of a milksop, apparently. No one had believed, at the time, that he'd last long. "Something to think about, definitely."

"And that is why we must increase tolls on the roads," Lord Alpine said. "The merchants need to pay a fair price …"

Isabella scowled, wishing – not for the first time – that Reginald had had a completely free hand when it came to choosing his councillors. He'd chosen Isabella herself, of course, and Princess Ruby, but the rest of the councillors were drawn from the ranks of men who were too wealthy and powerful to ignore. They weren't fools – mostly – yet they had their own interests, interests that were too important for them to put the wellbeing of the country first. It wasn't easy to keep them under control. And, with Reginald off teaching Baron Braddock a lesson, it fell to Isabella to try to keep them heading in the same direction.

"The problem, as we have discussed before, is that raising taxes, tariffs and tolls will inevitably reduce economic growth," Isabella said, coldly. "The merchants will, at best, seek to avoid the tolls. At worst, they will stop earning money and therefore stop paying any taxes."

She met his eyes, willing them to understand. They weren't fools – she reminded herself, again – but their experiences were very limited. They believed in land ownership, not trade and economic development and everything that seemed just a *little* insubstantial. And, given the chance, they'd strangle the economy rather than give up a tiny fraction of control. It wasn't easy to convince them otherwise. They'd sooner be powerful and poor than ... than risk their social inferiors making enough money to outshine men who could trace their families back thousands of years.

Her lips quirked. *And past a certain point, our records might as well be fiction ...*

"The matter can be tabled for another time," Lord Harris said. "A more important matter, Your Majesty, is the need for an heir."

Isabella forced herself not to introduce him to a particularly unpleasant curse. It boggled her mind, sometimes, to realise just how many ladies of the court had hoped to marry the Crown Prince. They honestly didn't realise the position came with all sorts of disadvantages, starting with noble lords asking pointed questions about pregnancy and maids inspecting one's underwear for signs of blood ... she'd dismissed a maid she'd caught in the act and threatened others with worse if they even thought about following in that maid's footsteps. And there were people openly wondering if she was barren, just because she hadn't yet conceived a child ...

She understood the logic. The days when it didn't matter who inherited the throne were long gone. Now, there had to be a legitimate heir as soon as possible ... a legitimate *male* heir. It made Isabella's blood boil. Ruby was Reginald's heir, technically, but she was a princess and a teenager beside. If the aristocracy refused to acclaim her as queen, who'd be the heir? It wasn't easy to say. Anyone with a close claim had been bumped off by King Romulus or Sofia, just to limit the number of potential challengers. A succession crisis could lead to outright civil war. Again.

And if I have a daughter, I'll have to teach her magic, she thought. *It might be her only hope.*

"You may raise the issue with His Majesty, when he returns from the wars," she said. It was hard to resist the urge to flay them with her tongue. "I'm sure he'll be happy to discuss the matter with you."

She doubted any of them would have the nerve, at least at first. Reginald – and she, if anyone cared about her – had only been married for six months. Later ... the pressure to have children would become irresistible, even if it meant putting Isabella aside and marrying someone who might be a little more fertile. She scowled at the thought. The idea there might be something wrong with *Reginald* was unthinkable, at least to them. They turned their eyes away from the cold fact that he hadn't had any bastards.

Which doesn't prove anything, really, she thought. *He's always been more interested in fighting than whoring.*

She dismissed the thought with a shrug. "We're done here," she said. She stood. "We'll reconvene two days from now."

A rustle ran around the chamber as the councillors stood and headed for the door. They didn't look best pleased to be dismissed so suddenly, but they couldn't challenge her. Not openly. She made a mental bet with herself that at least half were composing letters to Reginald, demanding that he return to put his termagant of a wife in her place. *That* wasn't going to happen. Reginald trusted her to handle the council. In hindsight …

"They're not going to give up," Princess Ruby said. She hadn't moved from her chair. "They want a male heir as quickly as possible."

Isabella nodded, curtly. She'd grown up in the Golden City. She understood the concept of marrying for dynastic purposes, instead of for love, but there were limits. There were questions one didn't ask unless one wanted to be hexed into next week. And pestering someone to have children because it would be *convenient* was just plain rude. Not, she admitted sourly, that it would have stopped her father. The old bastard had arranged his children's matches to suit himself and the family, laying the groundwork for what should have been a new era of power and prominence. Her lips quirked. His dream had died with the Grand Sorceress and the Last Empress.

And he didn't even live to see it, she thought. *How … terrible.*

"Reginald and I have been working on it," she said, curtly. She liked Ruby, but the girl was rather … weird. She'd been earmarked for a dynastic marriage before her father and older sister had died. "Right now, it doesn't matter."

"Quite." Ruby raised a hand. "Do you want me to handle the paperwork?"

"Yeah, please." Isabella rolled her eyes. Who would have thought a monarch had to do *paperwork*? "Reggie will check it when he gets home."

She stood, brushing down her trousers. The councillors had been scandalised, the first time, when she'd attended in trousers. The old ladies of the court had been even worse, although the younger girls had started to wear trousers themselves. Isabella didn't care. She felt a hell of a lot more comfortable in trousers and that was all that mattered. Besides, she could *fight* in trousers. A year ago, she'd believed her magic would save her from almost everything that might pose a threat. She'd learnt hard lessons since then.

"He'll have to make the final decision too," Ruby said. "Taxes are going to be a pain."

Isabella nodded, stiffly. Andalusia had been rich, once. Reginald's father had secured its independence and maintained its stability until the entities had sneaked into the kingdom and started to warp it into a nightmare. The combination of civil wars, rebellious barons and supernatural interference had drained the treasury dry. No one had any real confidence the country would remain stable, not yet. Perhaps not ever. It was hard to convince wealthy men to invest when there was no guarantee they'd ever see any return on the investment.

Perhaps the aristos have a point, she thought, as she stepped through the door and walked to her private chamber. *The land may not produce wealth, but it does keep them alive.*

The wards on the door glimmered, informing her that someone was inside. Isabella tensed, even though she knew only three people should be able to enter without her permission. She pushed the door open carefully, breathing a sigh of relief when she saw Princess Silverdale sitting at her desk. The little princess had been through hell, thanks to her older sister. Isabella didn't begrudge her the use of the chamber. It was one of the few places Silverdale could hide from her governess.

"Isabella." Silverdale stood and dropped a perfect curtsey. "How was the council meeting?"

"Boring," Isabella grunted. She poured herself a mug of coffee and sat on the sofa. The ladies of the court would be shocked to see her so much as fetch her own drink. They'd be horrified if they spent time in a mercenary camp. "You didn't miss anything."

Silverdale looked pensive, just for a second. She'd been earmarked for a dynastic match too, once upon a time. Now ... Isabella had exacted a promise from Reginald that he wouldn't arrange a match for Silverdale without her consent, but she was all too aware Reginald might not find it easy to *keep* his promise. Not, she supposed, that it mattered. Silverdale already knew enough magic to make life unpleasant for an unwanted husband. She might even have made herself unmarriageable.

"I've been studying the books on magic," Silverdale said. "Why doesn't it make *sense*?"

"Which *kind* of magic?" Isabella took a sip of her coffee. She'd never liked studying magical theory. She would sooner learn how to cast a spell than examine the theory behind it. "Ours or theirs?"

"Both," Silverdale said. "It just makes no sense!"

"I'm sure it does," Isabella said, although she wasn't sure it was true. The more they learned about the entities – and their magic – the more she suspected there were rules and laws that were pretty much beyond human comprehension. Some of the rules made sense, while others seemed to come right out of nowhere. "The more power they have, the more they can do."

She stared at the mug in her hand. She understood how to cast, manipulate, block and cancel trivial spells. She might not be as skilled as some of the others she'd known, back in the Golden City, and she might lack the raw power to make up for her weaknesses, but she'd known enough to make a name for herself. But the entities? The more she studied them, the more she was aware of how little she really knew. Common sense told her the laws should be consistent. Experience suggested otherwise.

The greater the contact between our world and theirs, the more they can do, she mused. *And the more we open ourselves to them, the more they can do for us – and to us.*

Her eyes lingered on the notebooks she'd placed on the desk. Her desk. She'd written down everything she'd found out, from the rules and laws she'd deduced through observation to the lessons she'd had from Mother Lembu. The entity hadn't lied, Isabella was sure, but Mother Lembu had barely scratched the surface of what she could offer her students. Isabella had been given the key to knowledge without the lock.

"I want to visit the astral plane again," Silverdale said. "If we go there …"

"No." Isabella shook her head. Reginald had flatly refused to allow Silverdale to explore the astral plane again. "It's too dangerous."

"And there's no other way to *really* look at the world," Silverdale insisted. "How *else* are we going to study the bastards?"

"Mind your tongue," Isabella said, without heat. She wasn't sure who'd taught the young girl such language, although she had a nasty feeling it might have been her. "If there's anyone who should go, it's me."

Silverdale looked mulish. Isabella had to smile. The young girl looked very much like her brother. And yet … Isabella winced, inwardly. No one could possibly accuse Reginald of being a coward. *He'd* jump into the astral realm first and think afterwards. She had the nasty feeling Silverdale would do the same, given the chance. And Silverdale *was*, Isabella had to admit, a natural. She was remarkably talented.

Anyone can use their magic, Isabella mused. *But some people are still better than others.*

"We should focus on your other lessons," she said, putting the coffee to one side. "Have you done your homework?"

"The governess said I did a bad job, and that she was going to tell you to beat me," Silverdale said. "Why do I even have to *have* a governess?"

"Because you need to study," Isabella said. She felt a stab of sympathy. *She'd* been raised by governesses too, at least until her father had taken a personal interest in her education. "And because no one else can be spared to educate you."

"I want to study magic," Silverdale said. She looked even *more* like her brother. "What else do I *need* to know?"

Isabella made a show of considering it. "A good magician needs more than just magic," she said, finally. She felt like a hypocrite. She'd had the same argument with her father and an endless series of tutors herself. "She has to be able to read and write, to put together a good argument … she even has to understand maths and theory as well as the spells themselves."

"And ugly face wants me to study estate management," Silverdale protested. "What does *that* have to do with magic?"

"You might wind up owning an estate," Isabella pointed out. "And even if you don't, you might find the information useful for something else."

She eyed the younger girl for a long moment. "I'll brew up some potion later," she added, slowly. "You can watch as I explore the astral realm."

"I should go," Silverdale protested. "I'm better at it than you."

Isabella swallowed the response that came to mind. The hell of it was that Silverdale *was* better than her when it came to accessing and using the astral realm. She had less to unlearn, Isabella supposed. The dangers of exploring such magics had been drilled into her so firmly that it wasn't easy to use them. In hindsight, it was clear that the empire had known far more than it had been prepared to admit about the entities. It had certainly worked hard to keep them from returning to the world.

She stood as she heard a knock at the door. A messenger, probably. No one else would dare disturb her, unless it was very important. She opened the door and frowned as the messenger hastily dropped to his knees. It was surprising that Reginald was so … *normal*. Anyone who grew up in such an environment might turn out poorly. But then, Reginald had been training for war from the moment he could walk.

"A letter from the king, Your Majesty," the messenger said.

Isabella took the letter, tipped the messenger and dismissed him as she turned back to her desk. The wax seal was untouched, although she was all too aware that was meaningless. Her husband had many talents, but magic was not among them. The letter could have been opened and read at any point along the journey.

"Well?" Silverdale looked up. "What does it say?"

"Patience," Isabella said. She opened the letter carefully.

"Let us see …"

She smiled as she scanned the first sheet. "He won," she said. She'd never really doubted it, but it was nice to have confirmation. "Baron Braddock is dead."

"Good," Silverdale said. "I knew his daughter. Stuck-up little tart."

Isabella snorted. "The poor girl is not going to have a happy life," she predicted. She read the rest of the letter quickly, then folded the paper and put it in her pocket. No one else needed to see the more intimate part of the letter. "And you'd better get back to your studies."

Silverdale pouted, but got back to work.

Chapter Four

"Lady Braddock, Your Majesty."

Reginald straightened as the young girl was thrust into the tent. The chivalrous part of his mind was horrified at putting a maiden in manacles, particularly a woman of noble blood and unquestioned chastity. She didn't deserve to be in irons, let alone marched around by men of low breeding. But the cold and hard part of his mind knew the poor girl could easily have been overshadowed herself... or worse. He still couldn't quite wrap his mind around the depths of Sofia's betrayal, but he knew what she'd done. Lady Braddock could easily have led her father into temptation herself.

His eyes narrowed as the woman prostrated herself before him. She was a terrible sight, her once-fine dress tattered, torn and stained with blood. Her hair looked matted, as if she hadn't had time to wash it in weeks. She'd been the only survivor amongst the Baron's family, something that aroused his suspicions. She looked ready to throw herself at his feet and beg for mercy, but he knew better than to take it for granted. *Anything* could be lurking behind her eyes.

"Helen, is it not?" Reginald was sure he'd met Baron Braddock's daughter at some point – she was certainly old enough to be presented at court – but he didn't remember her. A baron's daughter would have been outranked by most of the other ladies of the court. She would have been shoved to the rear, barely given a moment to pay her respects to the prince before she was put back again. "Your father is dead."

Helen bowed her head. "I'm sorry."

Reginald studied her for a long moment, trying not to feel contempt. It was difficult to imagine *Isabella* begging for anything. She wouldn't be so ... so weak. But Isabella was a sorceress, not a young girl who'd been raised from birth to be nothing more than a tool in her father's plans. She hadn't had any legitimate siblings, either. No doubt her father had used the prospect of winning Helen's hand in marriage to keep his followers in line. And then …

"What happened?" Reginald reached out and lifted her chin so he could peer into her eyes. "Why did your father rebel?"

Helen let out a sob. "I don't know," she said. "He … he just changed, he just … he locked me in my room until the castle was attacked. I don't know what happened to him."

"I suppose you might have been very lucky," Reginald said. "Your father rose in rebellion against me. I have crushed him in battle. Do you know what that makes you?"

"A prize," Helen said. The bitterness in her voice was almost palpable. She'd gone from being her father's tool to a prize Reginald could offer to his supporters. "I … I'll do anything …"

"My wife is a sorceress," Reginald said, before she could do something that would embarrass both of them. Didn't she know he was married? It was possible she didn't. The news should have reached her father, but he'd have felt no obligation to pass it on. "If you behave yourself, I'll treat you well and let you have some say in who you marry. If not … you won't enjoy the consequences."

Helen gulped. "Yes, Your Majesty."

Reginald studied her for a long moment. Isabella would take charge of Helen and the other Heiresses … perhaps. It wouldn't be *that* bad. Isabella was hardly likely to abuse them. Or to push them into getting married against their wills. Reginald sat back, suddenly understanding what his father had meant when he'd talked about how a king sometimes had to go against himself. Common decency said Reginald should let Helen choose her own husband. The demands of monarchy insisted Reginald had to have his say. If she married someone entirely unsuitable …

He nodded to the guards. "Keep her in irons," he ordered. He ignored Helen's squawk of protest. "Put her in the female carriage, alone, and make sure she has what few comforts we can supply. If she causes trouble, bring her back to me."

The guards bowed, then helped Helen to her feet and half-carried her off. Reginald watched them go, silently kicking himself for not making arrangements in advance. The courtly busybodies would have a bunch of nasty things to say about Helen being alone in the midst of an army … he snorted, rudely. It'd show him who needed to be sent back to their estates to *think*, or at least be out of his hair. He honestly didn't understand why his father had tolerated the endless backbiting, rumour mongering and everything else. It wasn't as if the ladies of the court were *that* important. They weren't even hostages.

And Helen is going to be a hostage, he reflected sourly. *If there's anyone still loyal to her father around, after everything, they might think twice about putting her at risk.*

He stood and paced over to the map on the wooden table. The campaign had been short, sharp and – for the moment – decisive. Baron Braddock's castle had been smashed flat, his armsmen killed and his remaining supporters scattered and demoralised. Reginald would leave a small garrison in a nearby town, just to make sure the supporters didn't try to rally the commoners against their king, but otherwise there was little to gain from reprisals. It wasn't as if the common folk could be blamed for their baron's deeds. Braddock simply lacked the common touch.

The tent flap opened. "Your Majesty," Captain-General Jones said. "A delegation of townsfolk wishes an audience with you."

Reginald raised his eyebrows. *That* was odd. In his experience, commoners tended to keep their heads down – and their daughters locked up – whenever their king and his army happened to be marching by. Reginald had hanged men for rape – and forced looters to run the gauntlet – but he doubted the commoners had any *real* faith in his justice. The poor bastards had suffered under Baron Braddock. It was unlikely they'd have any faith in *any* aristocrats.

"Send them in," he said. He had no idea what the townsfolk wanted, but he didn't have much else to do. The army was already breaking camp. He intended to be well on his way to Havelock by the end of the day. "And order the other Captain-Generals to attend upon me afterwards."

He sat down as the townsfolk were shown into his tent. They were a hard-bitten bunch, with worn faces and taut expressions that suggested they dared not show any hint of their emotions. Their clothes were well made, brushing against the limits of the sumptuary laws without ever quite crossing them. Reginald was mildly surprised to note that one of them was a woman. Women often owned businesses along the coastline, or in the bigger cities, but it was rarer in the hinterlands. She'd be one to watch, he reminded himself. A woman who had made something of herself, against family and social pressure, would be formidable. He'd met a couple who would have made great army commanders or naval captains if they'd been men.

They prostrated themselves. "Your Majesty."

"You may rise," Reginald said. He had no patience for empty flattery. "Get to the point."

If they were surprised by his bluntness, they showed no sign of it. "Your Majesty," the lead man said, once they were resting on their haunches. "We have come before you to beg your mercy."

"My mercy?" Reginald felt a tingle of alarm. He hadn't moved to attack the town. He hadn't even compelled the townspeople to sell the army goods at fixed prices. He'd given orders to make sure the army gave the towns and their populations a wide berth. Had someone disobeyed orders? Or … or what? "Why do you request my mercy?"

The man – the mayor, Reginald guessed – leaned forward. "Your men have given orders to destroy the Shrine of Pastuer, Patron of the Fields, Your Majesty," he said. "We beg you not to touch it."

Reginald shivered. "And you erected the shrine at your baron's command?"

"Yes, Your Majesty," the mayor said. "Since we started leaving gifts and offerings at the shrine, our fields have grown and … Your Majesty, we have enough to feed ourselves!"

They're worshipping one of the entities, Reginald realised, numbly. He cursed under his breath. The entities would keep their side of the bargain, but … the townspeople would become dependent on them. The entities would eventually have enough power to materialise and then all hell would break loose. Literally, perhaps. *And they're not going to listen to me.*

"The shrine has to be destroyed," he said, flatly. "You know not what you do."

"Your Majesty!" The mayor stopped and swallowed, hard. He'd seen enough to know there was *something* to the prayers and rituals he'd been taught, even if he didn't know precisely what. Questioning his king was enough to get him beheaded – or worse – and yet, he knew better than to cross the entities too. "Your Majesty, I ..."

He prostrated himself so deeply his next words were muffled. "Your Majesty, I beg of you. Please let us keep the shrine! Our children have enough to eat! Our wives ..."

His voice trailed off. Reginald winced, feeling a knife twist in his gut. He didn't *want* to hurt his people ... and he would, if he ordered the shrine destroyed. He didn't *want* to ruin their hopes and dreams and lives ... he didn't *want* to do something that would only end, that could only end, with ill-feeling that might draw the entities back to the region. But he had no choice. The danger was all too clear. The shrine had to go.

"My decision is final," he said, hating himself. "The shrine will be destroyed before the army goes."

He motioned for the guards to escort the townsfolk out, knowing the destruction might prove futile. The poor bastards knew how to carry out rituals now. Reginald could destroy the shrine – and his garrison would make sure the townsfolk didn't build another one – but there was no way to keep them from praying to the entities. They could even set up another shrine in the countryside, hidden so carefully that there was little hope of finding and destroying it. Reginald winced. He and his successors were going to spend most of their lives wiping out all knowledge of the entities, always knowing it was futile. It just took one person to invite the creatures back into the human world.

His heart twisted, again. They were going to hate him. They were going to pray for his death – or worse. And who knew who might be listening?

Captain-General Gars entered, followed by Captain-Generals Stuart and Jones. Reginald nodded to them, his trusted right hands. He'd need to promote them, he reminded himself; he'd need to reward them for their services, now he was king. One of them would probably be quite happy to marry Helen, if she consented. They weren't as well-born as she might have wished, but they enjoyed his favour. Who knew? Perhaps they'd be happy together.

He stood. "It's been a long day already," he said. "Are we ready to march?"

"Yes, Your Majesty," Gars said. "The troops are ready. We just need you to designate a company to remain behind."

"Pick one," Reginald ordered. He trusted Gars to pick a unit that could control the countryside without earning the ire of the population. If, of course, that was possible now. "Their first task is to destroy the shrines."

Gars nodded, curtly. "Yes, Your Majesty."

It was a lot easier when I was just the Crown Prince, Reginald thought. He'd been socially superior to everyone, but the gulf hadn't been insurmountable. He could drink with the lads – at least those of noble birth, or who'd earned a peerage – and no one had raised an eyebrow. Now? His only confidantes were his wife and his sisters, all of whom were on the other side of the country. *I could actually rely on people giving me good advice.*

"Tell the troops to be diplomatic, but firm," he said. "We're going to upset people."

"It doesn't matter, Your Majesty," Stuart said. "They'll do what they're told."

"Let us hope you're right," Reginald said. He was tempted to suggest that they drank, just like old times, but he knew better. Kings had died in drunken binges. "Are your men ready to leave too?"

"They're looking forward to it," Stuart assured him. "Being tied down wasn't much fun."

"I can imagine," Reginald said. "Have them disperse through the towns and villages as we pass, keeping their eyes open for shrines and other potential threats. If they see one, they're to report it. I'll decide what to do about it."

"Yes, Your Majesty," Stuart said.

Not that I have much choice, Reginald thought. *We'll have to destroy the shrines.*

He sighed. He'd never really believed in the gods. His father had been deeply cynical about religion, particularly the official hierarchy promoted by the Golden City. Reginald had come to agree with him when he'd pointed out how *convenient* the doctrine was for the sorcerers who ruled the world. Who could rise up against leaders descended from the gods themselves? He'd made sacrifices to the military gods, but he'd never really believed. His life was his own ...

... But it wasn't true for the commoners, was it?

He felt his temper darken. Isabella had pointed it out to him, time and time again. *Reginald* had been a Crown Prince, born to power and privilege. There was no way he could fall so far that he'd hit rock bottom, even if he drank himself senseless and indulged himself in each and every way. But a commoner didn't have that freedom … a commoner knew, all too well, that he could be cut down in the streets by his social superiors, that he could be robbed of all he owned or forced to watch helplessly as his wife and daughters were raped … to a commoner, the army had to look like a giant natural disaster. The urge to put one's faith in the gods had to be overwhelming, if one was powerless. And the entities would happily answer the call.

"We'll move as planned," he said. He wanted to get back to Havelock. Isabella was there, waiting for him. So was the council, but one couldn't have everything. "Dismissed."

The three men bowed, then retreated. Reginald stood and peered down at the map, wondering where the *next* bout of trouble would come from. The entities were still out there, somewhere. He had no idea where or what they were doing, but he doubted they'd remain quiet forever. They probably had something nasty in mind already. As knowledge of their nature spread, who knew what they'd do?

He stood and walked into the outside air. The army camp smelt of too many men, horses and suchlike in too close proximity. His eyes tracked the tents as they were dismantled, the soldiers either shoving them into carts or packing them into knapsacks for the march back to Havelock. Reginald nodded to a handful of soldiers he recognised, then started to walk towards the carriages. There weren't many. If there was one advantage to being king, to finally having all the authority, it was that he'd been able to ensure that everyone who accompanied the army knew how to ride a horse and handle themselves in a fight. The days when he'd had to put up with his father's commissioners, or his political allies, were long gone.

And here's hoping I don't repeat that mistake myself, he thought, as he walked up to the final carriage. A pair of guards stood outside, resting on their iron-tipped spears. *My son will probably chafe as much as I did.*

The guards stepped aside, allowing him to scramble up into

the carriage. It had been designed to transport prisoners, although Reginald had expected to be carrying Baron Braddock rather than his daughter. The inside had been crafted to give the prisoner some freedom of movement, and allow her to use the chamberpot, without giving enough room to escape. Or so he hoped. Reginald figured he could break out, given enough time.

Helen scowled, then hastily pasted a dull expression on her face. "Your Majesty?"

Reginald felt a flicker of sympathy. There was nothing to *do* in the carriage. There were no books to read – if she *could* read – let alone anything else. Helen had nothing to do, but brood on her likely future. Reginald hated boredom himself, even though he'd learned to tolerate it on campaign. Whoever had said war was long hours of boredom broken by moments of screaming terror had never said a truer word.

"We'll be on our way shortly," Reginald said. He silently kicked himself. He wasn't sure why he'd come. He eyed the manacles around her wrists, feeling a moment of relief. She couldn't call on the entities … if, indeed, she knew *how*. "Tell me something … what happened to your father?"

Helen's eyes narrowed. "I told you already," she said. "He just … *changed*."

"Why?" Reginald studied her thoughtfully. "What happened?"

"I don't understand," Helen said. "Why do you ask?"

"Your father's rebellion was doomed from the start," Reginald said. The entity had given them a few nasty moments, but he'd known how to handle it. "Why did he even try?"

"I don't know," Helen said. She laughed, bitterly. "Do you think he told me anything?"

Reginald shrugged. "I'll have some books sent to you," he said, as he opened the hatch. "And, like I said, you'll be treated well as long as you behave."

Helen rattled her chains. "Is this your idea of treating someone *well*, Your Majesty?"

"If there's one thing I've learnt in the last year," Reginald said, "it is that you cannot be too careful. Really."

And sometimes you can do everything right, his thoughts added, *and still lose.*

Chapter Five

Princess Silverdale knew, without false modesty, that she was a bright young girl.

She'd always been good with her lessons, the ones she'd cared enough to study. It was sometimes difficult to muster the enthusiasm to do anything when she knew, as the king's youngest child and a daughter to boot, it was unlikely her life would ever amount to anything. She'd loved her father – and she'd known he loved her, too – but she'd also been all too aware there would come a time when she was married to someone she might not know, for the good of the kingdom. Her governesses had made that clear, over the years. It wasn't until her eldest sister had gone mad, and her father had sunk into an enchanted daze, that she'd discovered her true talent. And she wasn't about to let it go without a fight.

She sat in her room, studying the small collection of ingredients the maids had collected for her. They were surprisingly mundane, something that had probably encouraged the maids to obtain them without asking too many questions or reporting the affair to Queen Isabella. Silverdale liked her sister-in-law – Isabella was certainly not the traditional wicked sister-in-law – but the older woman was too cautious for Silverdale's tastes. She would not approve of the younger girl experimenting, even though she'd done plenty of *that* when Sofia – and her master – had ruled the castle. It should be easier now, Silverdale told herself. The entity that had overshadowed the entire building, reaching into the hearts and souls of the entire population, was gone.

Her lips quirked as she mashed the ingredients together, pounding them into paste. Her governesses had occasionally threatened to send her to the kitchens to work beside the cooks and kitchen porters, but she'd known they'd been bluffing. A little princess could not be sent to the kitchens, no matter what she'd done. Now ... she knew that preparing the ointment personally was part of the magic, part of the rite that prepared *her* as well as everything else. It simply didn't work so well, if at all, if someone else prepared the ointment. She embraced the task wholeheartedly. There was no choice.

She finished grinding the ingredients into a pulp, drained the liniment and poured it into a small bowl. There wasn't much, but it probably didn't matter. She'd even heard hints that a placebo would work just as well, as long as the user didn't *know* it was a placebo. She wondered, idly, if she could trick herself into believing she wasn't using one. It didn't seem likely. She looked at the door, then the clock, as she walked into her bedroom. The governess had finished their lessons for the day. No one else should seek her out until dinnertime. She should have time to perform the rite and return before it was too late.

Reginald will be back soon, she told herself. The last message had stated the army would return within the week. *And won't he be pleased when he realises what I've done?*

She lay on her bed and dabbed the ointment on her eyes. The world started to blur around her, the room starting to fall apart … she tensed, then told herself to relax. She'd stepped outside her body before, time and time again. This time … she felt herself drifting up, and looked down. Her body lay below, breathing steadily. She could *see* the life pervading her cells, see the tendrils linking her astral self to her physical body. It felt oddly wrong, yet right. She allowed herself to drift up again, pressing against the ceiling. It offered little resistance as she passed through, as if it was nothing more than mist and fog. She found herself drifting within a servant corridor, one of the little passageways that kept the servants out of sight and mind. A pair of maids, carrying something heavy between them, walked through her as though she wasn't there. Silverdale's lips curved into a smile. As far as they were concerned, she really *wasn't*.

Her awareness expanded as she turned and looked around. The castle seemed to be little more than a ghostly building, as if it had hardly any presence within the astral plane. The inhabitants were points of light, moving to and fro in patterns that made little sense. She puzzled over it for a long moment, then realised they were pacing corridors that simply didn't exist to her. She glided forward, passing through walls and ceilings as though they simply weren't there. The people she passed showed no awareness of her presence. How could they?

They don't know I'm here, Silverdale thought. She giggled, the sound echoing oddly within the astral plane. *I could watch anyone from here ...*

She found herself looking at Ruby. Her older sister – her eldest sister, now Sofia was gone – was reading through a pile of letters. She looked bored, but intent. Silverdale leaned forward and planted a ghostly kiss on Ruby's neck, making her sister jump. Ruby stood and spun around, as if she knew there was someone behind her. Silverdale froze, hoping and praying her sister couldn't *really* see her. Ruby was known for bearing grudges. And if she thought to report the affair to their brother ...

A wash of guilt overcame her. Silverdale faded downwards, allowing the tendrils to draw her back to her body. She shouldn't be spying on her sister; not now, not ever. And yet, she knew that knowledge was power. Who knew *what* was in those letters? Silverdale was tempted to go back and look, even though she knew she shouldn't. She'd have to figure out another way to find out.

And it's probably boring anyway, she told herself. *Father was always complaining about the letters he had to read.*

The thought sobered her as she drifted back into her room. Her body still lay on the bed, unmoving. Silverdale looked down at herself, contrasting her astral form with her real body. The former was translucent, almost ghostly ... little more than a roughly humanoid cloud of mist. The latter was real, bound to flesh and blood ... she wondered, suddenly, if she could become a ghost permanently. She knew how to affect the real world, even though it was difficult. She wouldn't be dead, just ... absent.

A wave of ... *something* ... washed through the astral plane. Someone was calling. Silverdale turned, looking down. Voices were echoing through her mind ... no, a single voice. She found herself gliding down, passing through stone floors as if they weren't truly there. A wall rose up in front of her and ... she slammed into it. The force of the impact knocked the wind from her lungs. For a moment, she thought she'd materialised within the iron wall. Her body wasn't corporal, but it sure as hell *felt* corporeal. She hung there for a long moment, stunned. The iron seemed to repel her as much as it drew her.

She turned, suddenly very aware of where she was. She was in Isabella's chambers, the dungeons she'd adapted for her use and ... Isabella was *looking* at her. Silverdale turned to flee, but she knew it was already too late. Isabella had *seen* her. Silverdale swallowed and forced herself to look at her sister-in-law. She looked strange, as if two people were occupying the same space. Her astral form was ... different.

"I see you," Isabella said. Her voice sounded odd, but Silverdale had no trouble understanding it. "What do you think you're doing?"

She went on before Silverdale could think of an answer. "Get back to your body," she ordered. "I'll be up in a moment."

Silverdale fled, kicking herself. She should have known – she *had* known – that Isabella was the only one who could see her, when she was in her astral form. And she hadn't even thought to keep her distance! The voice had called her and she'd come and ... she looked back, sensing tendrils of alien thought reaching out of the iron walls and gliding into the distant realm, moving in ways no human could follow. Silverdale thought she could follow, but she feared she wouldn't be able to return. Her awareness kept expanding. *Things* were moving past, brushing against the edge of the human world. She didn't dare look at them too closely. Her instincts told her it would be fatal.

She crashed back into her body, gasping for breath. She felt as if she'd been punched in the stomach, even though she hadn't been. Her body seemed to have forgotten how to breathe. She took a deep, sucking breath, practically choking. The world felt strange, as though it wasn't quite real. She pressed her fingers into the bed, wondering – in her daze – why her fingers weren't going *through* the bed. It took her long moments to school her thoughts to calm.

"Here," Isabella said. "Drink this."

Silverdale took the glass of water and sipped it gratefully. Her body felt hungry, yet she didn't want to eat. The liquid felt heavy in her stomach. Isabella reclaimed the glass and refilled it, motioning for Silverdale to drink again. The older woman looked as if she didn't know whether she should be worried or angry. Silverdale had seen that look before, on the faces of innumerable governesses. It always ended with them going into retirement, if they weren't dismissed first.

"Thank you," she managed. "I …"

Isabella scowled. "What were you thinking?"

Silverdale hesitated, suddenly unsure what to say. Isabella had shown scant respect for Silverdale's birth, although she'd definitely shown *some* for her intelligence. She certainly *didn't* have any reluctance to scold a princess …

"I wanted to help," she said, finally. "And to practice magic."

"And I told you not to try," Isabella said. "Why did you visit the cage?"

"The cage?" Silverdale hesitated. "The iron walls?"

"Yes." Isabella's eyes bored into hers. "Why did you go there?"

"I …" Silverdale swallowed. "I heard a voice calling me."

"You're not the only one," Isabella said, tartly. She sounded displeased, although it didn't seem to be directed at Silverdale herself. "If you'd managed to open the cage …"

Silverdale frowned. "I can't touch iron when I'm a ghost," she said. "It's too heavy."

"Something like that," Isabella said. "Unfortunately, we cannot wrap the entire world in iron."

"Or even just line the castle walls with iron," Silverdale said. "We'd need ways in and out."

She paused. "What would happen if I entered an open room and then the door slammed closed?"

"I don't know," Isabella said. "And I don't want to risk your life trying to find out."

Silverdale swallowed. It was easy to forget, in the astral plane, that there were things that *could* hurt you. There was something about the realm that encouraged … complacency, perhaps, or just a general sense that nothing really mattered. She'd seen *things* that existed in the alien realm, creatures that could hurt or kill or corrupt her if they caught her, but it was still hard to believe they posed a threat. What would happen if her astral form wound up trapped? Would she fall back into her body? Or would she become a ghost in truth, permanently separated from her physical form? She shivered as she wrapped her arms around her legs. She didn't want to know.

Isabella studied her, coldly. "Magic is dangerous," she said, flatly. "And I *told* you not to use it without supervision."

"I know what I'm doing," Silverdale protested. "I wasn't using *your* magic!"

"You know enough to be dangerous and not enough to be safe," Isabella said. Her tone didn't change. "I'm not sure it's ever *safe*."

"I know what I'm doing," Silverdale repeated. "I used the magic to escape the castle and ..."

"And you could have easily been killed," Isabella said. "You don't know enough to be sure of anything. Nor do I. We're figuring out the rules by trial and error and that could easily get us killed."

Silverdale glared at her. "And what *else* am I going to do with my life?"

Isabella smiled. The expression didn't touch her eyes. "You have your entire life ahead of you," she said. "And you have the freedom to decide what you want to do with it."

"Hah." Silverdale snorted. If there was one thing she'd learnt, from a very early age, it was that she wasn't *free*. No one was *free*. Her father had been the king, a king whose every word was law, but even he had had his limits. An absolute monarch who wished to *remain* an absolute monarch had to be careful, he'd told her. He couldn't annoy his supporters without losing them and that would lead to inevitable disaster. "I'm not *free*."

"You're too young to be so cynical," Isabella said, although there was something in her voice that suggested she agreed. "You have more than enough time to master magic."

"And learn how to use it against the enemy," Silverdale said. She'd *seen* the creatures that had overshadowed her sister and enchanted her father. "If I keep practicing ..."

"Yes, under supervision," Isabella said. "Your brother will not thank me if you lose yourself in the other world."

Silverdale made a face. She loved her brother, but they hadn't had much time together since he'd taken the throne. Reginald just had too much to handle, from rebellious barons to securing the borders and sending reinforcements to the Summer Isle. Silverdale had a feeling the island was worthless

– she'd listened to a few of the debates, from the astral plane – but Reginald was determined to make something of it. He swore the Summer Isle would be very useful in the long term. And no one could convince him otherwise.

She looked her sister-in-law in the eye. "Did your parents try to stop you from studying magic?"

Isabella laughed, harshly. "Quite the opposite," she said. "My father was not a very nice man. He wanted a daughter who was both an important and skilled magician and completely subservient to him. He wanted his children to take up roles within society so, as a group, we could punch well above our weight. He spent decades convincing the Grand Sorcerer and the Grand Sorceress to support us, to promote us and our clients ... and you know what happened?"

"The Golden City fell," Silverdale said, quietly.

"Before that," Isabella said. "I ... I wanted to rebel against him. He'd set my life in stone before I took my first steps and ... I wanted to rebel. I wanted to hurt him. I fought time and time again, but ... it wasn't until I was an adult that I managed to break free. And he disowned me."

Silverdale shuddered. Disownment was the worst punishment anyone could suffer. She'd heard horror stories of boys and girls who were disowned and cast out to live in the gutters or find their fortunes somewhere else, somewhere well away from their former families. She had no idea what Isabella had done to merit disownment, but ... she didn't think she wanted to know. Did *Reginald* know? A disowned woman might not be the best choice of wife ... she felt a flash of shame. Isabella had risked everything for a kingdom that wasn't hers. She deserved better than petty suspicion.

"I'm sorry," she said. She meant it, too. "He made you study magic?"

"And everything else," Isabella said. "I rarely had a moment to myself."

"But I *want* to study," Silverdale said. "I need to study."

"You don't have the background to understand everything, not yet," Isabella said. She grimaced. "And I don't have the training to teach you everything. There are no books on practical magic in the castle library."

"Sofia probably had them burnt, along with the others," Silverdale said. She'd heard that every book on religion, particularly the approved religions, had been burnt to ashes shortly after Sofia had taken power. "I don't think she wanted anyone studying magic."

"No," Isabella agreed. "Although … the entities screw up magic. I don't understand how they do it."

"Then we have to find out," Silverdale insisted. She knew she sounded whiny, but she didn't much care. "We have to keep experimenting."

"Yes, *carefully*," Isabella said. Her voice grew colder. "And *you* chose to ignore my instructions."

Silverdale made a face. "What now?"

"You can copy out the first ten pages of your grimoire," Isabella said. "And afterwards, you can write a set of proposals. Experimental proposals. Perhaps we'll even try them."

"Ouch." Silverdale felt her heart sink. Her penmanship was good, but she'd spent long enough copying out entire sections – thanks to her governesses, who insisted it was the only way to learn – to know she hated it. She kicked herself, mentally, for telling Isabella how much she hated it. Perhaps she should have insisted she enjoyed it, instead. "Can't I go help the kitchen staff instead?"

Isabella smiled. "If you like," she said. She struck a contemplative pose that made Silverdale giggle, despite herself. "I can make the arrangements …"

Silverdale blinked. That had worked?

"You won't enjoy it," Isabella said. Her voice suggested she knew what was going through Silverdale's mind. "But perhaps it will teach you something about the value of hard work."

And how much you've rejected your birth, Silverdale thought. She knew little about sorcerous etiquette – she'd been six when the Golden City fell – but she doubted it was *that* different to the manners she'd been drilled in since she could walk. *No aristocrat would send her daughter to the kitchens …*

She told herself not to be silly. It was better than the alternative.

"And you can do your proposals too," Isabella added. "We might want to try them. Later."

"Yes, My Lady," Silverdale said.

Chapter Six

"The King! The King!"

Reginald pasted a regal expression on his face as the horse cantered through the gates and onto the streets. Havelock was turning out for him, the impression of spontaneity so extreme he *knew* the city council had lain the groundwork days in advance. They'd known the army was coming, of course, and they'd wanted to make a good impression. They feared what he might do to them, when he ran out of more important problems. It hadn't been *that* long since they'd given the keys to the city to Sofia …

But they didn't know what she could do with them, he thought, as he waved at the cheering crowds. Young apprentices, unmarried girls with flowers in their hair … they cheered so loudly he *knew* it must have been rehearsed. The people who'd been caught on the streets when the seemingly unplanned parade had begun looked far less enthusiastic, although they were trying their best to hide it. The city fathers wouldn't look kindly on anyone who didn't cheer loudly enough. *They were as surprised as we were.*

He kept waving as his eyes passed over the remains of a temple. It had been knocked down shortly after Sofia took power, the priest and his retinue taken away and probably marched through the Godly Realm. Or simply executed, their bodies cremated and their ashes dumped in the river. The entities had put up a handful of shrines, after the temples had been smashed, only to have them destroyed in turn when Reginald assumed the throne. His eyes narrowed, wondering how many of his people had sensed *something* near the shrines. All it took was one person to make contact and give the entities another chance at taking the kingdom …

A young girl stood near the castle gates, holding a bunch of flowers. Reginald slowed the horse to a stop, dismounted and accepted the flowers with as much grace as he could muster. The girl – she couldn't be any older than seven –

looked terrified, although she was doing her best to hide it. Common-born, he guessed, probably not from a wealthy or politically-connected family. The city fathers wouldn't risk putting *their* daughters in front of him, not when the slightest mistake could lead to ruination. He kept his face carefully blank, as the girl dropped a curtsey and turned and ran. Reginald didn't mind. He'd attended enough formal functions to understand the impulse all too well.

He spoke, briefly, to the city fathers before he stepped through the gate and into the castle courtyard. His bodyguards relaxed, the moment they were safe. Reginald smiled as he saw the line of aristocrats and wealthy commoners waiting for him, even though he found their presence a minor irritation. He wanted to see his wife again, not listen to insincere pledges of loyalty. If Sofia had won, they would have grovelled before her with just as much enthusiasm.

And if a random nobleman had captured the throne and imposed himself, he thought sourly, *they would have grovelled before him, too.*

He put the thought to one side as he walked down the line, nodding to those in favour and ignoring those who weren't. He'd never enjoyed playing the political game, in which he had to be nice to people he hated and cut dead people he liked; he had little interest in continuing, now he was king. He'd treat his friends and allies well. And if others had a problem with it ... he sighed, inwardly. Life had definitely been a lot easier when he'd been his father's strong right arm. There'd even been a safety net, of sorts. If he'd screwed up, his father could reprimand him and everyone would pretend to believe it was enough. He'd never liked being a legal child, even though he was an adult. It was odd to realise – now – that there'd been advantages to the humiliating status.

And my son will hate it too, he thought. *I wonder if he'll see the advantages before he inherits the throne.*

The Castellan stepped forward as Reginald reached the end of the line. "Your Majesty," he said. "Welcome home."

"Thank you," Reginald said. The castle didn't *feel* like home, not any longer. It was funny how he'd always wanted to leave, when he'd been Crown Prince. Now ... he couldn't move the throne without upsetting people. "You may accompany me."

He stepped through the curtain and into the corridor. Behind him, the Castellan dismissed the crowd. Reginald allowed himself a moment of amusement, knowing half of the guests would be unhappy the ceremony hadn't lasted longer. They hated the ceremonies as much as Reginald himself, but merely being invited was a badge of status. A man could be wealthy enough to buy the crown out of pocket change and yet he wouldn't be anyone, if he wasn't invited. The remainder, Reginald hoped, would be grateful. He hadn't *asked* them to wait for hours.

A messenger appeared in front of him. "Your Majesty, Her Majesty awaits you in your chambers."

Reginald smiled. "Good," he said. He was dirty and smelly, but he couldn't wait to see his wife. "Give a purse of gold to the flower girl, then inform the city fathers that her conduct was perfectly acceptable."

"Yes, Your Majesty," the messenger said.

Reginald felt his smile grow wider as he walked up to the royal chambers, despite an odd little pang that nagged at his mind. The chambers had belonged to his father ... in truth, they still felt like they belonged to his father. Reginald hadn't wanted to move into them, even after they'd been thoroughly cleaned and inspected for unpleasant surprises. But he'd had no choice. The rooms were the finest in the castle. He could neither leave them empty nor give them to someone else.

And Ruby didn't want to move into Sofia's rooms, either, he reminded himself. *She said the walls gave her bad dreams.*

He passed the two guards and stepped into the room. Isabella was sitting in a chair, making a show of reading a book. She put the book to one side as he entered, standing with a smile. She'd grown her hair out a little, he noted, as he took her in his arms and kissed her. The look suited her, although he wasn't sure he should *tell* her. She'd cut her hair short when she'd left the Golden City.

"I've been away too long," he said. There was royal business to attend to, but it could wait. He'd already issued orders for Helen Braddock's transfer to her suite. His staff could take care of it. "I've missed you."

"Me too." Isabella grinned at him. "Get undressed."

She drew back and removed her shirt. Reginald stared, savouring the moment when her breasts were thrust out. Her skin was tanned and scarred, her arms were muscular ... so very different from the fainting flowers of court. He felt his heart start to race as she undid her trousers and let them fall. It was suddenly very hard to get undressed without tearing anything. Their lips met, again ...

Afterwards, they lay together in bed. Reginald knew, dimly, that he had business to attend to, but he found it hard to care. He'd never had much time for the protocols of royal marriage and Isabella, of course, came from a very different society. The idea of having her in a separate room, waiting for him to attend upon her ... he smiled, wryly. Isabella would *never* go along with that. The traditionalists might howl, but Reginald didn't care. Besides, he'd always suspected the relative lack of royal heirs had something to do with the pressure to conceive. Pressure had never made *him* more inclined to do something. Why should it be any different for his wife?

"I definitely missed you," Isabella said. Her fingers traced a rune in the air. It glowed before fading into nothingness. "Your letters weren't quite the same."

"I could never write down what I wanted to say," Reginald said. He was all too aware that anything he wrote down could be intercepted and read by unfriendly eyes. His enemies might take something he wrote in confidence and turn it against him. "Your letters were pretty bland too."

Isabella elbowed him. "And someone would have said something, if I'd written a torrid description of what I wanted to do with you."

"Probably." Reginald scowled at the wall. There was very little privacy in the Royal Family and they both knew it. "I hope the maids haven't been giving you more trouble."

"No, but the ladies of the court still don't know what to make of me," Isabella said. "I've got a few of the younger girls wearing trousers."

"I'm sure the young men aren't complaining," Reginald said. "Their mothers, on the other hand ..."

She elbowed him, again. "Other than that, there are some issues we have to discuss," she said. "But do you want to discuss yours first?"

Reginald sat upright. Isabella might not be conventionally pretty, and she wasn't even *trying* to fit into the court, but she was devastatingly intelligent. He could rely on her, as everything from a sounding board to an advisor and bodyguard. The ladies of the court rarely understood the practicalities, when they weren't trying to turn him to their side or simply manipulate him. Her magic made her formidable, but it was her experience as a mercenary he truly valued.

"I encountered and banished another entity," he said. He briefly outlined everything that had happened when Baron Braddock's castle fell. "The baron was very definitely one of their pawns."

Isabella winced. "Do you think he knew the risks?"

Reginald shrugged. He hadn't known Baron Braddock very well, even before he'd become king. "His daughter says he changed suddenly, but she was kept out of the loop," he said, slowly. "We just don't know."

"And you brought her here," Isabella said. "Should I be worried?"

"Just check she's free of their taint, then we can put her up here for a while," Reginald said, dryly. There was no way he could have left Helen Braddock in the ruins of her father's castle and she knew it. Even if Helen herself didn't want to make trouble, someone could easily set out to take her by force. "I promised we'd treat her well as long as she behaved herself."

"Good." Isabella met his eyes. "Is that the worst of it?"

"No." Reginald grimaced. "I had a meeting with the townsfolk, or at least some of them. They were very insistent we should leave the shrines alone."

Isabella looked up, sharply. "What happened?"

"We destroyed them," Reginald said. "But the townsfolk weren't happy. They insisted the rites and rituals brought results."

"I don't doubt it," Isabella said. She looked down at her bare legs, scarred by years on the campaign trail. "I just worry about what *else* they'll bring."

Reginald made a face. "I don't know if we *can* erase all knowledge of the rites and rituals," he said. "Right now, they're already spreading out of control."

He leaned back, staring at the ceiling. "You've seen the reports," he added. "How do we keep people from *using* the rituals?"

"We tell them the truth," Isabella said, although she sounded as though she didn't really believe herself. "And we warn them of the dangers."

Reginald shook his head. Desperate people would do desperate things. It was easy to rationalise the most foolish of decisions, if one was so desperate as to believe there was no other choice. The rebel fighting against his lord, the wife lashing out at a brutal husband, the child striking an abusive parent, a maid trying to defend herself against a terrible mistress ... they could use the rites, in utter desperation, and unleash a nightmare. Peasants facing a combination of famine and grinding taxes were unlikely to think twice. Why should they? It wasn't as if there were many other options. And they'd give the entities an open door.

He felt cold, every time he considered it. He'd *seen* the dangers. He'd seen how much the entities could do. He'd seen them at work ... but others hadn't. They didn't believe the stories of creatures who might as well be gods, who were *worshipped* as gods. They'd learn better, too late. Reginald shuddered. There had been no shortage of monarchs and aristocrats foolish enough to ride a tiger, only to discover they couldn't get off.

"They wouldn't believe us," he said. "And we can't even rebuild the temples in a hurry."

"The Golden City was not built in a day," Isabella said, reassuringly. "It will take time, time and patience, but we can do it."

"I hope you're right." Reginald stood and started to pace. "Have you heard anything from your brother?"

"Not for quite some time," Isabella said. "The roads are a mess these days, as you know."

Reginald nodded, curtly. The mail service had once promised to take a message from one side of the continent to the other in a week or so. The network of crystal balls and trained magicians had allowed messages to be sent even faster, if one were prepared to pay. Now ... the Golden City was so far away it might as well be on the other side of the world. A message would take weeks to reach the city, if it got there at all. The dragons, and the civil wars, had torn up the roads, turned the population into refugees and generally smashed the work of centuries in a few short years. He'd heard the rumours, but he didn't really *know* what was happening to the east. It was unlikely to touch his kingdom for a good long time.

"We might have to send another messenger," Reginald said. He detested messengers, but they were useful. However, he didn't want to send one to certain death if it could be avoided. "Do you want to try?"

Isabella grimaced. She didn't like her brother. He found that hard to understand. His sisters had been sweet little girls. Even *Sofia* had been sweet, if a little too religious, until the entities had gotten their claws into her. But Isabella had had a very different experience. He suspected he'd never understand her childhood. It was hard to imagine coming to blows with his siblings.

Except I did, he reminded himself. *Sofia wasn't in her right mind, but ... she still killed our father.*

"We probably should," Isabella said, reluctantly. "He *did* say he'd be continuing his research."

Her eyes narrowed. "Speaking of which, you need to have a few words with Silverdale. She's been continuing her research too."

Reginald shivered. "I'll have a word with her," he said. His sister would listen to him, although ... she really *should* have listened to Isabella. "I take it she didn't listen to you?"

"She wants to move ahead too quickly," Isabella said. She shrugged. "Now you're back, I can spend more time with her. But she really shouldn't jump headlong into the unknown."

"I understand," Reginald said. He'd never listened to his early tutors either. It had taken his father – or the swordmaster – to make him pay attention. And his younger sister had gone through more governesses than the rest of her siblings put together. "She's probably feeling a little unsure of herself, now she's turning into a teenager."

"Quite." Isabella grinned, suddenly. "And now I understand why my mother was so cranky with me when *I* was a teenager."

"We always forget what it was like to be young," Reginald

mused. He had an entire list of mistakes, some of which had nearly killed him. His father had not been pleased. "Give her some space, please. Let her make her own mistakes."

He sighed, feeling old. He wasn't *that* old, not compared to his father, but he felt as if he had the weight of the world on his shoulders. The kingdom was his ... he understood, now, why his father had been going grey. The job had its perks, but it also made him the target for everyone with a grudge. He'd encountered people who'd insisted his father had set out to ruin them personally, even though the king had never heard of any of them. They'd been unable to imagine the simple fact they just weren't *important* ...

"Her mistakes might get her killed, or worse," Isabella pointed out. She shook her head, sharply. "What comes back from her experiments might wear her face, but it won't be *her*."

"I know," Reginald said. "But she's too stubborn to listen if you just keep saying *no*."

Isabella smiled. "Are we speaking about Silverdale, Lord Husband, or you?"

"Please don't call me that," Reginald said, with a mock shudder. "It sounds unnatural when *you* say it."

"Hah." Isabella stood, moving with a self-confidence he could only admire. The ladies of the court, the ones he'd bedded over the years, had been reluctant to undress in front of him and always insisted on dressing again as soon as possible. Isabella didn't seem to care who saw her naked. "I could call you worse things."

Reginald grinned. "Maybe later," he said. "Right now ..."

He allowed his eyes to follow her. He had to call a council meeting, if only to squash complaints about his wife before they got out of hand. And he had to have dinner with his family, what was left of it, and find a way to direct Silverdale's talents in a safer direction or two. But right now ... he stood and took hold of her. She turned and kissed him, her breasts pushing into his chest. It really *had* been too long.

I'll worry about it later, he told himself, as their kissing grew more passionate. *Right now, I want her.*

Chapter Seven

Isabella was still in a good mood hours later, when she left the royal suite and headed down to the guestrooms. Reginald was a fine husband in more ways than one, even if he *was* married to the kingdom as well as to Isabella herself. He took his duty seriously and that meant ... she frowned suddenly, remembering how badly they needed an heir. The council was probably nagging him about it now, the bastards. He needed a son, his sister needed to be married off to someone who would give *her* a son ... bastards. She cursed herself under her breath for letting them invade her mind. Her good mood faded as she reached the door.

"Your Majesty," the guard said. Isabella couldn't remember his name, but – thankfully – he wasn't one of the idiots who thought she'd faint at the merest hint of blood. Stupid, ignorant idiots. "The prisoner is secured, as per orders."

"Thank you." Isabella took a breath, centring herself. It wasn't the guard's fault she was in a vile mood. And to think she'd been in a good one only a few short moments ago. "Stay on guard, but don't enter without permission."

She braced herself as she pushed open the door. They'd lined the floor, walls and ceiling with cold iron, but she was ruefully aware there was no way to isolate the occupant completely, short of sealing the poor bitch in and leaving her to suffocate. There was no guarantee she'd been touched, let alone overshadowed, by the entities. Baron Braddock had apparently kept his daughter under tight control, but that was meaningless. Helen Braddock probably had just as many resentments as Princess Sofia. The entities could play on them until she allowed them into her heart.

Helen sat on the chair, a solid iron chain wrapped around her ankle. She had more than enough mobility to do anything she might reasonably want to do, apart from leave the chambers and escape. Isabella scowled. The suite was quite pleasant, but she had a feeling Helen Braddock had never been quite so restrained in her life. Isabella wasn't impressed. She'd spent time in the dungeons herself, thanks to Sofia, and she'd seen the cells under the Watchtower. They'd been nightmarish, cells designed to hold magicians who simply couldn't be killed. She'd had nightmares about ending up there herself ...

"Who are you?" Helen's voice was light, but Isabella had no trouble hearing the resentment underneath. "What are you ...?"

Isabella smiled as the younger woman's voice trailed away. She'd probably thought Isabella was a *man*. It was astonishing how many men – and women – looked at masculine clothing and thought *man*, even if the wearer had breasts. And a real man might have caused all sorts of problems for a young woman, whatever happened. The backbiters would have insisted the poor girl had lost her virtue ...

Even if she hadn't, Isabella thought. *That* was going to change, if nothing else. A woman's value didn't rest in her vagina, let alone her virtue. *And anyone who objects will spend the rest of their lives croaking on a lily pad.*

"I'm Isabella," she said. She knew she should probably make a grand pronouncement out of it, but she couldn't be bothered. She'd been a mercenary, one of the boys, for far longer than she'd been a queen. "And you must be Helen."

Helen stared at her, as if a live dragon had poked its snout into the cell. Isabella hid her amusement with an effort. Helen was a prisoner, effectively the ward of a king who might marry her off to the highest bidder. Isabella knew better, and she was sure Reginald had reassured the poor girl, but Helen didn't. She probably thought Reginald wouldn't keep his promise. He'd come under immense pressure to give her hand in marriage to one of his supporters. Isabella scowled at the thought. If she had a daughter, the girl was going to choose her husband ...

"Your Majesty," Helen stammered, finally. "I ... I ..."

"You may speak freely," Isabella said. She didn't know which faction was worse, the one that nagged her to leave politics to the men and concentrate on getting pregnant or the one that praised her in public and gossiped about her in private. Someone speaking freely would be quite refreshing. "I won't take offense."

Helen rattled her chain. "Can you take this off?"

"In a moment," Isabella said. "What happened to your father?"

"I keep being asked that question," Helen said. Her voice rose. "*I just don't know*!"

"I understand," Isabella said. She picked up a chair and carried it over to the wall, then sat down, mentally measuring the chain. Helen shouldn't be able to reach her, unless she'd been twisted into something utterly inhuman. It was possible, although unlikely. A Red Monk could have escaped well before it was shoved into the manacles. "Did he not say *anything* to you?"

"No!" Helen glared at her. "Why do people keep asking?"

"Because they can't see things from your point of view," Isabella said. She dug into her pouch and found the liniment. Silverdale had done a good job, although it would have been better if Isabella had made it herself. She wasn't sure why the liniment worked for her, when it didn't always work in reverse. "And they honestly can't understand your life."

She closed one eye, then dipped her finger in the liniment and gently dabbed it into her other eye. The world seemed to shift around her, as if it were slightly tilted off-kilter. She ignored Helen's gasp as she felt the ointment melt against her eye, a strange sensation spreading through her. Mother Lembu had cautioned her against using the liniment without proper precautions, citing the danger of seeing something a human could not see and remain sane. Ironically, she'd also told Isabella how to use the liniment to check for someone who'd been touched by the entities.

Her eye hurt, slightly, as she stared at Helen. The younger girl seemed to blaze with light and life, but there was no hint of taint. There was no suggestion that her mind extended into the astral plane, let alone the Godly Realm beyond. Isabella narrowed her eye as she studied Helen, trying to peer through her skin. She could see hints of Helen's personality, all sharp-edged and resentful, but nothing to suggest she wasn't her own woman. Mentally, at least. She was, to all intents and purposes, Reginald's ward.

Isabella opened her other eye … and instantly regretted it.

Helen's body seemed to split into two, two bodies that were occupying the same space … Isabella cursed her mistake as she scrabbled for a tissue and wiped her eye dry. *Things* hung at the corner of her vision, unseen eyes watching her … mocking her. She thought they couldn't get to her, but she knew she could be wrong. The astral realm was full of predators, of things that had crawled out of humanity's nightmares and now haunted the edges of perception, of things that could climb into someone's mind and do very real damage. She felt a hot flash of anger and fear for Silverdale. The danger of keeping an open mind was that something truly unpleasant might crawl in.

Helen coughed. "What are you doing?"

"Long story." Isabella felt her vision slowly return to normal. Opening her second eye had been a mistake. She hadn't felt so bad since she'd drunk herself silly, back during her first pub crawl as a young recruit. The drinking itself had been bad, but the hangover had been terrible. "You're clean."

"No, I'm not," Helen grunted. "I haven't so much as had a bath …"

Isabella stood, took a moment to make sure her legs could take her weight, then hobbled over to the chain and carefully removed it. Helen was a cross between a guest and a prisoner, but there was no need to keep her chained up like a dog. It was possible she'd still prove a threat, yet … she shook her head as she saw the red marks on the girl's skin. There was no such thing as *enough* precautions when the entities were involved, but … Helen wasn't touched, let alone overshadowed. She could be treated with some – more – dignity.

"There's a bathtub in the next room," Isabella told her. The castle had hot and cold running water, a rare luxury outside the Golden City. "You can wash and dress yourself."

"Myself?" Helen could hardly have sounded more shocked if Isabella had suggested going for a walk, completely naked. "I can't dress myself!"

"Of course you can," Isabella said, dryly. She opened the drawers under the bed and peered inside. The dresses were relatively simple, although still too expensive for the average family to own. "It's really very simple."

She adopted a tone that would have shamed a five-year-old. "Put water in the bath. Climb into the bath. Wash yourself in the bath. Get out of the bath. Dry yourself with the towel after the bath. Get dressed after the bath."

Helen reddened. "I ... I ..."

Isabella returned to a more normal tone. "You're a grown adult," she said. Silverdale was more mature, for crying out loud! There was at least five years between the two girls. "And you can act like one. I'll send a maid with a tray in an hour or two, so you have something to eat, but you'll have to learn to take care of yourself. We'll discuss the rest of your stay here later."

If I can't shove it onto Ruby, she thought, as she headed for the door. *This'll drive me mad if I have to deal with it every day.*

She pretended not to hear the sob behind her as she walked through the door and closed it behind her. Helen was weak, too weak. She wouldn't be able to take control of her life unless she learnt to take control of herself first. Maids could do everything, but ... it was easy to become dependent on them. Who was in charge if one depended on the other? And the shock of losing them would be so profound that the victim would agree to anything, if it meant a return to a life of luxury ... Isabella felt sick. The ladies of the court claimed they were in charge, but they weren't. Even the men of the court had far less power than they thought.

We'll see if Helen makes something of herself, she thought, stiffly. *Or if she jumps into the arms of the first man willing to provide for her.*

She dismissed the thought and addressed the guard. "When your relief arrives, send a message to the kitchen for a tray of food for the prisoner," she said. "And ensure that whoever delivers it is not alone."

The guard saluted. "Your Majesty!"

Isabella nodded and headed back to her chambers. She wanted to seek out Reginald, but she knew he'd be in the council chambers until nightfall. He'd probably be glad of an excuse to leave, yet ... she shook her head. The councillors would probably take it as a sign of weakness. Instead, she stepped through the wards and sat down at her desk. The latest set of reports were waiting for her, as were Silverdale's proposals. They were risky and yet … Isabella couldn't help considering them. They might be doable.

She looked up as the princess entered the room, looking surprisingly happy for someone who'd been cleaning pots and pans for the last hour. Isabella had spoken to the kitchen staff personally, giving them strict orders to ensure Silverdale actually did the work instead of passing it off to the scullery maids. She'd been suspicious – Silverdale had been entirely too happy about the punishment – but the young girl had set to work with a will. She hadn't even complained to her brother about her treatment.

"You look a mess," Isabella said. "What were you doing?"

"Cleaning pans," Silverdale said. "It was actually quite interesting."

Isabella frowned, feeling a flicker of suspicion. "And why was it interesting?"

"I have to clean my own tools, don't I?" Silverdale spoke as though it was the simplest thing in the world. "How else will I learn?"

"I see." Isabella conceded the point with a nod. "Very good, young lady."

Silverdale beamed. Isabella sighed inwardly, wondering if she'd ever been so young. She might have enjoyed her childhood a little more if she'd figured out a way to turn her father's punishments into an advantage. But her imagination didn't go that far. He'd taught her how to handle pain, emotional as well as physical, and that was about it. He'd never thought to put her to work preparing potion ingredients.

"I read your notes," she said, putting the past where it belonged. "You've got quite a few good ideas."

"Thank you." Silverdale sat on the other chair. "When do we start?"

"Now," Isabella said. "I want you to practice picking up objects from the astral plane."

Silverdale frowned. "Why that?"

"Because I want to know what happens when you try," Isabella said. She knew a hundred spells to pick up and move objects, but none of them seemed to work near the entities. "And perhaps a few other things."

She pointed at the sofa. "Your potion is there," she said,

indicating the collection of vials on the table. "Or should we wait for your brother?"

Silverdale picked up the vial and headed to the sofa. "Now," she said, quickly. "I'm ready."

Isabella smiled as she found the liniment and braced herself. She'd have to be careful to make sure she only had one eye open at all times, at least until she was ready to drink the potion herself. And yet ... she watched Silverdale as the little princess lay on the sofa, put the vial to her lips and drank. She didn't know it, but Isabella had replaced the potion she'd made with flavoured water. Isabella was curious to see if it still worked.

Silverdale closed her eyes. Her breathing faded to the point she looked almost dead. Isabella shuddered, then closed one eye and applied the liniment to the other. Her vision blurred, once again. When it cleared, the room looked decidedly odd, as if it extended in directions the human mind was not designed to grasp. And a ghostly form drifted over Silverdale's body. Isabella felt a shiver run down her spine. No matter how much she researched, no matter how much she experimented, she would always feel there was something wrong with the new – old – magic. It just didn't make sense.

"Try to pick up something," Isabella said. "Anything."

The ghostly form – Isabella could make out a face, but little else – reached for the vial and tugged at it. Isabella had no trouble seeing the frustration on Silverdale's face. The vial wasn't heavy, but she was having problems so much as touching it. Isabella reached out and brushed her hand against Silverdale's shoulder. A cold shock ran through her as her fingers passed *through* the girl's form. Silverdale started, her form blurring as if she'd been caught in a gust of wind.

"Try again," Isabella said. "And focus on the vial's shadow.

Silverdale drifted above the table, practically kneeling on the wooden surface as she pushed at the vial. It shivered, then rolled towards the edge of the table. Isabella closed one eye and opened the other. The vial seemed to be moving of its own accord. Isabella cast a pair of detection spells, looking for magic, but sensed nothing. She swapped eyes again and saw the vial running away from Silverdale. It fell off the edge a moment later, plunging towards the floor. Isabella cast a summoning spell without thinking. Nothing happened. The vial hit the floor and shattered.

"Interesting," she said. She silently forced herself to remember just *what* had happened when she'd cast the spell. The magic had reached out before fading away. She stared, convinced she was on the edge of a breakthrough. There was something there, nagging at her. But what? "I wonder …"

She washed her eye. The ghostly princess vanished. Isabella shivered. They were defenceless against attacks from the astral plane, at least without the liniment. Hell, even *with* the liniment, it would be difficult to defend against them. Silverdale's body had felt no more substantial than fog. There were spells designed to kill tracelessly by transfiguring a chunk of the victim's brain long enough for him to die, then snap everything back to normal. Could one do that – or worse – from the astral plane?

Silverdale's body jerked, gasping for breath. Isabella poured her a glass of water, then waited until the coughing was finished before passing the drink to her. The little princess looked torn between pride, fear and exhaustion. Isabella frowned to herself. If it took that much energy to move a vial – gravity had done most of the work – there was little hope of doing more. Silverdale was young, but – in the astral realm – she had more energy than anyone else. Anyone *human*, at least. The entities were far more powerful.

"I touched it," Silverdale said. She sounded as if she were trying to think of the right words. "The first time I touched it, my fingers went right through it. Like it wasn't there at all. The second time, I could *feel* it. It *was* there."

Isabella frowned. They were onto something, but what?

"I've had an idea," Silverdale said. "Can I try the rest of the potion?"

"Perhaps," Isabella said. "What do you have in mind?"

"Wait and see," Silverdale said. "Please."

"No," Isabella said. She kept her voice under tight control. "Tell me first."

Silverdale grinned, then reached for the vials, picked one up and drank.

Chapter Eight

Oh, she's going to be so mad, Silverdale thought, as her body crumpled to the floor. It should have hurt, but she was already halfway into the astral plane. *She's going to be really mad.*

She threw herself through the wall, hoping to vanish into the shadows before her sister-in-law could put more liniment in her eye. She didn't dislike Isabella, but her caution was … annoying. Silverdale had survived being a royal princess, then a prisoner. She could handle the astral plane. The walls posed no barrier to her astral self as she glided through the translucent building. It was weird to know the walls were thick – she'd watched, with interest, as newer towers were built on the edge of the complex – and yet see them as impossibly thin. They simply didn't exist in the astral plane.

Silverdale smirked as she looked around. The ghostly castle was filled with sparks of light and strange, shadowy creatures. One was attached to a spark of light, like … she shuddered as she realised it was a parasite. She looked closer, spotting one of the maids as she walked down the corridor. The creature was riding her, draining her. Up close, Silverdale could see … *something* flowing out of the maid and into the creature. It looked like a giant spider, but with far too many legs. The closer she looked, the harder it was to look away.

The creature looked back … and sprang. Silverdale flinched back as the creature came at her, impossibly quick. She had an impression of teeth and claws and an insatiable appetite for … she wasn't sure what the creature fed on, but she was certain that letting it latch onto her would be a mistake. Her back slammed into a wall, a wall that had been insubstantial a moment ago. For a horrible moment, she thought she'd fallen back into her body …

It's trying to trick me into thinking there's no way to escape, Silverdale thought. She saw it now. The astral plane was shaped by minds, human or otherwise. *I don't have to stay still.*

Her eyes narrowed. The creature was still coming ... it should have been on her by now. She controlled her disgust and fear as she focused her mind, widening the distance between them until it was practically infinite. The creature seemed to hesitate, then broke apart into nightmarish fragments ... it *was* a nightmare. It had latched onto the maid and fed on her fears and insecurities and ... Silverdale hastily looked at the young woman, only a few years older than Silverdale was. It was hard to be sure from the astral realm, but she looked happier now the nightmare parasite was gone. Silverdale smiled. It felt *good* to do something positive.

She turned, peering into the shadowy corners of the castle. The entity might be gone – she felt a pang as she remembered her older sister – but traces of its presence lay everywhere. It had warped and twisted the astral realm until ... Silverdale couldn't follow what it had done, but it had been apparently unsuccessful. Ghosts walked down the corridors, repeating patterns they'd followed in life ... she thought she caught sight of her grandfather, although she'd never known him. He'd died well before she was born. He didn't seem to notice her.

It might not be real, she thought. *It might not ...*

Silverdale forced herself to step back and study the realm objectively. It was separate from the human world and yet ... it wasn't. She saw tendrils and sparks of light everywhere, flashes of memory and emotion that pervaded the astral plane. The creature she'd killed wasn't alone, she realised numbly. They were everywhere. The more she looked, the more she saw. And, beyond them, she sensed great mentalities that bent the world to their will ...

She turned her gaze away, hastily. She was sure, without knowing quite *how* she knew, that looking at them would draw their attention. It was hard, very hard, not to even *think* of them. She glided away, spotting another maid as her spark of light glided down a ghostly corridor. Silverdale drifted after her, feeling torn between delight and guilt. The maid was a nexus of light and thought, images spilling out of her mind and into the astral plane. Silverdale could see them.

The sense she was doing something wrong overwhelmed her, but ... she couldn't force herself to move away.

A thought struck her. She glided forward until her ghostly lips were pressed against the maid's ears. "Drop your tray."

The maid's shock echoed through the astral plane as she let go of the tray she was carrying. It seemed to slip out of Silverdale's view as it fell and hit the ground, yet she had no trouble sensing the maid's horror. She'd dropped a tray. She'd broken a tray. She would be in deep trouble ...

"And that," a new voice said, "is quite enough."

Silverdale flinched. Isabella. Isabella was right behind her, one hand clutching Silverdale's arm. She tried to pull back, or to render herself insubstantial, but it didn't work. Isabella's will was too strong. Silverdale felt as if she was being stretched into toffee as she was dragged back to her body and thrust down. The real world enveloped her. She retched, helplessly, as she was suddenly aware of her body's aches and pains. She kicked herself for being surprised. Her body had fallen when she'd drunk the potion. Of *course* she'd hit the floor hard enough to hurt.

Her eyes opened. Isabella was sitting on the chair, rubbing her forehead. She'd drunk the potion herself to go after Silverdale, to ... Silverdale felt a pang of guilt. The maid would *definitely* be in trouble, even if her superiors believed it had been an accident. She'd be beaten or fined or simply dismissed without reference ... Silverdale stared down at her hands. She hadn't thought ... why hadn't she thought? Had she been so desperate to test her theory that she hadn't thought it through first? Or had she known, on some level, that she simply didn't have the *time* to think?

Isabella stared at her. Silverdale felt like a mouse, staring up at a cat.

"Tell me," Isabella said. "What were you thinking?"

Silverdale looked down. "I don't know."

"You don't know," Isabella repeated. "You ... *influenced* ... that poor girl."

She stood and started to pace. "Do you have any idea how much damage you could have done?"

Silverdale shook her head. The books hadn't said *much* about mind control and influencing spells, but they'd warned the side effects could be terrible. She hadn't tried to cast a spell … she shivered as she realised she'd done worse. She'd literally put a thought into the girl's head. She thought dropping the tray had been her idea, a moment of utter madness that could have cost her everything … *would* cost her everything, unless Silverdale did something. But what? She wanted to run to the Castellan and ask him to forgive the girl, yet …

"Please," she said. She felt about an inch high. "Please help her."

Isabella turned. "Do you understand what you did?"

"Yes," Silverdale said. "And … I'm sorry."

"You will be," Isabella said. "I'll deal with the girl. You …"

She pointed a finger at Silverdale. Magic flared. Silverdale flinched … or tried to. Her body was utterly immobile. She could neither move nor speak. She couldn't even blink! Panic yammered at the back of her mind as Isabella walked out, closing the door behind her. She was frozen and … she could *feel* the magic, locking her in place. She tried to push it away, to free herself – or at least to send her mind floating back into the astral plane – but nothing happened. She was stuck. All she could do was wait and think and …

Guilt nagged at her as she waited. She'd crossed the line and … she forced herself to think about everything she'd seen and done. There was an insight there, she was sure. The maid had been … guilt overwhelmed her, shame rushed through her. She'd heard the stories about what it was like to live below stairs – from Greta, who'd gone back to her family after the castle had been liberated – but she'd never mistreated a maid. Or had she? The maid had been more than a servant. She'd been a living thing … of *course* she'd been a living thing. She *was* a living thing. It was sheer stupidity to suggest otherwise.

I hurt her, she thought, numbly. *And there's no way I can make it up to her.*

***

Isabella felt unpleasantly drunk as she made her way through the corridors, even though she knew she hadn't touched alcohol in years. The castle felt strange, as if she wasn't sure if she was in the physical castle or the astral shadow. *Things* glinted at the corner of her eyes, corridors threatened to break or lead her in directions the human mind wasn't designed to comprehend ... she knew, all too well, that she should go back to her room and wait for the last remnants of the potion to wear off. The only thing that kept her going was a grim determination to do *something* to help the poor maid.

Cold anger flared through her as she walked on. It wasn't *easy* to tell where the maid was. The astral castle looked ... *different*, as if a ghostly building was overlaying the real one. Her head hurt every time she looked at it. She had the strangest feeling it would be easy to walk down a corridor that wasn't there and emerge ... somewhere. The Godly Realm? It was possible. The Red Monks – or the poor bastards who'd become the Red Monks – had walked through a corridor and emerged changed. She didn't want to take the risk. Not again.

She felt a pang of sympathy as she heard sobbing down the corridor. The maid was kneeling on the floor, surrounded by broken shards of china and pools of liquid. Isabella winced. The china alone was worth far more than the maid – and her entire family – could hope to make in a year. It was just a matter of time until someone came along, noticed the disaster and reported it ... the maid herself would have to report it. Isabella kept her face carefully impassive as the maid looked up, her face paling still further. She was only a couple of years older than Silverdale, yet ... her life might be about to come to an end.

"My Lady ..." The maid stuttered, scrambled to her feet and started again. "Your Majesty ..."

Isabella held up a hand and studied the remnants of the china. There were dozens of mending spells, but she doubted they'd work. The cups and teapot were just too badly damaged. She was almost impressed. They looked as if they'd shattered into dust. The maid started to babble, begging for mercy ... Isabella ignored her as she tested the spell anyway. It didn't work. She muttered a curse under her breath. Silverdale was going to be in a *lot* of trouble.

She glanced up as a senior maid came down the corridor. The older woman gasped when she saw the mess, her eyes moving to the younger maid as if she intended to dismiss her on the spot. She didn't even *try* to ask who was truly to blame ... Isabella was dismayed, although she wasn't surprised. Blame flowed downhill everywhere, it seemed. Besides, the senior maid had no way to know who was *really* at fault. Isabella was just so *tired* of it.

"The fault was mine," she said, straightening. She looked at the younger maid. "Clean up this mess, then take the rest of the day off" – her eyes moved to the other maid – "and you make sure she doesn't get into any trouble."

The maids gasped, in unison. Isabella turned and swept away, hoping they'd have the sense to follow orders without question. The younger maid might think it was her idea all along ... Isabella gritted her teeth. She'd practiced resisting mind manipulating and controlling spells from the moment a wand had been placed in her hand, but the maid was hopelessly vulnerable. The poor girl hadn't stood a chance. Isabella had seen enough to know she'd taken Silverdale's suggestion for one of her own thoughts. How could she have caught herself in time?

There will be rumours, she thought, sourly. The maids would approve of an aristocratic woman taking the blame for something she'd done, she was sure, but they'd be puzzled by her taking responsibility for the maid's actions. They might even wonder if the accident really *was* Isabella's fault. She'd heard enough muttering about the sorceress-queen to know they feared her ... she shook her head. *The sooner Reginald and I get out, the better.*

The world seemed to solidify around her as she returned to her chamber. She was almost relieved to press her hand against the stone without feeling her fingers gliding *through* the walls. The magic was so *different* that she doubted she'd ever understand it ... she wondered, idly, what would happen if she tried to use *her* magic in the astral plane. Nothing, perhaps. Or ... or what? She wished, not for the first time, that there was another trained sorcerer in the kingdom. But the handful of magicians who'd survived the last few years had been killed by Sofia and the Red Monks. They hadn't stood a chance.

And most of the other survivors are scattered, she thought, numbly. It still awed and terrified her, whenever she thought about how quickly the empire had collapsed. The Golden City was practically a backwater, these days. The Imperial

Palace was a pile of rubble and the Great Library locked away behind unbreakable wards. *There's no way to bring them together.*

She pushed open the door, revelling in its solidity, and stepped into the room. Silverdale stood there, utterly motionless. Isabella gritted her teeth, fighting an impulse to slap the younger girl into next week. Experimenting was bad enough, even when the experiments were carried out on victims who consented. Experimenting on someone who didn't even know was beyond the pale. The maid could have been seriously hurt or killed if Silverdale had pushed a little further. She might not even know what had happened to her. There were spells that could make people say or do or believe anything, but ... this was different. She might have gone to her grave blaming herself for smashing the china.

And the poor girl still might, Isabella thought. From the maid's point of view, Isabella had taken the blame for something she definitely hadn't done. *She doesn't know what really happened.*

She calmed herself with an effort as she sat down. Silverdale would find the punishment thoroughly unpleasant, but it wouldn't do any lasting harm. *Isabella's* father would have beaten or hexed her bloody, even if he'd been proud of her for doing something new. Her stomach twisted at the thought. The bastard was dead, and yet he still cast a long shadow over her life. It just wasn't fair ...

Her thoughts seemed to come to a halt. *A shadow ...*

She stared at the empty vial, still lying on the floor. Silverdale was more talented than Isabella, she acknowledged sourly, when it came to manipulating the astral plane, but she'd barely been able to move the vial. She hadn't been able to touch it until ... Isabella leaned forward as a thought struck her. The castle was a ghostly presence in the astral plane, but its inhabitants shone likes suns. *Everyone* had a link to the astral plane, even if they didn't know how to use it. She remembered brushing against someone's mind when she'd been exploring the astral plane, and shuddered. What was the point of mental defences if someone could read your thoughts by looking at you from the astral plane?

We can touch each other, but touching objects is hard, she thought. She was on the verge of an insight. She *knew* it. *And we can't touch cold iron at all.*

She considered it for a long moment. It made no sense. Every time she thought she understood the rules, they seemed to change on her. Unless … she forced herself to recall what she'd seen. Things – physical things – didn't really exist in the astral plane unless … unless what? Unless people believed in them, accepted their presence. The walls were there, but … useless. Insubstantial. It was the human *mind* that shaped the astral plane. And that meant …

We can open the link to the astral plane, and through that make contact with the entities, she mused. It made a certain kind of sense. Rites, rituals and liniments worked because the user *believed* they worked. Silverdale had had no trouble using a placebo, because she hadn't known it *was* a placebo. *And that brings more and more of their awareness into the astral realm and ... the more of themselves they bring, the more they can channel the power and rules of their realm.*

She smiled, despite herself. It wasn't everything, but – finally – she thought she had a solid insight into how the entities really worked. And how they influenced humanity and were influenced in return. Given time, who knew what they could do …?

"I know what we're going to be doing next," she said, to the frozen girl. She reached for a notebook and started to outline what she'd deduced, then stopped herself. "But first, you're going to explain yourself to your brother."

Chapter Nine

If my father had told me how much time was wasted in committee, Reginald thought sourly, *I might have thought twice about taking the throne.*

He kept his expression under tight control as the councillors wittered on and on. Two-thirds of them had been chosen for political reasons, rather than basic competence or a simple ability to talk for longer than a minute without getting on his nerves. He'd had no choice but to appoint them ... he groaned, inwardly. Isabella and Ruby had more intelligence in their little fingers than most of the councillors had in their entire bodies. And the men had had the nerve to suggest the princess be ordered out of the room. Reginald had dismissed that thought, immediately. He'd discovered, in the last few months, that Ruby's insights were valuable.

Baron Braddock would have been more useful, his thoughts mocked. The man addressing him was skilled at sailing with the political winds, but little else. *At least he wouldn't have been covertly undermining me from the start.*

He put the thought aside and forced himself to concentrate. There was more to running a kingdom than bashing heads and breaking skulls. The details were important, his father had said time and time again; a monarch who wished to *remain* monarch had to be aware of just what was going on at all times. And yet, they were boring. Tax policy? Land disputes? The disposition of heiresses and heirs ... the latter somewhat more complicated, as they couldn't be married off so easily. He allowed himself a brief fantasy of having the councillors flogged, or simply beheaded. Some problems just couldn't be solved quickly, if at all.

It was so much simpler when I was leading troops in battle, he thought. *I knew what had to be done to win.*

He breathed a sigh of relief when the meeting finally came to an end. "I trust that will be all," he said, in a tone that suggested it damn well *should* be all. "We'll reconvene shortly."

"With respect, Your Majesty," Lord Northerly said. "There is a matter that needs to be addressed."

Reginald managed, somehow, not to groan. Lord Northerly was the worst of the trimmers … which, his mind jested, put him up against some pretty stiff competition. He was still astonished Lord Northerly had survived Sofia's regime, particularly after he'd made unwelcome suggestions concerning her marriage. Perhaps he just hadn't been important enough for her to squash like a bug. Or, perhaps, he'd been tainted himself. Reginald had had all the councillors tested, repeatedly, but it was hard to be sure. The man could be stupid enough to think he could negotiate with the entities.

"Very well," he said. He met the older man's eyes. "What remains to be addressed?"

"The issue of the heir, Your Majesty," Lord Northerly said. "You have yet to designate someone to succeed you."

So you can start dripping poison in the poor bastard's ear? Reginald felt a hot flash of anger. It would be easy, so easy, to draw his sword and behead Lord Northerly before he could so much as blink. *And you can start laying plans for disposing of me?*

He took a long breath. His father had told him, time and time again, that most people wanted stability in their lives. Knowing who was king – and who would *be* king – was an important part of keeping the kingdom stable. It was why his father had forced him to learn kingship from the moment he was old enough to understand that being a prince involved more than riding, hunting, and courting the women of the court. His lack of a clear heir was a problem. He knew it, intellectually. But he didn't want to believe it.

"I have only been married six months," he said. "We have time to produce a child."

"Yes, Your Majesty," Lord Northerly said. "However, we must also discuss prospective nephews …"

Reginald raised a hand, cutting him off. "My sisters will marry in due course," he said, curtly. It was all he could do not to strike Lord Northerly down. "Right now, Princess Ruby is my designated heir. That will change when I have a child of my own."

He glared at the older man, silencing him before he

managed to get out a single word. It was easy to guess what Lord Northerly wanted to say. Isabella wasn't *old* – she was hardly a dowager – but she was older than the average royal bride. And they *had* to have at least one child, a child who would have a clear claim to the throne. It would get messy if Ruby inherited, even if she were married by then. She'd be expected to leave governing to her husband ... Reginald snorted. Ruby wasn't the sort of person to tamely step aside and let someone rule through her. The poor husband would be in for a world of hurt.

If she ever gets married, Reginald reminded himself. *If she doesn't, it will open up a whole new string of headaches.*

He stood, terminating the meeting. "We'll reconvene tomorrow," he said. "And the matter of the heir is closed."

The councillors rose, bowed and hurried to the door. Reginald stared at their backs, wondering which would be the first to betray him. They had ambitions of their own, ambitions that might – eventually – include the throne. They simply couldn't be trusted, not ever. Lord Northerly was too old to rule for long, if he somehow took the throne, but his son could take his place. And Reginald couldn't squash him without a very good reason. If the councillors thought he was turning into a tyrant, they'd band together against him ...

"He's never going to shut up about babies, is he?" Ruby was the only one who'd remained seated. "Or about an heir."

Reginald shrugged. An adult man, raised by a king who'd guided his realm through the greatest crisis in recorded history, would be capable of keeping the lords in check. *He* knew he could do it, although he had to admit it was harder than it looked. A child, on the other hand, perhaps one raised by someone without his best interests in mind ... he shook his head. Lord Northerly had a point. It was just one he couldn't do anything about. Not yet.

"I have a set of petitions for your attention," Ruby said. "One of them requires your *personal* attention."

Reginald lifted his eyebrows. Ruby had enough common sense to know there were matters that *didn't* require his attention ... and that she could handle them without it. If she thought something was important, he knew he should listen to her. She wouldn't have told him – in private – otherwise.

"Sergeant Theodore Ashworth requests an audience," Ruby

said. "I took the liberty of asking him to wait in the antechamber."

"I see." Reginald frowned, silently conceding that Ruby was right. Sergeant Ashworth was a good man, one of his loyal soldiers. Reginald could spare a few minutes for him, even though he wanted to go back to his wife. "Invite him in."

His lips twitched as Ruby stood, dropped a curtsey and hurried through the door. He really needed to get a proper secretary, someone to handle his correspondence, but it was hard to know who to trust. The nobility would be happy to suggest someone, perhaps a young man who'd been raised in their households ... he couldn't be trusted, of course. The very thought was absurd beyond words. Ruby might be stuck with the job by default. And that would make it all the harder when she finally got married.

And that's something we're going to have to discuss, sooner or later, Reginald thought, grimly. *That's not going to be a pleasant conversation.*

The door opened. Sergeant Theodore Ashworth stepped into the room. Ruby didn't follow him. Reginald was mildly surprised, although he knew his sister was canny enough to realise the sergeant and her brother might want to have their discussion in private. There were ways to eavesdrop on the council meetings, but Ruby didn't have to use them. She was already *on* the council. Besides, the councillors might not speak so freely if they thought they were being spied on.

"Your Majesty," Sergeant Ashworth said. "I have come to offer you my sword."

Reginald didn't try to hide his surprise. Sergeant Ashworth had always struck him as a lifer, someone who'd spend his entire life in the military ... someone who'd join a mercenary band if he didn't stay in the regular forces. He was completely trustworthy. For him to offer his sword, implicitly offering Reginald the chance to kill him ... Reginald's eyes narrowed. What had happened while he'd been gone? It couldn't have been anything disastrous, or he'd have heard about it already.

He met the sergeant's eyes. "What happened?"

"I allowed myself to be ... seduced ... by the prisoner," Sergeant Ashworth said. "The *special* prisoner."

The only prisoner in the dungeons, Reginald thought. The original prisoners had been killed or released when Sofia took power. Reginald didn't *have* any prisoners, save perhaps for Helen Braddock and the other heiresses. *He wouldn't be the first one to be seduced.*

He listened, feeling uncomfortably awkward, as the sergeant stumbled through an explanation. The entities could get into someone's head and warp them until they no longer had any concept of right or wrong or ... or their duty. Reginald understood, better than he was prepared to admit to anyone. The sergeant had been lucky. A weaker man might have freed the prisoner, only to be the first one to die. He'd failed in his duty, true, but it was an understandable failure. Reginald would have been a great deal less sympathetic if the sergeant had taken bribes or been threatened into submission.

"I see," he said, when the story was finished. "I cannot accept your sword."

The sergeant looked torn between relief and shame. Reginald didn't blame him. And yet ...

"You are a good man," Reginald said. The sergeant was old enough to be his father. "And you'll have your chance to redeem yourself."

He took a breath. "Report to Captain-General Gars. He'll assign you to the next punitive mission."

The sergeant bowed, then left the room. Reginald watched him go, his thoughts churning. His father would not have been amused, if someone had come to *him* with such a tale. Nor would many of the other lords. And yet, Reginald couldn't afford to issue massive, over-the-top punishments for men who failed through no fault of their own. It tended to upset people, to wear down their loyalty until they lashed out in self-defence. He could take some risks, but not with the army. It was the cornerstone of his regime.

And Lord Northerly and his peers will be happy to take advantage if I slip, he thought, as he headed into his private network of corridors. *They'll do everything in their power to undermine the army.*

He reached his bedchambers without incident and stepped inside. Isabella was seated at her desk, writing notes in a book; Silverdale was standing behind her, utterly unmoving. Reginald raised his eyebrows, surprised. A practical magic lesson? Or something else?

"She played a nasty prank on one of the maids," Isabella said, without looking up. "You'll probably hear something about *me* cursing the poor girl."

Reginald blinked. "You cursing the girl?"

"I took the blame," Isabella said, after she'd explained what had happened. "It was the easiest way to deal with the mess."

Reginald took off his jacket and sat down, trying not to smile. He couldn't imagine anyone else, save perhaps himself, taking the blame to spare someone else. There'd been noble youths who'd had whipping boys, youths who'd gotten in trouble just to see the boys howl ... bastards. The whole idea struck him as absurd. Too many noblemen regarded commoners as less than sheep or goats. The idea of taking the blame ...

He leaned back in his chair. "I'll talk to her later," he said. "Did you learn anything useful?"

Isabella smiled. "Did you?"

"Everyone wants us to have babies," Reginald said. He glanced at Silverdale. "Can she hear us?"

"Yeah." Isabella waved her hand at Silverdale. The girl collapsed to the floor, like a puppet whose strings had been cut. "She can hear us."

Reginald watched his sister struggling to her feet, face red and angry. "Go to your room," he said, gloomily aware he sounded *just* like one of the poor governesses. "I'll speak to you later."

Silverdale looked as if she wanted to say something cutting, but instead turned and stomped out. Reginald hoped she'd have the sense to follow orders, rather than running off and doing something stupid. He remembered his own teenage years, and cringed. He'd done a *lot* of stupid things. Some of them had nearly ended badly. His father had been particularly sarcastic when he'd pointed them out.

"She's keen to push the limits," Isabella said. "Right now" – she indicated the notebook – "we're still very much the blind leading the blind."

Reginald frowned. "Not like your schooling?"

"The Peerless School would be good for her," Isabella said. "And she's the right age to go, but ..."

She shrugged. Reginald understood. The Peerless School wasn't what it had been, during the glory days of empire. His father would have been reluctant to send his daughter, even if nothing had changed. It wouldn't do to give the poor girl ideas ... he shook his head. His sister deserved better. He'd have sent her himself if he could. But it was impossible.

"Right now, there's a lot we don't understand," she said. "But I think I'm starting to put it together."

Reginald smiled at her. "What have you found?"

Isabella took a breath. "Tell me if this makes sense," she said. "Life – intelligent or otherwise – has a presence on the astral plane. It casts *shadows* into the astral plane. Raw matter" – she tapped the table – "casts much less of a shadow, when it does at all. It doesn't have much, if any, effect on the other realm."

"Which is why you can walk through walls in the astral plane," Reginald said. His face twisted. Magic really wasn't his forte. "The walls don't really exist there."

"And so you can walk around them," Isabella said. "Or above them. Or ..."

She shrugged. "I suspect it'll take us years to decide on a precise terminology for this sort of thing," she added. "Point is, we have a connection to the astral plane. Our minds determine what it is ... they determine how we see it and therefore shape it ... if that makes any kind of sense."

"Just a little," Reginald said.

"Hah." Isabella frowned. "I think the same is true of the entities. They have a presence within the astral plane, too. That presence is what allows them to make contact with us and then cross into our world. Given time, they taint and then overshadow their victims, which binds them to our realm."

"I thought we knew that," Reginald said.

"It's bigger than we thought," Isabella said. "They can use the connection to effectively teleport by walking *through* the Godly Realm. Or change the rules, allowing them to work miracles. And I think ...

"I think their minds allow them to focus on our realm and influence it from the astral plane," she added, slowly. "I think we need to have our minds focused to manipulate objects in our world … we don't so much pick something up as we visualise picking something up, and that somehow does it – and that –"

Reginald held up a hand. "I think I've lost track of what you're saying."

"Sorry." Isabella managed to look a little shamefaced. "There are details, I think, that can't be explained. It's like trying to describe colour to a blind man when you're blind yourself."

"You'll figure it out," Reginald said. "You've already managed to trap two of the entities."

"And Mother Lembu is sure she'll escape one day," Isabella said. "The slightest slip, and she'll be free."

Reginald shivered. "Maybe you're looking at this from the wrong angle," he said. She was the sorceress, but he'd had the advantage of a very practical education. "If they can influence our world, can we influence theirs?"

"It's a very different world," Isabella pointed out. "And I …"

"In this world, physical strength is an objective measure," Reginald countered. "In the astral realm, things are different. Right?"

"Yeah." Isabella yawned. "And in the Godly Realm, things are different again."

"If they can take us into their realm and … *change* us," Reginald asked, "why can't we do that to them?"

"I don't know," Isabella said. "I think …"

Reginald stood and helped her to her feet. "I think you'd better go to bed," he said. "I'll be here when you wake."

"Are you sure you want to *sleep*?" Isabella smiled. "We could …"

There was a knock on the door. Reginald cursed under his breath as he let go of his wife and turned to the door. No one would disturb him in his bedchambers unless it was bad news, not even his sisters. *Very* bad news. He'd made that clear, the first day he'd slept in the royal suite. It wasn't as if Isabella and he slept in different beds.

He opened the door. The messenger took one look at his thunderous face and prostrated himself. Reginald sighed, resisting the urge to walk around the man and kick his backside. It was bad news. It *had* to be. And the messenger was terrified he'd be blamed.

"Get up," he snapped. "What's happened?"

"Your Majesty," the messenger gasped. "A man has arrived from the Golden City. He claims to be the queen's brother. He insists on speaking to her immediately."

Reginald glanced at Isabella, who looked astonished. "Show him to the small reception room," he ordered. "We'll be with him shortly."

Chapter Ten

Isabella's thoughts were churning as she splashed cold water on her face, then followed Reginald to the small – and very private – reception room. Her brother – if it really *was* her brother – was from a life she'd left behind years ago. They'd only met once since she'd departed the Golden City, when he'd asked her to keep an eye open for strange magic on the Summer Isle. She almost giggled at the thought. Poor Alden hadn't known the half of it. They'd exchanged letters since then, but ...

She sighed, inwardly. Alden had been their father's heir, but ... he hadn't *really* pleased the old bastard. None of his brood had, not really. Alden had been a bossy teenager when she'd been born and, since then ... he was better than their father, she supposed, but lacked the imagination to make use of his birth or the spark to rebel against it. She would have felt sorrier for him if he'd stood up for himself, let alone the rest of them. And now they were the last of their house. The name would die with her brother.

Reginald caught her eye as they reached the door. "Do you want to see him?"

"I suppose I must," Isabella said. "He wouldn't have come all this way unless it was urgent."

She pushed open the door. Alden sat in a comfortable chair. Isabella's eyes widened. Alden looked as though he'd ridden for days and nights without stopping, pushing himself and his horse to their limits. His clothes had been fine, once; now, they looked so tattered and torn she felt sorry for him. His gray hair was utterly unkempt. He didn't look like their father any longer. He looked like a man who'd been dragged through a swamp.

"Alden," she said. For a moment, she wondered if it truly *was* him. She performed a blood-rite charm of dubious legality, even in wartime, to confirm it. "What happened to you?"

Alden looked up. His eyes were dull, as if he was too tired to think straight. How far had he come? The Iron Dragons were long gone. If he'd taken one of the enhanced horses … she tried to calculate how long it would take him to get to Havelock from the Golden City, but drew a blank. It was impossible. He would have had to stop along the way, if only to rest and change mounts. Using magic to keep himself going would have caught up with him eventually. Isabella stared at him, all the resentments of twenty-eight years fading away. They no longer mattered.

"The Golden City is gone," Alden said.

"Gone?" Isabella was stunned. "Gone? Gone where?"

Reginald walked over to the drinks cabinet and poured Alden a stiff brandy. Isabella opened her mouth to suggest he didn't, then changed her mind. A drink would probably do Alden a great deal of good. Alden took the glass and drank it greedily, spluttering at the taste. He probably hadn't spent any more time drinking than Isabella herself. Their father would not have approved. She hoped he wouldn't simply pass out on them.

"We were attacked," Alden said. His voice was clearer now. "There was an army … it marched through the kingdoms without being stopped, then crossed the mountains somehow. I don't know how."

Isabella and Reginald exchanged glances. The Golden City was supposed to be completely impregnable. The mountain ranges that surrounded the city were incredibly difficult to climb. Even without the Watchtower and the network of defensive spells, the city was difficult to reach. But the entities could knock the mountains down or simply march the troops through the Godly Realm. And now they'd taken out the Golden City …

Her blood ran cold. They'd deduced how the entities had been cast out, thousands of years ago. The First Emperor, who spoke for the entire world, had banished them. But now … the Empire was gone. Even if the Last Empress returned, she didn't speak for *everyone*. Six months as Queen had been quite enough to convince her there was no hope of rebuilding the empire in time to save the world. They needed to find another solution.

"It was all so sudden," Alden said. "We didn't even get

any warning before they were swarming the city, storming and setting fire to the mansions. Our spells didn't protect us. Our wards collapsed as they pressed onwards. We ... I ... I had to flee. I had to get out before the mansion burned to the ground. I had ... I had no choice."

Isabella swallowed. She'd hated the mansion. It had been her father's domain. It had never been *home*. But now ... she felt an odd little pang, now it was gone. The family's private library was gone. Her bedroom ... her possessions, assuming the old bastard hadn't destroyed them out of spite ... all gone. And everything that had belonged to her siblings, to her parents and grandparents and ancestors who could be traced all the way back to the days of myth and legend ... gone.

"And you came to warn us," Reginald said. *That* was a more charitable interpretation than Isabella would have expected. "How did you get here?"

"Took the horse, got through the secret tunnels before they collapsed," Alden said. "Just kept riding, letting the sibling bond guide me. I knew you'd come back to Andalusia ... I hoped I could get to you in time. Everything's falling apart back there."

Isabella nodded, slowly. The kingdoms nearest the Golden City had been badly weakened by the civil wars. It was unlikely any of them would dare to attack the magical capital ... unless the entities were pulling the strings. She cursed under her breath as she remembered the creature that had escaped the rite ... had it gone east? There were a handful of kingdoms that could be subverted and turned into enemy states. The chaos after the fall would make it easy.

Reginald's thoughts were running along similar lines. "Who attacked the city?"

"I don't know," Alden said. "I ... they were burning what remained of the cities outside the mountains, so not them ... but I don't know who."

"They should have carried flags," Reginald said. "What were they wearing?"

"I didn't see them clearly," Alden moaned. "It happened so *quickly*."

"He's not a fighter," Isabella said, quietly. Her brother wasn't a coward, but ... he'd never had to fight without his spells and wards. Normally, he could have just sat within the mansion and waited for the enemy to go away. His wards, so ancient they dated back hundreds of years, could keep out anything. But the entities would laugh at them. "He's lucky to escape."

She forced herself to think as Reginald threw question after question at Alden. The entities understood the rules a lot better than she did. Taking out the Golden City made perfect sense. Even if the Last Empress was still alive, she could no longer rule. Ditto for any other lost heirs that might be bumbling around somewhere. There'd always been legends of missing heirs to the throne, but none had ever proven *real*. The ones that had made it to the throne had died when they'd parked their backsides on the seat.

And, given that they can teleport through the Godly Realm, they might not be close *to the Golden City*, she mused. Teleporting an entire army had been impossible, until now. *They might be a* lot *closer to us*.

Her mind raced. They *shouldn't* be able to teleport into Andalusia. Reginald was king and he'd ruled against it … that should be enough. She *hoped* it would be enough. A baron who sent his formal defiance would put himself outside the law, but not outside the kingdom. Right? She didn't know. There were just too many unknowns.

"I always thought the Golden City was untouchable," Reginald said, quietly. "The mountains alone would prove an impassable barrier."

Isabella nodded. "Yeah …"

Reginald looked at her, then shrugged and rang for a maid. "Escort Lord Alden to a suite and make sure he has everything he needs," he ordered, when the maid arrived. "He is to be treated as an honoured guest."

The maid curtseyed. "Your Majesty."

Isabella felt a twinge of pity as Alden staggered out. He *had* been using magic to enhance himself. He was not going to have a pleasant few days, if not weeks, when it all caught up with him. She mentally worked out the potions he'd need, if she could get the ingredients. She could brew them for him and then … he *was* a fully-trained magician. He might come in handy, if he hadn't been completely unmanned. Given his predilections, he would have been quite happy pottering around the mansion and playing politics in the Golden City. Now …

At least he had the wit to know something was wrong and ask me to deal with it, she thought, grimly. *And to seek out the Last Empress to ask for her insights.*

"Crap," Reginald said, when they were alone. "They destroyed the Golden City."

Isabella nodded, not trusting herself to speak. The Peerless School? Gone. The Great Library? Gone … or was it? The wards surrounding the library were the oldest in the city, far older than any others. Who knew? The mansions and workshops and everything else that had made the city tick … gone. She wanted to believe Alden was lying, or deluded, but she couldn't. He wouldn't have fled if he hadn't been in fear for his life.

"Fuck," she managed finally. "I … *fuck.*"

Reginald stood and started to pace. "There aren't any kingdoms within marching distance of the Golden City … none that could have produced an army capable of taking the city," he said. "How did they even get there?"

"They marched through the Godly Realm," Isabella said. She understood his point. An army from one of the more distant kingdoms could hardly have marched on the Golden City without passing through the nearer kingdoms, ensuring the magicians had plenty of advance warning. Hell, sending an army so far from home was asking for trouble. She didn't like the implications of *that*. "And they just appeared from nowhere …"

Someone must have betrayed the city, she thought, coldly. *Someone simply invited them in.*

She shook her head. The Golden City had been ruined well before the army had finished the job. There'd been no one in a position to bar the door. Not, she supposed, that that would have kept the entities from causing trouble. The Golden City had imported all of its food and drink. An army that was effectively immune to magic didn't have to do anything, but surround the city, barricade the tunnels and wait. The magicians would starve if they didn't surrender.

It doesn't matter, she told herself. *What's done is done.*

She stood and started to pace savagely. The entities had taken over a kingdom … *another* kingdom. And they'd clearly managed to lay the groundwork for a full-scale war of expansion. She gritted her teeth as she tried to figure out where the entities had gone, where they'd subverted … it could be anywhere. They'd sent warnings to every kingdom, but those warnings could easily have been ignored. Or someone could have been stupid enough to think they could barter with the entities and come out ahead.

"They'll be coming for us," Reginald said. "They have to know we're the greatest threat to them."

"Particularly after we snared two of them," Isabella agreed. "We'd know if they controlled the nearest kingdoms, wouldn't we?"

"Perhaps." Reginald didn't sound convinced. "If they've learnt to keep their presence a secret …"

He frowned as he opened one of the cabinets and produced a map. Isabella watched as he placed it on the table and unfurled it. The map was badly drawn – she'd travelled widely enough to see the mistakes, some of which looked to be deliberate – but it was accurate enough to use for brainstorming. She sat facing him and watched as he traced a line on the map. The Golden City – looking large enough to be a major country in its own right – sat at the centre of the map. That, if nothing else, was proof the map was over six years old.

"We have contacts in all the neighbouring kingdoms," Reginald said. "Sully, Janine, Halladale … we'd know if they were raising bigger armies. They can defend themselves, but they're not ready to launch a full-scale invasion of anyone. They didn't even think to raise more troops when Sofia was in control."

"They might not have known what was going on," Isabella said. "Or who was really in charge."

"Yeah." Reginald's finger lingered on a more distant kingdom. It looked small enough for a man to cross within a day. "The bigger kingdoms could raise armies without us hearing something, but … they'd have to come through lands that know the risks before they reached us."

"Unless they found a way to get through the defences," Isabella said. "Sofia got the keys to the city, remember, and used them against us."

Reginald nodded. "I'll have to send out scouts," he said. "The main roads should still be clear … it might lead to diplomatic headaches, but we can probably handle them. I'll send messengers to the neighbouring kingdoms too, ask if they've heard anything. They've been concerned about not having better relations anyway, so ..."

Isabella scowled. "Halladale wants Ruby's hand in marriage for their prince," she reminded him. "You said to stall them."

"I did." Reginald made a face. "That's something we'll have to consider later."

"Later," Isabella agreed. She stared down at the map. The Golden City was gone. How could it be? Even after everything that had happened over the last five years, it had survived ... until now. "I ..."

She felt her legs weaken. It couldn't be true. Her thoughts ran in drunken circles. She didn't want to believe it. She *really* didn't want to. But it was true. How could it be anything else? Alden wouldn't have come so many miles just to lie. And ...

"Six months," she breathed. "Six months since Sofia summoned the entity into the world. And in that time, it's taken over a kingdom, built an army and crushed the Golden City."

Reginald rested a hand on her shoulder. She leaned into his touch, a display of weakness she wouldn't have risked showing anyone else. Reginald was ... she trusted him, as well as loved him. She'd let *him* see, if no one else. He wouldn't use it against her.

"I'll take care of your brother," Reginald said. "Or do you want me to send him away?"

Isabella shook her head, not trusting herself to speak. Alden was her brother. As annoying as he'd been, when they'd been children, he was still her kin. And the past was in the past ... it was a shame, she reflected sourly, that the entities didn't agree *they* should stay in the past. Unless ... a thought struck her. If she turned time itself against them ...

"Take care of him," she said, quietly. She stood, allowing him to envelop her in a hug. She relaxed into his grip, something she would never have dared with anyone else. "He might be useful."

"How so?" Reginald sounded interested, rather than mocking. "He's a broken man."

"He knows a lot about magic," Isabella said. "And he has a lot of patience. He might be able to teach better than I."

"I doubt Silverdale will take him seriously," Reginald said. "She rebelled against each and every governess she's had, as well as her tutors and me."

"And me," Isabella said. She shook her head. "Give him time to get better first."

Reginald grinned, then sobered. "If the Golden City's fallen," he said, "what else is going to go?"

Isabella looked at the map. The Golden City stood at the centre of a continent-wide network of roads. It wasn't that important, in and of itself, but it might just be the key to conquest … if, of course, someone had an army large enough to handle it. Not, she supposed, that the entities really *needed* the roads. Given a handful of traitors in the right places, they could move armies from place to place in the blink of an eye. Her eyes traced the borders … Reginald's borders. What did it matter, if he forbade the entities from entering his kingdom, if they could just materialise an army on the far side and march across?

She held him tightly for a long moment, then lifted her lips to his. He kissed her back, his hands roaming over her back and into her trousers. She felt his passion, and his desperate desire to feel *alive*, as he pushed her trousers down. They'd been stunned by the news. They *needed* to feel human again. There was no time for foreplay. His stiffness pressed against her, then into her …

Reginald held her, afterwards. Isabella almost giggled, remembering the days she'd flirted with boys at the Peerless School. And girls, knowing it would upset her father. The thought of her entering a relationship that couldn't produce children … she shook her head. The old bastard was dead. The family was effectively dead.

"I love you," Reginald said. "I …fuck it."

Isabella did giggle. "You'd better call a council," she said. "And give them the bad news."

"After we get what we can out of your brother," Reginald said. "And figure out what to do."

"I think I've had an idea," Isabella said. The thought grew in her mind, despite her best efforts. "But you're not going to like it."

Chapter Eleven

Silverdale lay on her bed, staring at the ceiling.

It wasn't fair. It just wasn't fair! She'd learnt how to use magic, she'd mastered it to the point she'd been able to use it to escape the castle – with a little help, she supposed – but now that her brother was home, she was just a kid again. Worse than a kid! She couldn't even go riding or any of the things she'd done, before the nightmare enveloped her kingdom. And her sister-in-law was a pain.

She knew, deep inside, that she wasn't being particularly fair. Her brother had a kingdom to rule, a kingdom that had been twisted and traumatised by the entities that had enslaved her sister and imprisoned her. Her sister-in-law knew the dangers of magic – both kinds of magic – far better than anyone else. And she was trying to teach Silverdale how to use her powers. But … it felt as if she was being held back, again. As if … she gritted her teeth. She hadn't been fair to the maid – she admitted that, at least to herself – but she hadn't deserved such a punishment. It felt over the top.

It could be worse, she told herself. She didn't really believe it. *It could be a lot worse.*

She didn't move as she heard someone entering the antechamber. There weren't many people who could enter the chamber without her permission, which meant – she acknowledged sourly – her brother's permission. The guards outside had strict orders to prevent her from leaving and keep everyone else out, although she had no idea how they were supposed to carry out their orders if they weren't allowed to lay hands on her. She was tempted to try to leave, but she had a feeling that would only get her in worse trouble. Instead, she lay back on the bed and pretended to be asleep.

The door opened. "Silverdale?"

Silverdale felt herself twitch as Isabella stepped into the room. She wanted to keep pretending, but she knew it was futile. Instead, she opened her eyes and scowled at the older woman. Isabella looked tired and deeply worried. Silverdale tensed, feeling a tingle of alarm. It didn't feel as though Isabella was worried about *her*.

"I hope you've had a moment to reflect," Isabella said. "Do you understand why what you did was wrong?"

Silverdale nodded, sourly. The maid ... was more than *just* a maid. "I'm sorry."

"So you should be," Isabella said. She sat down on the bed. "My brother has arrived."

Silverdale sat up. "Your brother?"

She kicked herself mentally, a second later. It had honestly never occurred to her to wonder if Isabella had siblings. She'd had parents, of course, but ... Silverdale frowned. Siblings could be good or bad, as she knew from experience. Sofia had enchanted their father and taken control of the kingdom. And she'd heard worse stories from noble-born children, although it was hard to tell how many were actually *true*. She didn't want to believe there were such people in the world.

"My brother," Isabella confirmed. "He's not in a good state."

Silverdale sat upright. "Is he ... I mean ... is he *him*?"

"He doesn't appear to be overshadowed." Isabella understood the unspoken meaning. "He's just in a state of shock. I'm impressed he managed to get here."

"Oh." Silverdale thought about it for a moment. "Where was he?"

"The Golden City," Isabella said. Her voice broke, just for a second. "It's gone."

Silverdale thought about it. She was used to horseback riding – she'd been riding practically from birth – but she'd never ridden so far. She'd never even been allowed outside the kingdom. She wasn't *entirely* sure how long it would take to ride from the Golden City to Havelock, but she had a feeling it would be more than a week or two. Havelock had maintained a limited independence, in the days of the empire, because it was just too far from the Golden City. Now, of course, the city might as well be on the other side of the world. It had as little meaning to her as a common-born child from Halladale she'd never met and never would.

"I'm sorry," she said, more out of a sense it was something

she *should* say than genuine sympathy. She'd never seen the Golden City. "What happened to him?"

She wondered, suddenly, if Isabella had married without her brother's consent. *That* would put the dragon amongst the sheep! Reginald could authorise his own marriage, effectively granting himself permission to do the thing he'd intended to do anyway, but Isabella ... she might not be able to agree to the match. What would her brother say? Silverdale looked up at Isabella and knew, deep inside, that the older woman wouldn't *care*. She was old and powerful enough to make her own decisions. Silverdale almost pitied Isabella's brother, if he tried to stand in her way ...

"We're not sure," Isabella said. She grimaced, as if she was about to do something she didn't want to do. "Would you like to read his memories?"

Silverdale blinked. "Me?"

Isabella made a face, then pulled a vial out of her pocket. "You."

"Why me?" Silverdale started to reach for the vial before stopping herself. "I mean ... why me?"

"You have more natural skill with this kind of magic than me," Isabella said. She looked uncomfortable. "Normally, I'd never even consider doing this. There are laws ... I won't blame you if you say no. I don't know enough to warn you about the risks."

Silverdale didn't hesitate. "I'll do it."

"Be careful," Isabella warned. "And don't even *think* about digging too deeply."

Silverdale took the vial and opened it. The scent wafted up and brushed against her nostrils, tickling her. She wasn't blind to the dangers, but ... she wanted to prove she *could* be useful to her brother and sister-in-law alike. She put the vial to her lips and drank, then lay back on the bed as her head started to spin. It was suddenly very easy to close her eyes and drift up and out of her body. She turned slowly, studying her sister-in-law from the astral plane. A glowing line led from Isabella to Reginald. Another ...

She followed it automatically, finding herself floating in one of the guest suites. An older man, easily old enough to be her father, lay in the bed. It was difficult to be sure of his appearance – she wasn't looking through her physical eyes –

but he seemed to look very much like Isabella. His thoughts were a tightly-spinning knot of light, as if he were too fixated on everything that had happened to rest properly. She picked up aches and pains as she glided closer, a grim reminder of just how far the older man had ridden in the last few days. Silverdale felt a flicker of pity. If she'd been aching after hours in the saddle, she hated to think what it must be like after spending *days* on horseback.

 His thoughts reached up to her – or she reached out to them – as she glided closer. A whirlwind of images overwhelmed her, half of them beyond her comprehension. She found herself caught in his slipstream, watching his earliest memories. A tyrant of a father, imposing his will by belt and wand; a mother unable to stop him or to leave him ... Silverdale tried to pull back, but she couldn't. More and more images – and names – flashed through her awareness, as if she was being sucked into his mind. She reminded herself, sharply, that she wasn't really there. She knew it was a lie even as she thought it. Her body might be elsewhere, but her mind ...

The images grew sharper as they moved closer to the present day. Silverdale watched Alden's brief meeting with Isabella – she knew the older man's name, even though she'd never been told – and followed him on his journey to Ida. And then ... she shared in his horror as strange creatures, so *warped* they weren't easy to see, tore through the wards and destroyed the family mansion. She watched, unable to tear her eyes away, as the family and its servants died. She fled ... no, *he'd* fled, consumed with the knowledge he had to reach his sister and yet burdened by the grim awareness he'd abandoned his family at the worst possible time. Silverdale felt her heart go out to him, even as she sensed his strange mixture of feelings for his sister. Isabella and Alden had never gotten along, but they'd been family.

Sofia was family too, she thought, savagely. *And look what she did to us.*

Silverdale gathered herself, then tried to pull free. Alden's thoughts and memories were strong, a whirlwind threatening to suck her down. She felt as if she were caught in a trap, as if she were doomed ... as if something was pulling her into a grave. Horror flowed through her as she struggled, each moment making the pull worse. Alden wasn't *trying* to kill her, she thought; he wasn't even aware of her presence. And yet, she'd gone too close …

She kicked herself, mentally. She didn't have a physical body in the astral plane. She focused her mind, visualising herself as nothing more than an untouched and untouchable ghost. The pull vanished, allowing her to drift free and hover above his body. He was twitching uncomfortably in his sleep. Silverdale shook her head, then turned and allowed herself to glide back to her body. It was strange to see the lights and lines – links, really – running through the castle. She had the feeling she'd never again see the real world as truly *solid*. Given time, she might even be able to take her body through walls.

Her body jerked upright as she fell back into it, gasping for breath. Silverdale struggled desperately, suddenly convinced someone was sitting on her chest choking her to death. Her vision was blurred. She lashed out, flailing at an unseen opponent. Her fists passed through empty air. She caught herself a moment later, accepting a glass of water from Isabella. Her sister-in-law looked odd. It took Silverdale a moment to realise why.

"Your brother doesn't see you like I do," she said. Alden's image of his sister had been a good ten years younger than the reality, as if Isabella was eternally in her teens. "Why is that?"

"We all see different things, when we look at people," Isabella said. She looked as if she was about to say something, then thought better of it. "What you see isn't always what you get."

"I see myself as a ghost," Silverdale said. "What do you think that means?"

"That you're not so solidly bound to yourself?" Isabella shrugged. "What did you see?"

"There were … *things*," Silverdale said. She felt a twinge of frustration. She was sure she'd understand the invaders better if she'd looked at them through her own eyes. "They attacked the mansion. They were immune to magic and … physical force alike. Your brother had to flee."

She scowled, tasting – once again – the humiliation of a flight from danger. It wasn't something she understood, but … it wouldn't do a man's reputation any good if he ran, leaving others to die in his place. Alden would be called a coward, even if he'd had no choice. It was all too clear, from the memories, that the invaders had had the edge. The defenders couldn't so much as slow them down. She winced as she saw the jagged images, of burning buildings and slaughtered civilians and blood running like water through the streets. The invaders hadn't just taken the city. They'd destroyed it.

"It's gone," she said. The images mocked her. "They just wiped the city off the map."

"And we have no idea how they even came into the city," Isabella said. "Didn't they *listen* to me?"

Silverdale shuddered as the memories assaulted her once again. "He tried. He tried to convince the city council to listen. But they didn't …"

Isabella laughed, harshly. "I suppose they didn't believe him."

"No," Silverdale agreed. "Why not?"

"Imagine …" Isabella paused for a moment to think. "Imagine someone told you something you *know* to be untrue. Not just untrue, perhaps, but simply impossible. Perhaps someone told you that you were your own father. Would you believe them?"

Silverdale snorted. "That's impossible."

"That's the point," Isabella said. "You literally could *not* be your own father. Anyone who told you that … well, they *have* to be lying. They have to be making up nonsense. It just isn't the sort of thing someone could say, and mean, by mistake."

She shook her head. "We saw the entities. We *know* what they can do. But … someone who didn't see them at work will have problems believing us. The stories we've told them are literally unbelievable. They won't *want* to believe us. They'd sooner believe we made up the stories to cover for … for something."

Silverdale looked down at her hands. They felt … slightly translucent, as if they were still partly in the astral plane. She couldn't believe that *anyone* would disbelieve them, but … she knew *she* wouldn't have believed herself, a year ago. The story would have been too far-fetched to be true. She'd have been convinced that *someone* was playing a sadistic joke on her. Sofia had been humourless and strict, as sisters went, but she wasn't a monster.

"What now?" Silverdale forced herself to remember the maps. "If the Golden City has been destroyed …"

"Reginald and I will discuss it," Isabella said. "We don't even know who attacked the city."

Silverdale made a face as she tried to recall the images. The invaders had been so badly warped by the entities that they were no longer human, that the human eye found it hard to so much as register their existence. Merely *looking* at them brought pain … she rubbed her eyes as daggers seemed to stab into her brain. The pain was a memory – it wasn't even *her* memory – but it felt all too real. It made it hard to recall what she'd seen.

No wonder Alden is such a mess, she thought. *He wasn't remotely prepared for them.*

She gritted her teeth and forced herself to keep looking, but drew a blank. Her governesses had forced her to memorise an endless list of livery, insignia and flags – she'd been told, more than once, that making a mistake was a grievous insult – yet she couldn't pick out any livery on the invaders. They were little more than dark shadows … she wondered, suddenly, if they were creatures from the astral plane that had been marched into the physical world. It would explain how swords went through them, she supposed, without doing any actual damage.

"I don't know who they were," she said. The invaders hadn't talked amongst themselves, at least not in Alden's hearing. "They could be anyone."

"Yeah." Isabella let out a long breath. "Last year, they were saying the Golden City was protected by the simple fact that none of the kingdoms wanted to risk their rivals getting their hands on it. The kingdoms that wanted to annex the Golden City knew they'd be attacked by everyone else. But now the city has gone …"

Silverdale kept her thoughts to herself. She'd never seen the city … except she *had*, through Alden's memories. There'd been elegant mansions – she frowned, wondering how anyone had thought they could be defended – and a school and … she shook her head. Alden had loved the city.

He'd given his life in *service* to the city, to preserving the knowledge of magic that had been built up over countless generations. And now it was gone. She felt an odd, little pang. She'd hoped, despite everything, that she might have been able to go to the Peerless School. It was gone now, taking her hopes with it.

Isabella stood. "I want you to write down everything you saw," she said. "Put the memories down on paper before they fade."

"I won't forget," Silverdale assured her. "They're burned into my mind."

"They'll fade," Isabella predicted. "They're not really your memories."

Silverdale nodded. She hated writing, but ... Isabella was right. It had to be done. She forced herself to stand, brushing her fingers against the wall of cold stone. It felt reassuringly solid, even as her vision threatened to split into two. One eye showed the wall as solid as it ever was, the other ... suggested she could just walk *through* the wall. But if she did, she'd leave her body behind. Perhaps ...

"I want to help," she said, firmly. "I can help ..."

"Yes." Isabella let out a breath. "But you're too young."

Silverdale met her eyes. "And if I don't help, will I live long enough to see my next birthday?"

"I wish I knew," Isabella said. "I'll discuss it with your brother."

"He'll ..." Silverdale broke off as something dawned on her. "You didn't ask him about this, did you?"

"No." Isabella grimaced. "And he may not be happy."

Silverdale frowned. "What can he do to you?"

"That's not the point." Isabella sounded angry, although more as if she was angry at herself than Silverdale. "If you do something ... something someone else will see as a breach of trust, they will not be happy. They won't trust you. And that can bite you. Hard."

"Reginald will understand," Silverdale said. "Really."

"He won't be pleased," Isabella predicted. "I risked your life."

Her face darkened. "I know you've had to grow up quickly," she added. "But you should enjoy what remains of your childhood. Once it's gone, it's gone."

Chapter Twelve

The moon was rising, Master Henry noted as he reached the top of the ladder and clambered up beside the giant lantern, but the harbour was cloaked in shadow. Halladale City was falling into darkness as more and more households doused their lights, the shadows growing and lengthening as innocent men and women hurried home before footpads, thieves and rapists came out for the night. And other things too, things that only existed in whispered tales that made no sense. Henry had heard the rumours – and the fact they were officially denied suggested there was some truth to them – but he found the stories hard to believe. It was far more likely that a new and dangerous criminal gang was trying to make a name for itself on the streets.

He gasped for breath as he leaned on the metal lantern, then fumbled in his pocket for the firelighter. The oil was already floating within the bowl, carefully measured before nightfall. Henry let out a breath, remembering the days when the lantern had been magic and all he'd had to do was chant a handful of words to trigger the spell. Now ... it was just a matter of time before the city fathers replaced him with a younger man. The lighthouse post was supposed to be lifelong, but that wouldn't last if he couldn't do the job. Henry felt a flash of irritation, mingled with the grim awareness that there might be no choice. He'd been a fisherman in his youth and he knew the coastline all too well. Halladale City was the only safe port for miles. Everywhere else was lined with jagged rocks that were practically designed to tear the bottom from a ship. It was why there was a standing invitation to mariners to dock, day or night, and why the kingdom had invested so much money in the lighthouse. They couldn't take the risk of abandoning sailors to die.

Henry pressed the firelighter against the oil and clicked the switch. It sparked, flames steadily spreading through the liquid and up into the lantern itself. Henry smiled to himself as the chamber started to fill with light, even though the lantern was dull compared to the *magic* lantern. The sailors would be able to see it, he thought, as he started to scramble down the ladder. It had been a long time since his sailing days, but his eyes were still sharp. He wouldn't have been allowed to man the crow's nest if there'd been anything wrong with his eyes.

A shame I can't go back on the waves, he thought, as he reached the next level and stepped into the open air. The breeze smelled of sea air and rotting fish, an inevitable consequence of living too close to a fishing port. *Too old and too fat, I suppose.*

He smiled sourly as he walked around the lighthouse. The city was almost completely dark now, save for a handful of lanterns marking guardhouses, battlements and the castle. He'd been told the port was technically a free state in its own right, but he doubted anyone would dare make that argument to the king. The monarchy might be happy to take advantage of the ambiguity, yet they wouldn't allow it to last if it became inconvenient. There were just too many clashes with Andalusia and Zycrest for the nobility to be comfortable with too *much* ambiguity. And the rumours coming out of both kingdoms were far from reassuring. Henry had heard his fair share of tall tales – he'd heard sailors competing to tell the most absurd stories of daring voyages, back in his sailing days – but there was something about the rumours that bothered him. It could not be denied that refugees had crossed the borders before they'd been closed.

His eyes narrowed as he spotted a handful of men making their way through the streets. Sailors probably, either heading back to their ships or looking for a brothel now that the bars were closing. Not, Henry knew, that *all* of them would close. There were quite a few bars in places the guardsmen never ventured into, unless they had small armies behind them. The sailors could keep drinking and whoring themselves senseless if they wished.

And my days of doing that, too, are over, he thought. His wife would explode with rage if she thought he was so much as *looking* at a whore. He didn't blame her. *I picked up enough nasty stuff when I was a young man to know better.*

He dismissed the thought as he reached the far side of the lighthouse and peered out to sea. The waters were wrapped in inky darkness, utterly unbroken by light. No one in their right mind would try to sail so close to the coastline after dark, not here. And yet ... Henry frowned, suddenly convinced there was *something* out there. It was an instinct he'd learnt to listen to, when he'd been on his first voyage ....

His eyes probed the shadows. He could hear nothing, but the water lapping against the rocky atoll below the lighthouse. Perhaps he was imagining it. Perhaps ... he swallowed, hard, as a shape suddenly loomed out of the darkness. Alarm ran through him as the ship glided past the lighthouse and swept into the harbour. It shouldn't have come so close without lighting a lantern, giving the harbourmaster warning of its coming. There was no boom – the boom was only lowered in times of war – but it was still polite. Henry turned and ran back to the ladder, clambering up to the highest level once again. The bellpull awaited. There was a public flogging – or worse – for anyone who used it without due cause, but a mystery ship entering the harbour was more than good enough. Henry yanked on the rope, the sound of chimes nearly deafening him. The guards would hear it. Even the harbourmaster, a man renowned for sleeping soundly, would be jerked from his sleep.

Henry's ears rang as he ran back to peer at the ship. The captain was insane. He'd driven his vessel right into port and practically rammed it into another vessel, as if he'd been so desperate to avoid sinking he'd tried to ground her ... Henry couldn't believe it. What sort of idiot would try to ground a ship by ramming another one? The bastard would be lucky if he didn't sink *both* ships. He should have lit a lantern or ...

His mouth dropped open as he saw figures leaping from the first ship, swarming the second ship and running onto the port. The invaders – his eyes refused to track them properly – moved with an eerie grace, even as they hurled firebombs into the warehouses, hostels and port facilities. Flames spread rapidly, turning night into day. Henry saw more and more figures coming out of the ship, more invaders than he would have thought *anyone* could cram into a midsized sailing ship. He stared, feeling something twisting at the corner of his eye. The ship carried a crest ... a diplomatic crest. Zycrest ... Henry swallowed, hard. His kingdom had been plunged into war, his capital brought under sneak attack ... how? His mind spun in total disbelief. The invaders could *not* have brought an entire army in a single ship, yet they had. It was impossible.

The flames kept spreading as if they were living things. Henry saw a guard tower suddenly wrapped in fire, burning men jumping to the cobblestones below ... as if they wanted to die quickly. He thought he saw faces within the fires as they grew stronger, becoming a storm that washed over the city. The stone buildings weren't prone to fire – sailors knew the danger of fire better than anyone – but it didn't seem to matter. Tongues of flame were leaping up, licking towards the castle. Henry had no sensitivity to magic, but he didn't need it to know they were under magical attack. The invaders were magicians and ...

His eyes drifted back to the ship. Invaders were *still* leaping out of it, hundreds of men hurrying to the nearest ships and boarding them. Resistance was utterly futile. The invaders tore through the brave and the cowardly alike, slashing men and women down instead of trying to take prisoners for ransom, enslavement, or rape. Who *were* they? The city's wealth was more than just the gold in the king's castle. It was the skill of its people, the men who fished the ocean and the women who were renowned for their mercantile skills ... and yet, the invaders were slaughtering everyone. The city was dying before his eyes.

The invader ship seemed to twist, to become something *more*. Henry leaned forward, feeling as if his eyes were being twisted out of their sockets. It wasn't a ship any longer. It was a gateway to the darkest depths of hell. He felt liquid – blood – trickling from his eyes as it pulled at him, his head spinning helplessly as he kept leaning forward until he tumbled over the rail ...

... And plunged to his death on the rocks below.

***

Jayne allowed herself a tight smile as she sat in her office and reviewed the books. The business hadn't seemed *that* promising, when she'd married into the family and assumed control of the books, but business was starting to boom. She doubted it would get *that* much bigger, not unless something happened to their rivals, but there should be a nice little nest egg to pass down to her daughters and dowries for her sons. They'd marry well and … she allowed herself another smile. She hadn't had any children, not yet, but she was sure it was just a matter of time. As a younger daughter, she wasn't bound by quite as many rules as her older sister. She didn't *have* to spend her first year of married life desperately praying for a baby.

She grinned as she glanced at the stairs leading up to the bedroom. Her husband was up there, snoring loudly. She knew better than to complain. He had to be up at the crack of dawn, ready to take his ship out onto the bitter seas. It didn't seem fair, sometimes, that he had to go fishing while she ran the business, but it could have been worse. There were countries where the women were practically slaves, if not property. And besides, she was all too aware that the sea might make her a widow at any moment. Better to own the business and allow men to court her, rather than lose everything when – if – her husband died.

A clanging sound echoed. Jayne started. She was on her feet before her mind quite caught up with what was happening. That was the *emergency* bell, only rung when the city was in mortal danger. She hurried to her jacket, grabbed the dagger from the sleeve and held it as she ran back to the window. The entire city seemed to be coming to life. No, to *light*. The entire city was burning.

"Jayne!" Her husband hurried down the stairs, cutlass in hand. "What's happening?"

"I don't know!" Jayne was watching the fires. She'd seen flames before, everyone had, but there was something deeply wrong about *these* fires. "The city is under attack."

Her mind raced. She was a trader. She *had* to keep abreast of politics and yet … she hadn't heard anything that so much as suggested the kingdom might come under attack. Sure, there were tensions with Andalusia and Zycrest, with borders closed and traders banned on pain of death or mutilation, but not enough to start a war. Both kingdoms had their own problems, from what she'd heard. Had one of them decided to invade Halladale to distract their nobility from plotting against the crown? It was hardly impossible.

"How could they have gotten here?" Her husband, as befitted a sailor, was a very practical man. "Did they land an entire army in the port?"

"I don't know," Jayne repeated. She shuddered, helplessly. An invading army meant the city would be looted, the people raped and murdered and … she gripped the dagger tightly. She'd give any invader who wanted to rape her a very unpleasant surprise. The bastard would be castrated before he saw the blade in her hand. "I think …"

The ground shook. Lights flickered and flared. The flames seemed to be rising higher as they licked towards the castle … towards her. She thought she heard people screaming within the flames, people she knew …

"I have to get to the guard post," her husband said. "The lads will be massing there."

Jayne said nothing as he turned and left. Every man in the city was part of the militia, every man could and would be called upon to fight if his city came under attack. She couldn't have stopped him. And yet, she wanted to tell him to stay with her. She was too experienced to believe the city *wasn't* going to be sacked, even if the militia managed to assemble and take the field. They'd always assumed they'd have weeks of warning before an invasion, weeks to prepare for a siege … they'd never even *considered* an invasion that came out of nowhere. She gripped her dagger, suddenly wondering if she should leave herself. The flames were getting closer.

She walked upstairs and looked north, towards the port. Flames advanced steadily towards her, burning through houses and shops that were meant to be fireproof. She could feel the heat brushing against her bare skin, even at a distance. People ran, their clothes … and even their bodies … catching fire. She felt sweat trickling down her face as she peered into the flames. There were faces there, faces looking back at her. And, walking through the fires as if they were invulnerable, she saw the invaders. Her eyes refused to look at them. She just *couldn't* look at them and yet she couldn't look away. They drew her in and repelled her in equal measure …

Fire licked against her fingers. Jayne yelped, cursing out

loud as the pain yanked her back to reality. The bedding was starting to smoulder, as if it was on the verge of bursting into flames. The air was so hot she suddenly found it hard to breathe. She turned and fled down the stairs and onto the streets, too scared to even take a second to grab her coat. People would talk … no, they wouldn't. She saw a pair of naked people running past, their exposed skin already starting to char. The heat was growing worse. Behind her, the house burst into flames. She stared, feeling her heart sink as her life – their life – went up in smoke. Even if she made it out of the city, she'd have to rebuild from scratch. She'd lost everything.

She forced herself to run. The flames seemed to lick around her, as if the fires were toying with her. Two children ran past, screaming as their bodies caught fire. They were so badly burnt she couldn't tell if they were male or female, their blackened bodies crashing to the ground as they breathed their last. Jayne ran past, silently promising any god that might be listening that she'd spend the rest of her life in their service if they saved her now. She had never been particularly religious, but …

Something grabbed onto her ankle. She fell, hitting the ground hard enough to knock the wind out of her. Someone had grabbed her … she rolled over, drawing the dagger in one smooth motion. The would-be rapist was not going to live long enough to regret choosing her as his last victim. Her eyes hurt as she saw one of the invaders looming over her. He was … her head started to spin. He wasn't human. His arms were too long, his legs too thin and … his eyes were utterly inhuman. Her strength drained away, the dagger clattering to the ground. The figure raised a clawed hand and struck.

Darkness.

***

King Edwin of Halladale had known it was just a matter of time before his kingdom was attacked by one of his more powerful neighbours. Halladale was rich and weak, a dangerous combination even when the kingdom's society wasn't infinitely superior to the rest of the world. Here, a commoner could rise as high as a nobleman, if he – or she –

wished; women had rights and freedoms – and money – that they were denied elsewhere. He'd thought he'd laid his plans well, but …

He stood on the battlements and watched, helplessly, as a firestorm ravaged his city. Magic. It had to be magic. And yet, he'd never seen or heard of anything like it. The stories of ancient wars were horrific, but even *they* didn't come close. He thought he saw faces within the flames, directing them. They washed over the crowds of fleeing people, consuming them as easily as they consumed the city … he shuddered as the sickly-sweet stench of burning flesh drifted over the battlements. It was just a matter of time before the castle itself fell. There was no point in trying to escape.

The flames reached up and washed over the battlements. Edwin braced himself, wondering if he should jump. At least it would be quick. But instead, the flames receded. A man stood there, where they'd been. His eyes were so … *haunted* … that Edwin pitied him. A slave collar rested around his neck.

"Your Majesty," the newcomer said. "Will you bend the knee?"

Edwin swallowed, hard. He was a king. He bent the knee to no one. But … the war was already over. The city had fallen. And there was only one thing he could do for his people.

"Yes," he said. He dropped to his knees. "I surrender."

Chapter Thirteen

Isabella lay in bed, staring at the ceiling.

She'd never really *expected* that she and Reginald would enjoy decades of married life without a single row. Her parents had argued constantly, at least until her father had crushed her mother's soul; she'd had friends who'd confessed, often tearfully, that their parents had argued and fought and scared their children to death. And yet, the shouting match had been thoroughly unpleasant. Reginald hadn't realised what she'd had in mind. When he'd learnt the truth …

Her lips thinned. She wasn't used to backing down, not even in front of a king. A king who happened to be her husband … she snorted in disgust. She was a sorceress who'd grown up in a very different society, a society that had expected her to be more than just a silent helpmeet to her husband and mother to his children. She had magic. She was hardly as helpless and vulnerable as the average lady of the court, hardly dependent on a man to protect her and utterly submissive to his will. The thought *burned*. She'd spent too long establishing herself as a mercenary first – and a woman second – to think otherwise. And yet …

You wanted to spend your life with him, she thought, tartly. She could hardly say she'd been *forced* into the match. She could have stayed as his sorceress, his friend, or simply left. *And that means getting used to compromise.*

She sighed, inwardly. She wasn't used to admitting her faults either. Her father had made that impossible, damn him. And yet, she had to admit she *had* overstepped. She should have been more honest with Reginald. She should have told him precisely what she'd had in mind, instead of leaving him out of the loop. He might have said no, but … she made a face. He was, legally speaking, his sister's guardian. It was his bloody *job* to say no. And she'd trampled on him.

And you would have done it without hesitation, when you were twelve, Isabella thought. She still shivered to think of how many dumb things she'd done, in her bid to extract herself from her father's clutches. *You made the mistake of thinking Silverdale had grown up in the same place.*

She shook her head, tiredly. Reginald hadn't come to bed. That wasn't a good sign. The castle never slept, but ... there was a general lull after nightfall. She wondered, idly, if he'd gone to his old rooms to sleep. Hell, it was almost *expected* the king and queen would have separate beds. It made no sense to her, particularly given the endless demands for a legitimate heir, but it was custom. The castle staff wouldn't talk ... she hoped. Perhaps it was too much to hope for. She couldn't bind them with loyalty spells.

It isn't as if I was going to throw myself at his feet and demand forgiveness, she thought, sourly. *And he's not likely to do it to me either.*

Isabella willed herself to close her eyes. She was too stubborn for her own good sometimes, just like her husband. Neither of them was very good at admitting when they were wrong, that they'd overstepped ... she sighed. They'd have to talk about it at some point and perhaps apologise to each other. Her lips quirked. She'd apologise, if he apologised first. She had no doubt he felt the same way too. Her father had never apologised. She wondered if Reginald's father had never apologised either.

Her mind started to wander as she drifted off to sleep. She was on the verge of *some* kind of insight, something that nagged at her, but what? Something ... she couldn't put her finger on it. She was too tired and cranky to try. The argument had been just too nasty. She wasn't sure how she'd managed to keep from turning him into a frog or simply hexing him senseless. Hell, she was surprised he hadn't tried to hit her. She'd been a mercenary long enough to know that most men were happy to use their fists if their wives refused to fall into line.

She dreamed, aware – on some level – that she was dreaming. Mother Lembu was looking down at her, the three-in-one entity smiling as if she knew something Isabella didn't. The thought would have been maddening, if she'd been awake, but instead she merely took it in her stride as her mind drifted further and further away. She could feel unseen eyes looking at her from the astral plane, humanity's nightmares given shape and form as they waited for a human host. Isabella tried not to look at them too closely as her mind kept moving, drifting within the astral plane. They'd try to jump into her …

… She saw webs of power reaching across the land, across the globe. They weren't real, but they were… it made no sense, in the waking world, yet in the dream it made perfect sense. She saw giant spiders with too many legs, sitting in their webs and waiting. Waiting for what? Her eyes drifted over them, her body twisting slowly as if it were caught in a breeze …

… She looked down. The world lay below. It was a globe and it was flat and … it was a map. She was looking at a map that was also the territory … it made sense, she was sure, on some level. And yet … the map was folded and twisted and burning … her eyes narrowed as she realised she was looking at Halladale. The border kingdom sat between Andalusia and Zycrest, too large to be swallowed easily and too small to pose a major threat to either of the bigger kingdoms. Reginald had said something about the kingdom's prince wanting to marry Ruby or something … Isabella hadn't thought too much about it. The offer was unlikely to be serious. And yet …

… A flurry of images assaulted her mind. Halladale was under attack. The kingdom was burning, just like the Golden City. She could practically *see* the entities pulling the strings, smashing their way into the kingdom and laying waste to it … no, they'd won. They'd forced the king to surrender. And that meant …

Isabella sat up, body drenched in sweat. Her heart pounded like a drum. She'd seen … she wanted to tell herself it was a bad dream, that one of the nightmare creatures had latched onto her mind and disturbed her sleep, but she knew better. It had been real. The kingdom had been attacked and taken in less than a night. She muttered a spell as she swung her legs over the side of the bed and stood. The room filled with eerie white light. She was alone.

Naturally, she thought, crossly. Reginald was the only person allowed to enter the bedroom without prior permission. She'd made it clear to the maids that they were *not* to enter without asking her first. Isabella had had so little privacy in the mercenary camps that she had no intention of compromising it now. *He didn't come to me.*

She stripped off her sweat-sodden nightdress, threw it in the laundry basket and pulled on a robe. The maids could deal with it in the morning. She wanted to wait for Reginald to back down and come to her, but ... she scowled. It wasn't going to happen, not for a good long while. He'd been brought up to be even more stubborn than she was, to resist all attempts to pressure him into doing something ... anything. She gritted her teeth as she reached out gingerly, the way Mother Lembu had taught her. Reginald was just down the corridor.

Isabella opened the door, then hesitated. The ladies of the court had spent the first month, since Isabella and Reginald had married, trying to educate her in the ways of being a royal bride. Isabella had rolled her eyes at most of their advice, pretty much all of which struck her as being designed to *ruin* the match. She was meant to turn a blind eye to her husband's adultery? Really? She didn't think Reginald *would,* yet ... what if he had? What if there was another woman in his old bedchambers? What if ...

She silently cursed the ladies of the court as she made her way down to the bedchamber and opened the door. The wards posed no resistance as she stepped inside and peered into the semi-darkness. Reginald was lying on his bed, eyes wide open. Thankfully, he was alone. He turned his head to look at her, letting her have the first word. She just wished she knew what to say.

The truth, her thoughts advised. *And hope for the best.*

She swallowed her pride. "I'm sorry."

***

Reginald couldn't say he hadn't been warned, by the older men of the court, that there might be problems if – when – he made Isabella his bride. They'd pointed out that she brought nothing in the way of land and family ties, that – for all her magic – she didn't bring armies that would fight beside him if all hell broke loose. And they'd warned him that she hadn't been *raised* to be a noblewoman, let alone a queen.

The role was a demanding one. She might find herself caught in a morass she'd had no idea existed until it was too late.

He'd ignored the warnings. He'd pointed out the advantages of having a sorceress for a bride; he'd pointed out the number of other noble and royal women who'd managed to get themselves into trouble *despite* being raised for the role. And he'd told them that Isabella could and would give him helpful advice, unlike some of the ladies of the court. Reginald appreciated blind praise as much as the next man, but there were limits. He wanted – he needed – someone who'd tell him when he was being a fool.

And that, he thought, made the betrayal even harder to stomach.

Isabella had put his sister in danger. She'd known the risks – and she'd been evasive when she'd outlined what she'd had in mind – and yet … he shook his head in bitter frustration. The row had been terrible. He'd never heard his parents shouting at each other, not like that. He hoped Ruby and Silverdale hadn't overheard. He hoped the maids and guards hadn't overheard, although *that* was a faint hope. They'd keep their mouths shut …

He hadn't been able to sleep. He'd lain on his bed and brooded, his thoughts churning madly. Had he made a mistake in marrying her? Or had being angry with *her* been the mistake? He knew there would come a time, sooner rather than later, when he would have to arrange matches for his sisters … and for his daughters, if he had any. He would have to put the interests of the kingdom ahead of their interests … really, had Isabella done any differently? What would he have done, if he'd been in her place? And …

The door opened. Reginald tensed, bracing himself before remembering that only one person would have the nerve to open without knocking. Unless it was an assassin … Reginald knew, without false modesty, that he was probably *the* prime target for assassination in the kingdom, with Isabella a close second. He silently listened, assessing the situation, as he calculated the distance to his dagger. No one would fault him for killing an assassin. They'd cheer instead. The bastard who'd *sent* the assassin would cheer the loudest of all.

If only because dead men tell no tales, Reginald thought, although – with the entities involved – he wasn't sure that was actually true. *He'd be more worried if I took the assassin alive.*

Isabella's voice came out of the darkness. "I'm sorry."

Reginald blinked. Isabella was hardly a fainting flower, not like the ladies of the court and their daughters. She wouldn't swallow her pride so easily. She was stubborn enough to keep arguing for days, or simply turn away and sulk rather than bend the knee. The gods knew – he shivered, remembering the entities – she didn't need him. And she didn't have a family that would send her back if she tried to leave. She didn't have to stay …

He sat up, his eyes adapting rapidly to the darkness. "I'm sorry, too."

Isabella came closer until she was standing by the bed. "I …"

"I understand." Reginald had never been good with apologies either. The Crown Prince needed to learn from his mistakes, yet he wasn't allowed to admit them. Kings weren't allowed to admit their mistakes either. Most people would sooner cut their own throats than tell the king he'd made a mistake. It was one of the reasons he'd wanted Isabella for his bride. She wouldn't feel the same instinctive terror of monarchy as any of the other women in his life. "I forgive you."

"Hah." Isabella didn't sound impressed, even when he reached out, caught hold of her hand and pulled her onto the bed. She sat next to him, her face shrouded in darkness. "I shouldn't have done it, and I'm sorry."

"Me too." Reginald winced at the note of defiance mingled with regret in her voice. He'd sounded like that too, he was sure, when his youthful misdeeds had been reported to his father. A firm conviction he'd done the right thing, warring with the grim awareness that everyone else disagreed. "Next time, talk to me first."

He *heard* Isabella swallow a pointed statement as she put her arm around him. Reginald had no idea what she'd intended to say, but he could guess. He might have been tempted to point out that it was often easier to gain forgiveness than permission too.

"I had a bad dream," Isabella said. "Except it wasn't a dream. It was real."

Reginald tensed. "What happened?"

"Halladale was attacked," Isabella said, flatly. "The invaders took the entire country."

"… Shit," Reginald said. He didn't waste time asking if she was sure. He trusted her completely. "They forced the king to surrender?"

His mind raced. Halladale was small, but not *that* small. The kingdom was surrounded by mountains that were guaranteed to slow any invading army. It wouldn't be easy to get to Halladale City itself, not unless one managed to land in the port … he wondered, suddenly, if one of the kingdom's lords had turned traitor. The entities could have been invited in …

We'd have heard something, he thought, numbly. It simply wasn't possible. The entities were powerful, but they weren't *that* powerful. Were they? *How did they take an entire country so quickly we heard nothing?*

"I don't know how they did it, but they did," Isabella said. "And that puts them on our border."

"Yeah." Reginald cursed under his breath. He'd closed and barred the doors – the entities shouldn't be able to *teleport* into the kingdom – but there was nothing stopping them from simply marching their army across the border. Their slaves could take and hold enough of the kingdom to give the masters a chance to embed themselves … he shook his head. The bad news just kept coming. "They'll be coming for us."

Isabella cast a spell. The room filled with pearly white light. Reginald met her dark eyes and winced, inwardly. They shouldn't have had that row. It made it hard to think. And yet … he groaned. He might have to ask her to do it again – or something worse. The kingdom was at war. It was just a matter of time before the entities invaded.

"I'll have to convene the council," he said. He'd told his councillors about the fall of the Golden City, but – for most of them – the Golden City might as well be on the other side of the world. Halladale was a hell of a lot closer. "And …"

He shook his head. What if the councillors didn't believe him? It *was* unbelievable. If someone had attacked

Halladale, without provocation, it should still have taken time for their armies to reach the city. There should have been more than enough warning. Instead … he winced. The entities had teleported an army into the capital. It was the only explanation that fitted the facts.

"They'll need time to regroup," Isabella said. She sounded as if she was trying desperately to think of reasons to be optimistic. "We'll hear more tomorrow."

"Probably." Reginald was sure of it. People would already be crossing the border, if he was any judge. No commoner in their right mind wanted to be close to an invading army. "I dare say a messenger will arrive shortly."

She hugged him, tightly. Reginald understood, better than he wanted to admit. They were both stubborn, both unused to being defied … or simply told they were wrong. And all they had was each other. Isabella drew back, then pushed him onto the bed and straddled him, her fingers tugging at his trousers. Reginald smiled as she impaled herself on him, his hands reaching for her breasts and stroking them. She was far more aggressive, in bed, than any other woman he'd known …

And we only have each other, he thought, as he pulled her down for a kiss. His sisters wouldn't stay, once they married. Her brother probably wouldn't stay, either. And there was no one else he could trust so completely. The row had hurt – he suspected it would be a long time before they recovered – but they would get better. *There's no one else we can trust.*

He shivered, despite himself. The war was far from over.

In a way, he admitted privately, it had only just begun.

Chapter Fourteen

"It's good to see you again, Isabella," Alden said. He sat up in bed, eating breakfast. "I was afraid I'd be too late."

Isabella smiled. She'd brewed a dozen potions – with Silverdale's assistance – and encouraged him to pour them down his throat. Alden hadn't liked the taste, but he'd drunk them without a fight. She'd known men – mercenaries and soldiers, mainly – who'd sooner suffer than drink potions that tasted vile. She took advantage of his distraction to cast another set of sensing spells. Alden had burned his reserves to the very edge of the point of no return, to the point he'd nearly burnt himself out, but he'd survived. He was stronger, she acknowledged sourly, than she'd given him credit for. She guessed he'd felt their father's hand and wand, too.

"I'm glad you made it out," she said. "And that you made it here."

She winced, inwardly. The dream felt … her lips quirked. The dream felt like a dream, the shadow of something that wasn't quite real. Except … whenever she closed her eyes, she could see fires tearing through the city, smell people as they burned to death. She was no stranger to atrocity – she'd been a mercenary, fighting in a dozen civil wars – but burning an entire city was terrifying. How could anyone make use of the population, in any way, if one burned it to the ground?

Perhaps they wanted to keep their troops from running wild, she thought. She'd known commanders who'd *accidentally* set fire to the liquor stores. *Or perhaps they just wanted to make their mark on the land.*

"And I'm glad you're happy," Alden said. "I take it you didn't get my letter?"

Isabella frowned. "The last letter I got from you was six months ago," she said. It had been dated from weeks before the wedding. She'd written to Alden to tell him she'd gotten married, but his reply – whatever it had been – had been lost in transit. "The mail just isn't reliable any longer."

Silverdale leaned forward. "Why? Why did everything just ... break down?"

"The Grand Sorcerers kept everyone in line," Isabella said. She ignored Alden's snort. "They made everyone play nicely together, but they didn't do anything about the underlying grudges that had never been resolved. And so, when the Golden City lost its power, the kingdoms went straight back to war."

"It's a little more complex than that," Alden pointed out. "Really."

Isabella nodded, tartly. There'd been rebellious noblemen, who'd thought *they* could take the crowns and wield real power for the first time in centuries. Adventurers, who'd thought they could win glory by waging war; mercenaries, who'd seen a chance to earn money by keeping the fighting going until the kingdoms were drained completely dry. And too many of them had been right. Andalusia had been lucky. There were kingdoms that had gone through a dozen monarchs in the last six years. She rather suspected their populations were growing tired of a new king every few months.

"It doesn't matter," she said. "Right now, all that matters is stopping the entities."

Alden shivered. "They just destroyed the Golden City," he said. "Everything we knew and loved as children ... gone."

"It wasn't all good," Isabella said. In hindsight, the Grand Sorcerers should have spent more time working with the kingdoms than playing petty power games. Perhaps things wouldn't have fallen apart so badly if the kingdoms had truly *felt* they were partners in empire. "But yes, there was a lot of good in it."

She leaned forward. "I wish I had time to let you recuperate," she added. "Right now, though, we need you."

Alden nodded. "I am at your disposal."

"We've learnt some things about the entities," Isabella said. "And we're making progress on drawing them together into a coherent whole."

She took a moment to decide what she wanted to say, then started to outline everything they'd discovered in the last year. The entities, the nature of their power, their embrace of symbolic magic rather than *real* magic ... no, rather than *human* magic. There was power in the entities and only a fool would deny it. She told him about the first entity she'd captured, still buried under a city, and about Mother Lembu. The three-in-one goddess had been very informative, but much of what she'd said was misleading. Isabella wasn't sure if it was intentional or if she was simply asking the wrong questions.

"It's hard to believe," Alden said. "These creatures *feed* on worship?"

"I think so," Isabella said. "And our worship changes them, too."

She frowned, remembering how the human world and the entities interacted on the astral plane. It was quite possible the two worlds changed each other ... Mother Lembu had hinted as much. And humans who walked into the Godly Realm risked coming out changed. She shivered at the thought. She'd teleported through the Godly Realm once. She had no intention of doing it again.

"The laws of magic are different for them," Alden mused. "And our magic breaks down near them."

Isabella felt a flicker of irritation. Alden was taking the discovery of a new kind of magic surprisingly well. She'd expected him to have problems ... she told herself, sourly, not to be silly. She needed his insights. Perhaps ... it struck her, suddenly, that Alden might have regarded the Golden City as a prison. He could have left at any moment, if he'd been willing to give up the family once and for all. And now the choice had been taken out of his hands.

Perhaps he feels free to be himself for the first time ever, she thought. *It isn't as if either of us could continue the family.*

"You said their laws override ours ... sometimes," Alden said. "They can't be doing it deliberately or your trick with the transfigured blades wouldn't work. They wouldn't *let* it work."

"No," Isabella agreed. If the entities could have prevented her from turning their laws to her advantage, they would have done so. "I wanted to try a couple of experiments with you."

"I'd be happy to help," Alden said. "What do you have in mind?"

"I'll show you my workshop," Isabella said. "But first" – she made a show of wrinkling her nose – "you should probably have a bath."

She called one of the maids, ordered the young woman to help Alden wash and change into something more suitable, then led Silverdale back to the workshop. The little princess had been markedly subdued – Reginald had had a long chat with her, after he'd calmed down – but Isabella was sure she'd return to normal soon. Silverdale reminded her too much of herself, right down to the willingness to push the limits as far as they would go. And to put herself at risk.

"Let me help," Silverdale said, as soon as they were back in the workshop. "Please."

"I need to do this first," Isabella said. She didn't want to put Silverdale in danger. Not again. "You can try it after me."

She walked around the bench, laying out a pencil, a ruler and a small iron bar. It was no bigger than her middle finger, something she could normally have picked up with no effort at all. Silverdale followed, keeping her mouth shut. Isabella frowned, wondering if she was planning something stupid. It was what *Isabella* would have done.

There was a knock on the door. Isabella opened it. Alden stepped inside, wearing a dapper suit rather than aristocratic robes. She wondered, idly, what he should wear if – when – he was formally presented at court. A magician's robes? Or clothes befitting the older brother of a queen? She smiled at the thought as she beckoned him into the room, his eyes flickering around as if he expected trouble to come out of nowhere. A workshop was rarely safe, even for the owner. The tiniest mistake could lead to utter disaster.

"I'm surprised it's not bigger," Alden said. "Don't you need more room?"

"Right now, no," Isabella said. "I can get more space if I need it."

She allowed him to explore the room while she pointed out the handful of safety precautions, then motioned for him to sit next to Silverdale. "I'm going to try to move these items" – she waved at the table – "from the astral plane. I want you to watch and observe."

Alden nodded. "Of course."

Silverdale looked rebellious, but said nothing as Isabella sat on the sofa, put the vial of potion to her lips and drank. It tasted pleasantly sweet, unlike the more traditional potions she'd made for her brother. Isabella smiled to herself as the world started to swim around her. The potions Mother Lembu had taught her to make were the *real* traditional potions, dating all the way back to the days of myth and legend. The potions she'd learnt at the Peerless School were new ... and rare, now. The global trade network was gone. Once she burnt her way through what little stock she'd managed to find, it was gone.

We're going to have to find alternatives, and quickly, she thought. *Or else all our hard-won knowledge will be useless.*

She felt her mind drift up and out of her body. The astral plane felt ... quiet, too quiet. A shiver ran down her spine as she kept rising, her body spinning as if she was caught in an unseen current. She took a breath, then calmed herself and turned. The castle felt weirdly *wrong*, the walls little more than ghostly shadows. Alden and Silverdale were nexuses of glowing light. She was mildly amused to note that Silverdale was brighter than Alden, even though she was young enough to be his granddaughter.

And he never had kids, she thought. *The family bloodline will die with him.*

She put the thought out of her mind as she drifted back into the room. The workshop seemed to shimmer in and out of existence ... she had to concentrate to keep herself focused on the bench. It wasn't easy to so much as *see* the items she'd laid out for the taking. They were practically invisible. She braced herself, then reached out and tried to pick up the pencil. It should have been effortless. Instead, her fingers passed through the pencil as if it wasn't there.

Interesting, she told herself. There were other words she wanted to use. *I wonder if ...*

She gritted her teeth, then reached for it again. It didn't work. The pencil felt like ... like fog, like something she could *feel* but not quite touch. She glided forward until she was practically pushing her *head* into the pencil, reminding herself – not for the first time – that she was no longer bound by human rules. She could bend her body in ways that would be flatly impossible, even for a contortionist, in the human world. She brushed her mind against the pencil as her fingers touched the wood. This time, it moved. It felt like air, as if it wasn't quite there – and was constantly on the edge of falling *through* her hands – but it moved. She felt a flash of delight as the pencil hovered in the air. Silverdale might be able to see her ghostly form, but Alden ... she smirked. Her brother had to be utterly confused.

He knows what I'm doing, she thought, as she put the pencil down and reached for the cold iron. *I wonder ...*

Her fingers shattered. She felt pain, pure pain, crashing through her mind. Her hand had been smashed, her arm had been broken, her neck ... she bit her lip, hard. The pain wasn't real. It couldn't be real. And yet, it had come within seconds of killing her. She let go of the astral plane, plunging back into her body. It felt ... she shuddered, fighting to draw breath. The mere act of trying to pick up the cold iron had almost killed her. She stared at her hand, feeling tears prickling in her eyes. Her hand was normal, unhurt. And yet, she thought she could see another hand overlaying the first. That hand was shattered beyond repair.

Silverdale touched her arm. Isabella jumped. "I ..."

"What happened?" Silverdale looked worried. "I saw you touch the iron and then you ... you fell back."

"I think the iron was infinitely heavy," Isabella said. "It ... crashed through my hand."

She felt a twinge of pain in her fingers as she stared at them. It made no sense. The iron bar – the tiny iron bar – shouldn't have fallen *upwards*. It shouldn't have fallen at all. And yet, in the twisted world of the astral plane, it had hurt her badly. She thought she knew, now, why cold iron was an effective barrier. If Mother Lembu tried to escape, she'd be smashed flat before she could pull out ...

"Interesting," Alden said. He didn't sound too worried. To him, very little had actually happened. "I saw the pencil move. None of my detection spells worked."

"No," Isabella agreed. "I think ..."

She took a breath, trying to sort out her confused thoughts. *Nothing* made sense, not in human terms. And yet ...

"I think I imposed the rules of the human world on the astral plane," she said, slowly. Her thoughts ran in circles. "I think ... I brushed my mind against the pencil. I think that's what allowed me to pick it up. I was ... I was imposing my will on the pencil."

"As if you'd stood, walked over and picked it up," Alden mused. "Interesting."

"Interesting," Isabella repeated. "Is that all you can say?"

"Right now, I don't know enough to make any intelligent comments," Alden said. He frowned. "You'd be ... is that what *they're* doing? Twisting our world to allow *their* world, their rules, to exist? To allow *them* to exist?"

"I think so," Isabella said. She remembered Mother Lembu's description of what had happened when humans and entities had met for the first time. *Both* sides had been shattered by the experience. "I think ... you remember the mermaids that wanted to drown an entire town so they could live there?"

"Yes," Alden said. The incident had been a hundred years ago, but they'd learnt about it in school. "They had to drain the water to get rid of them."

He frowned. "The mermaids changed the environment so they could live there," he added. "And you're suggesting the entities do the same, just on a much larger – and stranger – scale. Magic breaks down near them because they change the rules to the point it can no longer work."

"I think so," Isabella said. "The poor bastards the mermaids drowned died because they could no longer breathe."

"And if that is true," Alden said, "then changing the environment *back* would get rid of them. Or kill them. Either way, we win."

"They have immense power," Silverdale reminded them. "Remember what they did to Sofia?"

"Yes," Isabella said. "But their power isn't what's important on the astral plane."

She considered it for a long moment. If the entities changed the rules, it raised the possibility – as Alden suggested – of changing them back. Hell ... given that the entities themselves were influenced, if not shaped, by the humans who worshipped them ... she made a mental note to look into the authorised temples and their designs. It was just possible that whoever had laid down the rules had done something to ensure the worship was directed *away* from the entities or grounded well before it could reach the astral plane. She felt her head spin at the sheer enormity of what had been kept from them. If the Grand Sorcerers had told everyone the truth, if they'd even *known* the truth ...

They might not have understood what they were doing, she thought, numbly. *And as long as the empire stood, the entities were barred from returning in any major way.*

"We're going to have to think very carefully about what to do next," she said. She entertained the idea of picking up an iron bar and throwing it at an entity, but she didn't think it would actually work unless the entity tried to pick the bar up itself. "The old barriers are gone. The entities might be able to feed on our worship ..."

She winced, remembering what Reginald had said. Baron Braddock's people had wanted to keep worshipping, despite the dangers. They'd been quite happy to offer worship for rewards, for miracles ... Isabella liked to think she wouldn't make that choice, if it was offered to her, but she knew better than to believe it. The poor peasants had very little to call their own. If worshipping an entity meant their communities grew and flourished, she couldn't fault them for worshipping. And yet, it was just a matter of time before they unleashed a horror beyond human imagination.

And we can't even stop them, she thought. She knew enough about human psychology to guess how the worshippers would react, even before the entities got their hooks in their souls. *They're unlikely to believe the warnings and they will defy any threats.*

There was a sharp tap on the door. Isabella frowned, opening the door with a gesture. A messenger stepped inside, looking nervous. He probably thought she shared her husband's attitude towards messengers. She didn't really blame either of them. Messengers generally bought bad news.

The messenger bowed. "Your Majesty, His Majesty requests your presence in the audience chamber."

Isabella frowned. It was rare, at least in her experience, for audiences to be arranged without any warning at all. "Why?"

"We have received an envoy from Zycrest," the messenger said. "His Majesty requests your presence ..."

"I understand," Isabella said. "Inform him I'm on my way."

Chapter Fifteen

It was a curious fact, Reginald had often thought, that – for all the talk of *the* throne – there were actually no less than *five* thrones within the castle. They all belonged to the king – it was death for someone outside the family to sit on them, even for a moment – but some were more important than others. The throne that sat in the audience chamber was, in some ways, the least of them. And yet, it was just as uncomfortable. Reginald's father had joked that sitting on the throne was just like sitting on a hedgehog. Reginald hadn't come to understand what he'd meant until he'd ascended the throne himself.

He sat, wincing slightly, as the audience chamber filled with the great and the good. The chamber had been thoroughly cleared and disenchanted after Sofia's death, but surprisingly few aristocrats felt comfortable in the room. Long custom demanded that Reginald invite *everyone* – or at least everyone who thought they were anyone – to the reception ceremony, yet half the nobility had failed to attend. He would have been insulted, if he hadn't been so relieved. It was easier to spin events the way he wanted if there were relatively few witnesses. He let out a breath as Isabella and Ruby joined them, Isabella wearing her workday clothes rather than a formal dress. The envoy wouldn't say anything, but he'd notice.

Reginald scowled as the herald blew his trumpet, then announced the envoy. There'd been no warning of his coming, no messenger to alert Reginald to make preparations. *That* alone was worrying. King Forsyth of Zycrest clearly *didn't* want to give Reginald the chance to keep the envoy's message to himself, given how openly he'd advertised the man's arrival. Reginald had never met King Forsyth, yet … either the man was a fool, or he wanted to back Reginald into an awkward position. Or … his scowl deepened. Zycrest was on the eastern side of Halladale.

There weren't many other kingdoms that would attack Halladale, certainly not so savagely. Reginald knew *he* hadn't done it and there weren't many other suspects.

The doors opened. The envoy stepped inside. Reginald felt Isabella tense beside him as the envoy came into view, pulling back her hood. She ... he blinked in surprise. She? It was rare for an envoy to be female. And yet ... her face was vague, obscured by ... his hand dropped to his sword. The envoy had been overshadowed. She'd given herself, body and soul, to the entities.

"King Reginald," the envoy said. "I speak with the voice of King Forsyth of Zycrest, the Imperator of All. He bids you greetings."

Reginald frowned. *That* wasn't a standard opening. The envoy was *meant* to acknowledge Reginald's supremacy within his own kingdom, showing him the respect of a fellow monarch ... diplomacy, his father had once said, was often little more than patting someone on the head and pretending you liked him, even if you hated him. Now ... a shiver ran down his spine as the overshadowed woman leaned forward. He couldn't see her face. She was utterly inhuman and it scared him to the bone. He gripped his sword. The cold iron helped him focus.

"I bid him greetings, too," he said. He had a nasty feeling he knew what the envoy was about to say. "What does he wish to say?"

The envoy seemed to smile. It was hard to be sure. Reginald had an impression of flashing teeth, jagged teeth ... too *many* teeth. "The Imperator wishes you to know that he intends to reunite the world under his banner, the banner of the true faith," she said. Every word dripped malice and condescension. "Your kingdom has a choice to make. You can bend the knee to the Imperator, or he will take your kingdom and put you all to the sword. The true faith will spread, whatever you may do. You can either join us, and submit to us, or you can die. Halladale has already fallen. The Golden City has fallen. You will not be allowed to stand in our way."

Reginald felt a hot flash of anger. No one, not even his father, had *ever* dared talk to him like that. No one. The envoy wasn't being remotely diplomatic. She certainly wasn't trying to salvage his pride … he gritted his teeth to keep from drawing his sword and beheading her on the spot. She should have approached him quietly and … and then what? He almost smiled. The iron fist might be inside a velvet glove, but it was still an iron fist. And there was no way he was going to surrender.

She's not here to convince me, he thought, grimly. *She's here to convince my followers that there's no point in trying to resist.*

He thought, fast. The aristocracy would switch sides in an instant, if they thought they were on the *losing* aside. Aristos who'd bent the knee to Sofia had pledged themselves to him as soon as he'd won the war. If he was overthrown tomorrow, the bastards would happily bend the knee to whoever had put a knife in his back. He wondered, idly, if the plotter would be foolish enough to trust them. The trouble with launching a coup – and succeeding – was that you gave other people ideas …

"Tell me," he said. "Who am I *really* speaking to?"

The envoy didn't show any visible reaction to the question. "You can open your borders to us and submit, or your land will be ravaged from end to end," she said. "There will be no further discussion."

Thank you, Reginald thought, sourly.

He forced himself to look at the envoy. "Your permission to be in this castle and country is hereby revoked," he said. "You will be escorted back to the border immediately, speaking to no one along the way. And you can inform your master, whoever he happens to be, that his demand for surrender and submission is rejected."

The envoy didn't curtsey or bow. Instead, she turned and walked out of the door, guards scrambling to follow. Reginald breathed a sigh of relief as the doors slammed closed, the air snapping back to something resembling normal. He'd been face to face with an entity … or, perhaps, with one of the human bodies it wore. The woman … who had she been? He told himself it didn't matter. Whatever she'd been, she wasn't now. She'd been completely overshadowed.

He gestured to a messenger. "Inform the councillors that we'll be meeting in ten minutes," he ordered, curtly. Word would already be spreading, he was sure. Rumours moved faster than anything else, except perhaps bad news. "And hurry."

Isabella nodded to him as he stood. "At least we know where the entity went."

"Zycrest," Reginald agreed. "And it took control of the kingdom."

He considered the problem as they made their way to the council chamber. He hadn't *heard* of any trouble in Zycrest, nothing that would give the entities an opening … he shook his head. It was meaningless. No one outside the castle would have known about Sofia's dissatisfaction, or cared if they had. He felt his heart twinge in pain. If he'd known his sister was so dissatisfied, he could have done something about it …

No, you couldn't, his thoughts mocked. *What does the happiness of a princess – or a prince – matter when the throne is at stake?*

Isabella and Ruby followed him into the council chambers, Isabella sitting beside him while Ruby sat at the far end of the table. Reginald suspected the councillors saw it as a demotion for Ruby, although they'd be wise not to say so out loud. Technically, Ruby was his heir and would remain so until Reginald had a child. It wasn't going to be easy for her to assert herself, if she *did* have to take the throne. And who could she marry? There weren't many men who'd serve her without trying to overrule her.

"Those of you who did not attend the audience will, no doubt, have heard what happened," he said, once the doors were firmly closed. "Zycrest has invaded and, apparently, annexed Halladale. They now want to do the same to us. And, thanks to their envoy, we know who – or rather what – is behind it. The entities have taken control of Zycrest and crushed Halladale."

Somehow, his thoughts added. *How did they get their troops into the city so quickly?*

"I will be blunt," he continued. "We will not surrender. We will not bend the knee. We will not invite them into our country, into our hearts and minds. And I say to you now, once and for all, that anyone who suggests otherwise will be stripped of his rank and power and banished to the furthest reaches of the Summer Isle. There will be no opportunity for *anyone* to invite them into our country."

He paused, allowing his words to hang in the air. "There's no hope of *them* building a true empire," he said. "We will become little more than sheep and cattle, harvested for our souls. We literally cannot surrender, because it means the end of the world. And so, we will fight. We know enough – now – to stop them. We *will* stop them.

"I will take the army to the border. I will stop the invasion, when it comes, and then liberate Halladale and Zycrest from the entities. And I expect each and every one of you to give me your full support. Anyone who feels otherwise is welcome to leave. Now."

There was a long, chilling pause. No one moved. Reginald wasn't surprised. Anyone who left would be branding himself as a fairweather friend, if nothing else. And yet, he was morbidly sure the councillors were already plotting their fallback positions. They'd want to make sure their families survived, if the entities won. They would be deluding themselves – he was sure of that, if nothing else – but there was no point in expecting otherwise. He'd have to settle for their half-hearted collaboration.

"I'll be issuing orders for a full mobilisation within the week," Reginald concluded. "Your levies will be summoned to join the army. I trust this won't pose a problem?"

He winced, inwardly. The feudal levies had been little more than a half-forgotten custom for centuries. Now ... his father had been reluctant to risk letting the aristocrats have too much independent military power. The levies might wind up being pointed at the king. Reginald knew he could squash any lone baron who waged war on him, but *all* of them? And he knew many of the young aristos leading the levies into battle. Some were experienced and capable, some were inexperienced and incompetent ... some had never seen war at all.

And I'll have to put the well-connected ahead of the experienced, he thought, sourly. *Half the aristocrats will have conniptions if their sons have to take orders from commoners.*

"Good," he said, when no one objected. "Are there any issues that should be raised now?"

Councillor Logan leaned forward. "Your Majesty, who'll remain at court?"

Reginald kept his face carefully impassive. "That will be discussed later," he said. He wanted to take Isabella with him. "You will be informed before the army marches."

He stood. "I expect each and every one of you to put the interests of the kingdom first," he cautioned. "I expect you to make it clear, to your clients as well as everyone else, that we are fighting for our lives. I will *break* the man, and his family, who dares try to take advantage of the crisis to push his own agenda. The world itself stands on the brink."

"Dismissed."

And I'll have your sons under my banner, he thought coldly, as the meeting broke up. *If you cause trouble, I can deal with them before I deal with you.*

He sat down, feeling years older. His father had aged rapidly when he'd assumed the throne ... no, he'd started ageing rapidly after the throne had suddenly come to mean something again. The Grand Sorcerers were gone ... Reginald shivered, wondering how many of the councillors understood what had changed. The Golden City was a blackened ruin ... the gods alone knew what was happening further east. He smiled, humourlessly. The gods really *did* know. They were the ones doing it.

"Some of them are already planning to put a knife in your back," Ruby predicted. She stood, brushing down her dress. "What are you going to do about it?"

"I'll have their sons with me," Reginald said. He made a mental note to keep a closer eye on the aristocrats who had more than two sons. "And I need you to stay here."

He looked at Isabella. "Will you accompany the army?"

"I have a hunch I want to try first," Isabella said. She grimaced. "Do you want me to come with you?"

"Try your hunch first," Reginald said. He did want her to come, even though her presence would cause complications. "And then you can rejoin the army."

Isabella nodded. "We can't let them get control of the borderlands."

"No." Reginald made a face as something dawned on him. "And we must seal the ports too."

"Pardon?" Ruby stared at him. "You'll destroy trade ..."

Reginald nodded. "They must have sailed a diplomatic ship into Halladale City," he said. He didn't *know*, but he was sure. It made sense. "A diplomatic ship would, technically, count as sovereign territory. They put the ship in the harbour, then teleported the army onto the ship."

Isabella sucked in her breath. "They bypassed all the defences."

"Quite," Reginald said. "That's another good reason to get the army east as quickly as possible."

He rested his hands on the table as he looked at Ruby. "I'm going to leave you in charge, with a handful of trustworthy men," he said. "And Lord Alden, if Isabella needs to go elsewhere. If I fall in battle, you will be the next monarch. Do you understand?"

Ruby swallowed. "You don't want to look for a more distant relative?"

Reginald shook his head. He had no children of his own. Sofia was dead. Silverdale was a child, Isabella was only related to him through marriage. Everyone else ... Reginald grimaced. His father had purged a bunch of people for being too closely related to the royal family, but not closely enough to be considered part of the main bloodline. The closest adult relative he had, as far as he knew, was someone who would not – normally – be in line for the throne. Ruby was the only real candidate. Anyone else ... there'd be too many competing claims for any distant relative to be accepted without a fight.

"It has to be you," he said. "And you need to start making contingency plans for what you'll do if I don't come home."

Ruby smirked. "Do I get to choose my own husband? Can I choose the pig-boy?"

"Right now, the pig-boy would have the advantage of pissing off *everyone*," Reginald said, mock-thoughtfully. "Should I send the guards to collect your future husband?"

He smiled at her glower, then sobered. The hell of it was that she *needed* a husband who wasn't connected to the aristocracy. If Ruby married an aristocrat's son, her new father-in-law would try to dominate her. Even if he didn't, the balance of power would start to shift and eventually topple as the other aristocrats allied against him. Ruby would find it difficult, if not impossible, to retain her footing and her crown.

And she can't remain unmarried either, he thought. *She*

needs an heir of her body if I don't have children myself.

"We'll discuss it later," he said. Perhaps a soldier … there were a multitude of good men, some of whom had aristocratic blood. Enough to be considered noble, not enough to give them a power base of their own. Or Lord Alden … he shook his head. The age gap was far too wide. "And you'd better think about it too."

Ruby took the hint and headed for the door. Reginald turned to Isabella as soon as the door was closed again. "And now we know."

"Knowing is half the battle," Isabella said. "Or so my old instructor used to say."

"Really?" Reginald hadn't heard *that* when he'd been studying war and kingship. "And was it helpful advice?"

"I believe so," Isabella said. She stood and started to pace the room. "The last I heard, the king of Zycrest was a weak man. There was a *lot* of speculation that the nobility was considering an uprising. A bunch of mercenaries I knew even headed in that direction … this was before you started hiring every mercenary you could find for the Summer Isle. You might have done the king a favour."

"At least until the entities arrived," Reginald said. A weak king might be easily and safely removed …. but he couldn't be left alive afterwards, for fear he would try to retake the throne. Or be used as a figurehead by someone else. "Isabella, if they have a whole country united under their banner …"

He stopped. He didn't have to spell it out. Not for her.

"The Golden City has been destroyed," Isabella said. "And now we have no way to keep them from infesting the rest of the world."

Reginald nodded. "I'll have to send more messages," he said. "If nothing else, we'll have to be very careful what we allow to enter our harbours."

"I have an idea," Isabella said. Her eyes turned contemplative. "Two ideas, really. And … I need Silverdale."

"Take care of her," Reginald said. He knew, even as he spoke, that it wasn't going to be easy. "Please."

"I'll do my best," Isabella promised.

Chapter Sixteen

Reginald took a deep breath as he walked into the army camp, his two bodyguards giving him some room to enjoy the scene. Hundreds of soldiers ran from place to place, their sergeants barking orders as they exercised and prepared for battle. Horsemen cantered around the camp, noblemen who'd learnt to ride before they could walk competing with commoners who'd joined Reginald's personal troops well before he'd become king; archers practiced firing salvo after salvo of arrows towards targets a goodly distance from the camp. The scene was organised chaos and Reginald loved it, even though they were going to war. It felt so *good* to be doing something *simple* again.

A trio of horsemen cantered past, hastily removing their caps and waving them at him in salute. Noblemen; they had to be. Reginald smiled, hoping they'd have the sense to *listen* to orders from their common-born sergeants and superiors. The trickle of levies was steadily turning into a flood, including sons who somehow managed to be snootier than their mothers and fathers. Reginald had heard a dozen reports of fighting between the royal troops and the levies, even though they were meant to be on the same side. He'd turned a blind eye, as much as he could. Hopefully, they'd get it out of their system before it was too late.

He allowed himself a curt smile as he walked past the sleeping tents. Aristocrats and officers got tents, but – otherwise – had surprisingly few privileges. It was a good way, he'd found, to separate the men from the boys. The ones who complained were too unreliable to risk putting in command of regiments, let alone entire armies. And besides, it often ended in unsuitable officers heading home without ever being formally dismissed. No one could blame him, not openly, for their failure.

The guards outside the command tent snapped to attention as he approached. They were well-trained, he noted with a flicker of relief; they didn't bow or kneel or do anything that might distract them from their job. He nodded to them both, then stepped inside. The three captain-generals were gathered around the table, pushing pieces of paper around as they tried desperately to fit the levies into the military command structure. Reginald didn't envy them. He'd done enough paperwork himself, when he'd been a mere prince, to understand the difficulties. It didn't help that the aristocrats who didn't get plum positions and commands would make a fuss ...

"Your Majesty," Captain-General Gars said. "Thank you for coming."

"It's good to be out of the castle," Reginald said. He'd spent the last few days dismissing suggestions he remain home, safe and well, while someone else led the army to the borderlands. There was no one else who could command the army, no one who could make the aristocrats behave ... no one who could be trusted not to turn the army around and lay siege to Havelock. "Are we ready to march?"

"We should have everything in place, ready to go, by tomorrow," Gars informed him. He indicated the paperwork with a wave of his hand. "The majority of the regulars have been dragged out of the pleasure dens and put back to work, regaining their edge. The remainder have been given a final warning to return by the end of the day or be charged with desertion."

Reginald nodded, scanning the paperwork with a practiced eye. Desertion was a constant problem, particularly when the recruiting sergeants weren't always scrupulous about how they convinced prospective soldiers to sign up. The army wasn't always a good place, either; it wasn't uncommon for raw recruits to take one look at the army life and flee, effectively becoming deserters. And there were too many people happy to help a deserter. And ...

"Give them their chance to return," he said. "How do we stand with weapons and supplies?"

"We've replenished the losses from the previous campaign," Captain-General Jones said, tactfully choosing not to mention that the last *major* campaign had been against Sofia. "The only real problem is supporting the troops once we reach the border. We simply couldn't pre-position supplies that close to the line without risking a diplomatic incident …”

“Which may have been a mistake,” Reginald said. He understood the logic, but in hindsight it had come back to bite him. Hard. “Can we keep the troops supplied?”

“As long as nothing interferes with the wagon train,” Jones said. “I’d be happier if we lived off the land.”

“Not if we can avoid it,” Reginald said. There was nothing more certain to turn the border folk against the army than ravishing their lands. Armies had been known to steal seed corn, leaving the local population to starve because they couldn’t raise next year’s crops. “Transport as much as you can eastwards. There’ll be limits to what we can take even if we *do* live off the land.”

“Yes, Your Majesty,” Jones said. “Do you want to ban camp followers too?”

Reginald grimaced. “They can come, as long as they’re useful,” he said. The army’s motley collection of wives, washerwomen and whores could be very helpful, but they could also be a major problem. “And as long as they don’t cause trouble.”

“Feeding them may be a problem, later,” Jones warned. “We simply didn’t plan for a full-scale campaign so quickly.”

“Particularly not one that requires a full-scale mobilisation and deployment,” Reginald agreed. “And the cavalry?”

“We’re ready to ride out on your command,” Captain-General Stuart said. He was the only high-ranking aristocrat amongst the three, an all-important qualification when half of the cavalrymen refused to take orders from commoners. “All our supplies are ready to follow.”

“Good.” Reginald let out a breath. Cavalrymen were required to provide for themselves, unless they’d signed up with him personally. It was a pain, particularly when they wound up with a dozen different types of saddle, but it saved money. “Make sure the newcomers understand their duties.”

“Yes, Your Majesty,” Stuart said.

Reginald reached for the map and unfurled the paper, laying it out on the rickety table. He smiled as he weighed it down, knowing precisely how shocked some of the aristocrats would be to see him doing his own work. They’d turn their noses up at the table too, even though it was vastly more practical than anything that might be found in an aristocrat's castle. It could be moved easily, or turned into a weapon or ... he felt his smile grow wider. They'd be arguing he shouldn't wipe his own arse next!

"I want cavalry patrols all along the road from here to the border, starting tonight," he ordered, as he traced a line on the map. "Your men" – he glanced at Stuart – "know what to watch for. Half of them have the ointment for their eyes. They are *not* to engage the enemy, be they warped men or simple worshippers. If they spot any trace of the enemy, they are to turn and gallop home. Make that clear to them."

Stuart banged his chest in salute, although Reginald had known him long enough to tell he had doubts. It wouldn't be easy to convince the cavalrymen not to gallop straight at the enemy, rather than following orders. They'd fear being branded cowards ... he shook his head. The days when he was willing to tolerate disobedience from glory hounds were long gone. He couldn't afford to focus on a single battle. He had to think about winning the war.

Which means keeping the entities out of the kingdom long enough to find a way to slam the door closed, he told himself. *And that isn't going to be easy.*

"The remainder of the army will depart in two sections," he continued. "I'll take the first section myself, tomorrow morning. The second will follow in two hours. If we run into trouble, the second section should be able to support the first. Ideally, we should be able to reach the border without trouble."

He made a face as he studied the map. The empire had built hundreds of roads to link the kingdoms together, but they'd been falling into disrepair over the last few years. None of the locals really *wanted* roads in their regions, knowing the disadvantages – taxmen and armies preying on them – far outweighed the advantages. The army might start marching in formation, but by the time it reached the border it was going to be spread out and vulnerable. If an enemy army had already crossed the border ...

We should have some warning, he thought. *Even if they teleported an army to the border itself, the army would still have to march across to gain control of our land.*

"We'll establish ourselves at Barr and decide what to do

next," he added. He had several ideas, but he couldn't make a final decision until he knew what was actually going on. He suspected they'd have to invade Halladale, if not Zycrest itself. "Our first priority remains keeping them out of our kingdom."

He leaned back, trusting them to handle the details as he headed back to the castle. Isabella was waiting for him … it felt odd to be departing on a major campaign without her, even though – two years ago – he hadn't even known her name. He'd put out a call for sorcerers, mages and even hedge wizards, but very few had answered his call. Sofia had destroyed what remained of the magical community in Havelock. Reginald suspected that any survivors weren't inclined to reveal themselves to the new monarch.

How the mighty fall, he thought, gloomily. Six years ago, magicians had practically ruled the known world. Monarchs had been little more than figureheads, puppets controlled by court wizards. Now … the Golden City was gone, the Peerless School was a pile of rubble, and very few magicians remained alive. *That could be us one day.*

He allowed the thought to torment him as he left the tent, walked back to his horse and cantered back to the castle. His bodyguards, recognising his mood, gave him space as they headed through the empty roads. The population was inside, sheltering behind locks and iron bars. Reginald scowled, knowing why they were hiding. They feared the army taking their sons, raping their daughters, and stealing whatever they wanted. And …

We need to set up our own school of magic, he thought. *And we need to find a way to prevent it from going bad.*

He sighed as the horse carried him over the drawbridge and into the courtyard. A stable lad bowed hastily and took the reins as Reginald dismounted, leading the horse back to the stables. Reginald felt a twinge of guilt – caring for his mount had been one of the lessons he'd learnt as a child – then turned away and into the castle. Servants bowed or curtseyed or scattered as he approached, as if they feared what he'd do to them. They remembered Sofia's brief reign all too well. They probably didn't think he'd be any better.

And too many noble boys get the maids into trouble, Reginald thought. *He'd* flirted with the ladies of the court, but not everyone had that option. *And then it's always the maid that gets blamed.*

He reached his suite and stepped inside. Isabella, Ruby and Silverdale were waiting for him, the latter reading a book on magic. Ruby herself was studying the latest set of crop reports from across the kingdom, Isabella offering helpful advice from time to time. Reginald allowed himself a smile as they looked up, feeling a sudden wave of affection. His family was all together ... his heart twisted. Sofia was dead. And even before she'd died, she'd been changed ...

Isabella stood. "How was it?"

"We'll be leaving tomorrow, as planned," Reginald said. They'd been lucky. The timing had been poor, if there was ever a right time for a war. "Unless something else goes wrong."

He removed his jacket and hung it by the door. "You'll be meeting us at Barr?"

"And I'll be coming too," Silverdale said. "You need me ..."

Reginald shook his head. "You're far too young," he said, with the private thought he *really* didn't want his sister anywhere near the border. Or an army camp. Technically, Silverdale was second in line to the throne. Anyone who took her captive would have the kingdom over a barrel. He shuddered to think what the *entities* would do with her. "You need to stay with Isabella."

Silverdale gave him a sweet, completely fake smile. "And when Isabella goes to Barr ...?"

"You can stay here," Reginald said. "Alden will teach you magic."

Silverdale looked rebellious. Reginald chose to ignore it as he glanced at Isabella. "Don't let her do anything stupid."

"I won't do anything stupid," Silverdale insisted.

"We do have a rough plan," Isabella said. "But we can talk about it later."

Reginald nodded as he rang the bell for the maids. He'd hoped to have a private family dinner ... something the nobility, no doubt, found insulting. Hosting two banquets in two days just wasn't enough ... he snorted, rudely, as he took his seat. The latecomers could be insulted, if they liked. He'd sent the missives in plenty of time. They'd chosen to dawdle and so … he knew he was being unfair, but he didn't care. Right now, he wanted to spend time with his family.

"The paperwork is getting worse," Ruby said. She put her papers to one side as the maid laid the table for dinner, then withdrew as silently as she'd come in. "Do I have to read *all* of it?"

"Make sure you know what's going on," Reginald said. He recalled his father's advice and smiled. "Even if you don't know the words, you have to hum the tune."

Ruby didn't sound impressed. "And what if you get the words wrong?"

"You couldn't get too far from the tune," Reginald said. The metaphor had its limits, but he'd yet to meet a metaphor that didn't. "Point is, the more you get a feel for what's actually going on, the harder it will be for someone to pull the wool over your eyes."

He sighed, promising himself that – if he had a daughter – she'd get lessons in estate management. Aristocratic girls got lessons from their parents, but *royal* girls … what little had been given, he recalled sourly, had been given to Sofia. Ruby hadn't been expected to be anything more than a pawn, someone who could be married for the good of the kingdom. The idea she would be one unfortunate death away from the throne had never crossed their father's mind.

Silverdale sat on the other side of the table. "You'd better watch your back out there," she said. "You never know who'll put a knife in it."

"I know," Reginald said. He carved the meat and served it himself, allowing Isabella to pass the potatoes, vegetables and gravy. It was a very basic dinner, but it would be head and shoulders above army fare. His aristocratic subordinates could hardly complain about rations if they watched him eat them, too. "And you watch your back here."

He put the coming march to the border out of his head and talked about nothing in particular as they ate. It had been too long since they'd managed to sit down and talk … hell, he really *hadn't* spent much time with his sisters since the empire's fall. He'd been too busy running around pissing on fires, securing the borders and making sure the noblemen knew the monarch had a strong right hand. He wished he had one, too. Even if Isabella were to get pregnant now, it would be fourteen years – at the very least – before their son was ready to lead troops in combat. Without a son …

Of course, there are sons who cannot wait to succeed their father, he reminded himself, sardonically. He'd heard of two monarchs who'd died under suspicious circumstances that suggested their heirs might have let it happen. He had never considered it. He'd always had too much to do. *And fathers who are terrible to their sons.*

Isabella said little until the dinner was finished and they were alone. "You will be careful out there, won't you?"

Reginald eyed her. "Are *you* alright?"

"I just have a bad feeling about this," Isabella admitted. "We still don't *know* how the entities managed to overwhelm Halladale so quickly. Or how they managed to get their hooks into Zycrest. And they have to be planning something."

"They have to come for us first," Reginald said. The rest of the world might not *believe* in the entities, which was deeply ironic, but Andalusia couldn't deny they existed. There was nowhere else that understood the dangers so well. "We know too much."

"I know," Isabella agreed. "And that means they'll do everything in their power to crush us."

Reginald said nothing for a long moment. He was entirely sure the entities had a trick up their sleeve. They'd leapfrogged an army right to his borders … at the very least, they'd send thousands of refugees fleeing across the border. And yet, what else *could* he do? The borders had to be secured or they'd start to dissolve, allowing the entities to move closer and closer to Havelock. It was just a matter of time until they won by default, unless they were stopped. He *had* to take the army east.

"I'll be fine," he said. He stood and reached for her hand. "You keep working on finding a way to stop them."

"I have a hunch," Isabella reminded him. "It may be nothing *more* than a hunch."

"I have faith in you," Reginald said. He pulled her towards the bedroom. "And, right now, I think we should be doing something else."

Isabella snickered, then spoke with heavy sarcasm. "How *romantic.*"

Chapter Seventeen

Silverdale hadn't been allowed out of the castle very often, certainly not without her family or a small army of bodyguards. She was too young, her father had said when she'd protested, to be allowed to explore the world. There were too many threats out there, waiting; there were too many people who'd do whatever it took to get their hands on a royal princess, on someone who had a claim to the throne. Silverdale had counted herself lucky to visit the country estates every few months. There, at least, she'd had a *little* freedom.

She smiled, delightedly, as the horse cantered down the street towards the distant city gates. Isabella rode ahead, showing less proficiency with her mount than Silverdale had expected. She – and her sisters – had learnt to ride at a very early age. Isabella, on the other hand, acted like someone who rarely so much as laid eyes on a horse, let alone rode one. The thought made Silverdale smile, even as she kept her distance. She didn't want to be too close when – if – Isabella's horse decided to throw her and run.

The streets seemed brighter, now the army had marched away. Silverdale had joined the crowd of noblewomen who'd stood and cheered as the soldiers left, blowing kisses and throwing garters at their crushes. The townspeople had seemed more relieved than impressed. Silverdale wasn't sure why, but she didn't care. Her brother was on his way to the border, leaving them alone. And Isabella had decided to take Silverdale with her!

She allowed her eyes to wander over the shops and houses as they reached the end of the road. There were more people on the streets, including girls little older than herself. She felt a twinge of envy for their apparent freedom, for their ability to walk the streets without bodyguards. The older girls looked up and watched as the horses cantered past, their brothers waving cheerfully. Silverdale wondered if the commoners knew who they were. They didn't really *look* like a queen and a princess. In their riding outfits, it was quite possible they'd been mistaken for boys.

The open air struck her the moment they passed the gatehouse and rode onto the main road. She took a long breath, tasting the fresh air as they picked up speed, galloping past a line of carts awaiting inspection. The guards were busy, checking the wagons for everything from illicit and undeclared goods to forbidden knowledge. Silverdale put the thought out of her mind as they passed the last of the carts and headed west. The air was delightfully clean. She liked the city, but she had to admit it stank.

"Keep close to me," Isabella called. "We don't want to get split up."

Silverdale was tempted to dig in her spurs and have a race. She swallowed the impulse before she could act on it. Reginald had given her a sharp lecture on taking care and following orders, particularly from her sister-in-law. Silverdale had to admit, privately, that he had a point, but she was damned if she'd admit it openly. Instead ... she concentrated on looking around, glancing into the astral plane from time to time. The forest seemed alive – more alive – in the astral world. She was sure she could see *things* looking back at her, things dark and ancient and very inhuman.

She felt sweat prickling down her back as she pulled back her gaze. The sunlight was bright and warm, but she felt cold. The world had changed. She'd heard the stories about people vanishing, about men and women refusing to go out after dark, about strange encounters ... it was hard to tell how many of the stories were actually *true*, yet ... she shuddered. The world was no longer wholly theirs.

Not that it was in the first place, she thought. She'd always known her fate. *Even those of us who rule are bound by rules.*

She felt her muscles start to ache as the horses galloped on. The road was starting to decay, tiny potholes and cracks appearing in the stone. Silverdale wondered, idly, who was responsible for mending them now. The locals? The crown? It wasn't as if the empire was going to do it. Alden's memories rose up in front of her, tormenting her. The empire was gone. Its capital was gone. And the magicians who'd once ruled the world were gone. She looked at Isabella's back and frowned, wondering how her sister-in-law had taken the news. Her family had effectively been destroyed.

Reginald would have talked to her about it, she told herself. *Right?*

Isabella said nothing as they turned off the main road and headed up a smaller road that was little more than a dirt track. The horses slowed to a walk, picking their way gingerly through piles of stones and puddles of muddy water. Silverdale shivered as she saw the puddles glowing in the astral plane, a grim warning that they'd been placed with malicious intent. If a galloping horse put a hoof in one of the puddles, there was a very good chance the poor beast would break a leg and throw the rider. Silverdale felt a hot flash of anger, mingled with fear and loathing. Who would do that to a horse? Horses were lovely creatures. But she knew the commoners might feel otherwise.

"We'll stop here," Isabella said, as they reached an inn. The wooden building was half-hidden within the foliage. "Let me do the talking."

Silverdale had never visited an inn before. Princesses didn't visit inns, except in bad stories her governesses had forbidden her to read. She was quite curious to see if they were anything like the inns in the stories, but Isabella didn't seem inclined to take her inside. Instead, she spoke briefly to the stable lad and allowed him to take the horse. Silverdale slid off her mount effortlessly and guided him over to the lad. His eyes flickered over her without showing much interest. It struck her, suddenly, that he *really* didn't know who she was.

Isabella caught her arm. "This way," she said. "Again, when we meet people, let me do the talking."

"He didn't know me," Silverdale said. "Right?"

"Why should he?" Isabella glanced at her, just long enough for Silverdale to see she was smiling. "Who are you to him?"

Silverdale stamped her foot before she could catch herself. "A princess?"

Isabella laughed. "Princess Silverdale is a sweet little girl with hair like chestnut who lives in a fairy-tale castle that might as well be on the other side of the moon. Queen Isabella is an exotic foreign woman from a kingdom no one has ever heard of, at least until now. Why should he connect a pair of strange women on horseback with such *regal* persons? If you went back and told him who you were, he'd laugh in your face."

Silverdale stared at Isabella's back. "Why ... why would he laugh at me?"

"He'd think you were lying," Isabella said. "You don't *look* like a princess right now."

"No," Silverdale agreed. She tried to wrap her head around the totally alien concept. "I ... everyone knows me."

"No, they don't," Isabella corrected. There was an odd note in her voice. "They have this ... *image* ... of the little princess and the foreign queen in their heads, but that image bears very little resemblance to reality. There's no reason they should draw a connection between those lofty personages and us. Why should they?"

Silverdale swallowed, hard. "If I changed into commoner clothes, would I be treated as a commoner?"

Isabella glanced back. "Yes," she said. "And you might never go home again."

She held up a hand as the path widened suddenly. "We'll discuss it later, if you like," she said. "For the moment, keep your eyes open. Both sets of eyes."

You want me to look into the astral plane, Silverdale thought. *And yet, you won't even tell me what I'm looking for.*

She kept her face under tight control as they stepped into the village. It was little more than a collection of grey stone houses, their roofs covered with grass that – she thought – would make them very hard to see from overhead. It struck her as pointless, although she *had* heard stories of dragons from the final days of empire. Maybe the people feared the village would be found by soldiers ... but why would soldiers come here? She followed Isabella as she walked towards a grey building near the edge of the town, a dark-skinned man standing guard outside. He scowled at them both, suspiciously.

"We have come to pay our respects to the goddess," Isabella said. She reached into her pouch and produced a bronze coin. "May we enter?"

The guard took the coin, bit it ... and then stepped aside. Isabella walked into the temple, looking neither left nor right.

Silverdale followed, her head spinning. A temple? This was a temple? It was nothing like the temple in the palace, the temple Sofia had ordered torn out and destroyed when she'd taken power. And yet … she looked around as her eyes grew accustomed to the darkness. A handful of young girls were kneeling in front of a statue of a hooded woman. Their quiet prayers echoed in the air, threatening to lull the listeners to sleep.

Silverdale frowned. The statue itself was … just a statue. It was a little exaggerated, as if whoever had carved it hadn't got the proportions quite right, but it was nothing like the entities she'd seen in the castle. The tiny handfuls of corn and barley at the statue's feet were … she frowned. She wasn't sure *what* they were. One of the girls stood and turned, her eyes flickering disinterestedly over Silverdale. She couldn't be more than two or three years older than the princess herself.

Isabella motioned for Silverdale to sit. Silverdale sat, feeling terribly out of place. She wasn't sure what to say or do … or even if she *should* say or do anything. Isabella seemed content to sit beside her and say nothing. Silverdale cursed herself as she realised she'd already been given her orders and opened her mind, peering into the astral plane. The temple didn't seem to exist within the astral plane. Silverdale frowned. The spot was quiet. Too quiet. There was something truly unnatural about it.

A shiver ran down her spine. The astral plane felt … dead. She lowered her gaze until she was looking at the worshippers. Their devotions rose, then faded into nothingness. The trickles of light that *should* have gone into the astral plane died before they could do *anything*. Silverdale stared at the girls. Their astral images should have been different – they should have looked as they saw themselves – but instead they looked unchanged. She was honestly unsure, just for a moment, if she really *was* looking into the astral plane. It wasn't until she looked at Isabella's hand that she *knew*.

Another girl rose. Silverdale looked at her through both sets of eyes. She was pretty enough, but her face was dirty and her feet were scarred and … she should have looked prettier in the astral plane. The girl walked past and left, without saying a word. Silverdale turned to watch her go, feeling as if she should try to say *something* to the girl. But no words came.

She concentrated, trying to leave her body completely. But … she couldn't move. Her mind refused to leave her body. She felt a flash of panic, mingled with confusion. She didn't need the potions now, did she? She didn't even *have* a vial … did Isabella? She wanted to ask for one, even though she knew it would be admitting defeat. And yet …

Isabella touched her shoulder. "Time to go."

Silverdale stood. Her legs felt weak. She felt weirdly drained, as if she'd walked for a hundred miles without actually moving. Isabella stepped up to the statue, studied it for a long moment, then turned and led the way out of the temple. Silverdale followed. Her eyes – both sets of eyes – had grown so accustomed to the darkness that the sunlight *hurt*. Silverdale stopped long enough to rub her eyes, wondering how Isabella managed to be unaffected. The older woman was already heading out of the village.

And you wanted her to treat you like an adult, Silverdale's thoughts mocked. *Be careful what you wish for.*

She followed Isabella, looking around with interest. The village was strange. Little children played together outside the houses, while their elder siblings helped their parents. There was a blacksmith's forge, but little else. No shops, as far as she could tell. The villagers eyed her warily, as if they knew she didn't belong. Silverdale kept walking, even though she could feel more and more people watching. She didn't start to relax until the trees had closed in around them again.

"I don't think they liked us," she said, as she caught up with Isabella. "Right?"

"We're strangers," Isabella said. "And strangers are often bad news."

Silverdale frowned. "What *is* this place? Why did you bring me here?"

Isabella stopped and turned to face her. "You tell me."

Silverdale made a face. She'd had governesses who'd played guessing games with her before and they'd *always* annoyed her. Whatever answer she gave was always wrong. And yet, Isabella was treating her more like an adult. She forced herself to think. The village had been strange, but it hadn't been overshadowed. The temple certainly hadn't been a direct link to the entities …

"That's an old temple," she said. "And you wanted to see what happened when people worshipped there."

"Yeah." Isabella nodded as she started to walk again. "The village is … somewhat off the beaten track. I figured there was a good chance the temple had been left untouched, when the temples in the bigger cities were smashed or burnt to ashes. And I was right."

Silverdale glanced at her back. "And what if you'd been wrong?"

"There were other possibilities," Isabella said. She sounded utterly unconcerned. "This one just happened to be close to our destination."

"I see," Silverdale said. "And what if they'd all been smashed?"

Isabella shrugged. "You can get into a lot of trouble by being wrong," she said, sardonically. "But you can get into worse trouble by being afraid to admit you *were* wrong. Or by allowing the fear of being wrong to keep you from doing *anything*. No one – sorcerer or general or monarch – is ever wholly right about everything. Yes, sure, whatever you do can go wrong. But doing nothing isn't always an option either."

Silverdale changed the subject, quickly. "What *was* that statue?"

"The statue represents the Goddess of Fertility and Fields," Isabella said. "She has many names, in many different places, but she governs everything from farming to pregnancy. The girls you saw, praying in the middle of the day, were probably pleading for good husbands and quick pregnancies. They have few others to turn to."

"I …" Silverdale frowned. "Why not?"

Isabella shrugged. "They have some choice in who they marry, but not enough. There aren't that many prospective husbands in the village. Their parents will … *encourage* … them to marry boys who own land or stand to inherit it. And the ones who are stubborn … well, sometimes they don't live to regret it."

She snorted. "Just like the aristocracy, only with poorer clothes and worse diets."

Silverdale said nothing. She didn't know what to say.

She'd hated how … restricted her life was and yet … and yet, it could be worse. It could be a lot worse. And yet …

Isabella seemed to read her mind. "There are girls here who would sell their souls to trade places with you," she said. "And, I dare say, aristocratic women who'd trade places with *them*."

"They wouldn't have to leave, would they?" Silverdale glanced back at the village, hidden within the trees. "I mean … they could just walk back to their parents if they wanted to visit."

"True," Isabella agreed. "But a great deal would depend on their new families. The new bride will be right at the bottom of the pecking order. Her mother-in-law will treat her like a slave, or worse. She'll be slapped if she steps out of line. Her husband will be expected to make it clear to her that he's in charge now, with his fists if necessary. Going home without permission would get her in real trouble. Believe me, you'd be horrified if you knew some of what goes on in the country."

"So it's *really* just like the aristocracy," Silverdale said.

"People are the same everywhere," Isabella agreed. "Rich or poor, noble or commoner, they have the same hopes and fears, the same moments of stunning generosity and disgusting malice … the same willingness to do whatever they have to do to get what they want and to hell with anyone who gets in their way. And the entities feed on that, using them as the keys to the soul …"

She shook her head as they reached the inn. "We'll get our horses, then carry on," she said. "I want to be in Frigg before nightfall."

Silverdale caught her arm. "Can we stay in an inn?"

Isabella turned to stare at her. "Are you mad?"

"No," Silverdale said. She refused to feel silly. "I just … every time we travelled, we never stopped at an inn. We always stopped at estates or castles or … places where they scraped and bowed and were glad to see the last of us. An inn would be much nicer."

"I suppose it would do you good to see how the rest of the world lives," Isabella said, slowly. "Very well. We'll stop at an inn. And don't come crying to me when you get bedbugs."

"I won't," Silverdale promised.

Chapter Eighteen

Isabella had to fight to conceal her amusement as Silverdale tried not to scratch. It wasn't really funny. The inn, the only one they'd been able to find near Frigg, had been grotty and smelly and, really, Isabella would have preferred to ride into town or simply find a place to sleep in the open. But Silverdale had insisted ... Isabella shook her head. The bedbugs alone would teach her a few lessons about how the vast majority of people lived.

And there was no bath, no proper shower, no nothing, Isabella thought. The food had been the best thing about the inn, but it was strikingly plain. *Perhaps we should stop at the garrison long enough for her to get a proper wash.*

She put the thought out of her mind as they approached the remains of the city hall. Frigg had been devastated by the fighting and, even now, the town had yet to recover. She'd read the reports very carefully and visited as often as she dared, despite the vast list of things she had to get done in Havelock. The locals had been reluctant to return to the centre of town, citing everything from bad feelings to constant nightmares. Isabella had a nasty feeling that, despite all her precautions, the entity she'd trapped under the building was slowly reaching out to the neighbours. Even the guards were having a hard time.

"Your Majesty!" Colonel Jackstay saluted. It had taken Isabella several weeks to convince him he didn't need to kneel. "Welcome back!"

Isabella nodded as she slipped off her horse. "Thank you," she said. The colonel didn't seem to be interested in Silverdale. Isabella had a feeling she could announce the princess by name and Jackstay wouldn't connect Isabella's apprentice with *Princess* Silverdale. "Have there been any problems in the last two weeks?"

"Nothing new," Jackstay said. "The city fathers haven't even *tried* to convince us to leave the hall."

Isabella nodded as Silverdale landed beside her. Frigg was meant to be semi-independent, the city fathers running the place as long as they didn't break the king's law. The city hall was a sign of their independence, yet … they hadn't tried to get it back. It was odd. Isabella would have expected them to try, under normal circumstances. The fact they'd done nothing bothered her. Either they had some idea of what was trapped under the hall, or they feared what the army would do. And that meant …

She pushed the thought aside. "We need to freshen up," she said. "And then I need to inspect the prisoner."

Jackstay nodded and led them into the commandeered house. The merchant who owned it had fled long ago, along with most of the townspeople. Isabella was surprised that most of them hadn't returned. The civil war was over. Reginald hadn't shown any inclination to purge anyone who'd backed the wrong side, pointing out – when his council had complained – that most of the loyalists had thought they were supporting the crowned king. And it wasn't as if Frigg was on an invasion route …

Except it was, she thought, wryly. *The town wouldn't have been attacked in the first place if Reginald hadn't marched through it.*

"I itch," Silverdale complained, when they were alone. "Do you have a spell to cure itching?"

"I'm afraid not," Isabella said. There *were* potions, but she didn't have the ingredients to make them. "Wash yourself thoroughly and change into new clothes."

She turned her back to give Silverdale privacy, mentally preparing herself for the ordeal ahead. She'd opened her own mind while they'd been in the temple, but she hadn't sensed anything useful. The temple had been designed – somehow – to keep prayers from drifting into the astral plane. She wasn't sure how it had been done, although she had a nasty feeling the answer was quite simple. Temples were designed to be strong, to stand against wind and rain and everything. Their framework might be made of iron.

And that might explain why some temples were missed, she thought. *They simply couldn't see them from the astral plane.*

Her thoughts churned unpleasantly as she waited. Taking

Silverdale to the temple had been a risk. Taking her to the inn had been a whim … not dangerous, she supposed, but not something Reginald would approve of, either. She wondered, suddenly, if he'd stayed in inns himself. He'd spent enough time with the military, sleeping on camp beds or the ground, to think the inn a very paradise. And *he* would have fewer illusions about the world.

"I'm ready," Silverdale said. She wasn't quite whining, but close enough. "I still itch."

"You can have a proper bath when we get home," Isabella said. She wasn't entirely unsympathetic, but the younger girl needed to learn before it was too late. "Give me a moment."

She splashed water on her face, then studied herself in the mirror. She looked … different, and yet, she couldn't put her finger on *why*. The mirror was mundane, without a single spell … she remembered, suddenly, how her older sister had cast a spell to make Isabella's reflection look terrible. The prank had made Isabella laugh, afterwards … her heart twisted as she remembered that her sister was dead. She and Alden were the last of the family.

Isabella turned, gritting her teeth to keep the memories from overwhelming her. She picked up her bag, checked the iron keys and led the way out of the room and down the stairs. The guards outside nodded to her as they left; the guards on duty outside the hall insisted on checking their eyes first before allowing them to enter. Isabella made a mental note to compliment Colonel Jackstay. His men knew their duty. A single overshadowed man could cause havoc, if he managed to free the entity. She picked up a pair of lamps and lit them, then passed one to Silverdale. The interior felt as dark and cold as the grave.

Silverdale cleared her throat. "I can feel it."

Isabella nodded as they walked through the hall. The entity might be trapped, but its presence was still damaging the fabric of reality. She could *feel* the corridors twisting, as if they were trying to move in directions the human mind was not prepared to comprehend. The paintings of long-dead city fathers hanging on the walls had taken on a truly disturbing aspect, as if they'd been vile monsters beyond the pale of civilised society. A statue of a king she didn't know seemed to move, whenever she glanced away. Isabella had been in a dozen war zones, since she'd left the Golden City, but this was different. The sense of threat was overwhelming.

Silverdale hung close to her, not daring to speak, as they made their way down the stairs and into the basement. The iron bars looked solid, as if they hadn't been touched since she'd had them welded into place. She'd been careful to ensure there was no way to escape. There were no doors in the cage, no way for the prisoner to believe it could leave without permission. It felt like overkill, but she knew better than to take it for granted. The entity was governed by inhuman rules. The entity might be able to depart if someone *said* it could go.

And it might be able to envisage itself as something no bigger than a fly, Isabella thought. *And a fly could pass through the bars without touching the cold iron.*

She stepped up to the bars and peered through. The ritual circle was still intact. The paint and blood shimmered under the light, as if it hadn't dried six months after she'd drawn the circle, summoned the entity and bound it in place. Beyond the circle … her eyes hurt as she peered at the prisoner. The entity wasn't pretending to be human – or humanoid – any longer. Two glowing red eyes peered back at her from a sheet of flame … she felt her face start to prickle, even though she *knew* it couldn't hurt her. The entity's rage seemed to burn, as if it were on the verge of setting fire to the entire world.

Silverdale stepped up beside her. "What *is* it?"

"You saw me binding it," Isabella reminded her. "It just looks a little different."

She put the lantern on the table and sat on the floor. There was no dust, even though the room had been largely untouched – and certainly not *cleaned* – since the entity had been taken prisoner. The shadows seemed darker, as if there were things lurking within the darkness … pressing against the light. Silverdale sat next to her, so close they were almost touching. The younger girl was putting on a brave face – a very brave face – but Isabella could tell she was scared. It was impossible to blame her. Even imprisoned, the entity dominated the room.

"Watch," Isabella ordered. She'd let Silverdale take some risks, but not *this* one. "You know what to do if something goes wrong."

Silverdale gave her a sharp look, but said nothing. Isabella stared back at her evenly. She'd been a teenager herself. She knew what it was like to want to defy one's parents. But there was a difference between sneaking out to go to a dance and challenging an utterly inhuman entity with powers that defied human comprehension. Isabella could and would put herself at risk. She wouldn't let Silverdale take the risk herself.

"Fine." Silverdale sounded sulky. "I'll do as you say."

"Good." Isabella took the vial from her pocket and stared down at it. This time, she'd been careful to make sure it wasn't a placebo. She couldn't try to fool herself, not here. "If something goes wrong, run. Don't look back."

She felt her heart start to pound in her chest as she drank the potion. A cold sensation settled in her chest and spread rapidly throughout her body. She was aware, on some level, that she was mentally falling to her knees, but it didn't matter. It was just a piece of abstract knowledge. She felt her mind shiver, then disconnect itself completely from her body. It felt …

The room seemed to lighten as she bobbled up. The cage wasn't restricting her, but … it seemed to pervade the astral realm without really being part of it. Her lips twitched as she realised what she was looking at. A person's self-image would often include clothes, even though their clothes weren't really part of them. The cage had grabbed and twisted the astral realm like a man might grab her arm. And, unlike in the real world, it actually *worked*.

She glided around the cage, studying the entity. It was immensely huge and infinitely tiny at the same time, a singular creature that was – at the same time – part of something much larger. She frowned as she saw traces of light – links of thought and prayer – reaching down to the entity, even though it was imprisoned. It was both trapped and not trapped, isolated and yet not isolated. Its sheer power was bending the astral plane around it, twisting it to its rule.

It thinks it exists, and so it exists, she thought. *It exists, and so it thinks it exists*.

She felt herself quail as the entity looked back at her. It was a towering presence, so bright she had the feeling that merely *looking* at it was enough to burn her to a crisp. The legends about long-dead sorcerers who'd flown too close to the sun suddenly felt very real. She drew back hastily, re-centring herself. The entity was threatening to infect her mind, to overwhelm her … she reminded herself, sharply, that it had no more power over her beyond what she chose to grant. Here, in a sense, they were equals.

Isabella held herself still, studying the entity as dispassionately as possible. Her head expanded, just enough to let her see how the Godly Realm was still feeding the entity … no, allowing it to exist. The entity was stamping its presence on the world through sheer power … she had a sudden vision of a kid jumping up and down on top of a frozen lake. It was just a matter of time before the ice cracked and the child died.

Fine, she thought. *It's time.*

She gathered herself, readying herself for a struggle. The entity was constrained, yet it was still drawing power. She scowled, mentally, as she realised why. She'd managed to trap the entity, yet in order to do the ritual she'd had to open a link to the Godly Realm … she'd really granted it permission to survive when she'd summoned it. Now … she glided forward, trying to stamp her own will on the astral plane. The entity was trapped within a cage that was both there but not there. Isabella pushed down, rewriting the rules.

No, she thought. *I'm reasserting the rules.*

The entity howled as she held it down while cutting the threads of power one by one. She felt its rage push against her, a very familiar emotion – panic, she realised numbly – battering her mind. She held steady, forcing the rules to reassert themselves as the links faded to nothingness. The entity battered against the cage, against her, even as the natural laws of the universe pressed down on it. The entity simply couldn't exist …

… And it didn't.

Isabella felt a surge of exultation as the entity blinked out. The cage rattled one final time, then fell silent. She fell back into her own body, just as the hall returned to normal. Her eyes snapped open. It was dark, but a strangely comforting darkness. She reached for her magic and cast a spell, summoning a ball of light. The cage looked thoroughly absurd.   And it was empty.

Silverdale giggled, although she sounded more relieved than amused.   Isabella wondered, suddenly, what it had looked like to *her*.   The younger girl would have seen everything … perhaps more than *Isabella* had seen.   They'd have to share memories, later.   Silverdale might have seen something Isabella needed to know.

"It worked," Silverdale said, as Isabella stood.   "You did it!"

Isabella nodded.   The entity was gone.   No, dead.   It hadn't been tossed back to the Godly Realm.   It was dead.   She remembered Mother Lembu taunting her, pointing out that it was only a matter of time until *something* happened and the circle was broken.   The entity could wait for decades.   Or centuries.   Sooner or later, someone would break the circle or the castle would crumble to rubble or *something*.   Isabella felt her smile grow wider as she wiped sweat from her brow.   She could kill the entities now.

And how many of them will we need to kill, she asked herself, *to keep them from invading our world?*

She scowled, wishing Reginald had accompanied them. There were things she could discuss with him that she couldn't discuss with anyone else, even Alden, Ruby or Silverdale.   They'd caught two entities through summoning rituals, but they couldn't perform a ritual without knowing the entity's names … she shook her head.   The entities couldn't claim worship without sharing their names.   How would anyone know who they were praying to?

"That's a problem for another day," she muttered.

Silverdale glanced at her.   "What?"

"Never mind."   Isabella felt herself flush.   She hadn't *meant* to speak out loud.   "I think we have to go upstairs."

She smiled as she turned and led the way back up the stairs. The hall felt reassuringly normal.   The paintings looked as dull as she'd expect from people who hadn't made any impact outside their communities.   She was fairly sure the paintings would have been taken down if the impact had been anything but good.   Isabella dismissed the thought as she stepped outside.   It felt as though the sun was shining for the first time in eternity.

Jackstay ran up to her.   "What happened?"

Isabella looked past him. The guards were grinning from ear to ear, as if they'd been relieved of a weight they didn't know they'd been carrying. The townspeople, those few that remained, were spilling onto the streets. It looked as if an impromptu party was about to begin, the guards abandoning their discipline and joining in. She had to smile ... she'd seen towns and villages pillaged and sacked by victorious armies, but this was the first time she'd seen civilians and soldiers practically dancing together. Someone struck up a tune ...

"I think we won," Isabella said, finally. "I think ..."

She put the rest of the thought firmly out of her head. It wasn't a victory, but it was a step forward. She'd discovered a way to kill the entities. Now ... all she had to do was figure out how to use it to get rid of the rest of them. And now ... they had to know what had happened, that one of their number was dead. The shock alone might be enough to convince them to back off.

"Tell your men to enjoy themselves," she said, instead. "Tomorrow, we'll be heading to the border."

She turned and hurried back to the garrison. A strange feeling was churning inside her, a sense of unease that was yet ... happy? She frowned in bemusement as they made their way back to the bedroom. She wanted to be sick and it was good ...

A thought struck her. She couldn't be? Could she?

"Isabella?" Silverdale sounded irked. Outside, the noise was growing louder. The crowd didn't know what they were celebrating, but that didn't stop them. "What's the matter?"

Isabella forced herself to think. Her cycles had always been irregular, but ...

"I think I'm pregnant," she said. She hadn't had a period for two months. That was ... *interesting*. "I'm going to have a baby."

Chapter Nineteen

"Your Majesty," Captain-General Gars said. "I think there's trouble afoot."

Reginald nodded as the army steadily marched towards Barr. The city had been heavily walled even before the empire's fall – the borderlands had always played host to bandits and rebels – but now the walls were surrounded by tents, makeshift shacks and countless people sleeping in the cold air. He scowled, wondering just how many of them were *his* people. They'd encountered a bunch of messengers as they'd marched east, each bringing grimmer and grimmer tidings from the borderlands. The trickle of refugees had turned into a flood.

He grimaced as the wind changed, blowing the stench of thousands of unwashed people living in too close proximity into his face. The city fathers had slammed the gates shut as soon as they realised what they were dealing with, too late to keep hordes of people from entering their city and refusing to be budged. Reginald tried not to wince. The city was large, but it was on the frontlines of a war. The more people in the city, the easier it would be for an invading army to starve the defenders out. He had a great deal of sympathy for the refugees, but he might have to order them to leave. Or try to move them further west.

We don't even have the resources to support them, he thought. *And even if we did, communities would refuse to take them.*

The smell grew worse as they reached the city itself. Reginald had seen refugee camps and settlements before, back during the civil wars, but there was something heartbreaking about the men and women in front of him. A week ago, they'd lived in a prosperous little kingdom that enjoyed cordial relationships with its neighbours; now, they'd been forced to cross the border, fleeing the nightmare that had engulfed their homeland. The messengers had made it clear that the kingdom had been invaded, that the capital had been burned and the king forced to surrender. It was just a matter of time before the invaders struck across the border.

He kept his face under tight control as they rode past men begging for bread and women offering their bodies for shelter. It was just a matter of time before someone started exploiting the refugees, if they weren't already. Reginald had seen it before. The men would be enslaved, for all intents and purposes; the women and children would be sent into service, if they were lucky, or simply marched straight into the brothels. He gritted his teeth, knowing there was little he could do about it. The hell of it was that he simply couldn't trust the refugees. How many of them, he asked himself, had come with bad intentions? How many would try to summon the entities into the kingdom?

The city gates opened. The guards looked nervous, their eyes flickering between the army and the refugees as if they didn't know who to fear more. They were better trained than Reginald had expected – city militias were rarely *that* well trained, for fear they might turn on the aristocracy – but probably no match for an army. The walls wouldn't even the odds if Reginald – or the Imperator – decided to take the city, not long enough to matter. And even the refugees might prove dangerous in a tight spot.

"Secure the walls," he ordered, quietly. Thankfully, the city fathers seemed to have decided to greet him with a minimum of pomp and circumstances. "I'll speak to the mayor."

He slipped off his horse as the mayor came forward, leading a small delegation of townspeople. The old man looked startlingly *civilian*. He wasn't even carrying a sword. Reginald guessed he was hopelessly out of his depth. He'd been elected to maintain stability, not deal with a border war and a flood of refugees that could easily turn into an army. His bow was shaky, suggesting he hadn't had the time to brush up on protocol. Reginald quietly forgave him. He knew there were aristocrats in his army who wouldn't be so kind.

"Your Majesty," the mayor said. "Welcome to Barr."

"Thank you, Mayor Boswell," Reginald said. He'd barely had a chance to do more than glance at the mayor's file, but he'd remembered the name. It would hopefully convince the mayor that Reginald would *remember* him. "My men will secure the walls and the garrisons, then mount patrols. And I need a briefing."

Mayor Boswell didn't protest. He didn't look as though he *wanted* to protest. Reginald felt a shiver run down his spine as the mayor introduced him to the rest of the town's council. Townsfolk stood on their dignities, on their ancient rights and privileges, for fear they would lose them. If the mayor wasn't objecting, it could only mean the situation was grimmer than Reginald had feared. The enemy army hadn't – yet – crossed the border, but the screws were already tightening.

He kept his eyes open as the mayor led him towards the city hall, wittering away with the air of a man who didn't want to broach a particularly grim topic. There were refugees and guards everywhere, the former sleeping in alleyways and the latter marching around the city as if they expected to be attacked at any moment. A cluster of men were practicing sword fighting with sticks, urged on by a sergeant who seemed to prefer shouting to actual training. Reginald silently wished he'd thought to send more trained men to the borders after he'd taken the throne, but there'd been too many other problems. And if he'd have trained and armed the townsfolk, they might have turned on him.

His bodyguards moved ahead, inspecting the chamber as they moved into the war room. It was reassuringly practical, as if whoever had designed it had military experience or at least a hefty dose of common sense. The table was slightly fancier than he would have preferred, but it was covered in detailed maps of the borderlands and the kingdom – the enemy kingdom – beyond.

"Your Majesty." Reginald turned to see an overweight man in a fancy uniform ... too fancy. "If you'll permit me to brief you ...?"

Reginald concealed his irritation. "And you are?"

"General Sidon, Your Majesty," Sidon said. "I was appointed commanding general of the militia after I came to live here."

After you bribed the right person, Reginald added, silently. Sidon's uniform was too fancy for anyone's peace of mind. A prowling archer would use him for target practice. *Unless you're trying to be very clever in the way only the very stupid can be.*

He dismissed the thought. "I'm waiting."

Sidon indicated the table. "Our first warning was when a horde of refugees crossed the border here," he said, tapping a spot on the map. "They overwhelmed the border guards and headed west, reaching Barr shortly after the news of their arrival. We did what we could for them, while trying to figure out what was going on. The tales they told were harrowing."

And familiar, Reginald thought. Smashed temples, forced worship, people being twisted into … *things. No wonder so many people fled.*

"Since then, we estimate that tens of thousands of people have crossed the border," Sidon continued. "They have effectively destroyed a number of villages. Others have greeted them with hostility, driving them away. The majority have made their way here. We closed the gates at once, barring them to all who couldn't prove they had a right to enter. However, they have refused to disperse."

He paused. "In short, Your Majesty, we have lost control of the border."

"If you ever really had it," Reginald commented. The border was hundreds of miles long. It was simply impossible to patrol the entire border and everyone knew it. The border people themselves paid as little attention to the border as possible. They saw no reason to honour the agreements between kings who cared nothing for anything, but tax. "Have you seen anything of the enemy army?"

"No," Sidon said. "The refugees claim the enemy army drove them from their homes, but we haven't seen any sight of it ourselves. However, we have lost control of the border. It could be right on the edge, or halfway here, and we wouldn't know anything about it."

"No," Reginald agreed. He studied the map thoughtfully. "We're going to have to do something about that."

"Yes, Your Majesty," Mayor Boswell said. "But we also have to do something about the refugees. They *cannot* stay here!"

Reginald looked at him. "Where would you suggest they go?"

The mayor waved his hands in the air. "Somewhere else. Not here."

"Really." Reginald didn't take his eyes off the mayor. "I

ask again. Where would you suggest they go?"

"Back home," the mayor said. "Your Majesty … we cannot feed and clothe them!"

Reginald indicated the map. "If they go home, they go to their deaths," he said. "Anywhere else, we'll still have problems. Here …"

He stepped back. "The able-bodied men will be drafted into the workforce," he said. "They'll help us to prepare the city for a siege. In exchange for their service, they and their womenfolk will be allowed to reside within the city. Those that refuse to work will be told to return home."

The mayor didn't look pleased. "Yes, Your Majesty."

Reginald understood why, although he didn't want to admit it. The refugees genuinely *were* a burden. The city couldn't feed them for long. And now the army had arrived, food was going to be shorter than ever before. Cold logic demanded that the refugees be expelled, even though it would be a death sentence for most of them. Reginald knew it might have to be done, but he intended to avoid it for as long as possible. He wanted to be able to look at himself in the mirror without recoiling in horror.

"My troops will maintain order," Reginald continued. "And we'll push patrols up to the border as quickly as possible."

He forced himself to think. He couldn't afford to sit on the defensive, not indefinitely. The entities knew they had to take him and his army off the board before he found a way to strike back. If Isabella's idea had worked, they might be able to take the fight back to the entities themselves. Even if it hadn't, his men had faced the entities before. They wouldn't panic quite so badly when confronted by magics that were supposed to be impossible and monsters out of legend.

"We'll consider what to do next, once the border is secure," he added. "Until then, keep your people calm."

"Yes, Your Majesty," the mayor said.

"My troops are ready," Sidon said. "But they have yet to see war."

Really? Reginald almost smiled. *Why am I not surprised?*

He turned back to the map and aimed question after question at Sidon. The civilian general answered surprisingly well for a man with little real experience, although Reginald rather feared he was more of a beancounter than a stirring leader. Perhaps not the complete disaster he'd feared – he tested the man's messengers by sending one of them with a message to Captain-General Stuart – but still a risk. Reginald made a mental note to ensure the man's subordinates were well-trained, well aware of what to do if they lost contact with their superiors. It was never easy to coordinate a pitched battle. It could be won or lost before the commanding officers on either side realised that the fatal blow had been struck.

The messenger returned, leading Sir Alaric and Sergeant Theodore Ashworth. The sergeant looked oddly tired for someone who'd been in service for most of his life, but Reginald knew he'd been practically killing himself to try to make up for his blunder. Reginald sighed inwardly. If he'd felt punishment was required, he would have administered it. The sergeant shouldn't beat himself up over it. He was hardly the first person to fall to the entities.

Sir Alaric snapped to attention, saluting smartly. Reginald looked the younger man up and down. His uniform was perfectly tailored, his bearing perfect, his horsemanship better than Reginald's own ... it was a shame, going by the report, that he was too brave to *think* before charging into battle. He might win the battle, but – in the process – lose the war. And he had too many aristocratic relations to be sent elsewhere. Reginald felt a twinge of irritation. The younger man – the thought made Reginald feel old – was too useful to be discarded, or assigned to a remote duty station well away from anywhere important, but too impetuous to be trusted with high command. Thankfully, he'd yet to realise that command of a cavalry squadron was a dead end.

"Your Majesty," Sir Alaric said. He was just a little *too* young to have served in the civil wars that followed the empire's fall ... Reginald rather regretted it. A taste of war would have tempered the young man before he did something foolish. "You summoned us?"

"Indeed." Reginald raised his voice. "Can we get the room?"

It was framed as a request, but no one took it for anything other than an order. The mayor, the general and their assistants filed out. Reginald made a private bet with himself that the mayor wouldn't come back. He'd have too many other things to do, none of which could be left to his staff. And besides, it would keep him away from the king. Being so close to the monarch wouldn't end well for the mayor, not after the war was over and the population forgot who'd saved them. He'd be kicked out of office in a landslide.

Reginald tapped the map. "We have very little accurate intelligence on what is happening here," he said, drawing his finger along the borderlands. "I want your squadron to reconnoitre the area and find out. Go to the border, go through the villages and towns … speak to the locals and find out what's happening. Do *not* cross the border and do *not* bother the locals any more than strictly necessary. We want them on our side."

Sir Alaric saluted. "Yes, Your Majesty!"

"If you see the enemy army, or run into trouble, break contact and run." Reginald's eyes bored into the younger man's, silently daring him to object. It was like looking into his own, a decade ago. "Your mission is to find out what's happening and report back, not to go looking for trouble."

"Trouble can find us, Your Majesty," Sir Alaric said. He didn't try to hide the subtext. "And we may be unable to break contact."

Reginald was tempted to clobber the younger man. He'd tolerate a great deal from experienced – and loyal – men, but not from an untried youth who probably bled blue when cut. The thought amused and irritated him in equal measure. He was a king, a king who'd inherited the crown. And yet, he'd fought since he was a boy. He'd fought for his father, then for himself. Sir Alaric had done little more than play at soldiers. He was a good horseman. But was he up to war?

"You're one of the best horsemen in the army," he said, calmly. "I'm sure you can simply outrun your enemies, if you encounter them."

He glanced at Sergeant Ashworth. "I have matters to discuss with the sergeant," he said. "Prepare your troop for departure."

Sir Alaric saluted. "Yes, Your Majesty."

Reginald watched him go, then looked at the sergeant. "I want you to advise him," he said, before the older man could say a word. "He's brave enough for ten, but not experienced.

Not yet. Try to keep him from charging straight into a trap."

Sergeant Ashworth said nothing, but his face tightened. Reginald understood. A sergeant was meant to educate the younger officers, but it wasn't easy at the best of times. Too many aristocrats thought their breeding made them automatically superior to their common-born subordinates. In hindsight, Reginald was astonished he'd been able to lose the attitude without getting himself or someone else killed. His father had made it clear he was to listen – or else – but Sir Alaric didn't seem to have had that lecture.

"It won't be easy," Reginald admitted. "But we don't have a choice."

"Yes, Your Majesty," Sergeant Ashworth said.

Reginald dismissed him with a nod, then turned his attention back to the map. The remainder of the army would straggle in, over the next two days. He was entirely sure that the enemy knew he was coming. Indeed, he'd drawn up plans on the assumption that Barr would be attacked and taken well before the army reached the city. The fact the enemy hadn't attacked the city bothered him. He knew he should be grateful – maintaining the army without the city wouldn't have been easy – but he disliked it when the enemy did what he wanted the bastards to do. It normally spelled trouble.

And the army itself is a priority target too, he thought. *Are they planning to hit us before we take up positions? Or what?*

A messenger entered the room and bowed. "Your Majesty, Captain-General Gars sends his compliments and invites you to inspect the walls."

"Very good," Reginald said. It was probably the first time he hadn't felt the urge to murder a messenger in hot blood. "Inform him I'll be on my way in a moment."

The messenger bowed again, then backed out. Reginald smiled and looked at the map one final time. Conventionally, they were in a pretty good position. Unconventionally …

They're up to something, he thought, darkly. He was sure of it. No enemy commander worthy of the name, human or otherwise, would let the grass grow under his feet any longer than was strictly necessary. *And we won't like what they're doing when it finally hits us in the face.*

Chapter Twenty

"You're pregnant?"

Isabella had to smile at Silverdale's shock. It wasn't as if it was impossible. She was, as far as she knew, perfectly healthy, perfectly capable of bearing children. And she hadn't been doing anything to prevent pregnancy. The odds of her catching, of him impregnating her, were quite high. She'd known she might have to do something to improve the odds at some point – she'd known she was expected to bear his children, when she married him – but it hadn't seemed necessary.

She touched her belly, muttering a spell she'd learnt when she started her cycles. The magic flowed through her, resonating with the baby growing within her womb. Isabella felt a surge of protectiveness as the baby seemed to smile at her, even though it couldn't have been more than a month or two since she'd fallen pregnant. There were at least seven months to go before she gave birth. She wondered, idly, when she'd caught. There'd been quite a few wonderful nights before Reginald had had to go off cracking skulls again.

Silverdale cleared her throat. "How?"

Isabella shrugged. She'd have to have a sit down with the younger girl and explain the facts of life, sooner rather than later. Silverdale had no mother to tell her how her body worked, let alone what happened between men and women in marriage beds. Isabella had heard enough horror stories about innocent brides not having the slightest idea of what was coming, or what was expected of them, to allow Silverdale to go the same way. *She'd* always found that advance knowledge made the event, whatever it was, easier to handle. And besides, it wasn't as if Reginald had been her first.

And I was hardly his first either, she thought, sardonically. *Not that the old goats on the council would find anything wrong with that, of course.*

She smiled, wanly. "The usual way, I assume," she said. "We'll discuss it later."

Silverdale sat back on her haunches. "Are you going to go straight into confinement?"

"No." Isabella laughed. "That's not for another seven months, at least. The baby needs time to grow."

It hit her, then, that she was going to have a baby. She'd known it would happen – she'd hoped it would happen – but all of a sudden it was *real*. Her fingers shook as she pressed them against her abdomen, wondering if she'd make a good mother. It wasn't as if she had many good examples. *Her* mother had been weak, utterly submissive ... she shook her head. She wasn't going to be like that. She would sooner take the child and run than let someone treat her like a slave. And Reginald ... would he be a good father? She thought so, but how did she know? The reality of parenthood was crashing down hard.

She composed herself with an effort. Right now, it hardly mattered. There was no reason to slow down, to take things easy ... she might have to remain at the castle when her belly started to swell, but until then ... she had things she needed to do. She sat on the bed, contemplating everything that had happened. An entity was dead. She'd killed it. Her thoughts ran in circles. The entities would know what had happened. And the gods alone knew what they'd do.

Her lips twitched. The gods *did* know what they'd do.

She stood. "We have to link up with Reginald," she said, standing. "He's going to need me."

"And me," Silverdale said. "I saw what you did ..."

"You're going back to the castle," Isabella said. "Alden will tutor you in magic and you ..."

Silverdale cut her off. "*You* should be going back to the castle," she said. "You're carrying the future of the realm in your belly."

"In my womb," Isabella corrected, absently. "And you are *not* to mention the baby to anyone until I've had a chance to tell Reginald."

"I'm coming with you." Silverdale stood, resting her hands on her hips. "You're going to need me."

Isabella nearly smiled. Silverdale and Reginald were very

different, but – in that moment – they looked almost alike. The same expression of stubborn determination, the same posture suggesting nothing – not even overwhelming force – would change their mind ... it was suddenly obvious, despite the age and gender gap, that they were siblings. And yet ... she let out a long breath. Bringing Silverdale to Frigg had been a calculated risk, one she'd reluctantly accepted. Taking Silverdale to the border, where – for all she knew – Reginald could be already fighting for his kingdom ...

"No," she said, firmly. "You're going back to the castle."

Silverdale met her eyes. Isabella could almost *see* the thoughts going through her mind as she sought a way to convince Isabella to change her mind. Pleas, threats, hints of blackmail ... Isabella waited, grimly aware she might have to order Silverdale tied to a horse and carried back to the capital. *That* wouldn't go down well, not with anyone. Silverdale had enough magic to make the trip a misery, even if she didn't really know how to use it. And there was a risk in sending Silverdale with only a handful of guards. Anyone who captured her would suddenly find themselves a player in the game.

"You need me," Silverdale said. "You told me to trust my instincts, sister, and my instincts tell me you need me."

Isabella hesitated. Six years ago, she would have flatly dismissed the comment and ordered Silverdale back to the castle. Now ... she wasn't so sure. Silverdale was far more *attuned* to the entities, and the changes they'd made to the laws of magic, than was Isabella herself. The younger girl might be right. If she was needed, and she wasn't there, who knew what'd happen? And yet, taking Silverdale would mean exposing her to unacceptable levels of risk ...

"If you come," Isabella said reluctantly, "you do as I say. Without backtalk. Without hesitation. Do you understand?"

Silverdale was too young to conceal her glee. "I understand."

Isabella scowled. She was tempted to pull a fast one, to order Silverdale home immediately on the grounds she'd agreed to obey. But ... she shook her head. "We'll be leaving tomorrow," she said. She waved a hand at the bed. After the inn, she doubted the younger girl would complain about the bed. "Get some rest. I'll be back shortly. And don't even *think* about leaving the room."

"What if I leave in astral form?" Silverdale smirked. "No one will see me …"

"That isn't true, and you know it." Isabella sighed. Silverdale reminded her of *herself*, when she'd been a little girl. She suppressed the thought ruthlessly before she could feel a twinge of sympathy for her father. "Stay here, or you can go straight back to Havelock."

She turned and stepped through the door, muttering a pair of spells to keep the room isolated and warded. Silverdale shouldn't be in any danger, but there was no point in taking chances. Besides, the kingdom itself was in flux. Someone thought to be loyal could turn on the royal family at any moment, if they saw an advantage for themselves. Or if they were merely overshadowed. The entities could offer the world, perhaps literally, to their servants. She'd be a fool to assume it couldn't happen.

The noise from the impromptu street party grew louder as she walked down the stairs and into the office. Colonel Jackstay was sitting in a chair, a topless woman kneeling between his legs. Isabella hid her amusement as the woman looked at her, squeaked and toppled over in an unconvincing faint. Colonel Jackstay wouldn't be pleased at being caught in such a position, although it could have been a great deal worse. They hadn't gotten to the good part yet.

"Your Highness!" Colonel Jackstay sounded shocked. "Ah … Your Majesty."

Isabella nudged the woman with her toe. "You can wait in the next chamber," she said, sternly. The woman opened her eyes, then remembered she was pretending to be in a faint and closed them again. "You can get back to it after I'm gone."

The woman grabbed her shirt and cloak, then hurried out of the door. Isabella made a mental bet with herself that the woman wasn't a whore. She certainly didn't *act* like one. It was far more likely she was someone local, someone the colonel had seduced … with or without her family's permission. Isabella sighed inwardly, remembering too many local arrangements that had ended badly … for the woman, at least. It was hard to believe there were worse fathers than hers, but they were real.

"Your Majesty," Colonel Jackstay said. He snapped to attention, hastily brushing down his uniform. "I ..."

"We'll be leaving tomorrow morning, after breakfast," Isabella said, curtly. There was no point in acknowledging his embarrassment. He'd have no trouble finding someone else, if the woman he'd seduced had run off. "Your men will escort us to the border."

"Yes, Your Majesty," Colonel Jackstay said. "What about the garrison here?"

"We can withdraw it now," Isabella said. Technically, it was Reginald's decision, but she doubted he'd say any different. The garrison was pointless, now the entity was dead. Frigg was hardly the kind of place to cause trouble. "The remaining troops can return to the capital and join the army there."

"Yes, Your Majesty," Colonel Jackstay said. "Is there anything else?"

Isabella smiled. "No," she said. "Have fun."

She turned and left the office. The noise outside was growing louder. She glanced through the window and saw men and women drinking themselves senseless. They were going to regret it in the morning, along with everything else. The cynical part of her mind wondered just how many bastard children were going to be born, nine months from now. Her more sanguine side recognised that the people needed to celebrate. They hadn't known what was going on – the entity had been oozing its way into their minds, even though it had been confined – but they'd *felt* it. And now it was gone.

And they'll have hangovers tomorrow morning, she thought. *Poor buggers.*

A sudden pang struck her as she made her way back upstairs. There'd been a time when she would have drunk and sang and started bar fights with the rest of the band. They were dead now, dead on the Summer Isle ... they'd died fighting for a cause most of them hadn't taken seriously. Some of her former comrades had talked about claiming land and serfs, others had just talked about the money. And none of them had realised what they'd encounter ... she mourned them all, even Big Richard. They'd died at the hands of creatures out of humanity's darkest nightmares.

She pushed the wards aside and stepped into the bedroom. Silverdale was lying on her bed, pretending to be asleep. Isabella was tempted to call her on it, but decided there was no point. The girl would be asleep – really asleep – soon enough. Instead, she undressed quickly, splashed water on her face and climbed into bed. It had been a long day and she needed her sleep.

Reginald is going to be thrilled, she thought, as she forced herself to clear her mind and meditate. *He wanted a child quickly ...*

Her lips quirked at the thought. Reginald would be happy, very happy. And yet ... he wanted a boy. He *needed* a boy. Isabella promised herself, silently, that any daughter she had would have the same shot at the throne as anyone else. She understood, all of a sudden, precisely where the wicked stepmother stereotype had come from. It was natural, and right, to want to promote one's children ahead of everyone else. The daughter – if it was a daughter – would learn magic, would learn to manipulate the world ...

You knew there would be cultural clashes when you married him, she reminded herself. She'd grown up in a world where men and women were considered equals. Magic was one hell of an equaliser. But Reginald had grown up in a place where women were expected to be one step above property ... if they were lucky. *You just didn't expect to encounter them so soon.*

She tossed and turned, even as she fell into sleep. Her dreams mocked her. She saw her father – she saw every bad father she'd known – looming over her, making her feel small and insignificant as he glared down at her. Her father had never considered her a *person* in her own right. He'd never treated her as anything other than clay, as something he could mould into ... into whatever suited him. And he hadn't even been the worst father she'd encountered. She'd killed a man, once, for molesting his own daughter. The bastard had deserved worse ...

"Isabella?"

Isabella started. Someone was in the room with her. She lashed out, all her nightmares bubbling to the surface as the darkness enveloped her. Someone jumped back, tripping and hitting the floor ... Isabella recoiled, casting a hasty lightspell. The room lit up. Silverdale was sitting on the floor, staring at her. The younger girl looked terrified. Isabella realised, dimly, that she'd come within inches of knocking a child into next week.

"You were screaming," Silverdale said. "What happened?"

"I was having a nightmare," Isabella managed. She sat up, feeling hot and bothered even though the room was cool. The sheets were stained with sweat. "I ... did I hit you?"

"No," Silverdale said. "What did you see in your dreams?"

"Old memories," Isabella said. Nightmares gave birth to creatures that lived on the astral plane. Had one of them latched onto her? Or was she simply overthinking it? Too much had happened in the last two days. "What time is it?"

Silverdale peered out the window. "Looks like dawn," she said. "The streets are deserted."

"Everyone's sleeping off their hangovers," Isabella said. "You go back to sleep. I'll wake you when it's time to go."

Silverdale looked as though she wanted to argue, but climbed back into bed and pulled the covers over her head instead. Isabella silently blessed her. She'd feared the younger girl would insist on asking questions, on knowing what shadows had pervaded Isabella's dreams. She had no idea what she would have said, if she'd been asked. Silverdale didn't need to know the truth, not yet. She was still innocent, despite everything. Isabella didn't want to be the one to ruin it.

Although she probably knows more than she lets on, Isabella thought. *She managed to make friends with a maid ...*

Isabella wanted to go back to sleep herself, but she couldn't force herself to relax. She sat in bed, arms wrapped around her legs, then stood and headed for the bathroom. The castle had spoilt her, she reflected sourly. Hot baths and clean clothes – and servants cleaning up the mess – were luxuries, not common necessities. The idea of a commoner having access to hot and cold running water ... absurd, outside the Golden City. Havelock had piped cold water, but hot? She shook her head as she washed the sweat from her brow before dressing and pouring more cold water into the tub. Silverdale would need it. She could even use magic to *heat* it.

She woke the younger girl, then headed back downstairs. Colonel Jackstay and his men were getting ready, looking somewhat the worse for wear after the previous night. Isabella suspected the poor colonel would be grouchy – there was nothing grumpier than a man who'd thought he was going to have sex *not* having sex – but there was nothing she could do about it. The men themselves looked happy to be on the road again. Garrison duty was either boring or extremely dangerous. They'd probably be happier in the open, where they weren't pinned down by enemy soldiers. They could outrun anything they couldn't outfight.

Colonel Jackstay saluted when he saw her. "Your Majesty!"

Isabella smiled. He looked more cheerful than she'd expected. "Colonel. Are you ready to depart?"

"Ready to leave in ten minutes," Colonel Jackstay assured her. "And yourself?"

"We'll be ready," Isabella said. Silverdale had been told to dress quickly. Thankfully, she was old enough to understand that *quickly* didn't mean an hour or two. "The rest of the garrison can decamp at leisure."

"Yes, Your Majesty." Colonel Jackstay bowed. "It will be done."

Isabella nodded, then returned to the room and hastily packed their bags. They hadn't brought much – a regular royal progress involved dozens of luggage carts, most of which were never touched – but they couldn't afford to leave anything behind. She passed Silverdale a piece of hardtack as soon as the princess was dressed, wondering if the younger girl would complain about not having a proper breakfast. Silverdale said nothing. Isabella nodded in approval. She'd met too many well-born girls – and boys – who'd thrown tantrums if they couldn't get their favourite food for breakfast. There was hope for the younger girl yet.

Of course, we used to bitch and moan about eating hardtack too, she reminded herself. She'd eaten hardtack during her mercenary days. It might not be very nice – even when it didn't include worms and weevils – but it kept people alive. *We just didn't have a choice.*

"I'm ready," Silverdale said. "Are you ... going to be sick?"

"I hope not," Isabella said, wondering where Silverdale had heard of morning sickness. One of the maids? It wasn't the sort of thing her governesses would be expected to teach her. Probably. "We have to leave now."

"I'm ready," Silverdale said, again. She clapped her hands in delight. "How long will it take to get there?"

"I don't know," Isabella admitted. It depended on factors outside their control. "It could be several days."

Chapter Twenty-One

It hadn't taken long for Sergeant Theodore Ashworth to decide he loathed Sir Alaric.

The man wasn't a *complete* idiot. Anyone who knew how to ride a horse and lead men into battle couldn't be a *total* fool. But Sir Alaric was too ignorant to know the magnitude of his own ignorance. He'd raised a cavalry squadron himself from scratch – fifteen men, all loyal to him – and yet, he knew little about how to actually *use* it. Or how it fitted into the military machine. Sir Alaric talked as if he was going to win the entire war by himself, as if his tiny squadron was going to gallop all the way to the Golden City without running into something they couldn't handle. Theodore knew better. The squadron would be wiped out in a heartbeat if they tried to charge a fortified position.

He gritted his teeth as the squadron galloped down the dusty road, tasting dust in his mouth. The borderlands had never been very well delineated, not before the empire had crashed into ruin, and it wasn't easy to say *precisely* where the line was actually drawn. The mountains in the distance should have made it harder to move an army from one kingdom to the next, but nothing was certain now. The entities could teleport an entire army behind enemy lines. He grimaced as they raced past a band of refugees, ignoring their pleas for help. Sir Alaric didn't give a damn about the poor bastards. He just wanted to win glory before he went home, married, and took over the family estate.

Theodore forced himself to calm down and wait. He had his orders from the king. He'd do his level best to advise the noble fool, then – if necessary – report what had *actually* happened to his superior. The king, at least, was smart enough to understand the totality of war. His father had made sure of it. Theodore wished he was back in the city, following a man who knew what he was doing. As punishments went, being assigned to Sir Alaric was thoroughly hellish. He'd almost sooner walk the gauntlet.

The air shifted, growing warmer as they plunged towards a small hamlet. Theodore tensed as he saw smoke rising from the cluster of buildings and patches of farmland beyond. They wouldn't be burning their own crops, would they? Not now … he grasped his sword, bracing himself as Sir Alaric led them down and into the hamlet. The entire settlement had been badly damaged, a couple of buildings still burning. A pair of bodies, both middle-aged men, lay on the ground. There was no sign of any survivors. Theodore guessed they'd been forced to flee. The locals had probably taken one look at the approaching party – both parties – and run for their lives.

Sir Alaric pulled back his horse, slowing to a stop in the exact centre of the hamlet. Theodore slowed too, looking around with growing concern. The damage was … odd. The raiders, whoever they were, hadn't done *enough* damage. The villagers would have no trouble in repairing the buildings. The burning croplands could be rejuvenated … next year. Hell, Theodore knew some farmers used controlled burns to fertilise their lands. He frowned, stroking his chin as he studied the nearest building. Raiders tended to be spiteful, if the villagers didn't stand still and let themselves be abused. He'd seen villages burned to the ground because the raiders didn't get what they wanted from the villagers. And yet, this village hadn't been badly damaged at all.

Maybe they were too dumb to know what they were doing, he thought. It was hard to be sure, but the raiders looked to have been and gone at least an hour ago. *They just decided to make a mess because they didn't know enough to do real damage.*

"We chased them off," Sir Alaric proclaimed. "They'll not show their faces here again."

Theodore resisted the urge to contradict the young fool in public. The horsemen hadn't *known* the hamlet had been raided. They hadn't been sent to chase the raiders away before it was too late. They'd only discovered the raid by sheer accident, at least an hour too late to do any real good. Sir Alaric could spin all he liked, but the blunt truth was that the raiders had been and gone before they could be stopped.

The king would know it, too, Theodore thought as he dismounted. He wouldn't be impressed by Sir Alaric's bragging.

He stepped up to the nearest hut and peered inside. The air smelt vile. It had clearly been abandoned in a hurry, judging by the way everything was scattered around. It was hard to be sure – again – but it didn't look as though the raiders had bothered to search the interior. It made no sense. The raiders might have thought the hamlet had nothing worth stealing, but … why bother attacking in the first place? His eyes narrowed as he slipped inside and looked around. An invading army would have done a great deal more damage.

You can't tax the village if you destroy the village, he reminded himself. He'd met too many noblemen who'd refused to grasp the point. *And if you drive them into penury, you'll just turn them into a plague on the land.*

He heard someone behind him and turned, just in time to see Sir Alaric following him into the hut. "This place stinks," Sir Alaric said, loudly. "Who would live here?"

People who have no choice, Theodore thought, sardonically. It wasn't something he could say out loud. Thankfully, Sir Alaric didn't seem to want an answer. *We can't all live in castles with a small army of servants.*

He stepped into the bedroom and frowned. It was larger than he'd expected, but still strikingly crude. A small wooden cage hung from the ceiling, the door hanging open in a manner that bothered him … although he wasn't sure why. The blankets had gone, if they'd ever been there in the first place. A wooden lattice at the rear of the chamber hid a chamberpot, he guessed. *That* was surprisingly sophisticated for a peasant household. The locals, like everyone else these days, were afraid to go out after dark. He didn't blame them. The days when he could take a nap in the dirt under a tree had died with the empire.

"Birds?" Sir Alaric sounded bemused. "They kept giant birds?"

Theodore glanced at him, feeling equally bemused. Birds? What was he talking about? The cage wasn't … he wondered, suddenly, if Sir Alaric was making a dreadful pun. But he was too ignorant to know what he was doing. The cage wasn't for birds …

"No, My Lord," he said. "That's where their women slept."

Sir Alaric blinked. "Their women?"

"Yes, My Lord," Theodore said. He was tempted to answer the question as stupidly as possible, but he resisted. "Traditionally, their women sleep in cages."

Sir Alaric looked disgusted. Theodore snorted. The noble lord didn't know the half of it. The household would probably have quite a few inhabitants, all of whom would sleep in the same bedroom. The women slept in the cage to protect them from the men ... it was very like an aristocratic household, without the thin veneer of civilisation that allowed them to pretend they were doing anything else. Theodore knew there was no point in trying to explain the sheer grinding brutality of peasant life, how it aged the poor bastards prematurely. He'd known women who were grandmothers at thirty.

They checked the rest of the huts, then mounted up again and rode out of the hamlet. Theodore silently composed his report for the king, meditating on precisely *what* the raiders had been trying to do. It made no sense. They'd burnt a handful of buildings and set fire to the fields, but little else. It didn't look as though they'd looted more than the bare essentials. They could have taken a great deal more and burnt the village to the ground, but they hadn't. It *really* didn't make any sense.

They might have been scared off, Theodore thought. He didn't want to admit it, but it was *possible* Sir Alaric had been right. *Yet ... they clearly left well before we arrived.*

He mulled it over as they rode through two more hamlets. They'd both been given the same treatment, right down to a handful of burned-out buildings and burnt fields. Sir Alaric insisted the horsemen were on the trail, hunting down the raiders, but Theodore had the uneasy feeling they were riding in the wrong direction. It was impossible to be sure. The handful of refugees they saw as they probed towards the border fled in all directions, the moment they laid eyes on the horsemen. Theodore didn't blame them. The poor buggers had no reason to expect any better treatment from the local authorities.

"We'll catch them soon," Sir Alaric predicted, loudly.

"And then we'll teach them a lesson."

Theodore kept his thoughts to himself as the road crested a hill and headed down towards a field. It had clearly been left fallow, but … dozens, perhaps hundreds, of people were gathered within the field. Theodore felt a shiver run down the back of his neck as he spied the man standing at the centre of the field, speaking to the crowd. His words were quiet, but Theodore had no trouble hearing them. He was telling the crowd about his god …

"And I say, put your faith in him," the speaker said. "Let him enter your heart and all your wounds will be healed. Let him sing to you and uplift your souls and …"

Shit, Theodore thought. The crowd was murmuring with reverence. They were already halfway to accepting the entities into their hearts. *And there's too many of them to stop.*

Sir Alaric didn't seem to notice. "Forward!"

Theodore opened his mouth to tell him to stop, but it was already too late. The horsemen were cantering forward, scattering worshippers as they charged onto the field. Theodore could *feel* the mood shift, from open reverence to outright hatred and anger. Peasant revolts were rare, but when they exploded they were *nasty*. His eyes flickered from side to side, silently gauging the crowd. Many of them carried makeshift weapons, holding them as though they intended to use them; many looked too angry and desperate to care about the consequences of revolt. He saw a man fall as Sir Alaric cantered past, his head cracking as it hit the ground. The crowd started to close in, raising its weapons. Sir Alaric didn't seem to notice. What harm could they do to him?

A lot, Theodore thought. He was no coward, but he knew better than to pick a fight he couldn't win. A melee against a crowd of armed peasants could – would – end very badly. The horsemen could kill ten times their number and still lose. *They can bring him down by stabbing the horse and then cut him to pieces.*

"This is an illegal gathering," Sir Alaric proclaimed. His voice, normally so loud, sounded weak in the face of the crowd. "You are ordered to disperse immediately!"

"Brothers and sisters," the preacher said. "You see before

you a tyrant! A man who steals your birthright! A man who denies the gods! A man who …"

Sir Alaric drew his sword. "Be quiet, or you will be damned!"

"I fear not death," the preacher announced. He still spoke quietly, but his words seemed to echo on the air. "I fear nothing, for *he* is with me."

Sir Alaric cut him down. His sword cut through the preacher's neck, sending his head flying in one direction and his body crumpling to the ground. Time itself seemed to stop, just for a second. The body fell, landing with a thud. Theodore blanched, realising that things were about to spiral out of control. The crowd seemed torn between anger and fear and …

"Kill!" Theodore didn't see who spoke, but it didn't matter. "Kill!"

"Get back to your homes," Sir Alaric ordered. "I …"

The crowd closed in. Theodore saw Sir Alaric's expression change from irritation to fear as the crowd tore at him. He lashed out with his sword, killing or wounding four men before the blade was torn from his hand. The horse kicked out, then bolted as its rider was pulled from the saddle. Theodore heard Sir Alaric cry out as the crowd surrounded him, too mad to care it was on the verge of kicking an aristocrat to death. Not, he supposed, that it mattered. They'd been committed from the moment they'd attacked Sir Alaric …

"Get back, now," Theodore snapped at the other horsemen. "Now!"

He hesitated, unsure if he really wanted to put his life at risk for Sir Alaric. The man was a fop and a fool and he'd probably led his men to their deaths. They were backing off, but the crowd had tasted its power. It wanted revenge. It didn't matter that most of the horsemen had done nothing to deserve being beaten to death and killed … he heard Sir Alaric cry out again and made up his mind. The king had ordered him to look after the fool. And he would sooner die than disappoint a worthy king.

Theodore dug in his spurs and charged forward. The mob scattered, just enough to let him roll his saddle and grab Sir Alaric by the belt. He was already bleeding, despite his armour … Theodore wondered, just for a moment, if he was risking his life for someone who was already dead. But there was no time to check. He yanked Sir Alaric up and held him close to the horse as he dug in his spurs again. The horse bolted, running across the field and onto the road. Behind him, he heard a roar of anger and the sound of running footsteps. The crowd was coming after them.

Sir Alaric yelped in pain. "I … stop them!"

"We can't stop them," Theodore said. He tried to pull Sir Alaric higher with one hand, while hanging onto the reins with the other. The noble lord was probably more concerned about dangling from a horse in a thoroughly undignified position than the mob chasing them. "We have to move!"

A handful of improvised missiles shot through the air. Theodore glanced back – the mob was still following – then dug in his spurs again. Sir Alaric, astonishingly, had the sense to go limp as the horse picked up speed, cantering down the road as if a horde of devils was after them. Theodore had no idea what had happened to Sir Alaric's horse, but there was no time to go after it. The poor beast would either make its way back to Barr or be caught and eaten by the mob. There were laws against eating horseflesh, but who'd give a damn when they were starving? It was just a matter of time until the refugees started eating each other.

And all of our taboos get thrown out the window when we have a choice between breaking them and dying, he thought, sourly. He'd never tasted human flesh, but he'd heard horror stories from the civil wars. *What choice is there, when our families are at stake?*

He kept galloping until the horse started to tire, putting as much distance as he could between himself and the angry mob. They'd been lucky, very lucky. He didn't know if Sir Alaric realised, but they'd come very close to death. The horse slowed to a halt, allowing him to lower Sir Alaric to the ground. The man looked remarkably shaken, legs unsteady. Theodore concealed his amusement with an effort. The last thing he wanted was for Sir Alaric to try to blame everything on him.

"They … they were going to kill me." Sir Alaric sounded stunned, as if he couldn't comprehend what had happened. "They …"

"They nearly did kill you," Theodore agreed, after a moment. He cast an eye over the younger man. The wounds looked bad, but – in his professional judgement – none were life-threatening. Not immediately, at any rate. "We have to get home and report to the king."

He motioned for the younger man to climb up beside him. Sir Alaric didn't argue, suggesting he really *was* shaken. Theodore suppressed a surge of resentment as they started to canter back to the city. If he'd screwed up so badly, on his first true mission, he'd be lucky if the sergeant didn't take him around the back and administer some rough justice. Why bother with a formal proceeding when you could just use your fists? Sir Alaric, on the other hand, would probably get away with it. The king might understand how badly he'd messed up, but the aristocracy …

At least he got trampled, Theodore thought. Sir Alaric *had* been insanely lucky. If there'd been fewer people in the mob, if they'd been working together … Sir Alaric would have been killed before Theodore could save him. The mob, thankfully, had been too large and too angry to think. *Hopefully, that'll teach him a lesson.*

He scowled as they picked up speed. The preacher's mere existence didn't bode well for the future. If the local peasants and refugees were desperate, they'd start listening and … Theodore wasn't sure how many of the crazy stories he believed, but they'd been warned about rogue preachers. They could be very dangerous. And the odds they'd encountered the only one were very low.

And the king has to be informed, he told himself. It was hard to escape the feeling they were running away … at least in part, he acknowledged sourly, because they *were* running away. *If the preachers are already out there, who knows what* else *is coming our way?*

Chapter Twenty-Two

"Your Majesty!" Reginald frowned as a messenger hurried towards him and bowed. "The patrol is returning in some disarray!"

"Some disarray?" Reginald felt his frown deepen. "They were attacked?"

"I don't know, Your Majesty," the messenger said. "They're racing towards the east gate."

Reginald glanced at Captain-General Gars, who shrugged. They'd spent the last two hours walking the walls, checking the defences and – where necessary – planning improvements. The townspeople were astonishingly pleased to see the army, something that bothered Reginald more than he cared to admit. The locals *had* to feel distressingly, if not disturbingly, exposed. It was just a matter of time until the enemy came over the border and attacked.

"Order them to report to my HQ," he said, finally. "And make sure they're checked before they're allowed to enter the city proper."

He winced, inwardly, as he turned and made his way back to city hall. There was very little they could do to keep astral spies out of the city. They'd rigged a couple of rooms with iron cages, as if they were practically prison cells, but he feared it wasn't enough. There was no way they could surround the entire *city* in a wall of iron. He wished, with an intensity that surprised him, that Isabella had come with them. She could have made sure that they weren't being watched, if nothing else. The fact he'd come to value her advice was purely inconsequential.

You shouldn't lie to yourself, he told himself, sharply. *You miss her.*

"Interesting," Gars said. "Where's the young fool's horse?"

Reginald blinked as he saw the horsemen being escorted towards city hall. Sir Alaric was riding behind Sergeant

Ashworth, his armour dented, crumpled and stained with blood. The young man – Reginald felt a pang of … *something* when he realised he'd thought of Sir Alaric as *young* – looked shocked, like a child who'd come face to face with blood and horror for the first time. Reginald had thrown up, badly, the first time he'd killed a man. It wasn't something he'd willingly share with anyone, even Isabella, but it was true. He was just surprised Sir Alaric had been so badly affected …

His eyes narrowed. Sir Alaric had lost his *horse*. His family could afford to buy and keep an entire stable of horses – they were known for breeding warhorses – but Sir Alaric would have raised his personal steed from childhood. They would practically have been one, when they rode to war. There was no way *that* could be replaced in a hurry. No new horse – bought or borrowed – would come with that link to its rider. Sir Alaric would have to train the poor beast and that would take time, time Reginald doubted they had.

"We'll meet them in the conference chamber," he said, curtly. His bodyguards would want to check the newcomers, just to make sure they hadn't been overshadowed. "And then we'll decide what to do."

"They clearly ran into trouble," Gars said, as they made their way into the building. "The invasion?"

Reginald shrugged. He'd deployed a dozen mounted patrols, and dispatched a handful of troops to potential vantage points, but the grim truth was that the fog of war had enveloped the borderlands. An army the size of his own – or ten times larger – could be bearing down on the city right now and he wouldn't know about it, not until the scouts returned or it hove into view. It had been so much easier, he thought, when he'd been on the offensive. He'd been doing *something*, forcing the enemy to dance to his tune. Here, he was the one who had to sit and wait to be hit. He couldn't launch an invasion of his own, not yet.

Perhaps not ever, he thought. *If the entire country has been overshadowed …*

He stepped into the conference room and took his seat as the heralds announced Sir Alaric and Sergeant Ashworth. Reginald was mildly surprised Sir Alaric hadn't protested, loudly, when Sergeant Ashworth had been summoned too.

The nobleman would want to make the first report, perhaps under the impression that Reginald wouldn't confer with the sergeant or the rest of the squadrons. Gars had already ordered two of his aides to interrogate the horsemen, to demand to know what had happened. Sir Alaric would have no chance to lie to him.

"Your Majesty," Sir Alaric said. He sounded badly stunned. "I ... I was attacked."

Reginald resisted the urge to say something cutting. Sir Alaric was wearing bloodstained armour. It was bleedingly *obvious* he'd been attacked. And ... he shook his head. He didn't have *time* to wait for Sir Alaric to sort himself out. Really, he should be visiting the doctors and letting them poke and prod him. The experience would do him good. If nothing else, it would give him time to calm down and organise his thoughts.

"Sergeant Ashworth," Reginald said, in his most commanding manner. "Report."

Sergeant Ashworth stood at parade rest, hands clasped behind his back. "Your Majesty. We rode along the border, passing through a number of damaged hamlets ... damaged, not destroyed. The raiders, whoever they were, seemed more interested in spooking the population and forcing them to flee than doing actual damage. We were unable, despite our best efforts, to run them down and bring them to battle."

Reginald frowned as he watched the sergeant draw a line along the map. He'd been a warrior long enough to know that pattern *was* odd. What was the point of random destruction? There was nothing to be gained by slaughtering the entire population, not if you wanted the population to feed your army. Damaging the hamlets struck him as singularly pointless, which meant there was something he wasn't seeing. But what?

"Eventually, we came across a rogue preacher, speaking to a crowd of refugees," Sergeant Ashworth continued. "Sir Alaric confronted the preacher and killed him. The crowd turned on us, nearly killing Sir Alaric before I could drag him away. We were ..."

"We retreated," Sir Alaric said. He sounded so certain that Reginald *knew* they'd run for their lives. "We had no choice."

"I see," Reginald said. "Sergeant? Do you have anything to add?"

He felt a twinge of sympathy for the sergeant. Sir Alaric didn't have a leg to stand on if he wanted to claim betrayal – Sergeant Ashworth could hardly refuse a direct command from the king himself – but would that stop Sir Alaric from making a fuss? Who knew?

"We retreated and returned to the city," Sergeant Ashworth said, stiffly. "I do not believe the mob was overshadowed, although the preacher *might* have been. Regardless, they were able to unhorse Sir Alaric and drive the rest of us away."

Reginald nodded, slowly. "I see," he repeated. "Sergeant, please escort Sir Alaric to the medical tents, then return to me and report on his condition. Sir Alaric's second can take care of the rest of the unit."

Sergeant Ashworth saluted. "Yes, Your Majesty."

And I've just given you a cast-iron excuse to return to me, Reginald thought. *If there's something you want to say in private, you can.*

He put the thought out of his head as he studied the map. The attacks seemed pointless, but … perhaps there *was* a point. What had they accomplished? They'd destroyed food stocks and unharvested crops, they'd driven the inhabitants into the forests or forced them to flee west … Reginald scowled, remembering the thousands of refugees camped outside the city. Perhaps *that* was the point. Send refugees fleeing in all directions, forcing him to either feed them from his limited stockpiles or drive them away with fire and sword. It made a certain kind of sense, he supposed. The more people in the city, the sooner it would run out of food. And if the starving people got desperate, they might even throw open the gates and surrender. They'd be too starved to care about the certainty the city would be sacked …

"Or maybe there's a more subtle point," he mused. "What if they want to make people miserable?"

Gars cleared his throat. "Your Majesty?"

Reginald mentally kicked himself. It had been a great deal easier to get good advice when he'd been the Crown Prince. The advisors had known he couldn't do more than refer them to his father, who'd been far more mature … he sighed, inwardly. He was king. Whatever he said was right by default, at least as far as his advisors were concerned. He could insist that elephants were orange and everyone would agree with him. And yet ... reality would bite, sooner or later. Elephants were grey. And the approaching horde of enemy soldiers was real ...

"They're making people miserable," he said. He'd been miserable on campaign, despite being the prince of the realm. He hated to think what it would be like to be forced to flee his hovel and hide in the countryside, or to be raped and murdered ... "They want to make everyone miserable so they will turn to the entities for salvation."

"That sounds possible," Gars said. "But how will the entities intervene?"

Reginald laughed, humourlessly. "It's the oldest trick in the book," he said. His distant ancestors had done it, before the empire. "You tell your subjects that, if they pay tax, you won't send your thugs around to harass them. And then, when they pay tax, all you have to do is sit on your ass and *not* send out the thugs. The entities control the raiders, directly or indirectly, so all they have to do is tell the raiders to leave the converts alone."

He sobered as he studied the map. If there was one preacher, there would be others. He was sure of it. And that meant ... he cursed under his breath. The raiders were forcing people into desperate straits, allowing the preachers to move in and convert them. And, afterwards ... what? His imagination provided too many possibilities. The entities could move the new converts into the Godly Realm, turn them into monsters and return them to the human world ... and then point them at the city. Or ... they could simply use the converts to spread the word still further. His finger traced lines on the map. They could keep sending preachers west until they reached Havelock ... or simply crossed the water to the Summer Isle. Again.

"We were thinking about an enemy invasion," he mused. "But the real threat may lie with the preachers."

Gars nodded, slowly. "That doesn't mean the enemy army *isn't* a threat."

Reginald frowned. "They win whatever happens, don't they?"

His thoughts spun in circles. If he broke up his army, if he sent a dozen men or so to each and every threatened hamlet, village or town, they'd be scattered. Easy meat for a full-scale invasion. But if he didn't take steps to protect the population, they'd be harassed by the raiders and converted by the preachers. And that would eventually cost him the kingdom anyway. He remembered what the locals had told him, after Baron Braddock's death. They'd wanted to keep their new shrines …

"We can put some additional patrols out there," Gars said, when Reginald had finished outlining his thoughts. "Or … we could start evacuating the area ourselves."

Reginald blinked. He hadn't thought of that, but he had no qualms about using someone else's idea. And yet … it would put immense strain on his resources. If he crammed everyone within twenty miles of the city *into* the city, how long would it be before they started to starve? He bit down a savage curse. There was no hope of tending for so many people on short notice. He'd be dragging them away from their farms, depriving them of any chance to feed themselves … and, at the same time, starving the poor bastards because he couldn't feed them. The preachers wouldn't have any trouble converting the starving into slaves. Desperate men would grasp at any straw.

"They'd win again," he said, sourly. He outlined his reasoning. "We simply couldn't feed them."

He rubbed his forehead in irritation. There was no way to produce food quickly enough to feed the current refugees, let alone the tens of thousands who'd be forced off the land if he tried to evacuate the entire region. It wasn't easy to produce food at the best of times. The peasants grew as little as possible, knowing their local aristocrats would take any excess. And there was nothing he could do about that either. He'd have a much larger rebellion on his hands if he tried.

"Fuck," he said. "What do we do?"

He wished, again, that Isabella had come with them. She might have an idea. She was certainly better at thinking outside the box. At the very least, he could talk to her …

"We really need to go after the raiders themselves," he said. "But how do we do that?"

"We'd have to get lucky," Gars said. "They can evade any

garrisons – or simply overwhelm them, if the garrisons are weak enough."

Reginald nodded, curtly. A small mounted patrol, something akin to Sir Alaric's squadron, could easily evade trouble, assuming it saw trouble coming before it was too late. There was little stopping the troopers from cutting across fields, crashing through hedgerows, jumping ditches and swimming rivers. They could be run down, given time, but … was there enough? The entire region was facing death by a thousand cuts. Reginald had no illusions. They could win a battle, perhaps two, and still lose the war.

He turned as the herald announced Sergeant Ashworth's return. "Sergeant," he said, before Ashworth could start saluting. "How is he?"

"Banged up, but mostly intact," Ashworth reported. "His armour took the worst of it."

"And his dignity took whatever was left," Reginald said. He smiled, although it wasn't funny. Sir Alaric's father would be proud if his eldest son died in honourable combat, but rather less so if his son was killed by a bunch of peasants. "How … unfortunate."

"Yes, Your Majesty," Sergeant Ashworth said. "The wounds have been cleaned and he'll be returning to duty shortly."

"Tell him to draw a horse from the reserves," Reginald said. "And to think, next time, before he jumps into a mess."

"Yes, Your Majesty," Sergeant Ashworth said.

Reginald stared down at the map for a long moment. "We need to stop the raiders, without weakening our position here," he said. His finger touched the city on the map. "What would you advise?"

The sergeant leaned forward. "The raiders will probably have set up camp somewhere within the countryside," he said. "Unless they *want* to waste hours riding back and forth across the border."

"I imagine they don't care," Reginald said. The thought of going after outlaws on their own territory made him wince. "We have to protect the population and …"

He looked at Gars. "We'll station units here, here and here," he said, tapping points on the map. "If the towns and villages come under attack, they can respond and hopefully trap the raiders. If not … they can try to trail the bastards home."

If that's possible, his thoughts added, soundlessly. *They might be hiding within the Godly Realm.*

"Yes, Your Majesty," Gars said. "I would also advise that you station additional units along the border. They will certainly cross sooner or later."

"Sooner rather than later," Reginald predicted. The entities needed to take him – and the kingdom – out of the equation as quickly as possible. "They know we know too much."

He allowed his eyes to wander along the map. "Sergeant, stay with Sir Alaric and his men for the moment," he added. "I want you patrolling the western edge of the border."

"Aye, Your Majesty," Ashworth said. "We could cross the border and raid too."

Reginald shook his head. In a conventional campaign, he would certainly have *tried* to make the enemy troopers as miserable as possible. A handful of well-timed raids could cause endless delays … as the entities were reminding him now. But Halladale was enemy territory. The entities owned it. They could probably twist the land itself against invaders. He shivered, remembering what he'd seen on the Summer Isle. The entities had laid claim to the land and made it theirs. His army had nearly been wiped out.

"I don't think we can risk it," he said. He wished, once again, for Isabella. Or Silverdale. He was reluctant to expose his younger sister to danger, but he might not have a choice. "It isn't our land."

"Yes, Your Majesty," Sergeant Ashworth said.

He didn't agree. Reginald could tell. He didn't blame the sergeant either. No one who hadn't seen the entities at work believed what they could do, if someone was fool enough to open their heart and let the entities in. A king – or a lesser aristocrat – could open the door for them to do worse. Far worse. And the hell of it was that the sergeant had a point. In a conventional campaign, raiding the enemy border was exactly the right thing to do.

"Take care of Sir Alaric," Reginald said. "Dismissed."

Sergeant Ashworth saluted and left. Reginald turned his attention back to the map. There were hundreds of settlements, from tiny hamlets to mid-sized towns, within the borderlands. He'd bet the crown that dozens of them had already been raided ... and dozens more were under threat. They hadn't heard anything, but that proved nothing. The locals might be reluctant to report to the city for fear of being victimised twice. It had happened, in other places ...

They've put a noose around our necks, Reginald mused, sourly. His army had taken the bait ... the bait they'd had to take. *Now they're trying to strangle us.*

His thoughts darkened. *And they might just succeed ...*

Chapter Twenty-Three

Silverdale threw back her head and whooped, allowing the wind to flow through her hair.

She couldn't help herself. It felt wonderful to be out of the castle, even if they were galloping towards a war zone. Silverdale had overheard a conversation between Isabella and Colonel Jackstay that had described, in graphic detail, precisely what could happen to them if they fell into enemy hands ... but she found it hard to care. She promised herself, as the wind blew stronger, that she would never let herself be locked up again. She was going to run wild and free because ... she *wanted* to.

The world seemed to glow, sparks of light and life dancing in and out of the astral plane. Silverdale drank it in as they galloped through a town, studying the people and the shadows they cast into the other realm. They seemed happy, but worried. The contrast between their physical forms and their souls bothered her, the more she thought about it. She saw a young woman curtsey to the horses, soul tinged with anger and resentment as she bent the knee. Silverdale shivered, even though it was a warm day. The girl hated her with a passion and yet the girl didn't even *know* her.

She sucked in her breath as the horses moved onto the road leading up to Barr and the borderlands. The world seemed a different place, more alien, as they left human civilisation behind. Here and there, they passed pockets of refugees heading west, but ... otherwise there were no humans in sight. She saw *things* lurking in the hedgerows, felt unseen eyes following them as they galloped on. Some felt friendly, reminding her of her teddy bear; some felt hostile or simply indifferent. She glanced at Isabella's back as she rode beside Colonel Jackstay, wondering what her sister-in-law saw. Perhaps nothing. Isabella had openly admitted she was unwilling to risk losing her mind in the astral realm.

Silverdale pressed herself against the horse, smiling. She

knew she should be concerned, perhaps even jealous, of her prospective nephew, but she'd never wanted the throne anyway. The throne had consumed her father and her oldest sister and it was currently consuming her brother. The lust for power had destroyed them. Her father had paid little attention to Silverdale, even when she'd been a little girl; her sister had tried to turn her into a pawn. Silverdale pitied the unborn child, even as she welcomed him. Or her. It would be nice to have someone to look up to her.

She reached out, peering into the astral realm. The landscape seemed to burst into light as she looked beyond the first and second layers of reality. She was pulled forward, soul threatening to tumble out of her body and go exploring. She wanted to go. She bit down on the impulse as she peered at Isabella. The sorceress queen was practically glowing with life. Silverdale smiled, knowing – as if she'd doubted it – that Isabella was going to have a baby. It was funny how Isabella's astral form was so alike and so different from the older woman's physical self. They'd never be taken for the same person in the real world.

Isabella turned to look at her. Silverdale flushed, feeling as if she'd been caught with her hand in the cookie jar. A wave of stern disapproval, tinged with amusement, washed against her mind. Silverdale pulled back hastily, blushing as the disapproval intensified. Isabella wasn't someone to take lightly. She might simply refuse to teach Silverdale any more magic.

And she might not be able to teach me as her belly swells, Silverdale thought. She wasn't quite sure on what had to be done to make a baby, but she'd seen pregnant servants in the castle. Some of them had barely been able to carry a tray. And there'd been awful whispers about a noble lady who'd lost a baby, although none of the stories quite made sense. *She might have to stay in bed.*

She looked around, admiring the beauty of the astral plane. There was life everywhere, if one knew where to look. Her mind glided through the fields and trees, skimming over a family of foxes in their lair. Silverdale felt a pang of guilt as she remembered the noblemen setting out to hunt wolves and drive them out of their lands. Wolves were predators, preying on sheep, but ... she shuddered. The noblemen had come home with corpses and put them on display. Her stomach churned. She'd never be able to watch *that* again. She might not even be able to visit the country estate. There was no way Reginald would let her go in the middle of a war.

A wave of darkness seemed to wash across the astral plane. Silverdale shuddered as it crashed into her, so cold it made her shiver. She felt as if she'd suddenly been plunged into a bath of cold water. No, something bigger than a bath. A lake. An ocean. The cold was leaching into her, making her shake helplessly … her arms and legs seemed to have turned to ice. She felt her stomach churn as she gasped for breath, convinced she was drowning. Panic nearly overwhelmed her before she remembered she was on the astral plane. She didn't *need* to breathe. Whatever was happening wasn't real.

Not quite, she thought. *But it isn't what it seems either.*

Silverdale gritted her teeth, concentrating. The darkness shrank rapidly into … something. A nexus of darkness, heading towards them. It was looking at her. She looked back, then turned away as it threatened to pull her soul out of her body. The darkness was coming … she fell back, straight into her body. Her heart almost stopped in shock. She'd been much further into the astral plane than she'd realised. The warm sunlight drenched her in light, but she could still feel the darkness. It was getting closer.

She forced herself to look further up the road, then behind her. Isabella, Colonel Jackstay and the seven horsemen rode in formation – Silverdale hadn't noticed she was at the centre until now – but there was no one else in sight. And yet, she could feel the darkness crawling towards her. She looked left and right, across fields and into forests, and saw nothing. The sense of imminent doom grew stronger. She *knew* they were coming.

"Isabella!" Silverdale's voice sounded weak and tinny, even in her own ears. "Isabella!"

Isabella turned, eyes grim. "Silverdale?"

"They're coming," Silverdale said. She saw a flash of fear in Isabella's eyes and shivered. Isabella wasn't scared for herself, but for Silverdale. Silverdale mentally kicked herself for insisting that she accompany the queen. She should have stayed in Havelock. And yet, her instincts insisted that she'd made the right decision. "I can feel them."

"I see nothing, Your Majesty," Colonel Jackstay rumbled.

Silverdale felt a hot flash of hatred that surprised even her. Colonel Jackstay was just another man who thought that being a man made him automatically superior. He'd pay respect to her rank, but he wouldn't *respect* her. He certainly wouldn't take her seriously. Silverdale could practically *taste* his lack of concern. He saw her as just another hysterical woman, no more important than the rest. Bile rose in Silverdale's throat. They were about to be attacked – the darkness was looming over them now – and the fool wasn't *listening*. They were about to die!

"That doesn't mean anything, not here," Isabella said. She, at least, was taking Silverdale seriously. "They could be coming at us right now …"

The darkness reached forward. Silverdale cringed, her attention unwillingly yanked front and centre. A set of horsemen appeared in front of them. She shuddered as she saw the dark horses, tasted the nexus of power and darkness surrounding the hooded riders. All the old tales of dark riders on the roads, of devils who would suck unwary travellers into their personal hells, suddenly felt very real. She felt the horse shift uncomfortably beneath her as it sighted the riders. Silverdale was a skilled horsewoman. She could *feel* the beast's sudden fear.

Colonel Jackstay raised his voice. "Ho! Stand aside!"

Silverdale doubted the dark riders would pay any attention. Legally, the royal family had right of way; practically, the kingdom was at war. The silent riders kept coming, faces hidden behind their hoods. Silverdale tried to peek at them through the astral realm and recoiled, feeling as if she'd just taken a bath in a cesspit. The riders were monsters. She felt as if she'd looked at something utterly beyond her ken.

"Deploy," Colonel Jackstay snapped. "We'll go through them."

"No," Isabella said, flatly. "We'll evade."

Silverdale sensed a flash of irritation and resentment from Colonel Jackstay. Isabella probably shouldn't have countermanded him in public. He wasn't fool enough to disagree, not in the face of the enemy. Instead, he barked orders. The formation altered course, leaping off the road and galloping across the fields. Silverdale sucked in her breath as they cantered through a field of barley and jumped over a ditch. Behind them, she felt the dark riders follow. Shadowy impressions wafted through the air, reaching out to encircle them. She didn't dare look closely. She had the feeling that would be the last thing she'd ever do.

"They're catching up with us," a voice said. A soldier … he sounded terrifyingly young. She wished, suddenly, that she'd thought to get his *name*. Reginald made a big deal about knowing names, about mentioning those who served well … she understood now, too late. "We can try to lead them through the morass."

"Too dangerous," Colonel Jackstay said. He glanced at Isabella. "Are there any others out there?"

You should be calling her 'Your Majesty', Silverdale thought, with a hint of spite. They might have escaped completely if Colonel Jackstay had listened to her. Even now, he was addressing the older woman rather than the princess. *Why didn't you listen to me?*

Isabella looked at Silverdale. Silverdale shrugged. The darkness was washing through the astral plane. If there was another enemy force, it was lost in the gloom. She looked around, hoping to catch sight of *something*, but saw nothing. The landscape looked undisturbed, save for the dark riders behind them. They felt like … they felt like they didn't belong.

"I can't sense anything," she said, quietly. She felt as if she'd been blinded. The astral plane was no longer safe. "There could be anything out there."

Colonel Jackstay nodded. "Your Majesty, take the princess and gallop for your life," he ordered. "We'll deal with them."

Silverdale stared, feeling a twinge of respect. Colonel Jackstay was going to risk his life to save her? It was his duty, she knew. And yet … he could have run. She wouldn't have blamed him. The dark riders weren't normal horsemen. She hoped he'd thought to arm his men with cold iron. It might be the only way to kill the horsemen.

"Understood." Isabella sounded grim. It was obvious she didn't believe Colonel Jackstay would survive. "Slow them down, then turn and run yourself."

Colonel Jackstay saluted, then wheeled his horse around.

Silverdale watched as the rest of his men followed, drawing their swords and raising a cheer as they cantered towards the enemy. The dark riders didn't flinch. They just kept coming in eerie silence. Silverdale stared, then jumped as a hand caught her reins. Isabella was riding right beside her.

"Gallop for your life," Isabella ordered. Her voice was sharp, leaving no room for disobedience. "And don't look back."

Silverdale dug in her spurs. The horse neighed, then put down its head and *galloped*. It couldn't gallop long, but if they could break contact, they could vanish in the countryside and make a run for safety before the dark riders caught up with them. She lowered her head, all too aware the horse would keep running if she tumbled off its back. Behind her, she heard a scream. It cut off abruptly. Silence fell, like a hammer.

"Don't look back," Isabella repeated. "Just *run*."

The horse galloped harder. Silverdale gritted her teeth. She could *feel* the dark riders as they gave chase. Colonel Jackstay and his men were dead, wiped out so quickly ... she didn't want to think about it. She could *feel* the dark riders behind her, even though she was trying not to *look* at them. Darkness was spreading ... she could sense the darkness reaching. She shuddered, knowing it was looking at her. It was just a matter of time until they ran out of places to run.

"I should never have brought you with us," Isabella said. The guilt in her voice was almost palpable. "I should have tied you to the horse and sent you back home."

Silverdale wasn't sure if Isabella was speaking or if she was somehow reading her sister-in-law's thoughts. She could sense the growing nexus of fear around Isabella, fear not for herself but for Silverdale. And for her child. Silverdale wondered, suddenly, if she should turn herself and slow the enemy, giving Isabella a chance to escape. She knew, deep inside, that Isabella wouldn't thank her. She couldn't run and she couldn't stay and ...

Isabella raised a hand and muttered a spell. A fireball flashed from her palm and darted towards the dark riders. Silverdale looked back, ignoring orders just in time to see the fireball wink out. The dark riders weren't letting them go so easily. She wished, suddenly, she'd thought to bring a dagger. She'd never been taught how to use weapons, not even a little knife, but it couldn't be *that* hard. Stick the blade in the enemy, right? But if the blade wasn't cold iron …

Magic flared, time and time again. Silverdale watched the dark riders shrugging off spells and projectiles with casual ease. They seemed utterly unconcerned, as if they knew it was just a matter of time before they ran down their prey. Silverdale sensed her horse starting to gasp for breath and knew it was running out of energy. The horse would have to slow soon, ensuring they were caught and trapped. She saw foam bubbling around the horse's mouth. The poor beast was coming to the end of its endurance.

"Turn the air to iron," she called. It was the only thing she could think of. "Quickly!"

"It won't *stay* iron," Isabella shouted back. Her horse was starting to foam too. "And there's nothing else we can do to slow them down."

Silverdale glanced east. The path was starting to get rocky. They might manage to make it to the road, but it would just be easier for the dark riders to catch them. There were meant to be army units making their way to Barr, yet … they wouldn't be able to help. The dark riders had effortlessly slaughtered Colonel Jackstay and his men. They'd go through a bunch of soldiers like hot knives through butter. And there was no hope of reaching Barr before it was too late. The horse was already tiring. Sooner or later – sooner rather than later – the horse would stop. There was nothing she could do about it. The horse would stop and she'd be taken …

The ground shook as the darkness enveloped them. Silverdale winced. She saw sunlight in one eye and darkness in the other. The dark riders were growing stronger, their presence reaching into the astral realm … she tried to look away, but it was too late. They were slowly reaching out to *take* them. The horse shook below her, the creature thoroughly spooked by the dark riders. She hoped it would encourage the horse to move faster, as they cantered onto the road. They might just make it to Barr and then … and then what? The dark riders would tear through the city and keep going.

Reginald would know what to do, she told herself. Her brother was the greatest warrior in the world, the one who'd beaten the entities and their servants twice before. He could stop them, if they could reach him … her thoughts laughed at her. *But we can't get to him in time.*

Isabella's horse jerked. Silverdale saw Isabella tumble back, hitting the ground as her mount fled into the distance. She pulled on the reins, but her horse was panicking, too. It didn't want to slow down, despite its exhaustion. She was torn, wanting to jump herself and also wanting to run. She couldn't leave Isabella behind. She couldn't!

"Run!" Isabella picked herself up, drawing her sword. Her *cold iron* sword. "Run!"

Silverdale barely heard her. The astral plane was … echoing with the sound of laughter. She felt sick as the dark riders closed in on Isabella, their presence polluting the air. She wanted to turn and yank Isabella onto her horse and run, but her muscles were frozen. They refused to move as the horse galloped faster and faster. She couldn't do anything …

"*Run,*" Isabella shouted. There was power in her voice. Silverdale felt it slam into her mind, a compulsion she couldn't ignore. "Run!"

Silverdale bent her head, feeling tears prickle in her eyes as the horse picked up speed. She tried to tell herself Isabella would be fine, even though she didn't believe it. She was powerful and cunning and carried a sword of cold iron. She could defend herself. She could … Silverdale shuddered as the laughter grew louder. The dark riders – or the thing behind them – was laughing at her. The darkness grew stronger, so … *dark* that she had to screw her astral eye shut and run. Behind her, Isabella was fighting for her life …

She didn't look back.

Chapter Twenty-Four

There was no hint, as the cavalry stood on watch near the border, that they were looking into another country. There were no markers, no guard posts ... nothing, not even a customs house, to suggest that the border was in front of him. The hills on the eastern side of the border were akin to the ones on the western side. Sergeant Theodore Ashworth was almost disappointed. The maps had always suggested the border was fixed, although he knew that wasn't true. Both kingdoms laid claim to land on the wrong side of the border and, of course, the locals showed scant regard to it. He'd been on military service long enough to know the locals didn't give much of a damn about the monarchs when there was family to see and profits to be made.

He leaned back in the saddle, eyes narrowing as he realised what was missing. People. No traders made their way up and down the road, no refugees fled across the border ... there weren't even any smugglers in obvious view. The last of these could probably see the cavalry, of course, but still ... he frowned. The smugglers might openly defy the cavalry, once they were on the wrong side of the border. They'd act as though the other kingdom had no interest in chasing them and they'd probably be right. He felt his frown grow deeper. There weren't even any birds in the sky.

His eyes slipped to Sir Alaric, mounted on his horse. His *new* horse. The aristocrat had been more than a little shaken, even though he hadn't been *seriously* hurt. His collection of bruises was enough to impress the ladies, but little more. Theodore had taken worse poundings in the fighting pits, back when he'd been a younger man. Sir Alaric was young enough to learn, Theodore supposed, from the experience. The only question was *what* he'd learn. To be a little more respectful, perhaps, or at least aware of uncommon dangers? Or to strike hard and run?

The latter wouldn't be a bad lesson to learn, Theodore

admitted. *We're not armed and trained to stand our ground.*

He frowned as he turned his attention back to the border. The last two days had been grim. The enemy raiders had continued their attacks, driving refugees towards the city; the enemy preachers had continued to preach, despite the best efforts of the king and his men. Theodore understood, all too well. The refugees were desperate. They'd turn to anyone for salvation and …

"Sir!" Theodore looked up, sharply, as one of the troops raised the alarm. "Look!"

Theodore peered forward as Sir Alaric put a telescope to his eye. The air on the far side of the border was shimmering. His eyes hurt, the more he looked at it. The road was twisting, as if it was suddenly heading in a direction his head refused to comprehend. He thought he saw … *something* … on the far side, gleaming towers and massive buildings and things he simply couldn't understand before the first soldiers stepped into existence. His stomach twisted, the hardtack he'd eaten for breakfast threatening to come up again. Behind him, he heard a horseman being noisily sick. The enemy soldiers were … he wasn't sure *what*. He remembered the Red Monks and shivered. They'd clearly marched through the Godly Realm.

Sir Alaric glanced at him, then raised his voice. "Mount up!"

The dismounted horsemen scrambled into the saddle as the enemy army advanced across the border. Theodore stared, everything he'd ever learnt about army deployments crumbling to dust. The army was a mob, yet … there was a hint of organisation about it that chilled him to the bone. There were no mounted horsemen scouting ahead of it, no officers in command … Theodore felt cold. The enemy army looked more like a horde of locusts than anything else, more of a natural disaster than something that could be stopped. He thought he saw something very inhuman in their shadowed, insistent forms.

"You three, go straight back to the city and inform the king the enemy invasion has begun," Sir Alaric ordered. "The rest of us will watch the enemy army from a distance."

Theodore nodded. Sir Alaric was thinking clearly for once. Good. Theodore supposed that seeing a giant enemy army advancing across the border was enough to concentrate anyone's mind. There was no hope of stopping it either, not until the king could get his army into position or it attacked Barr. Theodore made a face as the enemy army kept coming, advancing down the road with a strange combination of military professionalism and sloppiness that offended his sense of righteousness. No commander in his right mind would permit Sir Alaric's horsemen to shadow the army from a safe distance, not when he could easily drive them away. It was too late for the enemy to keep the horsemen from alerting the king, but ... he scowled as the enemy army kept growing, pouring out of the twisted road like an endless tide of warped soldiers. The enemy probably didn't care. They might even see it as a good thing. The king might take one look at the force advancing towards him and surrender.

The air twisted, again. Theodore's eyes were yanked forward as a ... *being* stepped out of the warped road. The being was quite some distance from the horsemen, but Theodore could see him clearly. He was ... the very embodiment of a warrior king, practically *glowing* with light and life and masculinity ... it was hard to make out his features amidst the glow. Theodore forced himself to look away. It wasn't human. Not any longer. It might have been human once, but it wasn't now. The poor bastard inside the glow had surrendered himself to the entities.

"By the stars," Sir Alaric breathed. He was staring at the entity, a disturbingly hungry expression on his face. "I ..."

"Focus," Theodore snapped. He wondered, suddenly, what Sir Alaric was seeing. If Theodore, a grizzled, experienced and profoundly cynical sergeant, could be affected so badly ... he knew Sir Alaric could be affected badly, too. Just looking at the entity made him want to follow it. "Whatever you're seeing, it isn't real."

Sir Alaric looked dazed. "It's real!"

"Your senses are lying to you," Theodore said. He'd heard horror stories about Princess Sofia's court, how she'd effortlessly controlled her courtiers. The entity in front of them seemed to be the same. Different, perhaps, but using the same technique. "That thing isn't real."

He reached forward and yanked on Sir Alaric's reins, turning him away from the entity. The younger man jerked, rubbing his forehead as the shock hit. The entity had burrowed into his mind without ever touching him. Sir Alaric let out an odd little sound, then motioned for the horsemen to canter away from the enemy army. Theodore was only too happy to obey. He could feel the pull, even when he wasn't looking at the creature. He shuddered to think what would happen if someone weak-willed were caught in its gaze. They'd fall to their knees within seconds.

They shadowed the army as it kept marching west, passing through countless hamlets and towns. Theodore wasn't surprised when most of the peasants, offered the flat choice between opening their hearts and being executed, chose to open their hearts. They probably didn't know what choice they were *really* making. Peasants would happily say whatever they had to say, just to make the swordsmen go away. If that meant pledging themselves to Andalusia one day, then some kingdom from the other side of the world the next ... they'd do it without a second thought.

This time, it would be different. They'd be worshipping the entities until the end of time.

"We should stop them," Sir Alaric breathed, after they watched the army crush the soul of a small town. The handful of remaining peasants didn't stand a chance. "Those traitors are going to let them in ..."

Theodore shook his head. "Sir ... you can't stop them."

He sighed, inwardly. None of the aristocrats had ever faced the risk of losing everything. Not really. Aristocrats were rarely killed on the battlefield, if it could be avoided. They were taken prisoner and – normally – treated well until their friends and families paid ransom. Peasants, on the other hand, were slaughtered out of hand. Theodore had read some reports that suggested only a handful of people had been killed in the war. The writers hadn't included the hundreds of common-born soldiers ...

"What would you say," he asked instead, "if someone held a sword to your throat? To your wife's throat? To your children's throat?"

Sir Alaric said nothing as the enemy army destroyed a handful of temples, then marched onwards. Theodore was glad of the silence. Judging by the plumes of smoke in the distance, the enemy army was advancing on a broad front.

He tried to calculate how many soldiers were marching through the borderlands, and drew a blank. Military tactics simply didn't *work* that way. A wise commander would focus on Barr and the roads that led west, towards the core of the kingdom. The entities seemed more intent on sweeping up villages and towns that were really nothing more than prizes for the winner. It didn't even look as though they were interested in looting or rape. It made no sense ...

Or perhaps it does, if they want worship, he mused. *They'll add thousands upon thousands of worshippers to their ranks ...*

He felt his heart sink. Kings didn't give much of a damn about hearts and minds. They didn't care if they were loved or hated, as long as they were obeyed. No one really bothered to convince the peasants to support their king. But now ... he shook his head as they watched another temple burn. The king could no longer offer even the bare minimum of protection. There was nothing to stop the peasants from selling themselves to the entities. Why should they not? The only alternative was death.

"They'll be at Barr within the day," Sir Alaric predicted.

Theodore nodded. The army was moving at a comparatively leisurely pace, but it wasn't slowing. It didn't look as though the warped soldiers needed to rest. And that meant they could just keep going until the city was under siege. Or worse ... they could try to storm the walls. The defenders had cold iron, but would that be enough?

"I know," he said. "And the king knows."

And it will have to be enough, he thought. *If we can't stop them quickly, we might not be able to stop them at all.*

***

Reginald dreamed.

He knew he was dreaming, even though he wasn't sure *how* he knew. He'd taken a nap, midway through the day, after spending half the night working on the defences and patting the mayor's head whenever he raised concerns. Now ... he saw the entire kingdom burning, his wife and siblings and children turned to ash in the blink of an eye. He saw ... *children?* He had no children. He'd been careful not to sire any bastards, his father's warnings about the dangers echoing in his ears. There might be noble lords who bragged of their fertility, who claimed hundreds of illegitimate children, but they were just lords. The king could not risk royal bastards. And he'd listened to his father …

His skin was on fire. He watched, utterly disconnected, as his skin turned black under the heat. There should have been pain, yet … his entire body exploded into fire. Flames licked his heart, reaching up to touch his mind … he smelt the sickly-sweet stench of burning flesh and boiling blood. He felt nothing. No pain, no concern … no nothing. The dream held him down, refusing to let him go. Reginald twitched, tossing and turning in his cot. He was in his room in the city hall, in Barr. He knew it. And yet he couldn't tear himself away from the nightmare.

"Your Majesty!" Reginald heard someone shouting, the voice so loud it made his skull ache. "Your Majesty!"

His head spun. The voice was male. No, female … he felt a twinge of annoyance. The mayor had offered him his daughter as an attendant, with a wink that suggested he had something more carnal in mind. Reginald had been revolted. He wasn't the kind of person who'd accept … his head spun, again, as he heard the voice. Someone was touching him, someone was …

Reginald snapped upright, one hand grabbing for the dagger under the pillow. He couldn't risk sleeping without it, even in the midst of his guards. No one could be trusted completely, when the entities were involved. No one. A messenger jumped back in alarm, his eyes going wide with fear. Reginald could stab him and no one would give a damn. He'd probably be cheered. The entire room lurched, so violently that Reginald thought he was back onboard ship. He'd heard of earthquakes and volcanoes, but he'd never seen one …

He brushed sweat from his brow. "Report!"

The messenger swallowed hard, as if he expected Reginald to order his immediate execution by torture. "Sire … an army has crossed the border, heading for the city."

Reginald took a moment to compose himself. "Details?"

"The picket reported at least ten thousand men, sire," the messenger said. "I don't know if it's accurate."

"No," Reginald said. He *hoped* it wasn't accurate. It

wasn't *easy* to estimate how many enemy soldiers were on the march. The vast majority of reports were either under or overestimates. He'd once read a report that claimed over a *billion* troops were on their way. "Inform the captain-generals that I want to see them in thirty minutes."

The messenger bowed and scurried out. Reginald stood on wobbly legs, feeling the world shifting around him. He'd never dreamed so intensely before. It was hard to draw the line between the walking world and the land of nightmares. He'd heard all the stories about the lords of nightmares dragging innocent children into hellish dreams, but he'd never quite taken them seriously. The stories had just seemed like lazy ways to get children to behave. Now ... it was possible there was a glimmer of truth in the old tales. The entities might have been the *original* lords of nightmare.

He splashed water on his face, then dried himself with a towel. The world had just become a simpler place. It was time to make war. And yet ... the nightmare hung in his mind, mocking him. He didn't have children. Did he? It was possible that one of his lovers had had his child and raised him in secret ... his heart twisted at the thought. He'd read those stories too. They never ended well.

Not for the kingdom, not for the king, and not for the poor bastard child, Reginald reminded himself.

He dressed, making sure to strap his sword within easy reach. The enemy army would concentrate a few minds. Unfortunately, a few of those minds would start thinking about opening the gates and surrendering. Normally, they might avoid a sack. Now ... he shook his head, sourly. The entities would crush the city's soul, then resume their advance west. They might even catch him too. And that would put Ruby on the throne. Reginald found himself brooding as he walked down the corridor. His sister had the strongest claim, but half the nobility would oppose her ... openly or covertly. They'd trigger a civil war at the worst possible time.

"Your Majesty," Gars said, as he stepped into the conference room. "Two more horsemen have arrived, with the same message."

Reginald scowled at the map. "These reports have been confirmed?"

"No, Your Majesty," Stuart said. "But the horsemen have been in service for years."

"And so we have *three* massive armies heading across the border," Reginald said. It looked like a full-scale invasion, yet ... one that offered him the chance to defeat each army separately. If, of course, he was prepared to take the risk of meeting the army in open country. "Where are they getting the men?"

He shook his head. It was a stupid question. They'd probably amassed thousands of worshippers, marched them through the Godly Realm and warped them into monsters. Thousands ... hundreds of thousands, perhaps even millions. Zycrest was a pretty big kingdom, bordered by several others. The entities shouldn't have had any trouble amassing the manpower they needed to take the world.

"They'll be here by the end of the day, if the latest reports are accurate," Gars said. "We'll have to face them here."

"Yeah." Reginald studied the map grimly. "There's no time for an effective retreat."

He glanced at Stuart. "Send a handful of messengers to Ruby. Inform her that she is to hold the remainder of the army, then have defence lines set up as planned. We may be unable to stop them here."

"Yes, Your Majesty," Stuart said.

Reginald cursed under his breath. Ruby needed a strong general who could be relied upon not to take her throne. She didn't have one. If something happened to Reginald ... or even if he were merely trapped or imprisoned ... the results might be disastrous. He wondered, suddenly, if he should send Gars or Stuart back before it was too late. Either of them would have the skills to take control. And he wouldn't have relied on them so heavily if he hadn't trusted them ...

"Stuart, I want you to go with them," Reginald said. He picked his next words carefully. "I'll need you to organise the relief army."

Stuart didn't look pleased. People would whisper that he was a coward ...

There was a sharp knock at the door. "Come!"

A messenger looked in. "Your Majesty! Your sister has just arrived!"

Reginald blinked. "My sister?"

Chapter Twenty-Five

The empire, Silverdale had been told, had insisted that the main roads be as straight as possible, even if it meant using magic and hard labour to cut through hills and bridge impassable ravines. She blessed their foresight now, praising generation upon generation of Grand Sorcerers and Sorceresses as she cantered down the road towards Barr. It would have been impossible, if she hadn't known the road would either take her to Barr or back to Havelock. She hadn't dared try to stop someone and ask for directions. Alone, she would have been an easy target. The person who knocked her out and stole her horse might not even know who she was.

Guilt gnawed at her mind as she passed through the refugee camp and rode up to the iron gates. She'd left Isabella behind. She hadn't had a choice – Isabella had compelled her, somehow – but it still hurt. She'd left Isabella and her unborn baby behind. And she might have been captured. No, she *would* have been captured. The entities would want her alive. Who knew? Threatening Isabella – and the child – might be enough to make Reginald bend the knee.

The guards stared at her, clearly stunned. She probably looked less like a princess and more like a ragamuffin. Or something worse. Silverdale had ridden for hours. Her body hurt so badly she wasn't sure she could so much as clamber off the horse without assistance. There was no disguising her fine clothes, but ... she didn't exactly *look* like a noblewoman. She wished, suddenly, she'd had the sense to tie up her hair under the hood. It might have been better if she'd looked like a boy.

"I am Princess Silverdale, daughter of King Romulus," she said, straightening as much as she could. Even *that* tiny motion made her body howl in pain. "Take me to King Reginald at once."

The guards eyed her for a long moment, then opened the

gate. Silverdale inched the horse into the city, then allowed one of the guards to help her to the ground. Her body was so stiff she found herself leaning against him, half-convinced she'd need to ask him to carry her like a baby. She gritted her teeth as they pressed cold iron against her forehead, the cool metal helping to centre her mind. The sense of guilt grew worse as they offered her a flask of water. She sipped gratefully, trying not to scream. Her brother was not going to be pleased to see her. She'd not only defied his orders, she'd lost his wife and unborn child …

She felt her eyes start to tear up as the guards escorted her through the streets. Her legs hurt so badly she wanted a pair of crutches. She knew she had to keep moving, but … she gritted her teeth against the pain and kept going. Hundreds of soldiers ran through the streets, followed by armed civilians; thousands of refugees haunted alleyways and half-empty buildings. She could practically taste the fear in the air. She didn't dare look into the astral realm. She was too scared of what she might see.

Her mind fussed, just a little, as the guards handed her over to another set of bodyguards. Reginald's bodyguards. One of them put a hand under Silverdale's chin and lifted her face so he could see her properly, the sort of thing she would have objected to – loudly – if she hadn't been so tired. The guard recognised her, then led her into a larger room. Silverdale felt her legs weaken, again, as she saw Reginald. His eyes went wide when he saw her. It dawned on her, too late, that he must have guessed what had happened. Isabella had been with her. She would hardly have sent Silverdale on her own …

"Silverdale," Reginald said. Only someone who knew him very well would have heard the quaver in his voice. "What happened?"

"I … I have to talk to you in private," Silverdale managed. She was going to start crying. She could feel it welling up inside her. "Please."

"Clear the room," Reginald ordered, curtly. "Now."

Silverdale breathed a sigh of relief as the room emptied. Reginald stood and walked towards her, hugging her tightly. She felt the sobs finally explode, her chest heaving as she cried into his sleeve. She hadn't broken down so badly since ... since ever. She hadn't even cried so badly when their father had died.

Reginald held her, gently. "What happened?"

"I lost her," Silverdale said. "I lost your child."

She felt Reginald tense against her. "My child?"

Silverdale kicked herself. Reginald hadn't known. Of *course* he hadn't known. Isabella herself hadn't known until a few days ago. He hadn't known his wife was pregnant or he wouldn't have let her go into danger ... Silverdale winced. A shouting match between a king and a sorceress was bound to end badly, but at least Isabella would have remained free ... she refused to believe Isabella was dead. The entities wouldn't kill her.

Reginald's grip tightened. "I think you'd better start from the beginning."

"I'll try," Silverdale said. What *was* the beginning? What came first. "We killed an entity ..."

She outlined everything that had happened, from the death of the entity to Isabella's discovery that she was pregnant, from the departure from Frigg to Isabella's fall. Reginald listened, his arms tightening as Silverdale described her flight. His wife being pregnant should be good news – it *was* good news – but now his wife was in enemy hands. And if the entities caught her, they'd know she was pregnant. Isabella wouldn't be able to hide it.

"And I followed the road here," she finished. "I ... I'm sorry."

"So you should be," Reginald snarled. The anger in his voice would have terrified her, if she hadn't been able to hear the worry and fear underlying it. "They're invading and they have my wife and ..."

He let go of Silverdale and started to pace the room. "I need to send you back, but I dare not," he said. "The roads aren't safe."

"They don't care about me," Silverdale said. She thought that was true. Sofia and Emetine might have cared about her, but they were both dead and gone. Probably. Nothing was ever truly certain when the entities were involved. "I can go ..."

"They shouldn't have cared about Isabella either," Reginald said. He glared down at the map on the table.

"They really shouldn't have …"

He shook his head. "She was the one who trapped two entities," he added. "If there's any of us they know and hate personally, it's her."

"She killed an entity," Silverdale said. "I felt it die."

Reginald sat down, hard. "And now they have her," he said. "What do you think they'll *do* to her?"

Silverdale hoped it was a rhetorical question. She'd heard horror stories of what happened to commoners who challenged their betters. The list of punishments seemed excessive – she thought the victim would be dead before the executioners had even finished the first item on the list – but horrible. They were meant to deter, she'd been told; they were meant to convince would-be rebels not to even *think* about it. The entities wouldn't take the death of one of their own lightly. They'd push back as hard as they could.

"I don't know," she said. There were just too many possibilities. They could drag Isabella into the Godly Realm and do *anything* to her. Anything, anything at all. "But I don't think they'll kill her immediately …"

Reginald glared at her. "And how do you know they won't?"

Silverdale shivered at the hopelessness in his gaze. "I …"

"Thought not." Reginald stood and rang the bell. "You need a long soak and a rest. I have to deal with the enemy army. Somehow."

"I'm sorry." Silverdale lowered her eyes. "Reginald …"

"Save it," Reginald ordered. "We'll discuss it later. If there is a later."

I can try to find her through the astral plane, Silverdale thought. *I do have a link to her …*

She stopped herself before she could say that out loud. Reginald would say no. He'd tell her, in no uncertain terms, that she wasn't to even *think* of risking herself like that. He'd tell her … she dismissed the thought of asking him anyway. She'd do it first, then tell him what she'd done. If it worked, it worked. If not … at least she'd have tried. She could put up with her brother's displeasure. It would be a small price to pay for saving her sister-in-law and her unborn child.

The door opened. A young woman, little older than Ruby, stepped into the room and dropped a curtsey. Silverdale almost smiled. The young woman was so unpractised it was absurdly clear she wasn't a trained maid. Her clothing marked her as middle class, if not upper class. Maybe not a born aristocrat, Silverdale decided, but certainly someone who aspired to greater things. She studied the woman with some interest. Such a person could be useful.

"Your Majesty." The girl fell to one knee. "How may I serve you?"

"This is my sister." Reginald indicated Silverdale. "Take her somewhere comfortable, get her a bath and something to eat, then let her rest. She needs it."

The girl bowed her head. "Yes, My Liege."

Silverdale stood and allowed the girl to lead her out of the room. Her stomach growled, reminding her it had been *hours* since she'd eaten something – anything. She'd eat, she'd wash and then she'd allow her mind to slip back onto the astral plane. And once she'd found Isabella …

She wasn't sure what she'd do then. But at least she had the *start* of a plan.

***

Reginald remained standing until the door was firmly closed, then sank into a seat and covered his eyes. His wife was captive. His wife … he swallowed, hard. It wasn't the first time Isabella had been taken prisoner – Sofia had managed to capture both of them, a few short months ago – but this time she was alone. No, she wasn't alone. She had a baby growing in her womb.

The thought tore at him. He'd hoped for a child. He'd prayed for a child … in hindsight, he wondered who or what might have been listening. He'd done everything in his power to ensure a child and now … the unborn child was a prisoner. His *wife* was a prisoner. He cursed under his breath, biting down on the rage that threatened to overwhelm him. He should have ordered Isabella to stay in Havelock. He should have ordered her to do her wifely duty and obey her husband. She wouldn't have listened or obeyed, part of his mind pointed out sarcastically, but …

His thoughts ran in circles. He was going to be a father. He was going to have a child. And that child was a prisoner. His wife was a prisoner. His wife … he recalled his father's lectures with a shudder, remembering the grim warnings of what could happen to a royal bride if she fell into the wrong hands. She could be raped, she could be impregnated ... the rumours alone could shatter a life beyond any hope of repair, even if nothing actually happened. Reginald had grown up in a royal court. He *knew* there was always *someone* willing to tell the most horrible lies, if it meant gaining a tiny morsel of influence. There would always be a question mark over the legitimacy of a royal child, if the queen fell into enemy hands.

You might have to acknowledge the child, even if it isn't yours, his father had said. *Or you might have to send your queen away.*

Reginald put the thought out of his head, savagely. There were spells to prove paternity. Isabella could cast them and ... he snorted as the thought mocked him. No one would trust the word of someone who had strong, indeed unimpeachable, motives to lie. She'd have to be insane, by the standards of the court, to tell the truth ... if, of course, the truth was that the child *was* a bastard. He knew better, but would they?

And she might be trapped within the Godly Realm, he thought. *What can they do to her there? What can they* not *do to her?*

He wanted to draw his sword and lead his men on a rescue mission. Every instinct demanded that he set out at once to recover his wife. But kingship demanded that he stayed in the city and did his duty. His father had talked about the price of kingship often enough, telling Reginald and his sisters that they had to make sacrifices to pay for their royal status. Reginald had known, even if he didn't want to admit it, that his sisters would pay the highest price. He'd never thought *he* might have to pay, too.

Not like this, he thought. He wanted to go to his wife. But duty told him he had to stay. *Damn it!*

Reginald stood, centring himself as best he could. The fear for his wife – and his unborn child – nagged at him, but he ignored it. He *had* to ignore it. There was nothing else he could do. Isabella was resourceful, perhaps the most resourceful person he'd ever met. She might escape or ... he shuddered. They might simply kill her out of hand. She'd killed one of them, after all …

He rang the bell for a messenger. "Tell the council to come back," he ordered. "And bring strong coffee."

"Yes, Your Majesty."

Reginald circled the table, never taking his eyes off the map. His councillors would have heard rumours, but … Reginald sighed. A royal princess arriving alone, looking like someone who'd been through hell? They'd be rumours. Of course there'd be rumours. Some of them might even be close to the truth.

"The enemy had troops operating in our rear," Reginald said. Silverdale's description of the dark riders had made them sound like Red Monks. Cold iron would kill them, but little else would even *touch* them. And yet … Colonel Jackstay's men had been armed with cold iron. They should have been able to put up a better fight before being overwhelmed. "We can no longer assume our supply lines will remain secure."

He briefly outlined what had happened, then went on before they could offer more than a handful of condolences. "Stuart, I need you to depart this afternoon … within the hour, if possible. Take a company with you and be ready to run, if necessary. You're in charge of readying troops to return."

"Your Majesty, I should stay," Stuart said. "You'll need me here."

"I need you more in Havelock," Reginald said. Stuart enjoyed his trust. He was a skilled commanding officer, experienced enough to pick subordinates who knew what they were doing, with enough aristocracy in his bloodline to convince the rest of the aristocracy to listen to him. "We'll hopefully link up when the enemy army is defeated."

"Yes, Your Majesty," Stuart said. He didn't sound pleased, but Reginald trusted him to do his job or die trying. "I won't let you down."

Reginald touched the map. The information was probably already out of date, unless the enemy had decided to take a break while he interrogated his sister, but the general thrust was clear. Barr was going to be attacked – or surrounded – within hours. And that meant they had to be ready.

"I want the refugees organised, quickly," he said. They

really *hadn't* had time for a proper survey. The refugees might be harmless ... or deadly. "Military-aged men are to be put to work on the defences. Their dependents are to be given shelter within the city. Those who are useless, from a military point of view, are to be ordered to head west or go into hiding. They can stay out of sight until the war is over."

Or they die, he thought. He felt another twinge of guilt. His orders were quite reasonable, from a military point of view, but there was no avoiding the simple fact that most of the refugees were about to die. *There's nothing we can do about it.*

He pushed the guilt out of his mind. "I want the city under strict martial law, as planned. Guards on all the food warehouses. Mandatory death sentences for looting or any other criminality, including illicit worship. The mayor and the city fathers will support us or be put in irons for the duration. We are *not* going to let them get their claws into the city. Is that clear?"

"Yes, Your Majesty," Gars said. He sounded confident. "And the defences?"

"We'll hold the walls as long as possible," Reginald said. They knew as well as he did what would happen if the enemy broke the walls, then thrust into the city. It wouldn't be easy to push them back out in a normal war. There was nothing normal about *this* war. "And we can let them batter themselves to death against our defences."

He felt his heart twist as he issued his final orders, then dismissed them. The first week would be relatively easy, as long as the enemy didn't try to storm the city, but afterwards ... starvation would *really* begin to bite. And the locals would be terrified of what would happen when the enemy army took the city after it refused to surrender. They might open the gates themselves, allowing the entities to flood inside. He grimaced at the thought. The bastards just didn't play fair. The merest chink in the defences would be enough to let them take the city.

And they have my wife, he thought. *What the hell are they going to do with her?*

Chapter Twenty-Six

She was … alone.

Isabella came back to awareness slowly, feeling oddly disconnected from the world around her. She could see nothing, hear nothing … there *was* nothing. She wasn't even sure she was alive. The silence enveloped her like a living thing. Her thoughts ran in circles. Was she dead? Was this one of the antechambers of the lands of the dead? Or … she felt a flash of suspicion as her thoughts started to clear. There were spells designed to plunge the victim into a world of sensory deprivation, a world of utter silence. She'd been taught to use them – she'd been forced to experience them – as part of her training. They were nothing short of torture …

If more subtle than hitting or cursing someone until they talk, she thought. She'd seen strong men break, after an hour or two of being deprived of their senses. It was a thousand times worse than merely being blinded. There was no input at all. She wasn't even aware of her own body. *They took me prisoner and … what?*

She reviewed her memories. The dark riders had surrounded her and … there was a blank. She'd fought. She *thought* she'd fought. And then … nothing. She tried to think, working her way through her memories in hopes of teasing loose something she'd been charmed to forget. Or merely repressed. She didn't *think* the entities could use memory charms, not the way she'd been taught, but they had their own magics. They could probably make her forget everything, if they wished …

Understanding struck. *I'm in the Godly Realm.*

The silence seemed to break and vanish, as if it had never truly been. Isabella groaned as a wave of sensations – aches and pains and a strange lassitude that bothered her on a very primal level – cascaded into her mind. Her eyes opened … no, they *were* open. She was kneeling on the ground, stark naked, wrapped in enough chains to tie down a dragon. She almost laughed at the sheer absurdity of the scene. What did they think she was? There were old tales of men who could shift into dragons – or the other way around – but none of them were real. They were just stories … her blood ran cold. The Old Gods had been stories, too.

She looked up. She was wrapped in darkness, but … she could feel *something* out there. The darkness was a living thing, pulsing with life … strange alien life. Her senses reached out and recoiled, as if she'd pressed her hand into a fire. The realm was so *different*, she realised as pain stabbed her mind, that she just couldn't comprehend what she saw. Her perceptions were very limited. And yet …

Her eyes narrowed as she sensed … *threads* ... of light and life passing through the realm and going … going where? Visions beyond her ken flashed in front of her as she tried to follow the threads, driving her back. Impressions of power and majesty that were more than merely human crossed her mind, each one a grim reminder that she was trapped. She couldn't escape her chains, let alone navigate the realm. There was no way out. Despair yammered at her mind as she remembered the child, the child in her womb. The child was trapped, too.

Silverdale will have made it out, Isabella told herself. The dark riders had surrounded her. The princess *should* have been able to get away. Or so she hoped. The dark riders hadn't shown any sign of being slowed down, even for a moment. They could have captured Isabella and then run Silverdale down with ease. *She will have gotten out and* ...

She shook her head, mentally. It didn't matter. She was trapped. She was a prisoner. Her eyes wandered over the chains, realising – for the first time – that there were no obvious weaknesses. She'd been taught how to pick locks and dispel charms, but here … she couldn't even see where to begin. The despair grew stronger as she tried to twist, to see what was behind her. She could hardly move. The last time she'd been a prisoner, she'd been able to work out how to manipulate the Godly Realm and use it to escape. This time … she was so weighted down with chains she could barely move.

The darkness pulsed, twisting. Isabella closed her eyes, just for a second. When she opened them … a man stood in front of her. Her perspective twisted, again. The man was now towering over her. He was hundreds of miles tall, larger than life … impossibly larger than life. She had the impression of great stratas of power plunging up or down or … moving, yet again, in directions she couldn't comprehend. She felt small, impossibly so, as the figure looked down at her. In her youth, during her training, she had been shrunk, or turned into a frog, and yet she'd never felt so miniscule. She was a tiny piece of lint under the gaze of a giant, a giant who stood so tall she couldn't make out his face …

It's not real, she told herself, sharply. *It's how it wants to project itself to me.*

She concentrated, refusing to allow herself to be intimidated. The entity didn't shrink, she thought, but it looked … more comprehensible. A shudder ran through her as she realised it looked like her father, right down to the forbidding stare and cold eyes that meant she was about to be punished. Again. It was for her own good, he'd said time and time again, as he'd drawn his wand or unbuckled his belt. She knew he'd believed it. It hadn't made it any easier to take.

"You're not my father," she said. "You're just … *you*."

The air seemed to grow warmer around her as the entity stared down at her. "I am the father of all."

"You're not *my* father," Isabella repeated. The entity's features grew vaguer. It – he – still looked stern and patriarchal, but no longer so much like *her* father. "You're just … a reflection of humanity's dreams and nightmares."

She felt a sudden stab of sympathy as she remembered what she'd been told. The gods had been shaped by human thoughts and desires. They wielded vast power, yet … they were shaped by their human worshippers. The entity in front of her was a representation of humanity's desire for father-figures, for a decent yet stern man who'd prepare his kids for adulthood and then let them go. Isabella *knew* it wasn't real and yet she felt the call. She'd always wanted a better father. The entity held out the promise of everything she'd ever wanted.

And it will end in tears, she thought. *The dream will turn into a nightmare.*

"You murdered one of my children," the entity said. "Why should I not kill you?"

Isabella had to fight to keep from kneeling at his feet and begging for forgiveness. The authority, the unquestioned and unquestionable, authority in his voice was overwhelming. It was easy to think she should bend the knee willingly, to take whatever came her way in the certain knowledge that – when she'd paid for her crime – it would end. Her legs wobbled. The chains no longer seemed so solid. They weren't quite real.

None of this is real, she reminded herself. *The creature in front of me isn't real either.*

She kept her eyes on his stern chin. She couldn't meet *his* eyes. "He killed thousands of my people," she said. "He was a murderer ..."

"They chose to follow him, or to stand against him," the entity said. "They made their choice."

"It wasn't a fair choice," Isabella said, angrily. The anger let her look *past* the entity and study the complex threads binding the creature to its worshippers. It was a puppet ... the entity and its worshippers were *both* puppets. But who was pulling the strings? Which one of them was really in charge? "They thought they were following a god."

"We are your gods," the entity said. "And you banished us."

Not me personally, Isabella thought. The entities stood outside time and space. Both were one in the Godly Realm. It was quite possible the entity didn't *know* thousands of years had gone by in the human world. There was a difference between knowing something and believing it. *And you haven't even told me your name.*

The thought encouraged her. She'd learnt the name of two entities ... and she'd captured and bound them both. The entity in front of her, the father of all, might fear her ... the thought seemed absurd, given that it could do *anything* to her, but ... could it? She hadn't opened her heart to the entities, let alone bent the knee. There were limits to what it could do to her ... directly. It could certainly do things that might kill her *indirectly*.

"You're not gods," Isabella said. She'd grown up believing that magicians were superior to powerless non-magicians, but ten years as a mercenary had knocked that out of her. The entities were no better. "You're just … powerful creatures."

The entity loomed over her. "It is childishly petty to refuse to accept that you will never reach our level, let alone surpass us."

"I will never be like you," Isabella agreed. She had the oddest feeling they were talking about two separate things. "But I don't think your sheer power makes you superior."

"You believe your *magic* makes you superior," the entity charged. "You still do."

Isabella blinked. She'd remembered that … she gritted her teeth, shielding her thoughts as best she could. The entity might be reading her mind or … she was in the Godly Realm. Her thoughts were clearly capable of influencing the environment, at least to some degree. Why else would the entity look like her *real* father? And that meant … she swallowed hard. The implications were terrifying.

"I did, when I was a girl," she conceded. There was no point in trying to deny it. "I have learnt hard lessons since."

"You still consider yourself to be superior," the entity said. "You have married into royalty, yet you refuse to accept the obligations. You have been given power, yet you refuse to take steps to maintain it. You have joined a new family, yet you refuse to honour its values. You consider yourself to be morally superior to the courtiers, male or female alike, and look down on them for playing the game. You refuse to accept that the rules are not the same for them. You refuse to believe that they cannot tip over the gameboard and leave."

Isabella said nothing, but her thoughts were churning. The entity had a point. She wasn't royalty. No, she hadn't been *raised* as royalty. She'd had obligations, but none of them had been as serious as the ones looming over Sofia and her younger sisters … and she'd been free to leave, too, when she'd grown up. The ladies of the court were pathetic, yet … what choice did they have? They had no real power. And the courtiers on the council weren't much better. As long as Reginald controlled the army, he'd be able to crush them like bugs. They had to play the game or risk losing everything.

But she … she had magic. She could impose her will on everyone. Or she could simply leave. Again. Why not?

She'd done it before.

"True," she said. The entity had probably spent years manipulating humans. It knew what buttons to push. And it could probably see her entire life from the Godly Realm. "But what else can I do?"

She rolled her eyes, something that had always annoyed her father. "Let them talk down to me, because they think I am a weak and feeble woman? Or simply someone who derives her power from her husband? Why do I have to put up with them?"

"You don't," the entity said. It looked displeased. "But you have to pay the price for *refusing* to put up with them."

Isabella snorted. "I didn't come here for a counselling session," she said, deliberately mispronouncing the word to sound like consoling. "Let me go."

The entity peered down at her. "Release my child."

"No," Isabella said. Mother Lembu. It had to mean Mother Lembu. "She lied to me."

"She never lied to you," the entity said. "She told you the price. You merely refused to pay."

"She wanted me to open my heart to her," Isabella said. She remembered how Mother Lembu had waited until she was at her most vulnerable, before making the offer. "What would I have become if I'd *agreed*?"

The entity leaned closer. "Release her."

Isabella felt a hot flash of anger. "She's not your child. She's not human. *You're* not human. Your whole pantheon is shaped by human thoughts and feelings. You aren't even real!"

"We are as real as you can possibly imagine," the entity said. The confidence in its voice was terrifying. "And you have welcomed us into your world."

Isabella felt her awareness widen, suddenly. The Godly Realm was infinitely huge, so big it seemed endless, and yet so small it was nothing more than a tiny point of light. And ... it was touching the human world. She had the impression of two soap bubbles meeting and merging, slowly, into one. Her head ached as the images pummelled her brain, as she realised the Godly Realm was absorbing the human world. The entire *planet* was about to fall into the Godly Realm. No, the two universes were about to become one. The scale was so big …

She whimpered, realising the true scale of the disaster. The entities had created their servant and sent him to take the entire world, to become the next emperor. The lands he invaded would be dragged into the Godly Realm, providing the manpower for the next set of invasions and the next … she recoiled in shock, her mind crashing back into her body. How did one fight something like *that*? They'd thought they'd bested the entities, back on the Summer Isle, but they hadn't even scratched the surface. The entities were winning.

Despondency overwhelmed her. The entities offered … *everything*. Humans prayed for food and drink, for love and happiness and … and everything. The entities fed on the worship, rewarding their worshippers with … with everything they wanted. And … she saw the entity in front of her, saw how it was shaped by the worshippers. It was more than just a parasite, she realised numbly. It was a parasite that actually helped its host. *Maybe it wouldn't be so bad,* she thought. Maybe they could learn to live with the entities. Maybe they could come to terms …

She bit her lip, hard. The entities would destroy everything that made the human race … the human race. They'd answer prayers and grant wishes and … the laws of reality itself would start to break down. Hard. They were already breaking down. She had a sudden impression of the entire human race feeding the parasites, being steadily drained until there was nothing left … of holy wars, waged between theocracies competing for the souls of worshippers. It could not be borne. And yet … the question hung in her mind. How did one fight something like that?

The entity seemed to read her mind. "Your people want us," it said. "Why not surrender to the inevitable?"

"We all die, in the end," Isabella growled. She'd known *that* from a very early age. "That doesn't mean we should just cut our own throats."

She kept her thoughts under tight control. The entities had been banished before, but now … the empire was gone. There was no authority that could tell them to go. Worse … Reginald had been right. People *would* pray for help, offering their worship to the parasites. They would … and, with each prayer, they'd tilt the world further and further away from the light and into darkness. No, into the Godly Realm. She could practically *feel* it spreading across the land. It was just a matter of time until the entities won.

That's what they want you to think, she thought, savagely. There was a way to win. There *had* to be a way to win. *They want us to think there's no hope ...*

"It matters not," the entity told her. "Your kingdom will fall. Your people will pledge themselves to us. My child will be freed. And you will spend the rest of eternity in this hell."

It didn't walk away. But it seemed to recede into the distance and vanish.

Isabella scowled as the darkness closed in again. The Godly Realm was pressing down on her, yet ... she thought she could touch the fabric of reality itself. The Godly Realm's reality. Her body ached, but ... she felt her scowl deepen as she started to work out what had really happened. Her mind had been yanked out of her body and imprisoned within the Godly Realm. She thought she could hear voices on the other side ... on the other side of what?

They have my body prisoner, too, she thought. The chains weren't real. They couldn't be real. They were just a representation of something holding her down. *And I have to get back to it.*

She composed her mind. Time wasn't on her side. She had to get out before it was too late and ... and what? She wasn't sure what she could do, when she did get out. The threat was impossibly large. There was no way she could fight something threatening to swallow the entire world ...

That's what they want you to think, she reminded herself, once again. *They're not gods. Not really. They're just ... entities.*

Chapter Twenty-Seven

"Your ... ah ... Your Highness," Savona managed. "What happened to you?"

Silverdale resisted the urge to make a cutting remark as she finished stripping, cast a spell to warm the ice-cold water and clambered into the tub. Savona – the mayor's daughter – was too old to be a friend, too old to realise that Silverdale wasn't a child any longer. She seemed torn between a belief that her age made her superior and a grim awareness that Silverdale *was* a princess and thus Savona's social superior. It didn't help, Silverdale thought, that Savona came across as dumb. Like most girls in her position, she was wary of appearing too smart.

"I rode for hours without stopping," she said, finally. "It left a mark."

She gazed down at herself as the warmth started to soak into her body. She didn't really blame Savona for being shocked. She looked as if she'd been beaten from head to toe. Her legs were black and blue, there were nasty red marks on her chest and arms ... she tried to imagine what could do *that* to someone and drew a blank. She'd ached before, after riding, but this was worse. Far worse.

"I can bring you more water, Your Highness," Savona said. "Or towels ..."

"Towels and food would be fine," Silverdale said. She wanted to be left alone, not mothered by someone who clearly resented the job. "And then you can go back to my brother."

Savona looked irked, but turned and left without comment. Silverdale wondered what was going on, then shrugged. It wasn't *her* problem. Savona's father probably thought his daughter could get a cushy post at court, if she danced attendance on the king and his younger sister. Silverdale doubted Savona would be happy, if she did. She'd move from being a big fish in a little pond to a tiny fish in a *massive* pond. Lake, more like. She'd be amongst the lowest-ranked girls at court, only a step or two above a servant. And she'd be treated as a servant, too.

Silverdale put the thought out of her mind as she relaxed into the water. The warmth soothed her aches and pains, but did nothing for the throbbing in her heart. She'd lost Isabella and her unborn child ... Isabella would be furious Silverdale had told Reginald about the pregnancy, yet Silverdale would have happily endured Isabella's displeasure if it meant she was safe and well. Silverdale's heart clenched. There were just too many things that could happen to Isabella, each worse than the last. She had to find Isabella before it was too late.

Savona returned, carrying a towel in one hand and a small tray of food in the other. Silverdale stood, dried herself with the too-small towel and stepped out of the tub. Savona showed no desire to stay, as she passed Silverdale a gown, but also no inclination to leave immediately. Silverdale felt a hot flash of irritation as the girl stood there. She sat down, then slipped – briefly – into the astral plane. Savona was a blaze of conflicting emotions. Silverdale's astral form brushed her ears and told her to go home. She fell back into her body just in time to see the door closing behind Savona.

She really must have wanted to go, Silverdale thought. Isabella would be furious if she found out about that – too – but Silverdale didn't care. *I guess she wants to be elsewhere.*

The thought nagged at her mind as she finished the food – a very basic dish she didn't recognise – then lay on the bed. It felt harder than the mattresses back home, but she found it difficult to care. She composed her mind, telling herself she didn't need potion to slip into the astral plane. She'd done it already, without thinking. Her mind bobbled loose, leaving her body to sleep. Silverdale drifted up and through the walls ...

... And winced as she sensed a presence approaching the city. It felt like a blinding light. She shielded her eyes with a ghostly hand, but it wasn't enough. The light seemed to stab into her very soul. It was roughly humanoid ... weirdly, it reminded her of herself. She puzzled over it as she looked away. The entity looked *nothing* like her and yet she couldn't shed the thought.

She drifted over the city, her mind brushing against the hopes and fears of the population below. They were terrified, all too aware that an enemy army was bearing down on the city. Barr had been peaceful for the last six years, but now ... Silverdale sensed grim resolution from some, mingled with fear and a reluctance to fight if there was any other choice. She shivered as she realised there were cultists already within the city. It was hard to locate them, but she knew they were there. Reginald would have to be warned.

Not yet, she told herself. *Find Isabella.*

Her mind expanded, slightly, as she looked down at herself. The link to Isabella was faint, but it was there. She told herself that meant her sister-in-law was still alive. It had to ... she followed the link, trying to ignore the gnawing fear in her bones as her mind wandered further and further from her body. If she lost her link, if she lost her way ... she wondered, suddenly, what would happen to her body without her mind. She smiled, feeling a flicker of dark humour. Some people would probably say it was a great improvement.

The link twisted around her. She was in darkness ... a darkened room. Her astral senses had problems grasping what she was seeing. Clever, she acknowledged sourly. The dark riders and their masters knew they couldn't put Isabella in an iron box, not one that would keep prying eyes from looking for her, so what did they do? They turned out the lights! She would have been more impressed if she hadn't known she was running out of time. The darkness was still dark, yet ... she concentrated, trying to see in the gloom. It wasn't dark outside, was it ...?

Isabella's body brushed against hers. Silverdale sensed the baby, but ... she didn't sense Isabella. Her earlier thoughts came back to haunt her. Where was Isabella's mind? She probed the body, trying to ignore the disconcerting sensations from the unborn baby as she looked for the link. There *had* to be a link ... something snapped and snarled at her, razor-sharp claws tearing at her soul. Silverdale screamed as the pain burned through her, then remembered she had no physical form. She dragged herself back, realising – grimly – that Isabella's mind was locked up and guarded. She had no idea how to get it out.

She rose up, allowing herself to pass through the ceiling

and look around. Night was falling. Dark was crawling over the land, the shadows bringing nightmares. Silverdale could still see the pulse of light in the distance, the humanoid form ... she shuddered, afraid to look too closely. It was like staring into the sun.

Her body jerked back to life as she followed the link and crashed into the human world. She gasped for breath as she sat up, trying to organise her thoughts. Isabella was alive, but where? She hadn't seen any landmarks nearby, certainly none she recognised. She promised herself, if she survived long enough to reach her next birthday, that she wouldn't let anyone lock her up again. If she'd known more of the country, she might have been able to lead a rescue party right to Isabella ...

Reginald will have to be told, Silverdale thought. Her brother was not going to be pleased, but ... hopefully, he'd *listen* to her. *And then we can figure out how to get Isabella back.*

***

Savona was still fuming, an hour later, as she slipped through the darkened streets and up to the rented house. No one took her seriously, no one. She might be the mayor's daughter, yet ... she clenched her fist in rage. First, she'd been expected to flirt with the king – never mind he was married to an actual *sorceress* – and then she'd been ordered to play servant to a little brat who'd been stupid enough to ride for hours ... resentment burned within her as she glanced up and down the street, then tapped on the door. The little brat had been laughing at her. Savona knew she'd been laughing at her. But she'd stop laughing soon enough.

"You're late," a hooded figure said.

"I got delayed at the hall," Savona said, as she followed him further into the house. The rest of the circle was already forming, a cluster of upper-class boys and girls who wanted something *more* for themselves. She knew half of them personally ... the other half, she was all too aware, weren't the sort of people she was *supposed* to know. Her father would have a heart attack if he knew what she'd done with them. "The little princess has arrived."

"Good," the figure said. She knew little about him, beyond

the fact he'd clearly tapped into a source of power and was willing to share. "Are you ready to make contact?"

Savona felt her heart starting to thump in her chest. They'd touched power – they'd touched a *lot* of power – but they hadn't been able to use it. Not until now. They would become creatures of light and magic, they'd been promised; they would be granted power beyond imagination and the writ to use it as they pleased. Savona smiled as she started to undress, clothes pooling on the floor. The others followed suit, as if they were guided by an unseen will. She felt her smile grow wider as she saw the naked men. Her father would have *two* heart attacks if he knew what she was doing. It was so delightfully transgressive. *That* was part of the fun.

And Father spends all of his time begging for scraps of power, Savona thought. She didn't hate her father, not in any real sense, but she hated the way he crawled for power. *Won't he be surprised to see me?*

She smiled, again. She'd always hated the rules. Breaking them meant nothing to her. She'd kissed boys and girls, she'd eaten forbidden foods and drank herself senseless … she didn't care what her parents thought. The rules never worked in her favour. After midnight, she wouldn't have to worry about them again. She'd be the one *making* the rules. Her parents could do what *she* said for once. Perhaps she'd even keep the princess as a slave. It would do her good to clean floors with her bare hands …

The circle formed automatically. Savona knelt and joined hands with the boys on either side of her. There was a hint of power already in the air, tempting her … calling her onwards. The boys didn't so much as look at her, even though she was naked. They'd moved beyond human lusts when they'd formed the circle. Savona herself barely noticed *their* nakedness. Her mind was elsewhere.

"We begin," the hooded figure said. He stepped into the centre of the circle. "We call …"

The group started to chant, their voices blending together into a single note. Savona felt it rising through the air, reaching out … *somewhere*. She felt as if she were on the cusp of true greatness, the power kissing her lightly as it flowed through them. The sound grew louder and louder, carrying her on. She knew she was doing something forbidden, that she'd be in real trouble if she were caught, but she didn't care. Her eyelids grew heavy and closed as the chanting reached a crescendo. Something was looking back at them. Something …

Her eyes snapped open. The hooded figure was nothing more than a shadow. No, a gaping emptiness. Something was coming towards them. No, something was already there. The shadows reached for them, tendrils of ice plunging into their souls. Savona felt liquid at the corner of her eyes and *knew* it was blood. She wanted to pull away, she wanted to escape, but the boys held her tightly. She couldn't break the circle … she heard a voice, whispering, at the very back of her mind. She knew, on a level she couldn't hope to defy, that she'd made a terrible mistake. That they'd *all* made a terrible mistake.

Savona opened her mouth to scream. But it was far too late.

***

Sergeant Theodore Ashworth kept a wary eye on the troopers as he led them down the road. It was never easy, preparing a city for the siege. The arrival of the enemy army had concentrated a few minds … unfortunately, as one of his superiors had jibed, it had started concentrating minds on the best way to surrender. Theodore had no doubt the city fathers were already considering ways to offer their fealty to the invading army, just to spare their population the rigours of a siege or a sack. He didn't blame them, but he knew what was at stake. They couldn't afford to give the entities a legitimate claim to the city.

He scowled as they passed a row of darkened houses. Soldiers, particularly raw or ill-trained recruits, couldn't be trusted with civilians. He would almost have preferred to be back with Sir Alaric and his men. If one of the soldiers decided to have a little fun, Theodore would have to do something and *that* could get nasty. The patrol might think he was nothing more than a spoilsport and turn on him … Theodore winced, silently relieved the streets were largely deserted. There'd be no chance for a dispute that could turn into something *really* bad.

Most people are smart enough to stay inside, Theodore

thought, morbidly. The king had announced a curfew, but there was always *someone* who didn't get the word. Anyone who admired the seamless efficiency of the army had never been a soldier. *And those who aren't are lying very low indeed.*

A chill ran down his spine, despite the warm summer night, as they turned the corner onto a residential street. The houses were made of grey stone, yet they cost more than he'd made in his entire career. They didn't look very big, he reflected, but they were close enough to the centre of town to allow easy access to city hall. Barr was just like Havelock, yet ... another chill brushed against him. His hand dropped to his sword. Something was wrong. Something was *very* wrong.

His eyes swept the houses. They'd been ordered to stay out of people's homes, unless there was no other choice, but ... he drew his sword, instinctively, as a door burst open. A naked girl stepped into the darkness, illuminated by ... she was glowing. Alarm rushed through him as he raised his sword. The girl was literally glowing with her own light. He heard two of the lads gasping behind him as the naked girl kept walking towards them. She was ... she was everything he'd ever wanted. His eyes were practically glued to her breasts. She seemed to have become the centre of his universe ...

"You're not real," he managed. His mouth was very dry. "Get back ..."

She smiled. A soldier – he hadn't had the chance to learn the man's name – ran past him and kissed her, hard. Theodore shuddered as he saw *something* shimmering around him, before the man crumpled into dust. The girl smiled. Theodore thought he saw fangs. A vampire ...? His limbs felt like lead. He knew the danger – he'd seen the danger – and yet it was hard to defend himself. It was all he could do to raise his sword and drive it through her heart. The girl fell into dust. It felt, absurdly, as though he'd killed himself.

Theodore swore as three more figures – two men and a woman – stepped out of the house. The men were ... he tried not to look at their naked bodies. They were just too perfect. And yet, their eyes were dead and cold. Behind them, the house itself twisted and released a horde of monsters. Theodore could barely look at them. They were just too different. The ground shook, again. He heard people start to scream as walls tumbled and doors burst open. The entities had gotten inside the city …

He grabbed his whistle and blew it as hard as he could. The king would know something had happened. The king would know the enemy was already inside the walls. The king would know … Theodore cut down a creature as it lashed out at him, then two more as they took its place. The line of invading … *things* … seemed never-ending. Theodore had no idea what they could do to stop it, if indeed there *was* anything they could do. The creatures were just swarming in all directions, tearing through civilians and setting fire to buildings. He realised, numbly, they were trying to drive the population onto the streets. And that meant the city was probably doomed.

"Retreat," he ordered, sharply. Two of his men had fallen … he wasn't even sure *when* they'd fallen. "We have to run!"

Behind him, he heard the sound of buildings toppling and people screaming. Men, women, children … they didn't stand a chance. There was an army outside the walls, waiting. Theodore had every faith in the king, but he didn't know how they were going to make it out. The army was bottled up, hopelessly trapped. He hated the thought of running, but … he shook his head, feeling sick. There was nowhere to run *to*.

Another scream rent the air. He didn't look back.

Chapter Twenty-Eight

Reginald knew, without false modesty, that he had no talent for magic. Either kind of magic. He didn't have the power for regular human magic, like Isabella, and he didn't have the mindset to use and exploit the *other* kind of magic. And yet, he could feel the entity on the far side of the wall. It felt as if he was standing in bright sunlight, even though it was practically midnight. He couldn't *see* the entity, but he knew it was there.

He stood on the battlements, peering down at the enemy army. His bodyguards had thrown a collective fit when he'd insisted on climbing the walls, pointing out that a single archer could shoot him down in a moment. Reginald had overridden them, grudgingly agreeing to wear a cloak just to keep them from holding him back. He understood the dangers – if he died, the army might break up and scatter – but he couldn't *not* get onto the walls. He owed it to his men to take some risks.

And make a show of sharing the dangers, he thought. *Men won't follow someone they consider a coward.*

He frowned as he looked down. The enemy army was just … sitting there. Reginald was an experienced soldier. The longer the siege lasted, the greater the chance of a relief force arriving or the enemy army becoming infested with disease. It might not apply to the entities, but … he frowned. He would have expected the enemy to take advantage of its superiority and launch an attack as soon as it arrived. It was what *he* would have done and *he* would have had to reorganise his columns first. The entities didn't have that weakness.

They have cut us off quite effectively, Reginald reminded himself. The enemy had sealed the city off from the rest of the kingdom, just by surrounding the walls and placing troops on all the roads. *They may think they can just wait for us to starve.*

He gritted his teeth, trying not to think about his wife in enemy hands. Isabella might be dead … or worse. She was probably number one on the list of humans the entities wanted to kill. Hell, they could probably kill her again and again and again … he cursed under his breath. He should have ordered her to stay …

A scuffle caught his ears. He turned and peered into the city. A small figure was wrestling with two of the guards, struggling against their grip. Reginald blinked, knowing – without knowing *quite* how he knew – that it was Silverdale. His sister … he hurried to the ladder and allowed himself to slide down, landing neatly as Silverdale broke free and ran to him. Her face was pale, even in the semi-darkness. Reginald swallowed hard. Silverdale could have easily been hurt, if the guards had wanted to hurt her. She'd been damn lucky she'd been caught by his elite bodyguards.

"Dismissed," he said, quietly. "Silverdale … walk with me."

The guards fell behind them as they strode back to the wall. Silverdale's face was cloaked in shadow, but Reginald had no difficulty telling she was nervous. He felt a surge of anger – his sister should have stayed home, where she was safe – mingled with a grim awareness that nowhere was safe these days. The city itself wasn't safe. And yet … if she hadn't been with Isabella, Isabella and the unborn baby might have escaped …

"I did something … something you have to know about," Silverdale said, carefully. She sounded as if she expected to be slapped at any moment. "I went onto the astral plane."

Reginald's eyes narrowed. He'd never been on the astral plane himself, unless he counted the moment Isabella had teleported them both out of Sofia's clutches, but he knew the basics. Silverdale had put herself in danger, for … for what? He clenched his fists, helplessness bubbling up inside him. He'd lost his wife and unborn child and he might be on the verge of losing his sister to a threat he couldn't *see*. The thought tormented him. How many of his loved ones was he going to lose?

"And what happened?" It was hard to speak calmly, but – somehow – he managed. "What did you see?"

"She's still alive," Silverdale said. "But she's a prisoner."

Reginald listened to the explanation as his head churned with emotions. Isabella was alive! The baby was alive! It was good and bad, he knew all too well. She was in *their* clutches and they could do *anything* to her. And the baby ... he remembered the stories about babies vanishing from their cradles, replaced by things that weren't remotely human. They suddenly seemed very real.

"You shouldn't risk yourself like that," he said, when she'd finished. He wanted to tell her to go back to her room and stay there until it was all over and yet he knew, all too well, that he might have to order her back onto the astral plane. "I ..."

Silverdale looked up, sharply. "They're here!"

Reginald felt the ground shake under his feet. How? He felt a flash of panic as whistles blew, trumpets summoning the men to their posts. He'd done everything in his power to bar the gates, to prevent the entities from teleporting into the city ... he realised, numbly, that he must have missed something. The mayor, perhaps, or one of the city fathers. They hadn't managed to conceal their resentment at losing control of their city, no matter what they said out loud. One of them could easily have invited the entities to step into the city ...

Or maybe one of the refugees was more than he seemed, he thought, as the ground shook again. He heard the sound of breaking glass in the distance. *They performed a rite and invited the entities into the city.*

He put the thought aside, grabbing hold of Silverdale's arm and half-dragging her towards city hall. Silverdale suddenly looked weak and tired, as if she could barely stand. It was hard to believe it had only been a few short hours since Isabella had been captured and ... Reginald drove that thought out of his head, savagely. He didn't have time to worry about it. Not now. A flash of light burst over the city, turning night to day for the briefest of moments. Reginald cursed under his breath. It was hard to be sure, but the source was too close to city hall for comfort.

His bodyguards fanned out around him as they reached the building. Reginald was tempted to find the mayor's brat of a daughter and order her to take care of Silverdale, but he simply didn't have time. Instead, he hoisted his sister over his shoulder and carried her into the war room. The ordered atmosphere was gone. Messengers ran in and out of the room, shouting their messages at the senior officers and then running again before anyone could demand clarification. One of the tables had been tipped over, spilling maps and bottles of expensive alcohol on the floor. Another was covered with figures, each one meant to indicate an enemy position. Reginald sighed when he saw it. The map wasn't so much out of date as it was completely inaccurate.

"Report," he bellowed. "What's going on?"

Gars looked up from where he was consulting with two infantry officers. "Your Majesty ... the enemy is within the city," he said. "The first report puts them on Havelock Street, but they've been sighted elsewhere and ..."

Reginald glowered at the map as Gars continued. The reports might not be accurate – the first reports rarely were – but it was pretty clear the enemy was *somewhere* in the city. He'd seen the evidence himself. The ground quivered under his feet as he traced lines on the map. Where would the enemy go? How many of them were there? If they had a small force, they'd be wise to try to open the gates. But they'd already declared their presence ...

"Send out messengers, try to determine where they are," he ordered. Havelock Street ... that was too close to city hall for comfort. "And be ready to evacuate this building. We'll go to the gatehouse keep."

"Aye, Your Majesty," Gars said.

"They're coming," Silverdale said. She felt absurdly light, as if her body weighed nothing at all. "I can feel them."

Reginald gritted his teeth. The enemy might know where they were. His eyes swept the room. A pair of city fathers – doddering old fools, in his eyes – stood against the walls, but the remainder – including the mayor – were gone. Dead? Perhaps they'd been the first victims of the *things* they'd summoned into the city. Or ... he shook his head. It didn't matter. Right now, they had to get out before it was too late.

There's nowhere to run, he reminded himself. The army sitting outside the walls would keep them from abandoning the city. *We have to make our stand here.*

"Send messengers to barracks one through three," he ordered. "The troops are to seal off the district centred on

Havelock Street, then advance from all directions until the last of the enemy forces has been destroyed."

He cursed himself as the messengers hurried away. A considerable number of soldiers were about to die. There was no helping it, but ... he knew it would gnaw at him for the rest of his life. The nasty part of his mind noted that wasn't likely to be very long. He'd sooner run himself through with his own sword than surrender to the entities.

Gars caught his attention. "Sire, they're pushing up the main road," he said. His face gleamed with sweat. "They'll be on us shortly."

"Then we'd better move," Reginald said. He took one last look around the chamber, then headed for the door. There was little point in taking anything with them. "Set fires before we leave."

"Yes, Your Majesty."

Reginald made a face as he carried Silverdale out of the building. Her body was twitching, as if she was being poked and prodded – or punched – by an unseen force. Her eyes were open, but seemingly stared at nothing. Reginald wanted to pour a sleeping draught down her throat, yet ... he had the idea that would only make things worse. He drew his sword as he stepped out of the city hall, feeling the ground shake again. The flames were spreading rapidly. He thought he saw faces within the flames, evil faces. They were laughing as they danced through the fires.

Elementals, he remembered. He'd seen something similar, back on the Summer Isle. To see them here ... he shook his head. The fire creatures were far worse. Now the flames had caught, they probably didn't need permission to consume the rest of the city. *They'll burn the city to ashes and kill everyone* ...

He yanked himself back to reality as a line of ... *things* ran up the streets and hurled themselves on the small group. Reginald felt his head start to hurt as one of the creatures thrust a blade at him, a blade that reeked of evil. He silently blessed his old swordmaster for his lessons on how to fight when distracted, even though he'd hated the bastard at the time ... he stabbed his sword through a creature, then cut down the next before it could react. The cold iron still worked ... he felt *something* from the far side of the wall, a flicker of ...

The ground heaved again. The flames grew stronger, reaching up to the heavens. Reginald cursed, again, as they hurried west. The gatehouse keep was the strongest fortification in the city … in hindsight, he should have turned it into a base and to *hell* with city hall. He hadn't needed to set up shop there, just to make it clear he was in charge. And he could have clapped the city fathers in irons. *That* would have made things so much simpler.

"It's coming," Silverdale said. Her breathing came in fits and starts. "Can't you hear it?"

"No." Reginald cut another creature down, earning himself a breathing space. "What's it saying?"

"A world," Silverdale babbled. She convulsed, spittle flying from her mouth. "Two worlds will be one …"

Her voice trailed off again. Reginald had no time to think about what she meant. The flames were getting closer, a sea of fire that was reaching out towards the city hall. The building was stone, not wood, but the flames didn't seem to care. Reginald thought he heard a groan, then a giggle, as fire leapt from house to house. The city hall was wrapped in fire … he prayed, heedless of what might be listening, that the building had been abandoned in time. The fires had spread too quickly. Anyone still inside was almost certainly dead or wishing they were.

Or crying out to the entities, Reginald thought. *They might offer safety, for a price.*

"Your Majesty," Gars shouted. "This way!"

Reginald nodded and started to run.

***

"Sir!" Theodore waved as he saw an officer on horseback, leading a troop of armoured infantry. "They're coming!"

The officer cantered to a halt and slipped off the horse. "What happened?"

"They spilled out of a house," Theodore said. He gabbled out a quick explanation. "And we had to run."

He turned and shivered as he took in the scene. The flames were spreading quickly, too quickly. They weren't natural. Theodore had done fire-fighting duties before, but here … he had a feeling that even tearing down the houses in the fire's path wouldn't be enough to stop it. The flames licked from

244

house to house, burning through stone and wood as if they were nothing more than paper. He saw a handful of people running, their clothes already catching fire as they fled. It was too late. The flames enveloped them as they ran.

"Get into formation," the officer shouted. He seemed to have thrown his unit together at short notice. Theodore had no difficulty recognising the signs. Too many men who were clearly unfamiliar with the men beside them, let alone their commander. "We have to stop them …"

Theodore raised his sword as a dark creature hurled itself out of the fire. The creature was already burning, the flames flickering and dying when Theodore rammed a sword through the creature's gut. He heard an unholy giggle as the creature died, realising there were more and more of the monsters coming out of the flames. The officer was babbling something about pushing through the fires, about putting them out, but it wasn't going to happen. Theodore could feel the heat. The stone beneath his feet felt as if it was melting. His skin was already starting to crisp. He gritted his teeth. Half his unit had fled. He didn't blame them.

"Forward," the officer shouted. There was a twinge of desperation in his voice, as if he knew he was about to make a mistake and yet intended to do it anyway. "I command you …"

One of his men brought his sword – the flat of his sword – down on his commander's head. The man crumpled, hitting the ground with an audible thud. Discipline vanished a second later, men running in all directions … a couple ran into the flames. Theodore swallowed hard, then turned and scooped the officer up as he also fled. Behind him, he heard the roar growing louder. It was impossible to escape the sense the fire was *angry* it had lost its prey.

The heat seemed to grow rapidly until his body was drenched in sweat. His armour felt heavy, the iron plates threatening to overheat … he did his best to ignore it, even though he wanted to take the armour off before it was too late. The officer moaned, clearly out of his wits. Theodore was tempted to drop him, to abandon him to his fate. The officer was a complete idiot. Ordering men to certain death was asking for trouble. He should have known there was no hope of driving the invaders back to hell. Instead …

He swallowed hard as he joined a crowd of refugees heading towards the walls. They probably didn't know where they were *really* going. They probably didn't … there was an enemy army outside the walls, yet there was a firestorm inside. Barr was a big city. Smaller than Havelock, to be fair, but quite big enough. And the entities had destroyed it practically overnight. The refugees weren't the poor souls from outside the walls or the kingdom itself, not now. There were men and women and children who'd lived in the city for their entire lives, from rich to poor … united in hopelessness, now, as they watched their city burn to the ground.

Theodore cursed again, telling himself he'd probably be doing the king a favour if he cut the officer's throat. The dumb bastard didn't need another chance to get more people killed. He could … he sighed and dumped the man on the ground as he groaned again. The officer was safe, for now. He could take his chances with the rest of the refugees. If he had the sense to ask for help … from whom? The question was almost funny. There was no one who could help, save the entities themselves. And the price was too high.

The ground shook, once again. He turned, just in time to see an immense column of light reaching up towards the sky. It would have been pretty, he thought, if it hadn't been so terrifying. No, it *was* pretty. The city was bathed in a shimmering blue-white glow. It was pretty …

But it felt like the end of the world.

Chapter Twenty-Nine

Silverdale's eyes *hurt*.

The pain tore into her very soul, threatening her with madness – or worse. She wanted to look away, but she couldn't. The world flickered in and out of her awareness, flashes of the human reality contrasting with the other realm ... the Godly Realm. It was above her, it was behind her, it was in front of her ... it was everywhere. She tried to withdraw into herself, as Reginald carried her towards the gatehouse keep, but it was impossible. The Godly Realm was just too loud.

Her head pounded as she looked east. A humanoid figure stood there, beyond the walls ... the walls themselves were little more than ghostly shadows that posed no more of a barrier than the air itself. The city was being sucked into the Godly Realm ... the Godly Realm was materialising in the human world. She saw the figure looking back at her, a glowing sense of superiority colouring its thoughts. There were flashes of something else – a sense that, perhaps, things had gone too far – but they were lost in the glow. The entities were winning.

Great creatures roared and danced over the city, directing the fires. Silverdale could see them, see the ties of light and obligation that bound them to the entities. Her eyes streamed with blood as she tried to look away, but she couldn't. It was a wonder no one else could see them. They were practically *part* of the human world now. She wished, suddenly, that she'd turned down the chance to learn the new magic. She might have been spared her insights into the hidden realms ...

"The far wall is breaking," someone shouted. Silverdale could barely see him. He was a whirlwind of panic and fear. "They're coming over the wall."

Reginald shifted. Silverdale could *feel* his determination ... and fear, gnawing at his soul. Her brother was a brave man who never backed down from a fight, but how could he stand against gods and monsters? The enemy army had surrounded the city. There was no way out. She closed her eyes and peered into the other realms, trying to find a way to get them out of the city. Isabella had teleported through the Godly Realm once. But the other worlds were too bright. Merely looking at them burned her soul.

"We have to run," she said. Eyes – unseen eyes – were looking at them. The entities knew where they were. "We have to move."

"A splendid idea," Reginald said, dryly. His voice was so calm she wouldn't have known he was afraid if she hadn't been able to sense it. "Which way do we go?"

Silverdale let her mind start to wander again as her brother barked orders to his men. The army was scattered, half the troops dead or … submitted. She could sense flickers of light sparking through the realm as they pledged themselves to the entities, their determination to serve their king breaking in the face of the onslaught. Silverdale wanted to scream at them, to curse them for cowards, but she knew there was no point. They couldn't stand against creatures out of nightmares. Their will to resist was steadily being broken down. She swallowed, hard. The heat was growing stronger. It was just a matter of time before the gatehouse keep was surrounded.

They want Reginald alive, she thought, numbly. It was the only reason the entities hadn't taken or killed them already. *He's the only one who can surrender.*

She pulled back, trying to look at the world from outside. The entities were steering their realm into the human realm, as if they were trying to merge two soap bubbles together. Silverdale could barely grasp the sheer immensity of their plan. The two worlds would merge, giving the entities complete control over the human world. And they would be unstoppable …

Reginald poked her arm. "Are you still in there?"

Silverdale opened her eyes, unsure when she'd closed them. "Yeah."

"We're going to make a breakout," Reginald said. He carried her into the courtyard. A cluster of horses, whinnying nervously, were waiting for them. "You ride behind me."

Silverdale shivered, despite the heat. The breakout was doomed. She *knew* it was doomed. Reginald knew it too ... but what choice did they have? They weren't fighting a war for land or glory or ... or anything *human*. Defeat didn't mean humiliation, but the end of the world. There would be no hope of resistance, no hope of rebuilding and then returning to re-negotiate matters ... there would just be endless servitude to nightmares given shape and form. She thought she saw the entities, giant humanoids, looking down at them from their realm. They thought they'd won. It was just a matter of time.

Reginald hoisted her onto the horse, tied her to the saddle and then clambered up himself. Silverdale would have been insulted, if she hadn't been so tired. She'd been riding practically since she could *walk*. The idea of being slung over the horse like a prisoner ... she knew, deep inside, that she could barely move. Her entire body hurt. She could slip and fall and hit the ground before she even realised she had to save herself. And there would be no time to save her. Reginald would have to run, leaving her behind ... just like Isabella.

The memory reminded her of something else, something Isabella had told her. Something ... Silverdale remembered, just as the horses started cantering towards the gates. The handful of men on the gatehouse were already pulling them open, taking the risk of allowing the enemy army into the city ... not, she supposed, that it mattered. They were already inside. She reached out with her mind, skimming over the hundreds of thousands of twisted slaves to make contact with the elementals. Their touch burned her mind, but she summoned all the gritty determination she could and held on. They were unthinking creatures of fire and destruction, not gods so much as ... tools. Isabella had managed to dicker with water elementals, Silverdale recalled. She could do the same.

I don't have anything to offer them, she thought, as fire burned her mind. She tried to think of a suitable offering – a bribe, Isabella had sneered – but nothing came to mind. Or ... her hand fumbled as she reached for her bracelet. It had once belonged to her mother, the mother who'd died giving birth to her. Silverdale had always been in two minds about wearing it, but ... her father had insisted. *If they want it ...*

She threw the bracelet into the air, then concentrated. Fire exploded in front of them – the horse reared, nearly throwing both of them to the ground – as the elementals tore through the enemy army. Flames roared in both directions, setting fire to the troops and burning them to ash. Silverdale sensed laughter, terrible laughter, and a strange sense of shock. She smiled, despite the ever-growing heat. The entities were surprised. *She'd* surprised them.

"Forward," Reginald yelled.

The horse galloped forward, kicking through the hot ash and running down the darkened road. Silverdale's mind expanded again, letting her see the burning city behind her. Barr was broken, effectively gone. The flames she'd summoned were already dying. She sensed the humanoid figure advancing into the city and knew, all too well, that they hadn't managed to do more than escape. The borderlands had fallen. It was only a matter of time until the rest of the kingdom followed.

Her head spun. Silverdale, gratefully, allowed the darkness to take her.

***

Reginald felt as if he'd gone beyond shock.

He wasn't sure why the fire elementals had suddenly attacked the enemy army, giving him and his bodyguards a chance to escape. It felt like a demented mind game, one played for the sheer thrill of making him twist and turn before his final – inevitable – defeat. And yet … he glanced back at the burning city as they made their escape. His army was effectively destroyed, burned to a crisp along with the city itself. He'd failed. He'd failed so completely that he'd lost the entire kingdom, that all he'd been able to do was flee.

Guilt burned through his mind. He'd spent his entire career fighting beside his men. Even as a king, he'd wanted to be on the frontlines. He'd wanted to share the danger. But now, he'd fled like a coward. He knew he hadn't had a choice. He knew the battle had been lost before they'd even known they were fighting. Once the enemy had got within the walls, once the walls had started to fall, it was over. He knew …

He wiped sweat from his brow as they plunged into the darkness. Silverdale was behind him, out cold. Reginald almost envied her. She would wake up in safety, or she'd never wake up at all. Reginald knew he'd failed her too, just as he'd failed his wife and sisters and everyone else. The kingdom was doomed, because of his failure. He tried to tell himself that he'd rebuild, that he'd meet up with the rest of his army and lead it back to recover the city, but he knew he was lying. The entities had taken the borderlands. It was surely inevitable that they would soon take the rest.

"Sire," Captain Archdale said, as he brought his horse closer. "We can't maintain this pace."

Reginald gritted his teeth. How could Captain Archdale and his men even stand to *look* at him? How could they not think him a coward? Or ... were they grateful he'd ordered them to flee the firestorm? They'd seen the faces in the flames too. They'd known there was nothing they could do if they stayed but die bravely. And uselessly. Reginald knew *he'd* been afraid, when the fires had been burning through the city. They'd all been afraid.

"We keep going until we reach a town," Reginald said, finally. They were running the horses ragged, but they needed space and time. Other men would have escaped, he was sure. He'd ordered the trumpets to sound the retreat before making a run for it himself. They could link up and ... if they cared to try. It was far more likely that the remnants of his army would simply go home. It was what tended to happen when soldiers lost faith in their commanders. "We need some time to think."

"Aye, Sire," Archdale said. "There's a town about thirty minutes ride away."

Reginald nodded as he peered into the darkness. Ruby was supposed to be gathering an army, but ... he doubted she'd had time. Captain-General Stuart might not even have *reached* Havelock by now, let alone taken command of the recruitment. And, as word of the defeat spread, it would be harder and harder to assemble a new army. The aristocracy would sooner bend the knee to the entities than risk total defeat. Why not? Too many of them had stood on the sidelines when Sofia had ruled, rather than stand against her and her master.

The darkness seemed to grow ... darker. Despondency raged at the back of his mind, threatening to overwhelm him.

He'd lost the battle. He'd lost his wife. He might even have lost the kingdom. There were stories – of course there were stories – of kings who'd been reduced to only a handful of followers, kings who'd somehow rebuilt their armies and retaken their thrones. Reginald knew most of those stories were utter nonsense, crafted by kings to suggest they could never truly be defeated. A broken king had nothing to offer his supporters, not even protection. The idea that a true king might still rule, even if he had no power, was absurd. Everyone knew the king was the one with the power. A usurper with an army outranked a legitimate king who lacked one.

And yet, the entities may feel otherwise, he thought. He was the king, in name if – no longer – in fact. He owned the keys to the kingdom. *They need me to complete their conquest.*

It wasn't much, he reflected as they rode on. But it was all he had.

***

Theodore gritted his teeth as the woman and her brats started screaming. He'd hoped to find his way to the walls, but the fires had blocked the shortest path out of the city. There was no longer any order, as far as he could tell. The aristocratic officers were either dead or had fled. The common soldiers weren't any better. He'd come across an infantryman trying to rape the woman in front of her children, as if he was trying to get one last fuck before he died. Theodore had beheaded him on the spot, then led the woman and her family towards the walls. He was starting to think that inviting them to stay with him had been a mistake.

The fires were growing stronger, licking through the remains of the city. They were unnatural, monstrous faces flickering within the flames as they consumed buildings and people with equal abandon. Theodore wasn't even sure how they were still alive. The heat alone should have killed them by now. He kept one hand on his sword as he turned around, unsure which way they were going. He'd always had a pretty good sense of direction, but the combination of flames and smoke had defeated him. He had a nasty feeling they were walking in circles.

A shape lurched out of the fire, burning. Theodore shuddered, unsure if the burning mass was male or female, friend or enemy. It didn't matter. The figure crashed to the ground and lay still. The body was still burning. Theodore swore, inwardly, as he tried to pick a path through the flames. The road beneath his feet was starting to crack. He just couldn't keep everything straight in his mind. He'd had a vague idea that he should be able to find a tunnel under the walls – there were always tunnels, in every walled city – but the ground was shaking so badly he was morbidly sure the tunnels had collapsed. If he'd even been able to find them …

"Where do we go?" The woman caught his arm. Theodore shrugged her off, wondering why he hadn't left her to her fate. He couldn't save her and her family. He couldn't even save himself. "Where do we go …?"

"I don't know," Theodore shouted back. He picked a direction at random and led them down it. The streets were starting to fracture, smoke and fog billowing towards him. He blinked, cursing himself as he glanced back. Flames had spread across the road, blocking their line of retreat. He had the sense that something was playing games with him, an intelligence so alien that … he thought he heard a giggle as the ground shook, again. "I don't know …."

The flames cleared, just for a second. He saw the wall in front of him, blocking their way out of the city. It cracked, then crumbled to ruin. Theodore stared, so far beyond shock that it was hard to feel *anything* as the enemy army marched into the city. They were humanoid, but not human. Their legs and arms were just too long, too gangly … he raised his sword, knowing it was futile. They were trapped. He might kill one or two, but the remainder would kill him and then continue their march. A glowing light appeared from behind the remains of the walls, slowly coming into view. Theodore felt a wave of awe as a man walked into the city. He was …

Theodore stared. The man was … a *great* man. A brave warrior, a noble leader … Theodore had to bite his lip to keep from hurling himself at the man's feet and pledging his eternal loyalty. The effect was almost overwhelming. The man's presence was so strong that Theodore knew he would have run back into the fire, even if it was certain death, if the man had commanded it. His body was almost absurdly muscular, yet there was nothing absurd about it. And yet, his face was just a little indistinct. Theodore felt his blood run cold. He wasn't staring at a human. He was staring at an entity.

The troops surrounded him. Theodore dropped his sword, knowing resistance was futile. The entity held out a hand, wordlessly inviting Theodore to join him. Theodore bit his lip again, hard enough to draw blood. He'd heard the stories. He knew what happened to those who opened their hearts to the entities. And yet … the urge to just open his heart and *follow* was so incredibly strong. The woman and her kids stumbled forward and prostrated themselves in front of the entity. Theodore understood. He couldn't bring himself to feel contempt for their choice. The entity was almost irresistible.

"No," he said. His voice wobbled. He hated it. He'd pledged himself to King Reginald and yet … he could feel his resolve being tested. He bit his lip, a third time. "I won't."

The entity looked … disappointed. Theodore felt as if he'd been stabbed in the gut. As if he'd displeased a stern, but beloved father. He knew it was an illusion, he knew the emotions were fake … and yet they tore at him anyway. The entity seemed to shift, its face becoming more and more indistinct. If it had been human once, like the poor bastard who'd carried an entity to Frigg, it wasn't any longer. Theodore tried to force his legs to move, to carry him away, but he couldn't. He felt as if he was trapped in a nightmare. Something – someone – was behind him …

Something struck the back of his head. He was unconscious before he hit the ground.

Chapter Thirty

Silverdale opened her eyes.

She was lying on a blanket, in a stable. A stable …? She sat upright, feeling her body ache as she tried to move. A grim-faced woman, old enough to be her mother, was cooking something in a cauldron. Silverdale stared, slowly realising that she wasn't in a stable. She was in a house, a commoner house. The woman turned, picked up a chipped mug and held it out to her. Silverdale winced at the taste – she wasn't sure what it was – but drank it anyway. It was hard, so hard, to stand up.

"Lie still, young lady," the woman said. Her voice was so slurred Silverdale had trouble following her. "You're safe now."

Silverdale cleared her throat. Her memories were confused. She'd been in the city, the city had been burning, she'd controlled the elementals … she looked at her wrist and shivered as she realised the bracelet was gone. She'd given it away … her heart clenched as she remembered how her father had given the bracelet to her. He wouldn't be pleased she'd given it away herself … he was dead. Tears prickled at the corner of her eyes. Her father was dead.

She forced herself to sit up, somehow. Her body ached, but she ignored the twinges of pain as she swung her legs over the side of the bed. The house looked like a pigsty. The air smelled terrible, as if the commoners actually let their animals sleep with them. She put the thought out of her mind as she tried to stand on wobbly legs. Her body still hurt, as if every last inch of her had been brutally beaten, but the pain was already starting to fade. She told herself it didn't matter. Everyone who'd been left behind, in the burning city, was in a worse state.

"You really should lie still," the woman said. "You're in no state to walk."

"I have to go," Silverdale said. "Where's Reggie?"

The woman looked blank. Silverdale stared back, then kicked herself. "The king," she corrected. Of *course* a commoner wouldn't know the king by name. "Where is he?"

"He's outside, with his men," the woman said. "I don't think you should disturb him ..."

Silverdale ignored her and headed for the door. She could hear men talking outside in low voices ... soldiers, she thought. The door swung open at her touch, allowing her to step into the village. It was larger than she'd expected, but otherwise ... just another collection of hovels. She glanced at the soldiers, looking for her brother. Reginald stood beside Captain Archdale, directing a pair of horsemen to gallop west. Behind him, Silverdale could see smoke rising to the east. The city was still burning ...

Her eyes hurt, suddenly. She could see the Godly Realm ... she opened her mouth to scream, to demand to know why they were so calm when the Godly Realm was dominating the sky, then closed it again. They couldn't see the alien realm. They didn't know what was out there, staring at them. They didn't know ... Silverdale blinked, trying to banish the image from her mind. It didn't work. Once she knew it was there, she couldn't *not* know it.

"Silverdale." Reginald called her over, his voice grim. "How are you?"

Silverdale wanted to ask him the same question as he led her into a barn. Her brother looked awful. She looked down at herself and winced. Someone had changed her while she slept, removing the tattered gown and replacing it with a simple village dress, but her face was scarred and her hair was so tatty she thought she'd have to cut it off and let it regrow. Her governesses would faint dead away at the sight ... she giggled, despite everything. She'd never have to worry about the governesses ever again.

"Sore," she said, finally. She looked at the wall. It was wood, but ... translucent. She had to touch it to be sure it was there. "The Godly Realm is out there."

Reginald nodded. She thought she saw despair in his eyes. "We had over seven thousand men, a day ago," he said. "Now ... we barely have two hundred."

Silverdale shuddered. "They're dead?"

"Or wishing they were," Reginald said. He waved a hand

at the door. "We barely have enough men to harass them, when they march west. And they will."

"They'll come for us," Silverdale agreed. "Have you told Ruby?"

"Yeah." Reginald scowled. "I don't know what she can do."

"No," Silverdale agreed. Her sister was clever, but … there simply weren't many options. "I … we need Isabella."

"I know." Reginald's eyes flashed with anger – and fear. His wife, and his unborn child, were in enemy hands. "Where is she?"

"I think I can find her," Silverdale said. "Her body, at least."

Reginald studied her for a long moment. "Are you sure?"

"I think so," Silverdale said. "It's worth a try."

"Do it." Reginald sounded guilty. "Please."

Silverdale sat down. "Give me some privacy," she said. "And I'll get right on it."

"Good luck," Reginald said.

He left. Silverdale looked around, half-wishing she had a proper bed. The straw stank … she didn't know what was normally kept in the barn, but it wasn't human. She grimaced, then closed her eyes. Her body felt sore, aches and pains returning in full force. She focused, trying to direct her mind out of her body. The pain dragged her back … no, it was holding her down. She needed the potion …

You don't need the potion, she thought, savagely. She found it hard to believe … she forced herself to believe it by dint of will alone. *You just need to focus your mind.*

The Godly Realm pulsed like the sun. Silverdale winced as the barn wall seemed to snap out of existence. The Godly Realm was right on top of her, as if it was going to crush her under its weight. She had a vision of a wall tumbling down, threatening to bury her … she pushed it aside as she sought out the astral plane. The Godly Realm was twisting the astral world … she smiled, despite the sense of imminent doom. Isabella had done something similar, when she'd killed the entity …

I'll find you, Silverdale thought. She liked Isabella too much to simply let her go. And her brother loved his wife. *Whatever it takes, I'll find you.*

Turning away, she began her search.

***

Reginald tried to paste an optimistic expression on his face as he walked out of the barn, even though he was fairly sure he wasn't fooling anyone. Soldiers weren't stupid, no matter what certain aristocrats claimed, and commoners weren't stupid either. It didn't take a genius to count the number of surviving soldiers, work out how many had died and then calculate the odds of surviving when the enemy army resumed its march. Reginald would be astonished if he hadn't already lost a few dozen soldiers, men who'd crunched the numbers and decided there was no point in fighting and dying for a hopeless cause. They'd seen the entities destroy an entire city. They knew the odds were no longer in their favour.

Captain Archdale met him outside. "A troop of horsemen just arrived," he said. "They were on patrol when the enemy army cut them off from Barr."

"Good." Reginald looked past him, at the tired men and their steeds. "Give them some water and food, then order them to patrol the approaches."

"Aye, Sire," Captain Archdale said. He hesitated, just for a second. "We can't stay here."

Reginald nodded. The village – he didn't think it so much as had a name – was tiny. It couldn't hope to feed the remnants of the army, certainly not for a day or so. He'd had to seize everything the villagers had, from seed corn to a handful of pigs and sheep, but it was nowhere near enough. They could not seize food the villagers didn't have. And besides, to take every last thing these peasants owned would only anger them. Who knew what they'd do? They might even betray the remnants of the army to the entities.

Or start worshipping the entities directly, Reginald thought. He'd been unable to keep people from calling on the entities when he'd had an army at his back. Now ... he couldn't so much as *try* to stop them. *We really can't stay here*.

"My sister is trying something," he said. If Silverdale *did* find Isabella, Reginald intended to go after her. He'd done his duty. He could afford to put his wife first. Once. "After that, we'll have to fall back."

He closed his eyes, visualising the maps they'd left behind. They'd be leaving the mountains – and rocky terrain – behind, if they headed west. They could slow an invading army, by destroying bridges and using rivers as natural strongpoints, but he didn't think they could *stop* the army short of Havelock itself. And even the walled city might not be enough to stop them. The entities were tightening their grip on the human world. It would not be long until some damned fool invited them in or their armies overwhelmed the defences and took the world by force. Reginald gritted his teeth. The entities just didn't play fair. They had overwhelming advantages and knew how to use them.

And we can't even call on the other kingdoms for help, he thought. *They have their own problems.*

"We'll set up lines along the Kingston River, centred on Kingston itself," he said. The town was protected by walls, but they wouldn't be enough. If he took out the bridges, the entities would bottle the defenders inside the walls and send the rest of their troops west. "We should be able to draw them onto the bridges."

"If they can't just march through the river waters," Captain Archdale pointed out. "Or create bridges themselves."

Reginald nodded. He'd heard the stories about the Last Emperor and the feats he'd performed with magic. Purely *human* magic. The entities could raise a bridge or a dam or *anything*, given time. He had a sudden vision of him fleeing from kingdom to kingdom, utterly alone, bearing warning of the coming disaster ... a warning no one would heed until it was too late. He groaned, inwardly. If he hadn't seen the entities, he wouldn't have believed it either. They were just too ... *different.*

"We'll have to slow them down, somehow," he said. He tried not to let the despair slip into his voice. "At worst, we can try to fall back to the Summer Isle ..."

He tried not to think about it as he moved from unit to unit, sharing a few words with his men in a desperate attempt to rebuild their morale. He had precious little to offer and they knew it. The ones who'd escaped the burning city knew just how badly they'd been beaten. It was rare for an army to be destroyed so completely, wiping out thousands of men and the cadre he needed to rebuild. He wished, suddenly, that he'd had the sense to withhold his most experienced men. Ruby could have used them as the core of a new army. But he'd needed them with him ... if only he'd known!

You couldn't have known, he thought, numbly. *You really couldn't have imagined what was coming.*

He sighed, feeling the weight of the world crashing down on him. He was the *king*! He was supposed to be the first in battle and the last in retreat, he was supposed to lead his soldiers to glory and protect his people from the wolves at the door ... he'd failed. He'd failed and now thousands – tens of thousands – of his people were dead or in enemy hands. His *wife* was in enemy hands. He'd failed so completely that he wouldn't really blame his people for turning on him, for throwing him to the enemy in a bid to get better terms. In a normal war, he'd be trying to sue for peace himself. In a normal war ...

His fists clenched. He'd seen the entities. He'd seen them warp reality and create monsters and break kings and shake the very ground itself. He'd seen them move armies across entire kingdoms in the blink of an eye. And yet, he hadn't grasped just what they could do. Their powers were still expanding. What would they be able to do next? It was starting to look as though humankind was utterly outmatched.

"Reginald!"

He turned. Silverdale was stumbling out of the barn, looking ghastly. Her blue eyes were strikingly bright in a face that was almost drained of colour, her hair hung in tangled ringlets around her face. Reginald felt a flicker of concern at the visible bruises on her skin. He'd never been that battered and he'd picked fights for fun! Silverdale looked as if she'd been through hell. And yet, somehow, she kept going.

"I found her," Silverdale said. "Well ... sort of. She's over there."

She pointed north. Reginald gritted his teeth, feeling a hot flash of anger. Somewhere along a line heading north? How far north? Ten miles? Fifty miles? A hundred miles? He could calculate, roughly, how far a man could travel on horseback, but the entities could teleport. If they'd taken Isabella through the Godly Realm, they could have taken her to the other side of the world. Reginald considered it, grimly.

If they marched north … it was impossible. Isabella could be anywhere between an unnamed village and the Great Salt Ocean. Hell, she might be *on* the ocean.

"Useless," he snarled. "She could be anywhere."

Silverdale scowled back. It struck him, suddenly, just how much she resembled their father. Not in looks – lucky for her, the snide part of his mind noted – but in general bearing. Their father had been a stubborn old cuss, moving from puppet king to actual monarch with a smoothness Reginald could only admire. Their father had never let anything stand in his way, not for long. He'd always found a way to go through or around a problem.

"There's a forbidden zone north of here," she said. "That's where they've taken her."

Reginald's eyes narrowed. "And how do you know about it?"

"Isabella and I went through a list of forbidden zones," Silverdale said. "She said there was one somewhere along the borders."

"I'll have to check." Reginald had to admit it made sense … but it was worrying. Sofia had performed her ritual in a forbidden zone. What could the dark riders do with Isabella in a forbidden zone? What could they do with his unborn *child* in a forbidden zone? "If you're right …"

"I have to come with you," Silverdale said. She crossed her arms as he shook his head. "You need me."

Reginald hesitated. He could order her sent back to Kingston, if not to Havelock. He could have one of his bodyguards escort her back, tied to a horse if necessary. She'd never forgive him, even though she'd be safe. Might be safe. And yet … he didn't want to send her away. Not again. If she was right …

"Very well," he said. "You'll accompany us. And I hope you're up to it."

He turned and marched back to Captain Archdale, forcing Silverdale to hurry after him. The captain looked up and snapped to attention. Reginald wished, again, that they'd saved at least one map. The peasants wouldn't have any, he was sure. Maps had been considered state secrets, even the ones that were completely outdated. In hindsight … he kicked himself. That policy would have to be revised, if the kingdom survived. So would a great deal of other policies.

"Captain, we'll be taking a mounted troop north, once we've had something to eat," he said. "The remainder of the army is to fall back to Kingston and establish defensive lines there. They are to hold until relieved."

Or until they're driven out, his thoughts added, treacherously. *They won't be able to hold for long.*

"Aye, Sire," Captain Archdale said. "We'll be ready."

Reginald nodded and accepted a plate of roast pork from one of the camp followers. The peasants looked unconcerned, but he could see the anger and despair on their faces. Pigs were expensive, by their standards; the cows even more so. The army had practically left them destitute. Reginald silently thanked the gods – something he wasn't sure he should do, now – that the commoners had had the sense to hide their daughters. Military discipline was a joke, now the army had been shattered. It wouldn't be easy to rebuild it ...

We'll repay them, he promised himself silently, although he knew he might not be able to keep his word. If they won, they'd have too much else to do; if they lost, they'd be dead. *I'll come back and repay them.*

He raised his eyes, spotting plumes of smoke in the distance. Enemy raiders were already heading west, pushing into towns and villages and burning them to the ground. There would be more refugees, more frightened and desperate people willing to open their hearts to the entities and invite them in. And, with each conversion, the process would continue to snowball until it was unstoppable. It might already be unstoppable ...

Don't think of it as unstoppable, he told himself, sharply. His father had taught him, time and time again, that he was not truly beaten until he gave up. Reginald had thought that was nonsense, but he understood it now. *That's one step closer to total defeat.*

"It's time," he said. He was tempted to order Silverdale to ride behind him, again, but she was a good rider. Besides, he might need to order her to flee. "Shall we go?"

"Yeah." Silverdale scrambled to her feet. "Let's go find your wife."

Chapter Thirty-One

The symbolism, Isabella decided, could not have been less subtle if they'd tried.

She found it a little reassuring, even though the chains wrapped around her naked body – her astral self – made it almost impossible to move. They wouldn't have bothered to tie her down so heavily, binding her to the Godly Realm, if they hadn't thought there was a chance she could escape. And they couldn't cut her link to her body entirely, not without her consent. She was a prisoner, but she wasn't *helpless*.

Her mind peered through the chains, studying the Godly Realm. It was strange, so strange, and yet it made a certain kind of sense. She had to put everything she knew about how the world worked out of her mind, she had to try to think like the entities themselves, she had to try to translate whatever she was seeing into human terms ... her head hurt from the effort, but she thought it was working. She could see the threads leading from the entities to their followers, she could see them drinking in the worship and rewarding it ... she swallowed, mentally, as she saw them draining the worshippers dry. They were addicts, she realised numbly. They were doing whatever they needed to do to get their fix.

She tested the bonds, trying to find a way out. The link back to her body was intact, yet ... she couldn't go down it. She thought she could hear voices through her ears ... voices saying what? What were they *doing* with her body? Her imagination provided a number of answers, none of them good. She wondered if they were so much as *feeding* her body. She wasn't sure how long she'd been a prisoner – there was no *time* in the Godly Realm – but her body couldn't survive without food. Or water. A woman could survive for several days without food, but water was a different story. She knew she would die very quickly without water. And what would happen to her soul then?

I might be trapped for the rest of eternity, she thought. *Or I might just blink out of existence and die.*

Her eyes hardened as she resumed her observations of the Godly Realm. It was shaped by intelligence ... by the entities themselves, but also by their worshippers. She thought she saw a multitude of heavens and hells, created by people who believed in them. Her heart twisted at the sight. Was that what awaited everyone, after they died? Or just the worshippers? Or no one? She didn't want to believe that human souls entered the Godly Realm when they died. The entities were powerful, but they weren't gods. They would have won by now if they were.

There has to be a way to stop them, she thought. An idea was starting to flicker at the back of her mind. Something she was seeing. Something she could *use* ... It might just work, if she could get out. *I might just know how to beat them.*

***

The last time Reginald had visited a forbidden zone, there'd been a barrier put in place by the empire ... a barrier Isabella had taken down so they could enter. Now ... there was no barrier, nothing to stop the horsemen from riding into the forbidden zone. The air grew strange as they slowed to a trot, then stopped to dismount. He thought he tasted hints of despair and fear in the air, droplets of *something* brushing against his soul. The entities had infested the forbidden zone once, he knew. And now they were back.

He glanced at Silverdale, who hadn't dismounted. "Take a look ahead," he ordered. "Let me know what you see."

His heart twisted as his sister closed his eyes. It still felt *wrong* to take her into battle, even if he couldn't spare her talents. Their father would never have approved. But ... he waited, listening carefully for the first hint of enemy presence. The forbidden zone was eerie. No birds sang in the trees, no animals moved in the undergrowth ... he looked down at the dirt and knew, deep inside, that it was dead. He touched a leaf and watched it crumble to dust. The life had been drained from the forbidden zone long ago.

Silverdale opened her eyes. "There's five ... *things* ... there," she said. She sounded more than a little unsure of herself. "And Isabella's body is there too."

Reginald nodded and glanced at his men. He'd brought ten of his best men – his best surviving men, his thoughts mocked – but he knew it might not be enough. Cold iron or not, the overshadowed were deadly foes. And they might have sensed Silverdale's intrusion. He braced himself, using hand signals to order the men forward. Silverdale would remain behind, out of sight. She knew to flee if the men ran into something they couldn't handle. Reginald hoped she'd be smart enough to follow orders. If he died, Silverdale would suddenly be Ruby's heir.

And you wouldn't have fled if you were in her shoes, he reminded himself. He'd done a whole bunch of stupid things in his life, because he'd thought he'd needed to do them. His father had beaten him often enough for not thinking before acting. *Why do you expect her to flee?*

His thoughts churned as they inched through the dying foliage. The forbidden zone nagged at him, sparks of pain stabbing into his soul as he moved closer. It felt wrong, as if an unseen force were trying to push him away without quite knowing what it was doing. He felt as if his very mind was slipping and sliding on boggy ground ... he pressed his fingers against the iron blade as he felt reality itself starting to break down. The shrine – whatever it had been, thousands of years ago – was little more than a pile of rubble. Reginald peered at it, warily. Isabella lay on a stone table in the exact centre of the structure, hands resting on her belly. Four hooded figures stood around her, his eyes hurting whenever he looked at them. Alarm shot through him. Four figures?

Something moved, beside him. He raised his sword hastily as the fifth figure hurled itself towards him. He stabbed once, planting his sword in the creature's gut and pulling it out in one smooth motion. The body was already crumbling to dust as it fell. Reginald kicked the hood aside and ran forward, yelling a challenge as his men followed him. The figures seemed surprised, as if they'd been doing something ... they spun, extending their claws and lashing out.

"Kill them," Reginald barked. He sliced off a figure's arm, then cut it in half. He had the impression of a body that was too small to contain its essence, of a life force that was utterly alien, a moment before it vanished. "Hurry!"

Panic yammered at his mind as another figure stabbed at Isabella's unmoving body. He jumped forward, crashing into the creature. It was like running into a wall that was made of both stone and jelly, as if the creature was both solid and insubstantial. A fist slapped his arm, nearly breaking it. He dropped his sword. The hooded figure's eyes, barely visible within the gloom, seemed to light up as a clawed hand stabbed down. Reginald kicked out, feeling as if he'd kicked another wall, then drew the dagger from his sleeve and threw it at the figure. The figure crumbled to dust. He breathed a sigh of relief as he stood and retrieved his sword, silently thanking his swordmaster for teaching him how to use both hands. His right arm wasn't broken, he thought, but it was practically useless. He suspected it would be several days before he could fight normally.

Captain Archdale walked up to him. "Sire, the site is secure."

Reginald had his doubts. The forbidden zone still felt eerie. He thought he could see ghostly traces of a bygone era everywhere he looked. Isabella still lay on the table, unmoving. Her eyes were closed. He felt a flicker of panic, wondering if she was dead. She was still breathing, but so quietly her chest was hardly moving. She seemed fast asleep.

"Isabella," Reginald said. The panic grew stronger. His wife was still a prisoner. "Can you hear me?"

Isabella didn't move. Reginald hesitated, then bent over and kissed her lips. Isabella had never *liked* being touched, not when she wasn't expecting it. She should have reacted ... he wouldn't have cared if she'd given him a black eye, if she woke up. But her lips were utterly still. She didn't seem to feel a thing. Reginald looked up and sent one of the horsemen to fetch Silverdale, then directed the others to patrol the edge of the forbidden zone. What was he supposed to do? Put his fingers under her shirt or into her trousers? Hit her? Make love to her?

He stepped back. Isabella looked unhurt, untouched. Some bastard would dare to suggest the child wasn't his ... Reginald clenched his fists, promising himself that the first person who tried would be beaten bloody. He'd do it personally and to hell with fairness. The child was his and that was all there was to it. Isabella had been pregnant before she'd been taken prisoner and … he looked up as Silverdale walked into sight. She looked nervous, even though the dark riders were dead. Reginald guessed the forbidden zone must be affecting her more than everyone else. She could see things that weren't there.

They are there, he corrected himself. *They're just in another realm.*

"She's tied up," Silverdale said. "I …"

Reginald shook his head. Isabella wasn't tied up. She was just asleep. Or was she …?

"Help her," he said. He couldn't think of anything else. "Please."

Silverdale met his eyes, then nodded. "I'll do my best."

***

Isabella looked … as if she were split in two. Silverdale's head hurt as she tried to make sense of it. There were two of her; one lying on the table, one naked, kneeling and chained so heavily that she couldn't hope to move. Silverdale recoiled in shock, even though she knew the sight wasn't real. Except it was, in a way. It was just a way of seeing what they'd done to her. Isabella might have been freed … no, her *body* had been freed. The rest of her was still a prisoner.

Silverdale touched Isabella's forehead lightly. She could feel a spark of life under Isabella's skin, but … no intelligence. No soul. The body was nothing more than an empty shell. The soul was elsewhere. Silverdale allowed her mind to sink into Isabella's body, searching for the link to her soul. It would be there somewhere, she thought. It had to be. She wouldn't be seeing double if Isabella's soul had been destroyed.

She'd brushed against minds and memories before, but this was different. Isabella's skull was a yawning emptiness. Silverdale had had governesses who'd accused her of having nothing between her ears, but this … she swallowed as she peered through the darkness. There were no defences, no barriers … no tidal wave of memories that threatened to push her out or overwhelm her. There was nothing, just a silence that gnawed at her mind. Isabella was gone. Her body wasn't *her* any longer.

You're looking in the wrong place, Silverdale told herself. Isabella's links might be gone, but the baby's links were still there. *Look elsewhere*.

The baby felt … strange. Silverdale had a sense of contentedness, a feeling of paradise that tore at her mind. The baby was aware and yet … she pulled herself free and searched for the baby's links. One of them *had* to lead to Isabella …

Silverdale shivered as her mind was pulled up, through the astral plane and into the Godly Realm. Isabella was right in front of her. The chains … there were layers upon layers of chains piled on top of her. Silverdale could see her eyes, but little more. Isabella couldn't move … Silverdale looked back, trying to see past the illusion. The chains weren't *chains*. They hadn't wrapped her in metal. They'd twisted the fabric of the Godly Realm itself to hold her in place. And it had worked.

"I'm coming," Silverdale said. Her fingers felt insubstantial. She tried to move the chains and failed. She wasn't even sure she was *touching* them. "Can you hear me?"

Isabella blinked, once. If she could speak … Silverdale heard nothing. She muttered a word under her breath as she examined the chains themselves. Unpicking them wasn't an option. Whoever – whatever – had crafted the raw material into chains had just been too strong. They'd bound Isabella solidly … they'd never intended to let her go. Silverdale wondered, morbidly, if they'd intended to keep her body alive long enough to have the baby. They'd turned humans into carriers before. Why not try with a baby?

Her mind raced. Isabella was trapped. Silverdale couldn't free her … or could she? The chains weren't real. She leaned forward, poking her fingers into the gap. They weren't long enough to touch Isabella's skin, except they were … if she visualised them as being long and strong. She felt the chains shifting underneath her, too late. Their skins touched … Silverdale pushed as hard as she could, twisting the Godly Realm around her. Isabella turned to liquid and flowed through the chains. Silverdale grabbed hold of her and pushed her down and out. The realm roared in anger …

Silverdale fell into her body, stumbling backwards.

Reginald caught her, a second before she could hit the ground. Isabella was choking, her entire body twitching violently. She'd been a prisoner for a day … it might have been longer, for her. Time and space meant nothing in the Godly Realm. She could have been inside for a few seconds, from an outside point of view, yet it would have felt longer. A lot longer. Silverdale had heard stories of people wandering into other worlds and returning within an hour, only to discover they'd been away for years. She thought she knew, now, the truth behind the myths.

"Isabella!" Reginald pounded on Isabella's chest. "Breathe!"

Isabella sat upright, panting heavily. "Reginald, I …"

Silverdale looked away, rolling her eyes as her brother and sister-in-law kissed. Disgusting. She couldn't imagine doing that … she wasn't entirely unaware of the facts of life, despite the best efforts of a succession of governesses intent on maintaining her innocence, but still … yuck. The slobbering noises were really disgusting. She made a mental note to tease Reginald about it later. He'd never be able to keep his throne if people knew he'd been doing *that*.

A hand touched her shoulder. "Thank you," Isabella said, quietly. "You saved me."

"I shouldn't have left you." Silverdale felt a pang of guilt. She was a good horsewoman. She could have scooped up Isabella before continuing to flee … if Isabella hadn't compelled her to go. "I shouldn't have …"

"I made you go." Isabella stood. "What happened to your face?"

Silverdale touched her cheek. "I rode for hours," she said. "And …"

She looked east. "The Godly Realm has started to materialise," she said. The glimmer in the distance might not be visible to anyone else, but *she* could see it. She thought Isabella might be able to see it too. "They're coming."

"They destroyed Barr," Reginald said. His voice broke, just for a second. "The army's gone."

Isabella nodded. "I think I know how to win," she said, once Reginald had filled her in. "I …"

Silverdale cut her off. "Don't say anything here," she said, sharply. The shrine was *theirs*. It was very far from safe.

"You don't know what might be listening."

She frowned. The forbidden zone was shifting. Changing. She hadn't paid much attention to the ghostly images, not when she'd been hurrying to help Isabella, but now ... she could feel *things* sliding into reality. The old masters were coming back, inching into reality ... she shuddered, a sudden wave of cold making her shiver. There were things beyond the entities, things so incomprehensible they were utterly beyond her. She felt as if something was wrenching her eyes open, forcing her to look ...

"We have to run," Isabella said. "Now!"

Silverdale turned and sprinted back to the horses. The world was starting to blur, as if it were starting to pull them back to the old shrine. Captain Archdale and his men were already gathering, horses whinnying nervously as reality itself started to scream. She had the impression of huge tentacles reaching into reality, teeth and claws snapping as they searched for prey. Reginald helped Isabella onto his horse, then mounted behind her as Silverdale scrambled into her own saddle. The horses neighed as they galloped away, not a moment too soon. Behind her, reality gave one final scream and collapsed into nothingness. The shrine was gone.

Sweat prickled on her forehead. *They just tried to kill us.*

"We need an iron cage," Isabella said. She sounded remarkably composed for someone who'd just been rescued from enemy clutches. "Do we have to go all the way back to Havelock?"

"I hope not," Reginald said. "There should be something suitable in Kingston."

And if we find a cage, we can discuss our plans, Silverdale thought. She had no idea what Isabella had in mind. *And if we can't ...*

She shivered. They'd rescued Isabella, but ... so what? The Godly Realm was still visible, still touching the human world. And it was expanding steadily. She dreaded to think what would happen when it overshadowed Havelock and the remainder of the kingdom. It would be the end of the world ...

Chapter Thirty-Two

Sergeant Theodore Ashworth shuddered, mouth hopelessly dry, as he came back to himself.

He was kneeling in a muddy field, his head and arms trapped in a wooden yoke. The city itself was a blackened ruin, a handful of men and women being escorted out of the wreckage by enemy soldiers. The fires seemed mostly to have died, but a handful of plumes of smoke still rose in the distance. A faint ghostly glimmer seemed to overhang the city, despite the brightness of the day. Theodore swallowed, hard, as he looked from left to right. He was a prisoner, and he wasn't alone.

His heart sank as he tested the cangue. There was no way to break it, no way to do much of anything as long as his hands were trapped. His legs weren't shackled, as far as he could tell, but it hardly mattered. He'd be easy prey if he managed to get away, an easy target for enemy soldiers, bandits or locals seeking their chance for a little revenge. Theodore had no illusions about how the commoners regarded the army. The chance to crack his skull would be irresistible. If nothing else, it would be a good way to prove their loyalty to the new regime.

He tasted smoke in the air as he studied the other prisoners. They were mostly soldiers, although there were a handful of mercenaries and civilians amongst them. The mercenaries looked calculating, clearly wondering if they could change sides; the civilians looked stunned, as if they couldn't quite believe what had happened. Theodore didn't blame them. The city was effectively gone. It would be a long time, if ever, before it rose from the ashes. He had a feeling it would never recover. The population – the craftsmen and merchants who'd made the city work – was gone. And yet, the ghostly glimmer hung at the corner of his eye. It looked as if the memory of the city was not yet gone.

Theodore gritted his teeth, trying to find a pose that was

marginally comfortable. His arms and legs were aching. He supposed he should be grateful his captors hadn't rammed the board against his chin hard enough to force him to look up. That might not have hurt much, at first, but in the long term it would have hurt dreadfully. It was one of the ways to torture captives that were technically forbidden, never mind that everyone did it anyway. The old laws had died with the empire. King Reginald might preach charity, justice and fairness to all, but soldiers in the middle of wartime had their own rules. No one would treat a captive gently for fear said captive would turn on them, given half a chance.

He kept a wary eye on the sun as it climbed towards midpoint. Mid-morning then, trending towards noon. He'd been out for hours. He wondered, idly, just who'd knocked him on the head and taken him prisoner ... and why the attacker had bothered. Theodore wasn't important. Theodore didn't have a wealthy family that would have paid a staggering ransom for his safe return ... Sir Alaric's family might have paid through the nose for his return, but Theodore's family didn't give a damn if he lived or died. They'd probably be glad to be rid of him, if they knew what had happened. And the army – or the king – wouldn't pay a ransom.

Which means they have no use for me, he thought. *Shit.*

His mind raced. No one in their right mind would take him as a slave. He knew too much. He was too used to looking after himself to be safely enslaved. The days when wizards had churned out slave collars were long gone. And no one would take him as a pleasure slave ... he shuddered at the very thought. No, they were probably going to kill him. Theodore briefly considered pretending to switch sides, but the thought was appalling. Unthinkable. He was going to die, and the king would never even know what had happened to him.

Theodore winced as he looked back at the remains of the city. The king's army – the strongest army the kingdom had ever produced – had been quartered there, only a few short hours ago. Now ... Theodore tried to tell himself otherwise, but he couldn't hide from the simple fact that the army had been effectively destroyed. A few hundred men might have escaped the burning city and cut through the enemy army, but so what? They couldn't stop the advancing tide as it headed west. They'd become bandits or slip into civilian communities or … Theodore shivered as it dawned on him the king himself might be dead. Did Theodore's oaths to the king end with the king's death? He wasn't sure. He certainly hadn't sworn loyalty to the kingdom as a whole.

Not that it matters, he thought. He was surprised his throat hadn't been slit while he'd been unconscious. The enemy wanted him alive, but for what? *What are they going to do to me?*

He shook his head, slowly. There were no good answers.

His eyes narrowed as he saw a troop of enemy soldiers walking towards him. Their faces looked reassuringly *human*, without the indistinct haze he'd learnt to fear, but there was a disturbing fanaticism around them that worried him. Fanatics could be very dangerous, given the chance. They feared nothing, certain that their gods were on their side. He snarled at the thought. *These* fanatics might just be right. Their gazes suggested they were long past the stage of questioning their orders. He shuddered, inwardly, as they came up to him. Perhaps he was going to be sacrificed, to inspire the faithful. He'd broken up cults in days of yore … in hindsight, the first hint that the entities were returning. The cults moved quickly to quash any sense of independence amongst the new recruits, tainting them to the point where they couldn't hope to go home and seek forgiveness. They did awful things and became awful people …

"On your feet, scum," the leader ordered.

Theodore snorted. "Do you think I can move with this … *thing* … on me?"

He'd hoped to irritate them, just a little. Perhaps they'd give him a quick death, instead of slow torture or … something. Instead, they merely took hold of the yoke and yanked him to his feet. Theodore's limbs screamed in protest. He gritted his teeth, trying not to show any sign of discomfort. He had the feeling that showing weakness would be a very bad idea. It was unlikely they'd relax around him, not if they'd plucked him from the fires. They wouldn't have to do more than look at his muscles and scars to know he was a trained and experienced soldier. There was no way he could pretend to be helpless.

The Lady Joan poisoned her captors when they took her prisoner and forced her to cook for them, he recalled. *But they didn't see a weak and apparently helpless female as dangerous.*

The thought made him smile as they shoved him across the field and into the makeshift camp. No one would be asking *him* to cook for them ... the smile slowly faded from his lips as he looked around the enemy camp. There was something slapdash about it that offended his sense of what was right and proper. The tents were scattered everywhere, without even the merest stockade to protect them from enemy cavalry. Sir Alaric and his men could charge through the camp, kicking down tents and throwing firebombs in all directions ... there was nothing, not even a concealed murder pit, that could have slowed them for a moment. Theodore allowed himself to hope, just for a second, that Sir Alaric was on the way. He knew better. The aristocratic fop had probably roasted within the burning city. His ashes would never be found.

We are all equals in death, Theodore thought. Bitterness warred within his soul. *And she comes for us all, in due time.*

He tried to keep himself centred as he studied the enemy army. They looked more like a mob than a trained and disciplined band, walking around casually instead of marching in formation. From time to time, a man would throw himself on the ground in full prostration ... even though there was nothing in front of them. A chill ran down Theodore's spine as he saw another man knocking his head on the muddy ground. Was there something there, invisible to his eyes? Or were the enemy soldiers so consumed with their faith that they couldn't help themselves? He shivered, again. The camp might not be as undefended as he thought.

They reached the centre of the camp and stopped. A figure – a glowing figure – stood in front of a giant throne, peering down at them. He was hundreds of miles tall and yet ... Theodore's head swam as he tried to make sense of what he saw. The figure was perfect, inhumanly so. He – it, perhaps – looked to have been carved from marble, the very image of the heroic warrior king that didn't exist outside bad adventure stories and worse romances. Theodore had known too many aristocrats – and even a king – to put much faith in those stories. Reginald was a good king, as kings went, but even *he* had to use the toilet and put his trousers on, one leg at a time. The entity in front of him …

It was hard to see the entity as a coherent whole. Theodore saw flashes – blond hair, a strong chin, golden armour, muscles on his muscles – but he couldn't see the whole creature. It felt as if he were seeing hints of something much greater. It felt … he felt a hint of admiration, even worship. The figure gave the impression of being … utterly reliable, the kind of leader he would follow into the gates of hell itself. Theodore told himself, firmly, that the feeling wasn't *real*. The entity was playing with his emotions, manipulating his thoughts. And yet, it was impossible to escape the feeling of awe. It went beyond anything he'd ever felt for anyone *human*. His father, his first sergeant, his king … anyone.

"On your knees," his escort ordered. He gave Theodore a push. "Now!"

"There's no need to be harsh to our prisoner," the entity said. "Release him."

Theodore allowed himself a moment of relief as the cangue was removed and tossed to one side. His arms and legs ached badly, so badly that he almost dropped to the ground. It was all he could do to hold himself upright as he took stock of his situation. His armour had been removed – surprise, surprise – as had his weapons. Someone had searched him thoroughly and removed both his sword and the daggers he'd concealed up his sleeve. He couldn't check, but he'd bet what little remained of his monthly pay that the dagger in his boot had been stolen too. Not, he supposed, that the faithful would let him take a blade of cold iron anywhere near their god. A single dagger would be more than enough to banish the entity back to … back to wherever it came from.

He forced himself to stall, trying to drag matters out as long as possible. The entity showed no visible reaction. He had the feeling that the entity thought it had time enough to spare on … on whatever it intended to do. The thought didn't bring him any cheer. The remnants of the army had to be scattered, then. Or, perhaps, the entity was just too powerful to be threatened by anything merely human. An assassin with a blade of cold iron would have to get through layer upon layer of fanatical bodyguards before he took his shot at the entity.

An arrow would be just as good, he thought. *But the trick would be getting close enough to take the shot.*

He raised his eyes. "What are you?"

"I am King Forsyth of Zycrest, Imperator of the World," the entity said. The absolute confidence in its voice was staggering, even though it *had* to be an illusion. "And your kingdom is falling to me."

Theodore gritted his teeth. Every word practically *compelled* him to bend the knee. There was something ... warm and comforting in pledging himself to the entity, in serving a lord who would never betray him, in fighting for a good and decent cause. He wanted to submit, even though he knew he shouldn't. The entity was very far from human. The very thought of surrender made him feel unclean. It was far worse than merely going home at the end of the war ...

"I will take the entire world," the entity informed him. "Your kingdom will become part of my empire. You will fight for me, will you not?"

Theodore found himself caught in a maelstrom of emotion. He *wanted* to serve the entity. He wanted to fight. There was nothing wrong – he *knew* there was nothing wrong – with abandoning his oaths to his king and throwing himself at the entity's feet. Indeed, he feared he would be called a coward, or worse, if he failed to join the war. The effect was so overwhelming that he felt his knees wobble ...

He bit his lip, hard. "No."

"Admirable," the entity said. "But quite futile."

There was no hint of mockery in its tone. No suggestion it was making fun of him. Theodore had the feeling it genuinely *admired* his stance. And yet ... he forced himself to look into the glowing face. The eyes were human ... and there was something damned and suffering within their gaze. Theodore recoiled, helplessly. King Forsyth of Zycrest had been overshadowed, just like Princess Sofia. Perhaps he'd been willing, perhaps not. It hardly mattered. The entity was wearing him, using him like a puppet. And yet ...

Theodore could *feel* the call. He wanted, on some level, to surrender. He couldn't deny it, not to himself. It would be *glorious*. He would be a soldier fighting for the righteous cause, with everything he did – he would do – being right because it was for the *right* ... he had a vision of marching through an endless series of burning towns and cities, trampling the infidels and aristocrats under his feet as he raged on. The war would never end. It would be an eternity of fighting beside boon companions and matching himself against honourable enemies and … it wasn't true. It couldn't be true. He'd commit endless *atrocities* for a creature that was not even human.

"No."

The entity, somehow, managed to look *impressed.*

Theodore bit his lip, once again. The hell of it was that he was *sure* the entity really was impressed. He didn't think, not for one moment, that it was faking it, or trying to lure him into a false sense of security or *anything*. It really *was* impressed. Theodore stared, suddenly aware that the entity was shaped by its worshippers as much as it shaped them. The thought was almost enough to break his resolve as he looked into the golden face. He could almost feel himself bowing his head in worship.

"I wish you to perform one simple task for me," the entity said. "If you agree to do so, you may leave the camp freely. You will remain unhurt as long as you do not take up arms against me again."

Theodore knew, on a level he couldn't quite comprehend, that the entity was telling the truth. It didn't have to play mind games. Theodore had known quite a few sadists during his long career, and the entity didn't look to be one of them. And yet … he felt a certain, basic fear at its words. What did it want him to do? Something that would put him beyond the pale? Something that would ensure he had nowhere else to go?

"You are to take a message to your former master," the entity said. "Take the message, give it to him, and then you will be free of all obligation."

Theodore's eyes narrowed. He couldn't see the trap, but that didn't mean there wasn't one. The entities broke the world just by existing. The message might be designed to force the king to surrender. Or … or something. "And what is the message?"

"You will inform him that I have defeated his army and won the war," the entity said. "If he comes before me and opens his heart and bends the knee, I will accept him and his kingdom as part of my growing empire. There will be no need for any further bloodshed. The conversion will be accomplished easily. But if he refuses to take this chance, there will be not be another. I will put his land to fire and sword until his people surrender and accept me into their hearts. Do you understand me?"

"Yes," Theodore managed. His mouth was dry. He could feel his hands shaking. He'd been fighting for years, ever since the fall of the empire, and yet ... the devastation the entities had unleashed was an order of magnitude worse than anything the remaining sorcerers and kings had caused. He didn't want to think about how many people had died in the fires. The bastards hadn't even bothered to *sack* the city before setting light to everything. "I understand."

The entity turned away. Theodore felt his heart twist in pain. Part of him was with the entity now, whatever it said. He gritted his teeth as the guards took hold of his arms and dragged him back. He should have been happy he was being released. He should have been happy and relieved he wasn't having his throat cut or being tortured to death ...

... But it felt, as they shoved him on his way, as if he was leaving behind all that truly mattered in the world.

Chapter Thirty-Three

Reginald wasn't sure what he'd expected, when he rode into Kingstown. The town wasn't much bigger than the village they'd used as a rendezvous point, after they'd fled the city, but it was emptier. The advance elements – the advance elements of a retreat, the nasty part of his mind pointed out – had probably arrived only a few short hours ago, long enough for the townsfolk to decide to lock up their daughters or take to the hills. Reginald didn't blame them, he decided, as the horse stopped outside the local tax collector's mini-mansion. Soldiers were dangerous to civilians at the best of times, but these soldiers had just lost a battle. They'd take their anger out on the civilians if strict discipline wasn't maintained.

Colonel Hastings saluted as Reginald half-carried Isabella into the mansion, Silverdale trotting at his heels. "Sire, we've cleared two of the rooms for you," he said. "I've got the remainder of the troops working on defences, save for a cavalry troop. They're watching the approaches."

"Good thinking." Reginald rubbed his forehead. He didn't know Hastings that well – he'd inherited the man from his father – but the colonel had clearly risen to the occasion. "Has there been any word from Havelock?"

"Not yet, Sire," Hastings said. "I ordered a messenger to ride to the city as quickly as possible, but he may not have reached Havelock by now."

Reginald nodded, sourly. There was no way to get a message to the capital any quicker, not without using the Godly Realm. He was desperate enough to consider it, but he knew the dangers far outweighed the advantages. Instead, he dismissed the colonel and allowed a maid to show them up the stairs to their rooms. The mansion was larger than he'd thought. He suspected the tax collector was abusing his power. If the man was still alive – uncertain, now all hell had broken loose – he'd have to do something about it.

"Get some sleep," he ordered Silverdale. "And don't let

your mind go wandering."

His sister entered her room without a fight, a clear sign she was tired beyond the limits of endurance. Reginald was morbidly impressed, despite the gnawing guilt at repeatedly taking Silverdale into danger. His father would have clobbered him for even *thinking* of exposing his sister ... he grimaced as he remembered that his father was dead. His father was dead, his sister, Sofia, was dead ... the kingdom itself was at stake. He pushed open the doorway to the master bedroom, clearly abandoned and then tidied in a hurry, and dismissed the maid with a wave of his hand. The bathroom was surprisingly modern. They even had cold running water.

Better than bothering the maids, he thought. He'd always felt guilty about forcing the poor girls to carry buckets of steaming water up to his suite. *Isabella can heat it herself, if she wants*.

Isabella pulled free of him and stood. "I need a wash," she said, very definitely. "Wait outside."

Reginald didn't argue. Instead, he walked back into the bedroom and lay on the bed. They'd saved his wife – he'd count that as a victory, under the circumstances – but lost the army. He was experienced enough to know it wouldn't be more than a day or two before the enemy army reached Kingston and either stormed the town or simply enveloped it while fording the river. The river wasn't even *that* deep. A skilled army could easily build a handful of pontoon bridges and cross, all the while mocking the town and its defenders. Reginald could envisage the entities plunging onwards, sowing defeatism as they headed towards Havelock. They might not even have to fight for the city. *Someone* would open the gates.

The bathroom door opened. Isabella stood there, naked. Reginald sat up, eyes wandering over her muscular body. There were scars ... new ones. He winced, hoping he'd killed the bastards who'd beaten her. Isabella hurried forward and kissed him deeply, then started to fumble with his trousers. Reginald felt a surge of lust as she pulled them down ...

Afterwards, they lay together on the bed. Reginald smiled, not quite able to believe they were going to have a baby. He believed it and yet … it was hard to believe. He was too young … no, he was easily old enough to have children. He'd known lads who'd become fathers when they were in their late teens. And … he wondered, suddenly, what sort of father he'd be. What sort of example would he set for his child? He promised himself he'd be at least as good as his father, even if it meant not making things too easy for the child. The kid would need to learn through doing and that meant, perhaps, learning through failing. Reginald had done it himself. It hadn't been easy. Hell, he'd resented it at the time.

He put the thought aside as she turned to look at him. Her dark hair was streaked with sweat and her face was bruised, but he'd never seen her look more beautiful. She seemed to glow … he felt a surge of protectiveness that surprised him. He wanted her – by all the gods, he wanted her – but he also wanted her to be safe and well and *happy*. He felt his smile grow wider, even though he knew there were things they had to talk about. And quickly.

"You should have told me," he said, reluctantly. "If I'd known …"

"I didn't know myself," Isabella said. "It wasn't until after killing Mali that I realised the truth."

Reginald frowned. "I thought girls always knew."

Isabella snorted. "My cycles have always been a little irregular," she said, tartly. "Missing one or two cycles wouldn't have been *proof* I was pregnant."

"I suppose not," Reginald said. His father had explained menstrual cycles to him, but the old man had been long on vague generalisations and short on specifics. It hadn't been something he'd *wanted* to talk about, not to anyone. "You shouldn't have gone into danger, either."

Isabella gave him a sharp look. "There was no reason to think I'd be in danger, not then," she said. "We didn't even know the invasion had begun until … until it was too late."

"It hadn't," Reginald said. It had all fallen apart so *quickly*. Isabella had been captured in the morning, Silverdale had made it to the city in the afternoon, the entities had burned down the city in the night … they'd escaped, rescued Isabella and fled to Kingston the following day. He still couldn't believe it. "They kicked our asses so hard …"

His voice trailed off. The gods alone knew how many men had died in the fires. Or been taken prisoner. Or been forced to serve their new masters. He didn't want to *think* about it, or about what had happened to the townspeople. The ones who'd been burned to death might have been the lucky ones. The survivors might find themselves at the mercy of monsters from beyond the human realm ...

Or human monsters, he thought, coldly. *It isn't as if we need the entities to be monstrous to each other.*

"Yeah." Isabella let out a breath. "That might have been my fault. I panicked them."

"By killing an entity." Reginald didn't have it in him to be angry. "At least you proved you can kill them."

Isabella sat upright and stared down at him. "I saw things, while they were holding me prisoner," she said. She drew signs in the air as she spoke. "I think we can do more than *just* kill them."

Reginald felt a flicker of hope. "What do you have in mind?"

"They want us to think of them as gods," Isabella said. "I think ... I'm not sure if that's intentional, at least on their part. In their base form, they're living *ideas*. I think, from what we were told, that they were shaped by us as much as they shaped us. Possibly more so, actually. Mother Lembu and the others are aspects of our collective perception of ... of gods, creatures that are so far beyond us as to be untouchable. And that keeps us from thinking of them as what they really are."

Her voice hardened. "Parasites."

Reginald shivered. "They feed on their worshippers."

"I believe so," Isabella said. "I saw ... *threads* linking the entities to their worshippers. They feed on the worship and, in return, work miracles. I think they're addicted to worship, to the point they're actually trying to merge their realm and ours into one. They can do anything, grant any prayer, within the Godly Realm. This way ... there will be an endless source of worship for them."

"Because everyone will *know* the gods exist," Reginald said. "And yet, they need our permission to do it ... right?"

"Yes," Isabella said. She paused, clearly choosing her next words carefully. "Imagine ... a cheese sandwich. One layer of bread is the human world, the other is the Godly Realm; the cheese, in the middle, is the astral plane. Our minds are linked to the astral plane by dint of intelligence, as are theirs; our worship reaches into the astral plane and touches them, influencing them. I think that's how they managed to get back into our world, after the empire collapsed. They were able to make contact with desperate worshippers and push them into rituals that widened the chinks in reality."

"And the more worshippers they get, the more power they have in all three worlds," Reginald said. It made a certain kind of sense. "They can warp the astral plane to influence our world."

"Yes." Isabella smiled, although there was little real humour in the expression. "I think that's how they killed King Hereford. There would have been a thread linking him to Queen Emetine, enough for them to twist the astral plane and *kill* him. Much like I did to Mali, more or less."

Reginald scowled. King Hereford's death had started everything. And yet, it felt as if it had taken place centuries ago. Reginald found it hard to believe just how much things had changed in the last couple of years, from the invasion of the Summer Isle to the invasion of Andalusia itself. If he hadn't gone to the Summer Isle, if he hadn't pressed his claim to the island, would things have been different? He knew he'd never know. And yet, he also knew the question would haunt him for the rest of his life.

"The entities need worship to get their hooks in their worshippers," Isabella said. "But they also need to overshadow a willing victim, someone who can become their puppet. That allows them to remain in contact with our world, at least until they manage to merge the two worlds into one. If we kill the imperator, we'd buy some time …"

"If," Reginald said.

"If," Isabella agreed. "I think there's another option."

She met his eyes, evenly. "We poison the well."

Reginald's eyes narrowed. "What do you mean?"

"They're parasites," Isabella repeated. "Like most successful parasites, from ticks to taxmen, they don't kill their hosts. Not immediately, although they do trigger a steady decline. There are limits to how far they can push things, if only because they need the worship. But … if we were to find a way to *poison* the worship, to turn it against them, it might *kill* them. Or, at the very least, dissuade them from feeding on us."

"I see," Reginald said. "And how do you intend to poison the well?"

"I have a couple of ideas," Isabella assured him. "I might need Silverdale's help ..."

She paused. "And I think I might need magic, too."

Reginald blinked. "Magic?"

"Magic may be poison to them," Isabella said. "I think ... I don't know. But it won't be easy to poison the well otherwise."

"We don't know too many things," Reginald said, tiredly. "And ... I should be mad at you for involving Silverdale."

"She's already involved," Isabella said. There was a hint of waspishness in her voice. "And I'm sorry."

"Me too," Reginald said. "How old were you when you went to the Peerless School?"

Isabella smirked. "Twelve."

Reginald raised his eyebrows. "And were you put in dreadful danger on the very first day?"

"A careless magician is a magician who will kill himself, if not others, sooner rather than later," Isabella said. "The Peerless School is supposed to be safer than studying at home, but ... it has its dangers. The slightest mishap can blow an unwary student into pieces or leave him croaking on a lily pad or ... something worse. I was never *safe*."

"And she wouldn't let us exclude her," Reginald said. He wondered, idly, how one tied up a girl who was perfectly capable of slipping onto the astral plane. A cage made of iron? Or ... or what? Isabella had been held prisoner by entities that couldn't so much as *look* at cold iron. "You have to take very good care of her, understand?"

Isabella nodded. "Tomorrow, I want to find a handful of cultists," she said. "And we need to take them alive."

Reginald frowned. "Is that possible?"

"I dare say we're about to find out," Isabella said. "We have to try."

She straddled him, then pressed down on him. Reginald's hands rose to her breasts as she began to ride him, trying to banish the nightmares through pleasure. He wanted to point out that she was pregnant, that she should go back to Havelock where she'd be safe ... but he knew she'd never listen. And besides, where *was* safe these days? The entities had burned an entire city to the ground. The remainder of the kingdom would throw the gates open as soon as the enemy army arrived, if only to ensure that their city wasn't burned, too. They'd surrender their former masters in an instant ...

Isabella kissed him, deeply. Reginald smiled and let himself go.

***

She should be sleeping.

Isabella lay in the borrowed bed, her eyes wide open despite the tiredness pervading her every thought. Reginald was beside her, one leg covering hers ... it wasn't enough to keep her awake. She was used to sharing a bed, used to having him cuddling up to her at night ... she knew, with a flicker of amusement, that he'd deny it if she ever told him he did it. Men could be funny that way, as if they thought cuddling their wives was somehow wrong. And yet ...

Her mind wandered as she recalled everything that had happened from the moment of her capture to her release. She knew, deep inside, just how vulnerable she'd been. She worried – she feared she'd always worry – that they'd done something to her or her unborn child. She'd performed what tests she could, once she'd been in the bathroom, but she was painfully aware the damage might not be obvious. They'd held her in the Godly Realm. They could have done *anything* to her.

And yet, they didn't do anything beyond holding me prisoner, she thought. The chains, whatever they'd been, hadn't so much as marked her skin. They hadn't been *real*. *Why didn't they do anything to me?*

She frowned as she leaned into Reginald's sleeping embrace. It was the nightmare that nothing, from wild sex to her husband's strong arms, could banish. The entities could have warped her into a monster or worse. They could have made her say or do or believe anything they liked. They could have penetrated her reality at any point – the thought made her shudder – and warped it so badly she couldn't have hoped to recover. Hell, if her personal reality had been changed – and all her ways to assess reality had been changed too – would she even know? There was no shortage of dire warnings about spell-controlled traitors, about people who were forced to betray their friends and allies ... people who didn't even *know* they were being controlled until it was far too late. If merely human magic could do that, what could the entities do? How would she even know she was being controlled?

You didn't snap Reginald's neck, she told herself. *You didn't put a knife in his back.*

Paranoia warred with common sense. The entities couldn't have *known* she was going to be rescued. They could have merely thought there'd be time enough to break her resistance later. Or ... perhaps they'd been focused on burning the city and invading the kingdom. They might just have considered her unimportant, at least until it was too late. She'd been a helpless prisoner, held fast in chains formed from the fabric of the realm itself. She wouldn't have made it out if Silverdale hadn't been there ...

Unless that was what they wanted to happen, she thought. *They wanted me to be rescued ...*

She groaned. There was no point in second-guessing the entities. Their worshippers probably made excuses for them all the time. It wasn't just a parasitical relationship. It was an abusive one. She shuddered in bitter disgust. The entities probably took pleasure in granting or withholding their boons, as the fancy took them. Their powers weren't *magic*, as humans understood the term. They were living things, entities shaped by the human subconscious mind. No wonder they were so strange.

Isabella rolled over and cuddled up to Reginald, putting the thought out of her head. She was fine. She was unharmed. She was untouched. She wasn't overshadowed ... but that was what they'd want her to think. Wasn't it? She couldn't be anything like as effective a weapon if she knew they'd done something to her and she took precautions. And yet ... she hadn't thought to warn Reginald or to ask Silverdale to take a look at her from the astral plane ...

It was a long time before she finally drifted off to sleep.

Chapter Thirty-Four

Silverdale woke, unsure where she was.

She was in a mid-sized bed, clearly designed for someone a little bigger than herself. The windows were closed and covered with heavy curtains, thick enough to block her view without quite hiding the brilliant sunlight. The blankets were finer than she'd expected ... memory came back to her in a flash of light. They'd escaped the city, rescued Isabella and fled to Kingston as night fell again. And she'd been shown into a room and left there.

Her stomach rumbled as she pushed the covers aside and forced herself to stand. The makeshift clothes were in rags, practically falling apart as she headed for the washroom to splash water on her face. Her entire legion of governesses would have had a collective fainting fit if they'd seen her ... she giggled at the thought as she looked around for something to wear. The dressing robe hanging behind the door was clearly designed for an adult. It was too long for her. She hesitated, then undressed, washed herself with ice-cold water and donned the robe anyway. She didn't have anything else to wear.

That might be a problem, she thought. She'd had a pair of dresses and riding outfits in her saddlebags, but they – and her horse – had probably been burned to ashes. She felt a pang of guilt at the thought of her poor horse, dead in the flames. *What am I going to wear?*

There was a knock as she stepped back into the bedroom. "Come!"

A young woman stepped into the room, carrying a tray of food. "Princess," she said, in a tone that suggested she wasn't used to serving royalty. "His Majesty commanded me to feed you."

"And me to eat," Silverdale said. She took the tray and placed it on the table. She was too hungry to care about proper etiquette. "Can you find me something to wear?

Something suitable for riding?"

The maid dropped a very imprecise curtsey, then backed out of the room. Silverdale barely noticed. She was too busy digging into a bowl of oatmeal sweetened with honey. It wasn't much, but she had a feeling there was little for anyone. Kingston was a small town suddenly expected to play host to the survivors of an entire army. She doubted they'd have much of a stockpile of food, even if they hadn't hidden half of it already. She'd heard the grumbling during Sofia's brief reign.

There was another knock on the door. The maid returned, carrying a handful of outfits. Most of them were utterly unsuitable for anything, except perhaps sitting on a pedestal and being worshipped from afar. Sofia would have loved them, Silverdale thought, but she wasn't so impressed herself. She wasn't sure if the maid had misunderstood what she'd been told, or if she was trying to be cheeky, or if there was honestly nothing suitable. The only things she could wear were a pair of riding trousers, under a skirt that would probably start to tear very quickly. It would have to do.

"Thank you," she said. "I ..."

She sensed, more than heard, Isabella stepping into the room. The maid didn't seem to recognise her at first, then practically tumbled over herself to curtsey as it dawned on her she was looking at the *queen*. Silverdale hid a smile as Isabella dismissed the maid with a shrug and a wave. Her sister-in-law had very little patience for servants. Silverdale didn't understand why. Servants could be annoying, but they were also necessary.

"Isabella," she said. "Did you sleep well?"

"Well enough." Isabella hesitated, as if there was a topic she didn't want to broach. "Can you tell me if they did ... *something* ... to me?"

"I can try." Silverdale sat on the chair, then peered at Isabella through the astral plane. There was a complex network of emotions surrounding her, and the unborn baby was a ball of light within her womb, but there was no hint of *taint*. "I think you're clean."

Isabella relaxed, slightly. "We're going to catch a handful of cultists," she said, sitting on the bed. "Interested?"

Silverdale blinked. "Did you bother to ask Reginald?"

"He knows," Isabella assured her. "As long as you follow orders, you can come with me. Us."

"I'll follow orders," Silverdale said. She stripped off the too-long robe and changed into riding trousers. She was tempted not to bother with the flimsy dress, but there was no point in tempting fate. Reginald was probably already terrified of sending his little sister into danger. "Where are we going?"

"Stay behind me, let the cavalry do their thing," Isabella said, as they headed for the door and down the corridor. "We'll only intervene if things go to hell."

Silverdale shivered. It was the middle of summer and yet … a cold air was blowing from the east. She could see hints of smoke in the distance … she shivered as she sensed the Godly Realm touching the human world. It seemed to be biding its time, for now, but it was still there, still heading towards them … she swallowed, hard, as she pulled her cloak around her shoulders. The entities were growing more and more powerful. Before long, they would be messing with the weather too.

A nobleman knelt to her. "Your Highness!"

"Sir Alaric," Isabella said. There was a hint of faint disapproval in her tone, although Silverdale didn't understand why. Sir Alaric looked the very *picture* of a hard-charging cavalry officer. "Do you understand your orders?"

"Yes, Your Majesty." Sir Alaric stood and thumped his chest in salute. "We're to find a handful of cultists and take them alive, if possible."

"If possible," Isabella echoed. She indicated a pair of horses, patiently waiting for their riders. "Mount up."

Silverdale nodded and scrambled into the saddle, taking a moment to get comfortable before taking hold of the reins. The beast made a faint noise – it sounded almost like a growl – but didn't seem inclined to throw her or make a bolt for it. Silverdale tensed, bracing herself to show the horse just who was in charge. Horses wanted – needed – to be shown that their rider knew what she was doing. If they scented weakness, they'd take advantage of it. She felt a sudden pang at the thought. Her father, who'd put her on her first pony, had said it was a useful lesson to learn. She hadn't understood what he'd meant until after his death.

Sir Alaric barked a command to his troop. The horsemen wheeled as one and cantered away from the mansion, heading towards the gates. Hundreds of soldiers were strengthening the walls, digging trenches and generally doing whatever they could to prepare the town for a siege. Silverdale glanced at the churning river and wondered if the enemy was already within the walls. There were gods of waves and water. It stood to reason there were entities that could control water too.

She felt her good mood evaporate as they followed the river north. There was no sign of the enemy, but she could *feel* a shadow steadily spreading across the land. Eyes glinted at her from the undergrowth, eyes that were very definitely not human. She gritted her teeth, forcing herself to concentrate as the road grew steeper and rougher. They were practically galloping up the side of a mountain, passing small clusters of young men as they rode. Sir Alaric shouted angrily at them, at least until Isabella reprimanded him. Silverdale guessed the young men were deserters.

The horses slowed as they reached the top of the hill and peered down into the valley. A small town sat at the bottom, surrounded by small fields and green hills studded with white spots. Sheep, she thought. She stared at the town and saw a handful of people standing in the centre of the village green, speaking to a growing crowd of villagers. Her blood ran cold as she realised they were cultists. The villages were being invited to worship the entities.

Isabella nudged her. "Do they have a connection to the entities? Or are they overshadowed?"

Silverdale passed her the reins, then carefully peered into the astral plane. The cultists definitely had ties to the entities – she could see the threads linking them to their master, threads linking their listeners to them and *then* to their master – but they didn't appear to have gone through the Godly Realm. She puzzled over it for a moment, then decided the overshadowed probably looked monstrous – if not threatening – to everyone, even those who couldn't see into the astral plane. Purely *human* preachers would be much more convincing, at least at first. Her eyes narrowed as she widened her mind, her awareness drifting over the crowd. Some of them, at least, were listening. Others were scared to listen, but also scared to run. They knew *something* bad had happened to the east, even if they didn't know *what*.

"They're not overshadowed," she said, softly. It was impossible to be sure ... no, she was sure. They didn't feel as if they were puppets. "They're just ... linked to the entities."

"Good." Isabella passed back the reins. "Stay here. If this goes wrong, ride back to the river and follow it back to the town. Don't look back, don't make any attempt to help us ... just get back to Reginald and tell him what happened. Understand?"

"Yes," Silverdale said. She didn't like the idea of just abandoning Isabella – again – but she'd agreed to follow orders. And yet, Reginald would *kill* her if she ... she told herself, sharply, that it wouldn't end that way. "I understand."

"Good." Isabella winked at her, then frowned. "Do *exactly* as you're told."

***

Isabella knew that she'd faced a *lot* of dangers from the moment she'd been able to walk. Her father's steady demands had been bad enough, but her first year of school had been a series of reminders that she could either be the victimiser or the victim and it was better, if not *right*, to be the victimiser. And yet, she still felt guilty for bringing Silverdale with her. The little princess had one hell of a talent, a talent Isabella doubted she'd ever match, but the risk was alarmingly high. She didn't blame Reginald for worrying. If Silverdale fell into enemy hands, the enemy would be just two lives from the throne.

"Your Majesty," Sir Alaric said. He sounded just a *little* bit too eager, for someone who'd nearly been killed by enemy cultists. He should have learnt a few lessons from *that* near-disaster. "We're ready."

"Remember the plan," Isabella said. She removed the charmed netting from her saddlebag and held it in her hands. The plan was for the horsemen to go first, but she knew they might not make it. "Don't go after the audience, unless they try to fight."

She held his gaze, silently daring him to defy her. She'd

met too many young aristocrats who just couldn't get over slights from their social inferiors. Anger was a good servant, but a poor master; bitterness and resentment were worse. He'd have been eaten alive at the Peerless School. He was having quite enough troubles coming to terms with taking orders from *her*. The nasty part of her mind wondered if he'd dreamed of marrying Sofia before the shit hit the fan. He would have thought he could rule through her ...

Which is the sort of stupid thing a young fool would think, she thought, crossly. Sir Alaric was just old enough to think of it and too young to realise it would never work, that he'd have to deal with opposition from older nobles and Sofia herself. *And you don't have time to worry about it.*

"Go," she ordered. There was no time to be subtle, either. The town was too small to sneak men onto the streets without being noticed. Sir Alaric and his men couldn't pass for commoners, not unless whoever spotted them was blind and deaf. "And don't stop for anything."

She braced herself as they cantered down towards the village green. There didn't seem to be anything in their way – and the cultists probably didn't have any *real* powers of their own – but it was hard to be sure. She'd seen the entities control storms, create earthquakes ... they'd even destroyed a whole city. The cultists looked up as the horsemen picked up speed, eyes glowing with hate. She wondered, idly, what they'd been saying. The promise of better crops and lower taxes would have gone down very well indeed. And the townspeople would probably consider the promise worth a prayer or two.

The townspeople scattered in all directions, save for a handful of determined worshippers. Isabella felt a pang of guilt as a young man was trampled under a horse, someone – his mother or his wife – howling behind them as Sir Alaric and his men closed on their targets. The cultists were roaring and chanting, saying words in a language Isabella didn't recognise ... the words echoed in the air, thudding against reality itself. Ice washed down her spine. They were calling on their patron. Their master ...

"The nets," she shouted. Their eyes were glowing. She could see sparks of fire dancing around them. They were drawing power from the remaining worshippers, using the power to manipulate the astral plane ... she wasn't sure they understood what they were doing, but it was impressive. "Now!"

Sir Alaric threw the first net. The cultists smirked as it flew through the air and crashed down on top of the closest man. Their smirks turned to shock as the net reverted to its normal form – cold iron. The sudden weight pushed the victim to the ground. The remaining cultists started to turn and run, their power broken, but it was too late. They were taken down quickly, before they could gather themselves or escape. She wondered, too late, what would happen if they lost faith in their masters. Would they stop worshipping them? Or would they convince themselves that they were just being tested?

"Grab them," she ordered. The townspeople had scattered, but it wouldn't be long before they tried something stupid. She didn't have time to deal with it. "Hurry!"

The horsemen dismounted, cuffed the cultists with iron cuffs and shackles, then hoisted them onto the horses. The beasts made protesting noises, but submitted without a fight. Sir Alaric whooped and led his men back towards Silverdale, galloping away from the town without a care in the world. Isabella followed, feeling another surge of guilt. The man they'd trampled was already dead. She had a nasty feeling their crime would come back to haunt them sooner or later. And there was nothing she could do about it.

Silverdale was perched on her horse, her eyes unfocused. She didn't look at Sir Alaric as he and his prisoners galloped past. "They're cut off. I think ..."

Isabella scowled at her. "You think?"

"They still believe," Silverdale said. Her eyes focused as she came back to herself. "But the iron is hurting them."

"Good." Isabella glanced at the younger girl, silently checking that she was fine, then dug in her spurs. "Follow me."

She resisted the urge to glance back at the town as they galloped away. The townspeople would never know how lucky they'd been. They'd never know just how close they'd come to becoming food sources for alien entities. They'd never know ... Isabella shivered. The entities could take advantage of it, if they knew what had happened. They could send a force to protect the town or forcibly convert the townspeople or … she shook her head. There was no point in worrying. She had too many other things to worry about. The cultists might be shackled, but who knew what they could do? She had to get them into an iron cage before they managed to recover. There was no guarantee the cold iron around their wrists would render them powerless.

Her eyes lingered on the river as they followed it south. Was it her imagination or … were there *things* in the water? Fish? She tried to tell herself they were fish, even though … the water looked too choppy for fish. Her expression darkened as she studied the river itself. It was quite wide, but the entities wouldn't have any trouble fording it. They could get around Kingston quite easily … Reginald had said as much, over breakfast, but she hadn't understood what he'd meant until now. Their defence line was so flimsy it was hard to imagine it lasting long enough to get the soldiers out before the town was either stormed or simply isolated.

She felt a grim awareness that time was running out as they reached the town and passed through the gates. It looked as though more stragglers had returned to the fold, sergeants and officers barking orders as they tried to rebuild units that had been shattered in the previous battle. Reginald's archers were reforming themselves too, even though two-thirds of the once-proud brigade were missing or dead. They couldn't be replaced in a hurry. There'd always been a *lot* of opposition, from what Reginald had said, to the suggestion that commoners would be required to own and practice with a bow. The aristocracy had seen it as a possible threat. They hadn't cared about the kingdom as a whole.

The world is never going to be the same again, she thought. There was definitely no hope of reuniting the empire. *And that means we have to find a way to come to terms with the entities.*

She shook her head. It didn't seem possible.

And yet, if they failed, it would be the end of the world.

Chapter Thirty-Five

"They don't look very impressive," Reginald said.

Silverdale glanced up at her older brother as he peered into the prison cell. It was not the sort of place she would normally be allowed and she suspected that her brother and his wife had had some pretty heated discussions before Silverdale had been invited into the cells. The prisoners really *didn't* look that impressive, at least to those who looked at them with normal eyes. Indeed, they looked revolting. But, when she looked at them through the astral plane, she saw hints of ... taint. *Their* taint. The entities were slowly, but steadily, starting to overshadow the cultists. It was just a matter of time until they were consumed.

She frowned as she studied the prisoners. They didn't look tough any longer. They looked like ... drenched rabbits, as if they'd been hit with a disaster they couldn't even begin to comprehend. And yet, they hadn't chosen to step into the light. They were clinging to their faith, clinging to the stench that hung around them like ... she couldn't put it into words. The cultists didn't think they were beaten, she decided. They saw their imprisonment as nothing more than a test of their faith. She might have considered it admirable, if she hadn't known what was manipulating them. Their perceptions and souls had been warped to the point where they would do anything, as long as it was in their god's name.

Not a god, she reminded herself, once again. *A monster that cloaks itself in godly guise.*

"I want you to be careful," Reginald said. His voice was very cold, but Silverdale could feel the underlying worry. Her brother feared for his wife and unborn child. "If there was someone else ..."

"There isn't," Isabella said. "There's just me."

Silverdale opened her mouth to point out that *she* could do it, then closed her mouth again when Isabella shot her a sharp look. Her brother would be furious if she tried ... she knew, without having to ask, just how much he feared for her, too. She felt a pang of irritation, mingled with a grim awareness that it was Reginald's job to worry. If something happened to her … he'd never forgive himself. And she was, technically, second in line to the throne. Her death would throw the succession into question again.

But only if Reginald and Ruby die before settling the issue, Silverdale thought. *Reginald's child will be the first in line the moment he's born.*

She frowned as her brother turned on his heel and left the chamber. Reginald had too many other things to do to stay and watch, but she thought he would have stayed if he'd been asked. Isabella hadn't asked … Silverdale wasn't sure if she wanted to work without interference or if she wanted to make sure her husband didn't have to watch her die. Silverdale wasn't blind to the risks they were about to take, in hopes of striking back at the entities. She'd seen death now. They were risking both their lives and their souls.

Isabella stepped forward. "I want you to watch," she said. "Whatever happens, do not interfere."

Silverdale gritted her teeth. "And if you run into trouble? Again?"

"If this fails, you may be the only one who can try again," Isabella said, flatly. "I want you to watch and learn from my failure."

"You're not going to fail," Silverdale said. "Just … be careful."

Isabella nodded as she opened the cage door. The prisoners looked up, their eyes tinged with fanaticism. Silverdale could feel their utter faith in their master, a faith shaped by real miracles … by a real reason to believe. She remembered Sofia suddenly and felt sick. Her sister had thrown herself to the gods a long time before the entities had made their presence known. She thought she'd had no choice. Perhaps she was right. She'd had very little control in her life. But she'd made herself vulnerable to entities that had exploited her.

"He is coming," the lead cultist said. He'd said nothing since he'd been captured, even when he'd been threatened with torture or death. "He is coming for you, little witch."

"Really?" Isabella knelt beside the cultist. "Who's coming for me?"

"He is coming, to put you where you belong, to grind you under his heel," the cultist informed her. The conviction in his voice was striking. "He is coming."

"Really?" Isabella smirked. "What sort of god is he, if you cannot speak his name?"

"His name is not spoken in front of infidels," the cultist said. "It is a holy name ..."

"And if I had his name, I could summon him to me," Isabella said. "And if I summoned him, I could bind him and imprison him and even *kill* him. He knows I can do it, too. That's why you're not allowed to mention his name."

She leaned forward. "Do you even *know* his name?"

The cultist merely glowered at her. Silverdale winced at his brooding presence. He'd seen wonders. He wasn't about to let anyone, particularly a sorcerous queen, shake his faith in his god. She could see the logic. Whatever happened to him, whatever he had to endure, he would be rewarded with heaven. His god's heaven. Silverdale felt a flicker of sympathy. She doubted the Godly Realm would be very welcoming. It was far more likely the cultist would be drained dry and left to wink out of existence. There would be no afterlife for him.

"Release me," the cultist said. "Release me, or your torment will be eternal."

Isabella said nothing as she checked the chains. The cultist was chained to the point of absurdity, chained to the point that he could barely move. Isabella had insisted, pointing out the symbolism of pinning the prisoner in place. Silverdale had thought it was pointless – the prisoner didn't appear to be able to control the astral plane – but Isabella had been firm. She might have been right, too, for more reasons than one. The prisoner couldn't attack her when she slipped into the astral plane.

"Watch me," Isabella said. "And don't interfere."

She produced a vial from her pocket and pressed it to her lips. Silverdale was surprised Isabella still needed the potion. *She'd* moved beyond needing it months ago. But she supposed it helped the older woman focus. Silverdale found it hard, sometimes, *not* to look into the astral plane. She sat on her haunches and watched as Isabella's astral self detached itself from her body and drifted towards the prisoner. The prisoner looked … *small* in the astral plane, even though he was a big man. Silverdale guessed it was because he'd given himself to his master.

Watch, she told herself. *Watch and wait.*

***

Isabella could not escape the sense she was doing something wrong as she brushed her astral self against the prisoner's soul. There were spells to read a person's mind, but they were regarded as dark or dangerous or both. The trouble with keeping an open mind, her tutors had joked, was that it was impossible to be sure what might crawl in. The jokes had been funny during training, back when the world had made a certain kind of sense. Now, knowing what lurked in the astral plane, the humour was gone. There were living ideas – nightmares – prowling at the edge of human awareness. They might crawl into someone's mind and lay eggs at any moment.

And there were people who thought commoners couldn't handle the truth about magic, Isabella remembered. *They'd faint if they saw the universe now.*

She tried to smile, but there was no humour as she skimmed the top of the prisoner's mind. His presence was strikingly small, without the life and light she'd sensed from Silverdale and others. He had very few links, very few connections to anyone else. She guessed his faith had weakened his connections to everyone outside the faith, destroying ties his family might have used to draw him back from the brink. The one solid link led up and outward, into the Godly Realm. Isabella breathed a sigh as she studied the link, allowing her awareness to widen without actually *following* the link to its master. The entity didn't seem to be aware of her. She had the oddest feeling it didn't care about her. It pulsed, contentedly, as it drained energy from its victims.

Isabella scowled as she studied the connection. The cultist had practically surrendered everything to the entity. She should have picked up a hint of self-awareness – a name, if nothing else – but his mind was practically blank. There were no memories of his life before accepting the entity into his soul, no sense of hopes and fears, of desires and lusts … she shivered, suddenly cold. The cultist was being drained.

It was quite possible – her mind shied away from calculating the odds – that he'd be drained completely before he sired children of his own. There would be no replacements when he died.

They're eating their seed corn, she thought, as she examined the link closely. *They won't be bound to us for eternity. They're going to kill us. They're going to exterminate us.*

She leaned forward, summoning her magic. The cultist shifted uncomfortably as the power grew stronger. She tasted his revulsion … his *tainted* revulsion. She'd met plenty of people who hated, feared or resented magicians, but the cultist was different. The people she'd met had feared what she might do to them – or, more generally, feared a woman with power. The cultist seemed to hate magic because of his tie to the entity. She braced herself, then forced the link open and forced magic up and into the Godly Realm. It might just work.

The entity recoiled in shock. Isabella tasted the creature's agony as it surged down the link. Her ears hurt … it took her a moment to realise that, back in the physical world, the cultists were screaming. A wave of nausea slammed into her, as if the entire world was vomiting helplessly. She tried to hold on, to keep feeding magic into the link, but it was growing harder and harder to keep the link open. The entity was pushing down on her, trying to shove her out … the cultist's head was threatening to explode. Isabella forced herself to hold on as the push grew stronger. The entity was effectively trying to perform surgery on itself, trying to cut something out of its heart without killing itself in the process. She could feel hints of other entities looking down at her … no, looking at the creature she was trying to kill. They didn't understand what was happening …

A wave of frustration and hate shot through her. *Die*, she thought. *Die. Die. DIE. DIE.*

The link fractured. A whirlpool enveloped her, threatening to drag her down into the darkness. The entire world was shattering around her. Isabella panicked, trying to fly away from certain death. It didn't work. She was being dragged down. Her vision started to dim … she remembered, barely in time to save herself, that she didn't have a physical form within the astral realm. She could fly as fast as she liked. She darted away and crashed back into her own body, the whirlpool fading from her awareness ... no, snapping out of existence. Her eyes snapped open. The cultist was dead. Blood leaked from every orifice and pooled on the ground. Isabella retched, despite herself. She didn't stop retching until her stomach was completely empty.

"Isabella!" Someone was screaming at her. It was hard to be sure. Her thoughts were fractured ... the cultist had died and she'd been almost sucked down too. She thought ... it was hard to be sure of anything. "Isabella!"

Isabella tried to stand. Her legs failed. She forced herself to look up as her chest contracted painfully. She thought, just for a moment, that she'd been punched repeatedly ... panic shot through her as she remembered the baby. What had she done? She swallowed hard, tasting bile and the remnants of half-digested potion. Reginald would never forgive her if she killed their child. She would never forgive herself.

"Isabella!" Silverdale. It was Silverdale. "What happened?"

"I ... I think I hurt it," Isabella said. Her memories were a jumbled mess. Had she *killed* the entity? She didn't think so, but she'd very definitely made it notice her. The other cultists were staring at her in shock. "I think I hurt it badly."

"I'm getting Reggie," Silverdale said. "You lie still."

"No," Isabella managed. She stumbled to her feet, telling herself time and time again – in the hopes she'd believe it – that she'd had worse. "Give me a moment to recover."

She leaned against the wall, trying to breathe. Her breath kept catching in her throat, as if ... as if she were on the verge of choking. She didn't dare try to check on the baby. She was too fearful of the results. Silverdale stood beside her, wringing her hands. The younger girl didn't know what to do. Isabella understood, better than she cared to admit. Whatever choice Silverdale made, someone was going to be upset. Isabella had been in enough spots like that to know they were never easy to resolve.

"You look terrible," Silverdale said. "I mean, really terrible."

Isabella snorted. "The charm school was a waste of money, wasn't it?"

She felt a stab of regret as soon as she said it. Her father had often threatened her with charm school, although – given that the schools seemed to specialise in turning brains into mush – she was fairly sure it had always been an empty threat. Silverdale was too young to attend, even if the schools still existed. Besides ... she *was* young. She had an excuse for lacking the tact and grace of a woman ten years older. And ... Isabella sighed, inwardly, as she straightened up. The poor girl had watched from a distance – a safe distance, Isabella hoped – as her sister-in-law had tried to murder an inhuman creature in cold blood, only to be nearly killed in the process. She could be excused for being impolite.

And I probably do look terrible, she thought. *Reginald is not going to see me like this*.

The cultists started to chant. Isabella jumped. They were there ... she'd forgotten they were there. Alarm ran through her as she stared at them, hastily checking the chains were still in place. They were, but ... the chant was growing stronger. She could *feel* something in the air. Her hair tried to stand on end, an unholy prickling running down her spine as the chanting grew louder and louder. She could feel the entity massing its power. She could feel the astral plane start to shudder. She could feel ... a storm. A storm was building on the edge of reality.

Silverdale moaned, pressing her hands to her temples. Isabella winced in sympathy. The little princess was getting the brunt of it, even though the entity wasn't doing anything. Yet. She could feel its presence growing stronger, she could taste malice hanging in the air as the entity reached through its pawns. The astral plane was twisting, ghostly fingers reaching out towards her. The entire mansion started to shake. She heard something crashing in the distance.

"He is coming," the cultists said. They spoke in eerie unison. "He is coming. He is coming."

"No," Isabella said.

She was too weak to draw her sword, but she still had her dagger hidden up her sleeve. She drew it, the cold iron reassuringly solid as the world started to fracture around her, and cut their throats in one smooth motion. Reality seemed to hang on a knife-edge for a long, chilling moment, then snapped back to normal. The presence vanished. She breathed a sigh of relief as the three bodies fell to the floor. That had been too close.

Silverdale groaned, again. "I … I didn't know they could do that."

"Neither did I," Isabella said. She cursed under her breath. She'd assumed the cold iron would be enough to keep the captives prisoner. It had worked, she supposed, but it hadn't deprived them of *all* of their tricks. "I think we have to rethink our approach."

Her mind raced as she turned and headed for the door. The entity hadn't been killed. She guessed, from what she'd sensed, that she'd given the creature one hell of a belly ache. It had killed its cultist rather than keep eating poison … she wondered, suddenly, why it hadn't let the poor bastard go. Perhaps it couldn't. They needed human permission to enter the hearts of men. They might not be able to *leave* without permission, too.

We hurt them, she told herself. *And we can use it to hurt them again.*

Silverdale looked as if she was going to be sick herself. "What now?"

"First, we get washed," Isabella said. She was all too aware her shirt was badly stained. She needed a wash and a change of clothes. "And then, we sit down and work out how to do it again."

She smiled, despite the throbbing in her head, as a thought struck her. The entities were, for once, at a disadvantage. It was unlikely they knew where she was. The Godly Realm was so tiny, in human terms, that they didn't consider distances … they would have to warn all their cultists, even the ones who were so far away there was no hope of catching them. If she was lucky, she'd slowed their plans enough to give the kingdom time to catch its breath …

Or push them into taking the offensive now, she thought, sourly. The Godly Realm was coming closer. She could feel it. *They still have advantages, if they have time to use them. And there's nothing we can do about it.*

Chapter Thirty-Six

Theodore had known, somehow, that his passage from the remains of the burnt-out city to Kingston would be unimpeded. He had no idea *how* he knew. The enemy cavalry was probably already probing west, trying to keep the remnants of the king's army from reforming and setting up new defence lines; the local civilians were probably licking their lips in anticipation at the thought of knocking a handful of stragglers on the head, stealing everything on them and slitting their throats. They'd have the chance to take a little revenge – Theodore was too experienced to think King Reginald's orders would have been heeded – and endear themselves to the invaders at the same time. A flicker of contempt, oddly dulled, ran through him. Civilians could be relied upon to support whoever looked stronger at any given moment, then switch sides the moment that changed. It was pathetic ...

And yet, it felt right.

A sense of unease ran through him as he made his way down the road. The civilians, the few he saw, largely ignored him. There was no sign of the enemy army. A handful of villages looked abandoned, as if the inhabitants had downed tools and run into the forest. They probably had. The enemy army was even less likely to behave itself than the *king's* army, or so they'd think. Everyone knew that looting, raping and pillaging their way through enemy communities were perks of the job. They made up for low pay, aristocratic officers and the risk of death ...

Theodore recoiled at the thought. The idea that the entity he'd seen would order such atrocities was ... hard to believe. No, it was impossible to believe. His mind twisted itself in knots as it tried to understand what was happening. Atrocities would happen – he knew that, as surely as he knew his name – and yet, he was sure they wouldn't. It just made no sense at all.

The thought tormented him as he made his way down the long road to Kingston. There were more and more people on the streets, heading west in hopes of finding a little safety. The civilians who'd objected to taking care of refugees were now refugees themselves, all too aware they'd be shown little more consideration than the people they'd turned away. Here and there, he saw wounded soldiers and deserters amongst the crowd. He said nothing. There was no point. Most of them weren't fit for service any longer. The remainder would probably be swept up when they tried to cross the bridges …

Unless they head north or south and cross somewhere out of sight, Theodore thought. The river wasn't an impassable barrier. There was nothing stopping a relatively fit man from swimming across. *The enemy army will follow in their wake.*

He felt an eerie sense of despondency as he followed the road down to the bridges. The king's army had taken control of the town and started to set up defences, but his experienced eye told him they'd be worse than useless. There just weren't enough men, within eyeshot, to hold the trenches and walls. There didn't seem to be any defences at the rear, either. The enemy army would ford the river and attack from the rear, if they bothered to attack at all. The town's sole value lay in the bridges and they weren't important enough to force the enemy to attack along a narrow front. Hell, the enemy could simply walk through the Godly Realm and *then* attack the vulnerable rear.

"Halt!" A guard raised a spear as Theodore approached. "Who are you?"

"Sergeant Theodore Ashworth, attached to the Royal Bodyguard," Theodore said. He wasn't sure if that was still true, but it was the quickest way to see the king. No one would dare claim to be part of the Royal Bodyguard unless they *were*. It would be an automatic death sentence. "I have a message for the king."

He sighed, inwardly, as the guard called another guard, who called a sergeant, who – finally – called an officer. The army might have been soundly thrashed – by supernatural fire, no less – but discipline had to be maintained. If he'd been in charge, he would have frog-marched himself to the king at once … probably after strip-searching and binding his hands just to be sure he couldn't do any harm. Instead … he shook his head in irritation as he was finally escorted into the town. They should have searched him, at the very least. They hadn't even bothered to blindfold him!

"Sergeant," a voice said. "You're alive!"

Theodore stared in disbelief. Sir Alaric was alive? How … he felt as if he'd been punched in the gut. Hundreds – thousands – of good men had died in the fires, burnt to ashes … and Sir Alaric had survived? How? He wondered, savagely, if Sir Alaric had made a deal with the entities … or if he'd just been protected by sheer dumb luck. It was pretty much the way the world worked. People could slave for years and never enjoy the fruits of their labour; others – aristos – could laze around all day and still wallow in the best the world had to offer. He felt a surge of sheer bitterness as he looked at the fop. The urge to just bury his fist in the man's throat was overwhelming.

"Yes," he managed, finally. "And I have a message for the king."

Sir Alaric visibly swallowed a handful of questions as he led Theodore into a mansion that had clearly once belonged to someone with a very high opinion of himself. Theodore glanced from side to side, noting how few defences were visible. A trained squad could probably take the mansion in less than ten minutes. The owner – or at least the designer – probably wasn't a nobleman. A city father, perhaps. Theodore dismissed the thought as utterly immaterial as he was marched into the hall and, finally, searched. He resisted the urge to crack jokes. The searchers probably didn't have much of a sense of humour.

He felt tired, tired and worn, as he was finally shown into the war room. The king was still young, seemingly unchanged by the defeat, but … there was something *faded* about him. Theodore couldn't put it into words. It felt as if he'd been staring into the sun, then into the moon. The sun had been so bright the moon was just … he felt his head start to ache as he put it together. King Reginald was impressive, for a human. But he was just *human*. The entity that had sent Theodore on his way was … not. Theodore felt a yearning he couldn't put into words either. He *wanted* to go back.

"Sergeant," the king said. Behind him, his little sister looked alarmed. "I'm glad you made it out alive."

"I didn't, sire," Theodore said. The words felt like ashes in his mouth. "They took me prisoner. And ... and *he* sent me back with a message."

The king's eyes narrowed as Theodore relayed the message, then detailed everything that had happened over the last two days. He showed no visible reaction, but ... there was something cold and hard in his eyes. King Reginald wouldn't surrender, even though the situation was hopeless ... Theodore swallowed, hard. The entity had twisted his mind. It was hard, so hard, to believe there was a hope of actual resistance. He felt as if he'd lost a part of himself. No, as if he'd given it to the entity.

"There was something suffering in the king's eyes," he finished. "I don't know what happened to him."

But that wasn't true, he reflected sourly. Theodore prided himself on being deeply cynical, on always looking a gift horse in the mouth, yet even *he* had been overawed by the entity. The entity was a perfect warrior king ... he knew he was being manipulated, that his emotions were being twisted, yet it was hard to believe it. The poor king – a weak man, if the stories were true – hadn't stood a chance. He'd probably *welcomed* the entity when it had revealed itself to him. He hadn't understood the price until it was too late.

"I can guess," the king said. "Does *he* want you to return with a reply?"

"He didn't say," Theodore said. That was odd. He felt a yearning to return that terrified him to the bone. "I don't know if I should return."

"He has to want some kind of reply, even if it's just *nuts*," the king said. "You have a rest. I want to talk to my council."

He nodded to one of his guards. "Escort the sergeant to a room and give him something to eat. I'll speak to him later."

And keep me prisoner if I want to leave, Theodore added, silently. He'd been in the Royal Bodyguard long enough to know the score. *You might be wiser chaining me to the wall.*

He winced, inwardly, as he was shown out of the chamber. The yearning was wrong. He felt as if he was eying the wife or daughter of a wealthy and powerful nobleman, the kind of forbidden fruit he shouldn't even be *thinking* about touching. And yet, the sheer love for the forbidden was burning into his mind. He wanted to go back to the entity and throw himself at its feet, even though he knew it would be the end of him. Once, he'd mocked weak men who allowed themselves to become dependent on drugs. Now, he understood how their cravings had grown to dominate their lives. They hated it – they hated what they'd become – but they went back to the drug dens anyway.

I won't go back, he told himself. *I won't.*

But he knew, all too clearly, that he might well be lying to himself.

***

Reginald kept his face under tight control as Sergeant Ashworth was shown out of the war room, only allowing his lips to tighten when the door was firmly closed. The sergeant might or might not know it, but he'd clearly been affected by the entities. Reginald knew through grim experience just how easily they could warp the human mind, no matter how determined their victims were to resist. He'd seen what they'd done to Sofia. Sergeant Ashworth probably had his own weak points, his own hopes and fears and bitter resentments that could be used to weaken his defences. Given time, the entities could do whatever they liked to him.

Or to anyone, Reginald thought.

Silverdale nudged him, gently. "Can we talk?"

Reginald nodded, steering her towards the side room. The war room itself was practically useless. They'd found a handful of maps, but most of them were so poorly drawn that there was no way to safely estimate distances. In some, Havelock was practically touching the Golden City; in others, they appeared to be so far apart there was no hope of a messenger from one ever reaching the other. Reginald was all too aware the distances between kingdoms had grown wider – practically, if not literally – in the last six years, but there were limits. There *had* to be limits.

He closed the door and peered at his sister. Silverdale was growing up, he thought with a sudden pang. She was still young, but she'd seen and experienced more than he had when he'd been her age. There was a hardness in her eyes that bothered him. She was no longer his kid sister. She was no longer a pawn on the international marriage market. She was … she was her own person, for better or worse. He made a mental note to treat her as something more than a child, even if she wasn't an adult. Not yet.

"That man has been overshadowed," Silverdale said.

Reginald tensed, one hand dropping to his sword. Sergeant Ashworth had clearly been affected by the entities, but … overshadowed? He hadn't *felt* overshadowed. The signs of someone who'd given himself so completely to the entities had been absent. His face hadn't been a blur. And yet … there'd been something about the sergeant that had worried him. The man he'd known had been a lot more … loyal.

"How so?" He wondered, suddenly, if he should order the man killed. "What did they do to him?"

"Not completely," Silverdale added. "But the entity tainted him. Like" – she struggled for words – "like it stuck a thorn in his side. A poisoned thorn. Given time, it will overshadow him completely."

Reginald felt a pang of guilt – and fear. "How?"

"I don't know," Silverdale said. "I can try to read his memories …"

"No," Reginald said, sharply. There was no guarantee the taint couldn't spread to Silverdale and infect *her*. Even if it didn't, Sergeant Ashworth would be furious at the invasion of privacy. Reginald knew what *he'd* do to anyone who had his mind read and *he* had to think about the kingdom first. A loyal man could become a deadly enemy through abuse. "You are not to try."

Silverdale rested her hands on her hips. "I could ask him …"

"No," Reginald repeated. "I will not have you take the risk."

He started to pace the room. It was odd, to say the least, that the entity hadn't made any provision for a reply. Why bother sending an ultimatum if you didn't want to hear the response? Reginald knew the conventions as well as anyone. There were plenty of ways to offer safe conduct agreements, keeping them in being just long enough to ensure the messages reached their destinations. Did the entity think he'd send the sergeant back to the remains of the ruined city?

Or … would the sergeant *want* to go back? Or …

Is it trying to lull me into a false sense of security? Reginald considered the possibilities for a long cold moment. *It might be trying to convince me it doesn't intend to take the offensive in a hurry.*

He shook his head. His men were already doing everything in their power to strengthen the defences. Given time, he could make the enemy pay a heavy price for Kingston … or simply fall back on the next walled city. It would be costly, but he could force them to bleed themselves white trying to take Havelock. And yet … given the nature of the enemy, a conventional plan might end badly. They had a near-unlimited number of soldiers to throw at the walls. A single traitor in the right – or, rather, the wrong – place would be enough to let them inside the defences. The thought tormented him. He might be unable to hold them back long enough for Isabella and the others to come up with a more permanent solution.

Silverdale cleared her throat. "What are we going to do?"

"I don't know," Reginald said. Something was nagging at the back of his mind. Something the sergeant had said. Something half-lost in his praise of the entity. "Did Isabella's idea even *work*?"

"It made the entities take notice," Silverdale said. She'd said as little as possible about what had actually happened, something that worried him too. "It certainly *hurt* the … them."

"You've been spending too much time around me," Reginald said. He was sure she'd intended to use a word she wasn't supposed to know. "Where is my wife?"

"She's getting cleaned up," Silverdale said. "She'll be along when done."

Reginald scowled at her. Isabella could get up and dressed within minutes. She didn't spent hours washing, getting dressed and applying cosmetics. Even if she'd had to change her entire outfit, she could have done it – she should have done it – by now. She should have joined him before the sergeant arrived. He would have welcomed her insights. He felt as if he was advancing into the darkness, inching forward and yet morbidly sure the enemy was creeping up behind him. The rules kept changing. He had a feeling they would never be able to grasp the underlying basis, if indeed there *was* an underlying basis …

And if she's taking hours to change, he thought, *either something went very wrong or she's stalling.*

There was a knock on the door. He looked up. "Enter!"

A messenger peered into the room. "Your Majesty, Captain-General Stuart and a mounted troop has arrived from Havelock," he said. "Your brother is amongst them."

Reginald blinked. His brother? He didn't *have* a brother. A trick of some kind? It hardly seemed likely. The kingdom might not know *much* about their rulers, but they certainly knew the previous king had only one son. Reginald's father had made the entire kingdom swear an oath to uphold the succession, when Reginald had come of age. There was no point in pretending to be his brother. No one would be fooled for a moment.

Alden, he thought, suddenly. Isabella's brother, Reginald's brother-in-law. *He's meant to be back with Ruby.*

He stood. "Have them shown into the dining room," he said. It wasn't much of a conference room, but it would have to do. He'd see what Stuart – and Alden – had to say for themselves before he passed judgement. If they were here … it boded ill. "And invite my wife to join us."

"Yes, Your Majesty."

Reginald headed for the door, then stopped as his earlier thought snapped into sharp focus. It was a plan … it was a *crazy* plan, but it might just work. It might …

Silverdale coughed. "Reginald?"

"I've had an idea," Reginald said. She wouldn't approve, he thought, but … it was worth a try. Isabella probably wouldn't approve, either. But she'd understand. "And if it works, we'll win outright."

And if we lose, his thoughts pointed out, *we'll lose outright, too.*

Chapter Thirty-Seven

Isabella could sense Reginald's displeasure as Captain-General Stuart explained why he'd led the reinforcements personally, defying his king's orders in the process. It was wise to have a commander who was aristocratic enough to keep the other aristos in line, but Reginald had needed a strong officer at Havelock to safeguard Ruby's position. The princess was in no danger – probably – as long as her brother was still alive, yet if he died ... Isabella glanced at Alden, frowning inwardly. *Her* brother should have stayed with the princess, too.

Talk about that later, she told herself, firmly. *You don't want to have that discussion in public.*

She kept her face under tight control as her eyes swept the table. The council of war was *much* reduced. Captain-General Gars and Captain-General Jones were dead or in enemy hands. Colonel Hastings and Sir Alaric represented the infantry and cavalry respectively, but neither of them had the authority or experience to dominate the table. Stuart was the only survivor of the previous council, save for Isabella herself. And Silverdale, by normal standards, shouldn't have been allowed anywhere near the council table. Isabella was surprised someone hadn't told her to leave war and politics to the men.

They're taking their lead from Reginald, she reminded herself. *They know better than to question him openly.*

"The scale of the disaster was such, we believed, that getting reinforcements up to you was vitally important," Stuart finished. "Your sister insisted on it."

"Good," Reginald said. He wasn't happy. "We'll discuss that later."

He took a breath. "Now we're all up to date with everything that's happened over the last two days, it should be clear that we won't be allowed to remain here much longer. The enemy has already demanded our surrender.

They'll start marching within a day."

"Perhaps sooner," Isabella said. "We gave the entities a nasty shock."

Reginald nodded. "I think we have one chance to win this," he said. "At the very least, we should buy ourselves some more time and make them take us seriously. And time is precisely what we need."

Isabella frowned. Reginald hadn't discussed his idea with her. *That* didn't bode well. Her husband wasn't foolish enough to dismiss her opinion as automatically worthless. Whatever he had in mind, she feared she would not approve. She touched her abdomen lightly. The child was growing within her womb, apparently unharmed. She felt a sudden stab of fear. The thought of losing her husband, and the father of her child, was just too much.

"The entities are shaped by our perceptions," Reginald reminded them. "Sergeant Ashworth's ... gushing praise of the entity that overshadowed King Forsyth suggests that *this* entity sees itself as an honourable warrior. Reports indicate it certainly *isn't* devastating the surrounding countryside. It even allowed some of our men to go free, once they were unarmed. I believe it cannot help itself."

"It had no trouble burning an entire city to the ground," Silverdale said, in a tone that suggested she didn't know where Reginald was going either. "*Two* entire cities, to be exact."

"Yes," Reginald agreed. "But that is a perfectly legitimate tactic of war."

Isabella wasn't convinced. She was no fool who thought war could be rendered bloodless. She was no idiot who assumed soldiers could avoid killing civilians. But ... there was a gap – a gulf – between accidentally hitting a child with an arrow, fired blindly into a city, and burning the entire city to ashes. It was a ruthless tactic, horrific beyond words. It spoke of a kind of warfare that cared nothing for human life, just practicality. She shuddered in disgust as she tried to calculate how many people had died in the flames. There was no answer. There *couldn't* be an answer.

"I'll take your word for it," Alden said. He sounded tired, as if he was still drawing on his magic to keep himself alive. It hadn't been *that* long since he'd fled the Golden City.

"What do you have in mind?"

Reginald smiled. "I intend to challenge the entity to a duel," he said, "with the kingdom itself as the stakes."

Isabella blinked. "What?"

"Clever," Stuart said. "If you won, the entity would be dead."

"Are you mad?" Silverdale stood, her voice rising hysterically. "You'll die."

Reginald tapped the sword on his belt. "Cold iron."

Isabella swallowed, hard. "Cold iron or not, the entity will still be stronger and faster than you," she said. "And if you lose …"

"The entity is bound to a human body," Reginald reminded her. "It cannot move *much* faster than the average human."

"And there's no guarantee it will play fair," Isabella added. The whole plan struck her as madness. Reginald might die, opening the doorway for the entities to stroll into his kingdom and take it. "If you lose, the entire kingdom will be lost."

"I know." Reginald met her eyes, evenly. "You've been in war. What are our chances if – when – the enemy armies come here?"

Isabella lowered her eyes. She didn't want to admit the truth. "Low."

"Quite." There was no triumph in Reginald's voice. "I think the entity will have no choice, but to accept my challenge. And … no, it probably won't play fair. But we're not going to play fair either. For starters, I'm going to abdicate in favour of my unborn son."

You don't even know the child is a boy, Isabella thought, coldly. There were spells to check an unborn child's gender, but she'd never been taught how to use them. *It could be a girl.*

"And you're going to jab the entity, just as it goes onto the field," Reginald continued, calmly. "You're going to distract it long enough for me to kill it."

"By poisoning the link with magic," Isabella realised. She could see the plan now, but … it depended on too many factors outside their control. "How do you intend to send the challenge?"

"Sergeant Ashworth can take the challenge," Reginald said.

Silverdale shook her head. "We need him to give the entity a jolt," she reminded him. "There are no more cultists …"

"And none we know to be tied to that *particular* entity," Isabella finished. She winced at the thought of what they were going to do. "We need him here."

"Perhaps not," Alden said. "We can craft a blood link."

Isabella's eyes narrowed. "And you know how to do it?"

"Yes." Alden made a face. "Father taught me, years ago."

"Why am I not surprised?" Isabella grimaced. Blood magic wasn't precisely forbidden, not when all the great families made use of it, but it was borderline dark. It was very easy to twist someone through blood-based spells. That their father had known even some of those spells … she wasn't remotely surprised. "Can you make them work?"

"Yes." Alden looked pale, but ready. "I know how to use them."

"Good," Reginald said. He stood, indicating the matter was closed. "This is what we're going to do …"

***

Theodore felt as if he was going mad.

He sat on the hard, wooden chair, trying to focus his mind. It didn't work. Every time he thought he'd calmed himself, he remembered the entity and found himself spinning into madness again. He cursed under his breath, silently kicking himself for each and every time he'd made fun of opium fiends. He'd mocked them for not breaking the habit … it had been hard, he realised now. Their bodies had demanded their fix and … the only real solution had been to lock them up and keep them in chains until the cravings finally stopped. Now …

His eyes flickered to the door. It wasn't much. The room hadn't been designed as an actual *prison*. He didn't have any weapons, but the door was nothing more than a flimsy layer of wood. A single kick would be enough to knock it down. There would be a guard on the far side, perhaps more than one, but Theodore *knew* the guards would be no match for him. He'd put them down, take their weapons and run east. He'd be back with his master, bathing in his glorious light, in no time.

Disgust and revulsion rose up within him. He was no … he

was no slave, beaten into helpless submission. He was ... he was a free man, a loyal servant of his mind ... he was ... it was growing harder and harder to keep that in mind. He didn't want to surrender, yet ... his will to resist was leaching away into nothingness. Theodore raised his hand and pinched his arm, hard enough to leave a bruise. The pain made it easier to focus, for a few brief seconds, before the yearning started again. He was a good servant of his master. He was a good servant ... he retched, trying to catch hold of his treacherous thoughts. Perhaps it would be better if he hurled himself through a window and plummeted to his death. He was fighting as hard as he could, but he was all too aware his will was fading.

I will not give in, he told himself, savagely. *I will not give in.*

Sweat beaded on his brow. Unseen forces – imaginary forces – seemed to pull him towards the door. The walls felt thin, even though he wasn't touching them. His imagination told him he could walk right *through* the doors. The chair felt painfully insubstantial, as if he was about to fall on his arse. He stood, aware – too late – that he was on the verge of giving in, of breaking down the door and running back to his master. It was all he could do to keep himself still. Sitting down was not an option. Not any longer.

The door opened. Theodore bit his lip so hard it bled as the king stepped through, followed by a grey-haired man who looked ... odd. Not overshadowed, but ... *wrong*. He wore a simple tunic, yet held himself like a titled aristocrat. In earlier days, Theodore would have enjoyed the puzzle. Now, he could barely keep himself from running through the door and out into the open streets.

"You're bleeding," the older man said. He drew a handkerchief from his belt and wiped Theodore's mouth before he could say a word. "Do you want me to heal it?"

Theodore glared. "Who the hell are you?"

"It doesn't matter," the king said. "Will you take a message for me? Back to the entity?"

"I ..." Theodore felt his heart leap and knew he was lost. An excuse to go home, back to his master ... he couldn't say no. "I ... yes."

"Good," the king said. "Tell him I challenge him to a duel.

He and I, fighting for the kingdom. If I lose, if I die, my patrimony will become his. If I win, he and his armies withdraw from my lands."

Theodore blinked, utterly surprised. The king's patrimony was his until he passed it down to his son. He couldn't simply hand it over … could he? His thoughts were lost in a whirlwind of emotion. He was going to go back to his master. He was going to be his …

"I understand," he said. "Can I go?"

The king glanced at the older man, who nodded. Theodore took it for dismissal and ran past, throwing caution to the winds. The mansion was oddly designed, but he had no trouble finding his way downstairs and onto the streets. No one tried to stop him as he picked up speed, running past soldiers and civilians who'd been pressed into military service. They didn't matter. Only his master mattered …

His master … and the message he was carrying for him.

***

Isabella braced herself as she stopped outside the makeshift lab, feeling oddly uncertain of herself. There'd been too many shocks in one day, from Reginald's suicidal plan to the grim discovery that Sergeant Ashworth had been almost completely overshadowed. Silverdale had sworn blind that, when the sergeant had entered the mansion, he'd been barely tainted. A thorn, she'd said. And the thorn had grown into a dagger.

She told herself she was being silly as she pushed the door open and stepped inside. Alden was sitting at the table, his fingers pressed against a bloodstained handkerchief. He'd been sure the combination of the blood and the link between the sergeant and his liege lord would be enough to maintain the connection, but it was impossible to be sure. The entities broke all the normal rules. Alden looked up at her and smiled, nervously. She felt her resolve weaken, again. He looked too much like their father for her peace of mind.

"I understand you're having a baby," Alden said. "How did *that* come about?"

"I'm sure *someone* told you about the birds and the bees when you were a little boy," Isabella said, tartly. She pulled out a chair and sat down, eyes lingering on the charm dancing around his fingertips. "Reginald and I enjoy a happy and fulfilling sex life, thank you very much."

Alden coloured. "I'm sorry I asked."

Isabella felt a twinge of regret. "I'm sorry too," she said. She changed the subject before the conversation could get any worse. "Why did you come here?"

"I had nowhere else to go," Alden said. "Coming to you … where else would I go?"

"I thought you were going to stay in Havelock," Isabella said. "Princess Ruby might have needed you …"

Alden looked at his hands for a long moment. "I didn't fit in," he said. "This new world … it doesn't have a place for me."

Isabella frowned. "What does *that* have to do with it?"

"I …" Alden shook his head. "I wanted to tell you I'm sorry. I … I should have protected you. I should have tried to tell our father that … that he didn't *need* to treat you like a slave, like something he could mould to suit himself. I should have tried to reach out to you …"

"You should have," Isabella agreed, tonelessly. She allowed none of her inner consternation to show on her face. "Why didn't you?"

"I was scared," Alden admitted. "He was such a great man, at first. The family was going places. We were going to be top of the heap. Kingmakers, if not kings ourselves. And then things started going wrong. He'd moved too far, too fast. Too many families were allying against us. He started to get desperate. He made deals that threatened to come back to haunt us. He became obsessed with planting his people in useful places …"

"Like me," Isabella said.

"Yes." Alden sighed. "He thought he could put you in the Inquisition. He thought he could still come out ahead, even after you left. The Grand Sorcerer was dying. He might not be able to influence who won the contest, but he might be able to shape the names and faces around the winner. Everything started to work, finally …

"And then the empire collapsed," Isabella finished. She snickered. "It was all for nothing."

"Yes," Alden echoed. "It was all for nothing."

Isabella stood and started to pace. "Everything," she said.

It would have been easier, she thought, if her father had *just* been a sadist. She would have found it much easier to walk away from someone who abused his children for kicks. "The lectures. The beatings. The endless sessions with an endless stream of private tutors ... all for nothing. The family is gone."

She swallowed, hard. "What happened to the others?"

"Dead," Alden said. "A couple were hostages, killed during the fighting. The others ... I don't know what happened to them, but they're dead. I couldn't form a blood link with them when the rubble stopped bouncing. They're gone."

Isabella looked at the blood. It was possible, she thought, to cut a blood link ... but difficult, almost impossible, without the proper training. She would have done it, if she'd known how; she'd always assumed her father had disowned her so completely that her name had been expunged from the family book. And instead ... ice curdled around her heart as she wondered if her father had always thought she'd return to him. It wasn't impossible. He'd certainly seemed confident that, in the long run, she was firmly under his thumb.

She shook her head. Their father was dead. He couldn't hurt them anymore.

Her voice hardened. "What do you want from me?"

"I don't know," Alden said. "I have no right to ask for forgiveness. I failed you and I admit that and ... and there's no way I can make it up to you. And you're carrying the future of the family ..."

"My family," Isabella snarled. She wasn't sure if Reginald's mad plan to crown their unborn child would actually *work*. Perversely, it might cripple the entities while doing nothing to stop their human enemies. It was hard enough to keep a child-king on the throne, now the Grand Sorcerer and the Court Wizards were a distant memory. She hated to think how hard it would been to keep an *unborn* child in power. "Our family is dead."

She clenched her fists as she turned away. "I had the courage to walk away and build a life for myself," she demanded. "Why didn't you?"

"I thought it was worth something," Alden said. "I was wrong."

"Yes." Isabella felt her anger drain away, to be replaced by numbness. "You were wrong."

She shrugged. "I can't forgive you for not helping," she said. "But at least you're trying to make things better."

"I ..."

Isabella cut him off. "Now, if you'll excuse me, I have to see my husband," she said. She had no doubt the first part of the plan would work. It was the second part that bothered her. "It might be our last night together."

Chapter Thirty-Eight

Reginald hadn't felt quite so keyed up since the day he'd been knighted.

He couldn't help following as much of the old ritual as possible from the moment the cock crowed in the morning. He rose, bathed in cold water and dressed, slowly and carefully, in a suit of light armour. The smiths had woven a mesh of cold iron into the metal so it was touching his skin, sacrificing comfort for protection. Reginald knew he'd be bruised and battered by the end of the day, win or lose, but it didn't matter. He walked back into the bedroom, picked his sword from the table and started to clean it. He'd been taught to take care of his weapons. The task was not one he could pass to a servant.

Isabella sat up in the bed, hands folded over her breasts. They'd spent the night together, after the second messenger arrived to confirm that King Forsyth – and the entity possessing him – had accepted the challenge and proposed the field outside Kingston as a suitable arena for their duel. Reginald had been mildly surprised the entity hadn't suggested somewhere further east, but he figured it wanted to prove that it had won fairly. His lips quirked at the thought. *He* wasn't intending to fight fairly. The blade of cold iron was the *least* of his weapons.

"You'd better come back to me," Isabella said, sternly. "Or I'll dig you up and put you back to work."

Reginald nodded, not trusting himself to speak. They'd had a long argument about the risks of challenging the entity to a duel. Isabella had pointed out he might lose the kingdom anyway, even if he *had* abdicated in favour of his unborn son. The entity might see nothing wrong with taking the kingdom if it won, if only because it had entered the contest in good faith. There were just too many unknowns. Reginald honestly couldn't remember the last time *anything* had been settled by a trial of combat. His father had always discouraged duels. They didn't prove who was right, he'd argued; they'd merely proved who was better with a sword.

He watched as Isabella stood and headed for the bathroom, then picked up his sword and buckled it to his belt. His stomach growled, reminding him he hadn't eaten for hours. He didn't feel like eating anything, but he knew he had to. He'd felt the same on the eve of his first battle, back when he'd been a young and untried man. His father had made him eat …

The thought caused him a pang. His father was dead. His sister was dead. He knew, deep inside, that everything rested on the duel. They had to stop the entity, even if it meant his death. He knew he was leaving his wife and siblings a ghastly mess – he knew the kingdom might shatter, if they failed to secure the regency – but there was no choice. A purely human struggle for power would be bad, yet it would be better than a world dominated by the entities. Silverdale had told him the Godly Realm was inching closer. She'd tried to explain, in a manner that suggested she didn't have the words to explain colour to a blind man, but it didn't matter. All that mattered was that time was running out.

Isabella stepped back into the bedroom, her hair – longer, now – shining under the light. She dressed quickly, donning a simple tunic and sword. It was far from conventional, but no one would dare say a word. Not today. Besides, she might have to saddle up and gallop away if – when – the entity realised it had been tricked. Reginald had given the orders to have horses at the ready, for his wife, sister and brother-in-law. They should be able to make a clean break … he hoped. It was quite possible the Godly Realm would envelop them before they escaped.

The maids entered, carrying trays of food. Reginald felt repulsed, almost, as he looked at the meal. Rabbit stew, with bread … the sort of dinner at which he would have turned his nose up, once upon a time. It smelt good, but he had to force himself to sit and eat. He barely tasted anything. His mind was churning, wondering if it was his last day. The entity wanted – needed – to kill him to claim the kingdom. He looked at his wife, wishing – suddenly – that they'd had more time together. The baby might grow up in a world dominated by the entities, never knowing his father. Or *her* father.

Reginald wanted to pray the child would live. He didn't dare. He didn't know what might be listening.

He drank a sip of heavily-boiled water, then stood. He didn't want to drink too much. Going to the toilet in full armour was something that was left out of the stories, for extremely good reasons. The bards glossed over such details, while caterwauling the praises of whoever was paying their wages. Reginald had to smile, despite the growing emptiness in his stomach. The songs were awful and they left out all sorts of things, from marching through mud to blood and gore and everything no one wanted to know about before they donned armour for the first time. Isabella stood beside him, her face pale.

"Here," she said. She held out a piece of lacy cloth. "Take this."

Reginald blinked. A garter …? "My lady's favour," he said. "Thanks."

Isabella nodded, blushing slightly. "I thought it was … fitting."

"It was," Reginald said. He'd had too many ladies of the court offering him their garters, if not their underclothes, but *this* was the first time it had actually *meant* something. He'd never had to fight for a woman's attention, let alone her body. What did the practice of courtly love mean, when he outranked everyone at court? "I'll wear it with pride."

Isabella snickered, although it was clear she was still deeply worried. "Are you going to hide it under your armour?"

"No." Reginald smiled as he wrapped the garter around his arm. "Everyone will know it's there."

He took her hand, then walked through the door. The armour was light enough not to impede his movements, thankfully. He might have been willing to risk catching a blow on his armour if he'd been facing a human, but the entity was probably strong enough to drive a sword right *through* cold iron. He'd given serious thought to wearing nothing more than a simple tunic and padding, on the grounds it would make it easier to dodge. Isabella had talked him out of it. The armour might not protect him from a blow, but it would shield him from the entity's influence.

His bodyguards formed a line as they left the mansion and

strode through the deserted streets towards the gates. He could feel his soldiers watching him, their eyes burning into his armoured rear. He wondered, grimly, what they were thinking. Did they think he was putting himself in needless danger? Or were they thinking it was right and proper for the matter to be decided by an honourable duel, rather than army against army? He felt a twinge of guilt, remembering all the men who'd died under his command. Would it have been better, he asked himself, if those wars had been settled by duels, too?

Probably, he thought. *But Sofia would never have faced me ...*

The thought would have made him smile, once upon a time. Now ... the flicker of humour drained away as they passed through the gates and crossed the bridge. The entity was already standing at the far side of the field, a humanoid form wrapped in glowing life. Reginald scowled, unable to resist a flash of naked hatred. The entity was larger than life, embodying the promise of a good and true warrior king. Reginald feared that, if things had been different, he would have been sucked into the entity's glow. The allure was too strong to easily resist.

Silence hung in the air as he let go of Isabella's hand. The audience – the handful of soldiers and city fathers summoned to watch the contest – neither cheered nor booed. The stillness mocked him. He told himself, sharply, not to be silly. Everything depended on the duel. Everything. He heard a faint whisper as he advanced, feeling completely alone. Isabella knew what she had to do. She wouldn't watch ...

Good, Reginald thought. *If I die, she won't have to see me fall.*

His eyes sought out the entity. Sergeant Ashworth stood beside it, looking up with all the awe and admiration of a toddler staring at his father. Reginald groaned, knowing the sergeant was lost to them. If a man as stubborn and cynical as the sergeant could be induced to surrender his will, what chance did the *rest* of them have? Sweat prickled across his forehead as he stepped onto the field, raising his sword in challenge. The air felt uncomfortably hot.

The entity advanced, leaving the sergeant behind. Reginald

tried to peer past the glow in hopes of picking out the overshadowed king's features. They were lost within the light, leaving only the faintest hints of eyes and a mouth. King Forsyth had been a weak man, if the stories were true. He hadn't been strong enough to keep his nobles in line. Rumour had it that they'd even been on the verge of overthrowing their king when the entity arrived. Reginald felt little sympathy for them, but his heart ached for their king. He hadn't deserved to be swallowed up by a monster.

"I have come," the entity said. It spoke quietly, but Reginald *knew* everyone could hear every last word. "Let us duel for the kingdom."

It raised its sword and charged.

***

Silverdale wore, for the first time in her life, a pair of trousers. They felt oddly confining against her skin, as if they needed to be worn regularly before she could move freely, but they were so much better than dresses that she was determined never to go back. It was hard to care what the people thought, if they saw their princess in a pair of trousers borrowed from someone's young son. She could run, if she had to; she could run without tripping over herself and landing in the mud. She could run without being caught ...

She felt cold as she stood beside the gatehouse and watched as her brother and his wife advanced across the river. The audience was riveted, watching intently to be sure they didn't miss a single moment. Silverdale cringed, inwardly, as she remembered throwing tantrums because she hadn't been allowed to attend the tournament as a young child. She hadn't been deterred by the warnings they weren't suitable for little girls ... now, she was going to watch her brother fight and perhaps die. She wished, suddenly, that she could go back and tell her younger self to be careful what she demanded. She might get it.

The wind seemed to blow colder as it shifted. She could see the entity in the distance, a creature that was not even remotely human. It looked ... her head hurt every time she looked at it. The Godly Realm glowed around the figure, a pinprick of light that was infinitely huge ... she couldn't make sense of it. And yet, beneath the light and glowing threads linking the entity to its worshippers, there was someone screaming in pain. The host hadn't known what he'd been agreeing to, when he'd accepted the entity into his soul. He did now.

A hand touched her shoulder. Silverdale jumped. Isabella stood there ... how had she crossed the bridge and crept up on Silverdale without being noticed? She wanted to snap and snarl at the older woman, but the silence was all-consuming. No birds sang as the contestants raised their blades, the metal glinting under the sunlight. The entity seemed to be playing fair. Silverdale supposed it didn't have a choice.

Isabella steered her into the gatehouse, closing the door behind them. Silverdale blinked, her eyes adjusting to the darkness. Alden sat at a table, eyes closed as his fingers played with a bloodstained handkerchief. Silverdale shuddered as she saw the complex network of spells, old and new, playing around the blood. She could *see* the link leading to the sergeant ... her stomach churned as she realised what they were doing. She'd known the plan, but ... seeing it was different.

"They're starting," Isabella said. She sat facing her brother, resting her fingers on top of his hands. Silverdale couldn't help noticing Alden's hands were as smooth as her own, without the calluses and scars she'd seen on her father's hands. "We have to hurry."

Silverdale sat. "I'm ready," she said. She knew the risks, but ... the alternative was leaving her brother to die. Her skin crawled as she looked at the blood. She couldn't escape the feeling they'd have to pay a price for breaking the laws of gods and men. "Let's go."

Isabella looked at her. "You remember how to run?"

"Yes." Silverdale scowled. "I know what to do."

She ignored Isabella's sharp look. She had her orders. Get to the tunnel, get out of the town, get onto the horse and don't look back. And don't wait for anyone, even the king's wife and their unborn child. She had privately determined she wasn't going to obey *that* order. She'd sooner put herself in danger than run, again. The unborn child *was* the king. It was her duty to save it, even at the cost of her own life.

"Good." Isabella put a vial to her lips and drank. The blood started to smoulder moments later. "We begin."

***

It was hard, so hard, to think straight.

Sergeant Theodore Ashworth knew, deep inside, that something was very wrong. He couldn't put it into words. They just escaped him as he bathed in the light of his master. He wanted nothing more than to spend his life in service to the warrior king, to follow him across bloody battlefields and burnt-out cities until there were no worlds left to conquer. His master favoured Theodore, particularly after Theodore had returned to him with the promise of an entire kingdom. And yet ...

He watched, his eyes shining with light, as his master contested with the king. The former king. His master had been clear, although he hadn't spoken a single word, that King Reginald was doomed. He was already a former king. King Reginald didn't seem to know it as he fought. They thrust at each other, parrying blows in a dance that could only have one ending. Theodore knew, deep inside, that his master would walk away victorious, with an entire kingdom under his thrall. And yet ... something was wrong. He knew something was wrong.

His eyes hurt as he looked away, sweeping towards the distant audience. His master had come alone, save for Theodore himself; King Reginald had brought a handful of spectators to watch the duel. Theodore peered into their eyes and knew they were on the verge of bending the knee, just waiting for the warrior king to emerge victorious once again. And yet ... his gaze travelled over a pair of young women and stopped, dead, when it alighted on Sir Alaric. A flash of hatred shot through him. It focused his mind ...

Theodore bit his lip, hard, as he fought to stay ... awake. It felt as if he was being dragged down into darkness, into ... into *something*. He could barely keep himself *aware* of himself as the pull grew stronger, yanking his awareness back towards his master. His mind spasmed in shock as he realised how far he'd fallen, how far he'd submitted himself to the entity. It was like the first time he'd gotten drunk, only worse. By the time he'd realised he was drunk, he'd already drunk too much ... his stomach churned, his knees wobbling. Resistance was painful. The urge to just let go, to let himself be sucked into the entity's spell, was overwhelming. He had to clench his fists hard enough to dig his nails into his palms to keep from giving in.

No, he thought. The memory of kneeling before the entity, of bathing in its warm regard for him, was terrifying. He knew it was a lie, he knew the entity didn't care about him, and yet it *called* to him. *I won't give in.*

He raised his eyes, somehow. The duel was still going on. King Reginald was holding his own, but ... it was just a matter of time before he tired and fell. The entity was playing fair – it *had* to play fair – yet it had the whip hand. It just needed to wait for the king to exhaust himself and move in for the kill. King Reginald's blade was cold iron, enough to kill the host and dispatch the entity back to the Godly Realm, but he hadn't managed to land a single blow.

Theodore felt a flicker of admiration, almost despite himself. King Reginald was no fop. He was no entitled brat, using his family name to get what good men couldn't earn in a lifetime of loyal service. The king was fighting bravely, putting his life on the line to save the kingdom from an endless nightmare. There was nothing wrong with his technique either, nothing to suggest he'd been taught by a prissy dancing master rather than a sergeant who knew all the tricks. He fought like someone who'd fought for his life – for real – time and time again. Theodore clung to that admiration, using it to centre himself. King Reginald was human. And that made all the difference.

And someone was whispering at the edge of his awareness ...

Chapter Thirty-Nine

Isabella plunged into a whirlwind of emotion as she allowed the blood to carry her awareness towards Sergeant Ashworth. The astral plane was a maelstrom of light and power, warped and twisted by the presence of the entity and its link to the Godly Realm. The sergeant was still fighting – Isabella could sense his desperation to save something of himself – but he was losing, and losing badly. He was drowning in bloodstained mud, his desperate struggles only making him sink faster. She breathed a sigh of relief as she sensed him looking at her. His awareness was already halfway within the astral realm.

She hoped the entity couldn't sense her as she brushed her soul against the sergeant's. It felt as if she was doing something wrong, as if she was allowing herself to become intimate with a man who wasn't her husband. She knew there was no choice – she knew Reginald understood what she had to do – but it still bothered her. She could sense the sergeant's shock as the link grew stronger, a mingled surge of emotions blasting out at her. He hadn't particularly liked her, she noted. She tried not to take it personally. A man who'd spent most of his life struggling for even the slightest shred of respect wouldn't be happy if someone waltzed in and *took* it.

The memories grew stronger as she hunted for the link to the entity. She could *sense* the taint crawling through the sergeant, steadily overshadowing him … she had a hint, all of a sudden, of a moon steadily eclipsing the sun. His inner landscape was shading to black … she pushed the morbid thought aside as she followed his memories, sensing the link that led straight to his new master. The thought felt wrong, badly so. The sergeant knew he'd been manipulated into surrendering his soul.

"Help me," he said. "Please."

"Don't speak," Isabella said. She couldn't tell if he was

verbalising his words or not. Direct mental contact had never been her forte. She'd feared the loss of privacy too much, even if she was supposed to be in control. "Think at me."

She gritted her teeth. The sergeant was drowning ... and threatening to drag her down into the mud, too. She reminded herself that whatever she saw, on the astral plane, wasn't entirely real. No matter what it looked like, it only had as much power as she gave it. But ... the sergeant was dying, his soul steadily being absorbed into the entity. The thought seemed to spur her towards the link. She could *feel* the entity looking back at her. And, beyond it, King Forsyth. The unwilling host was crying helplessly.

I'm sorry, Isabella thought. *But I have to kill you.*

The sergeant held himself together, barely, as Isabella formed a link and started to draw magic from both Silverdale and Alden. It was hard, so hard, to hold the link together and direct the power towards the entity. She wasn't even sure it would *work*. The entity was pinned to the mortal realm by King Forsyth, held firmly in place ... changing the rules around it might kill the creature or it might not. Isabella wasn't sure. It was quite possible she'd kill the sergeant, while the entity itself went free.

"Kill me," Sergeant Ashworth said. Or thought. "Kill me. Free me."

Isabella nodded, silently thanking the other man for his service even as she nearly drowned in a tidal wave of emotion. The sergeant thought he'd been ... broken. He thought there was no way to recover from what he'd become. Isabella tried to argue otherwise, but the emotions were just too strong. The sergeant thought he'd been defiled forever. There was no point in disagreeing. Instead, she drew on his will – what remained of it – and stabbed power deep into the entity's very soul.

And it screamed.

***

Reginald felt sweat trickling down his back as he parried a blow that would have cut him in half, then stepped back to avoid a second thrust from the entity's blade. It fought in a manner that made little sense, seemingly impossible to predict. Reginald couldn't help feeling it was a strange mix of drunken flailing and skill that matched, if not exceeded, his own. His old swordmaster would have beaten him with the flat of a blade, if he didn't *accidentally* cut off an arm, if he'd tried to fight like a drunken master. And yet, he had to admit it was working. The entity was keeping him off balance with ease.

He leaned forward, aiming a thrust at the entity's throat. It darted back, somehow remaining upright despite a set of clumsy movements, then slashed back at him. Reginald had no time to dodge. He had to parry the blow, the force of the impact sending pains shooting through his hand and up his arm. It was all he could do to keep hold of his sword as the pain grew worse. The entity seemed to smile as it glided forward again.

Reginald straightened, then moved around the entity. Wearing armour might have been a mistake. It was just slowing him down, making him tired ... he swallowed, hard, as he parried another blow. The entity was showing off ... in a normal fight, trying something as stupid as that would end in broken bones if not outright death. It was the sort of trick idiot boys tried before they learnt better. But the entity made it work. Somehow.

Not this time, Reginald thought.

He thrust himself forward, raining blows on the entity's blade. Sparks flashed as it blocked every blow. It was hard to be sure, but it felt as though the entity was laughing. The glow was getting brighter and brighter ...

... And then the entity screamed.

***

Isabella recoiled at the sound, feeling the sergeant's mind – his much-abused mind – snap completely under the pressure. She tasted madness raging through him, an insanity that was completely beyond her comprehension. The entity's anger had effectively killed him ... she had to fight, twisting the astral plane around herself, as the sergeant's soul evaporated. But the link remained intact.

She focused, feeding enough of the power into the sergeant's body to keep it alive even as she continued to poison the entity. No one knew what would happen if one used blood from a mindless body, but ... they didn't have time to figure it out. The link was fracturing, breaking under the strain. She needed to reach out and forge her own link to the entity, but she didn't dare. She *knew* it would lead to her death. Or worse. And yet, she was caught between two fires.

"Hold the link in place," she ordered. Silverdale – bless her – was reshaping the astral realm around them, while Alden kept feeding her power. "Don't let it go."

The entity howled as they held it in place and directed magic into the core of its being. It was thrashing about – she saw glimpses of Reginald, as if she was looking through its eyes – utterly unable to focus or do anything. And yet … somehow, it was warding off her husband. Isabella didn't understand it …

Shit, she thought. The entity was bound to a human form. King Forsyth wasn't overshadowed so much as he was a host. And the entity was using him to survive. *I* …

The entity's sword slashed the sergeant's head off. His body collapsed, ice spreading through its veins. Isabella knew, beyond a shadow of a doubt, that it had won. The link was already breaking up, now the sergeant's mind was gone. It would collapse completely once his body was dead, throwing her back into her own body or turning her into a ghost. She could sense the vultures already gathering, inhuman creatures lurking within the astral plane waiting for her … the cold grew worse, seeping into her. She was about to die.

It struck her, then, that she could win. She could take herself into the Godly Realm, burning with magic, and impose her own rules on the entity. Its form would shatter as easily as her spells, back when they'd first encountered the entities. She could kill it, at the cost of her life … at the cost of her child's life. She knew she had to do it, to save her husband and his entire kingdom, and yet she couldn't bring herself to kill her son. And she would, if she threw herself into the Godly Realm like a stone from a catapult …

Power surged through her. She saw Alden, glowing with light; Alden, as – perhaps – he wanted to be seen. Her brother looked like … his own man as he flew through her mind and up the link. The entity recoiled, too late. Isabella grabbed hold of its fabric, heedless of the risk, and held it in place. The touch burned her soul, but she held on as her brother slammed into the entity and exploded. The world crumbled around her, the rules that allowed the entity to exist no longer effective … it winked out of existence, just like a candle. Isabella had no time to watch. She threw herself back into her own body, just in time. Behind her, the astral plane burned with the entity's death throes. She knew, all too well, that its worshippers were dying, too.

Her eyes snapped open. Alden – Alden's dead body – was smiling. She stared down at their joined hands. He'd given his life for her. He'd thrown himself into the fire for her. For her and for her child, the last of the family … she swallowed, feeling a lump in her throat as she pulled her hands free. Alden had failed her, right up until the moment he'd given his life for her. She wished, suddenly, that they'd had more time together.

"Isabella?" Silverdale was bleeding, blood streaming from her eyes and nose. "Did we win?"

"I think so," Isabella said. Her vision was blurring. It struck her, as she started to collapse, that she was bleeding, too. "I think …"

"It's still there," Silverdale said. "The Godly Realm is still there!"

Isabella barely heard her. The darkness reached out for her …

***

The golden glow faded, but didn't vanish entirely as the entity slashed its sword through Sergeant Ashworth's neck. Reginald felt a flicker of guilt at the sergeant's death, then concentrated on fighting as the entity resumed the offensive. The glow was changing, becoming something else. He could feel the world shifting around the creature as it stood straighter, as if …

He had a moment of awareness, an instant before the entity attacked again. It was no longer moving like a drunken master, but a puppet whose strings had been taken by someone else … someone deadlier. Reginald felt the ground shift under his feet and knew, deep inside, that the first entity was dead. It hadn't slowed the overshadowed king for more than a few seconds, if that. He gritted his teeth, hacking away at the entity's arms and legs. Whoever was in charge, now, wasn't anything like as powerful but made up for it in skill. Reginald would have laughed, if the entire world wasn't at stake. Who'd have thought that killing the entity that had burned at least two cities to the ground would have made things worse?

Hold out, he told himself, savagely. *Hold out and wait for your chance.*

***

Silverdale had seen ladies of the court pretending to faint before, normally to draw attention to themselves. It had never failed to irritate her, if only because she *knew* they were faking. She'd even gotten in trouble, once, for poking a woman who'd pretended to faint … she gritted her teeth at the memory as she stood and hurried to Isabella's side. Her sister-in-law had *really* fainted. Blood was streaming from her eyes. Silverdale wasn't sure what to do.

She shouted for help, but there was no answer. The guards outside had strict orders not to enter or intervene, whatever they heard inside. Alden … she knew, without looking, that he was dead. He'd died bravely … Silverdale had picked up enough to know Isabella was of two minds about her brother, but he'd died bravely. There would be time enough to cremate his body, bury the ashes and remember him later.

Panic flickered through her as the Godly Realm continued its advance, brushing against the walls. They suddenly looked insubstantial … her heart quailed at the sheer power hammering against her mind. It wasn't *fair*. They'd killed the entity controlling the king. They should have won, not opened the gate for further invasions. They should have won! She checked Isabella could breathe safely, then sat back and threw her mind back into the astral plane. The entities were opening the chink wider through sheer force of will …

They still have their link to the king, Silverdale thought. *And they're using it to drag our world into their realm.*

She forced herself to leave her body and fly towards the king. He stood at the centre of the storm, his mind frozen in the astral plane. It was a little like when Isabella had been held prisoner, she thought, but more complex. His body was back in the human world, fighting Reginald to a standstill.

And his eyes were damned and suffering. He wasn't a prisoner in the sense he was held in a prison, one in the centre of his mind. He was a prisoner who'd been hollowed out and turned into a puppet.

Memories brushed against her as she closed on him. He'd been the third son. He hadn't been expected to inherit. He hadn't even been prepared for the throne, for fear the training would give him ideas. Silverdale wondered, suddenly, what would have happened if she'd had a second brother. Would he have been prepared for the throne or quietly marginalised to prevent him challenging Reginald? And then, Forsyth had become the king anyway. He hadn't been remotely ready for the task.

Silverdale's heart went out to him. He had to be at least six years older than she was, but his astral self was no older. He was a boy wearing adult clothes, clothes that were too big for him. He looked pathetic and weak and helpless, the kind of boy who'd be mocked by peers and grown adults alike. Silverdale remembered Sofia, as she pressed her lips against King Forsyth's ears. Her older sister had been a maelstrom of bitter resentments, too. She knew, without having to ask, precisely what the entities had offered. The dream of being strong had seduced far weaker men.

He jumped as she whispered in his ear. "Is this what you want?"

His head turned. He was young … suddenly younger than her, a boy who didn't understand the way of the world, who didn't understand what he'd done that was so bad. Silverdale winced, unable to keep from understanding. The entity had taken King Forsyth's soul and opened it up, somehow allowing the other entities to control him even after the first entity had died. And now …

"Let me go," King Forsyth whispered. "This isn't what I wanted."

"Then retake your body," Silverdale said. She touched his hand, allowing some of her memories to flow into his mind. She thought it would work. "Hold still."

The king smiled at her, then vanished.

***

Reginald cursed as he blocked another stroke that nearly cut him in two. He was running out of room, the ground turning to a swamp beneath his feet. The entities were no longer playing fair. Perhaps they'd realised *he* wasn't playing fair. Perhaps they'd just decided they didn't need to follow the rules any longer. Why not? They could use the astral plane to rewrite the rules on a massive scale. Anything humans could do, they could do too.

The glow vanished. He found himself staring at a man only a few years younger than himself, a man silently begging for death. Reginald hesitated, suddenly unwilling to strike with cold iron. King Forsyth might have been an innocent victim, just like Sergeant Ashworth …

He winced as the glow started to return, then slipped forward and sliced his blade through King Forsyth's neck. The glow vanished again, a faint smile covering the king's face as his head hit the muddy ground. Reginald felt the air clear, as if an oppressive presence had suddenly vanished. He heard the crowd cheering behind him, cheering for their king … cheering for the winner. He had no illusions. They would have cheered for whoever won, but – for the moment – it lifted his heart. He clung to the feeling as he turned and left the field.

"Have the bodies collected and buried, with all the honours of war," he ordered. Sir Alaric would do as he was told, or else. "And then dispatch patrols to the east."

He ignored the cheers as he walked across the bridge and headed for the gatehouse. His wife was in there, along with his sister and brother-in-law … he pushed open the door and stepped inside. Silverdale was crying. Alden was dead. Isabella was bleeding, but breathing. Her eyes opened as he peered down at her.

"It's over," Reginald said. The entity was dead. Its army would be broken – or dead. It was a shame he didn't have the manpower to boot the enemy out of the nearby kingdoms, but he was fairly sure their inhabitants would do it for him. Zycrest and Halladale were probably already on the brink of civil war. "We won."

"Not quite." Isabella struggled to her feet, leaning against him as if she'd aged in the last few hours. "We have to get back to Havelock. And there … we can *really* put an end to it."

Chapter Forty

Isabella felt as if she'd been beaten to within an inch of her life, then held prisoner in a cell that had been carefully designed to ensure the captive didn't manage to get so much as a moment of sleep. She wanted, needed, to close her eyes and rest, but too much had happened over the last few hours for her to take the chance. The entities knew they'd taken a pounding. They knew their chosen servant had been defeated, that one of the most powerful amongst them had been killed. It would take some time, even in a timeless realm, before they got over the shock and pushed back.

Silverdale and Reginald had offered to accompany her, as she made her way down the stairs and into the dungeons, but she'd declined. The risk was just too high. Reginald would be needed to run the country – it was going to be one hell of a headache if the aristocrats decided to take his abdication seriously, particularly if Isabella and their unborn child didn't return – and Silverdale knew how to manipulate the astral plane. And besides, Isabella wanted – needed – to be alone. It would be harder to negotiate with an audience.

She felt her heart start to pound as she opened the outer door and stepped inside. The inner door was still locked and bolted, but she checked it carefully just to be sure. There was no telling *what* Mother Lembu might have tried in the last two weeks, no guarantee she wouldn't have found a chink in the defences that she could widen into a crack and then a gaping hole. It still puzzled her that the entity couldn't simply change her form ... although, she supposed, it didn't matter. The prison didn't have to be literally airtight to be symbolically airtight. It just had to *feel* like a prison.

Isabella stood outside the door, bracing herself, then opened it. The air inside felt stale, a grim reminder that the entity didn't need to breathe. A faint glow, with no visible source, illuminated the chamber. Mother Lembu stood inside the cage, her shadowed eyes bowed in mourning. She knew,

Isabella was sure, what had happened to her fellows. Isabella tried not to feel too sorry for her. She had tried to seduce Isabella into opening her heart and surrendering ...

"We have to talk," Isabella said. "I think you know what I've come to say."

Mother Lembu raised her head. "Nothing may be known ..."

"Until it is spoken," Isabella finished. "I think we should talk as equals, don't you?"

The entity smiled. "We are not equals."

Isabella shrugged. "A long time ago, our worlds met. The result was utter disaster for both worlds. You shaped us, and in turn we shaped you. We became dependent on you and you became addicted to us. It may be wrapped up in myth and ritual and religion, we may see you as gods and you see us as worshippers, but that's what it really is. A mutual dependency that is bad for both of us."

"You gain much from us," Mother Lembu said. "We gain much from you."

"At a price," Isabella said. "We surrender our free will to you. You are reshaped – you reshape yourself – to suit our needs. Our desire for gods that are really nothing more than bigger humans, for genies who'll grant our wishes without twisting them."

"You hardly need *us* to twist your wishes," Mother Lembu observed. "You do that very well without our help."

Isabella conceded the point with a nod. "The empire banished you because it knew you were just too dangerous," she said. "We forgot you. You, creatures from a timeless world, never forgot us. Eventually, the empire crumbled and you started to make your way back into the human world. The results have been disastrous."

"Quite." Mother Lembu looked bored. "Is there a point to this history lesson?"

"We know how to hurt you," Isabella said. "We know how to poison the worship you demand from your followers, forcing you to either die or withdraw in agony. We know how to impose our rules on you, when you're in our world, and we know how to reach into your world and turn it into a weapon. We no longer have an emperor who speaks for all of us, who can drive you away, but we can destroy you."

"There are untold millions of us," Mother Lembu said. "Do you believe you can kill us all?"

"Yes." Isabella put as much conviction into her voice as she could. "But it won't be necessary. You see, too much … awareness … of you has leaked out already. People are praying to you, asking for favours in exchange for worship. We cannot stop it all. The empire had power and reach that far exceeds ours and yet the empire couldn't completely erase knowledge of you. Given that our minds reach onto the astral plane, there's simply no way to do it."

"We will meet in dreams," Mother Lembu said.

"We'll let you have your small cults and worshippers," Isabella said. "You can offer them small miracles, if you like. But we won't let you get established on a bigger scale. Not again. If you do, we'll kill the entities responsible. Respect our limits and we'll let you draw a little worship, from those who wish to offer it. Try to go beyond it and we'll crush you."

"We are eternal," Mother Lembu said.

"And yet, you have no real perception of time," Isabella said. "It isn't *just* magic that poisons you. It's time."

She took a breath. "Go back to your people. Go back to your … father. Tell him what I've told you. Tell him what the rules are. Tell him … if he wants to live, to enforce the rules on his people. And tell him that, this time, we will not forget."

Mother Lembu smiled. "You've grown up."

"We know what the rules are," Isabella said. "You see, you limited yourself when you reshaped yourself. You have been warped to the point where you can no longer be sure who's really in charge. We've moved beyond you. We can use all three realms to develop ourselves. If we have to, we can destroy you."

She opened the cage. "Go."

Mother Lembu looked at her for a long moment. "Take care of your child," she said. "He will have a very special destiny."

Isabella blinked. Mother Lembu was gone.

She stared at the cage for a long moment. She wasn't *entirely* sure they could stop the entities, let alone destroy them, if they came back. She was all too aware there would be others, hundreds of others, who'd risk playing with fire if it meant getting a little more power for themselves. And ... she shook her head, her fingers brushing against her abdomen. Her child ... she shivered, despite herself. A special destiny ...?

It's time to go, she thought.

She left, not looking back.

***

Reginald stood in the crypt, looking at the two new inscriptions that had been added to the wall. Alden of House Majuro wouldn't raise eyebrows, if anyone saw it, but Sergeant Theodore Ashworth definitely would. Sir Alaric and his men had already held a wake, toasting the sergeant and then forgetting him as they drowned their sorrows in beer. Reginald hoped, as he studied the single line of carved text, that the sergeant would be remembered by more than just him and his family. He'd deserved better.

"I'll be studying magic," Silverdale said, breaking into his thoughts. She was still wearing trousers. "*Someone* is going to have to monitor the astral plane."

"Just be careful." Reginald knew there was no point in arguing. Silverdale was too much like him. Stubborn, determined, all the more likely to want something if she thought she'd be denied it. "And make sure you follow Isabella's instructions."

"That'll be a first." Isabella stepped into the vault, looking tired and worn. "She's fond of making up her own mind."

Silverdale flushed. "I am not!"

"Yes, you are," Reginald said. He ruffled his sister's hair, then pointed at the door. "You'd better get ready for the big party."

"I thought I'd go as I am," Silverdale said. She stuck a determined pose. "I'm dressed just like the queen!"

Reginald smirked. "That should make for some interesting arguments," he said. "But now ..."

Silverdale curtseyed, then hurried out. Reginald felt cold, knowing he'd failed her. His sister was not supposed to be exposed to danger, let alone forced to help kill a god. And now she was a changed person, unwilling to let anyone control her any longer. Reginald pitied her future husband.

He also feared, unwillingly, that she might never marry. Her reputation was already souring.

She'll always have me in her corner, he thought. *And the rest of the family.*

He grinned at his wife, then sobered. "How did it go?"

"I gave her the message," Isabella said. "And she'll take it back to the Godly Realm."

Reginald nodded. The entities *had* taken a bloody nose. Their overshadowed servants had died when their master had been killed. The remnants of their armies had scattered, fleeing into the countryside or running back to Zycrest and Halladale. He'd read reports that suggested the kingdoms were already starting civil wars, as the surviving noblemen fought over who was going to take the throne. His lips quirked. If his army had been bigger, if he hadn't had too many problems at home, he might have been tempted to try his chances. The locals would probably have welcomed him as a liberator.

He dismissed the thought with a flicker of irritation. He had to secure his throne. He had to send troops to the Summer Isle, to remind the local lords that they'd sworn themselves to him. He had to raise and train a new army, before one of his neighbours looked at his weakened borders and started thinking greedy thoughts. And he had to repair the damage the invasion had done to his kingdom. An entire city and countless towns and villages needed to be rebuilt from scratch …

And we don't know if the entities will listen, he thought. *They may continue the war.*

"We'll see," he said. "Are *you* ready?"

"We can start training magicians and cunning folk soon," Isabella said. "By the time this one is born" – she touched her abdomen – "we should have the basics laid down."

"And we'll be well on our way to establishing a magic school of our own," Reginald agreed, as he took her arm. "I wish we had more tutors."

"So do I," Isabella said. She hesitated. "Mother Lembu said, before she left, that our son would have a destiny. A special destiny."

Our son, Reginald thought. It was a relief, despite the near-certainty that any daughter they had would have magic.

The lords would have hesitated to follow a girl … damn them. *Our son will be great …*

He looked at his wife. "Whatever it is," he said, "we'll deal with it."

"Yes," Isabella agreed. "We will."

And they walked out of the crypt, leaving the past behind.

The End

Elsewhen Press

delivering outstanding new talents in speculative fiction

Visit the Elsewhen Press website at elsewhen.press for the latest information on all of our titles, authors and events; to read our blog; find out where to buy our books and ebooks; or to place an order.

Sign up for the Elsewhen Press InFlight Newsletter at elsewhen.press/newsletter

Christopher G. Nuttall's Royal Sorceress series

Book I: The Royal Sorceress

In an alternate history, the principles of magic, discovered in the 1770s, saw Britain win the American War of Independence. Master Thomas, the King's aged Royal Sorcerer, needs a successor with mastery of all magical powers. The only candidate, untrained & unacknowledged, is perfect in every way but one: the Royal College of Sorcerers has never admitted a girl before.

But even before Lady Gwendolyn Crichton can begin her training, London is plunged into chaos by a campaign of terrorist attacks co-ordinated by Jack, a powerful and rebellious magician.

ISBN: 9781908168184 (epub, kindle) / 9781908168085 (400pp, paperback)

Book II: The Great Game

After the uprising in London, Lady Gwendolyn Crichton is settling into her new position as Royal Sorceress and fighting the prejudice against her gender and age that seeks to prevent her from fulfilling her responsibilities. But when a senior magician is murdered in a locked room and Gwen is charged with finding the culprit, her inquiries lead her into a web of intrigue that combines international politics, widespread aristocratic blackmail, gambling dens and personal vendettas... and some of her discoveries hit dangerously close to home.

ISBN: 9781908168375 (epub, kindle) / 9781908168276 (400pp, paperback)

Book III: Necropolis

The British Empire is teetering on the brink of a war with France that may, for the first time, see magicians in the ranks on both sides. As Royal Sorceress, Gwen will be responsible for the Empire's magical resources when the time comes. But her adopted daughter Olivia, the only known living necromancer, has been kidnapped. Intelligence soon establishes that it was Russian agents who took Olivia, so an incognito Gwen joins a British diplomatic mission to St Petersburg.

ISBN: 9781908168726 (epub, kindle) / 9781908168627 (416pp, paperback)

Book IV: Sons of Liberty

War! South East England has been invaded, and Gwen and the Royal Sorcerers Corps are helping to fight off French magicians and drive the invaders back into the Channel. When an inexperienced major disobeys orders, sending two hundred hussars to their deaths, Gwen compels him to sit down and shut up but, in doing so, permanently damages his mind. Afterwards Lord Mycroft suggests she needs to be less prominent for a while. The colonies are also under attack, so he sends her to New York to train the few locals with any magical talent. She sets off on HMS Duke of India, along with Irene Adler and Irene's new apprentice Raechel Slater-Standish, accompanying a naval squadron and a regiment being sent to reinforce colonial defences. But even before they reach New York they meet armed opposition.

ISBN: 9781908168986 (epub, kindle) / 9781908168887 (416pp, paperback)

Visit bit.ly/RoyalSorceress

Now available as audiobooks from Tantor

The Magic Fix

Mark Montanaro

The Known World needs a fix or things could get very ugly (even uglier than an Ogre!)

"Did we win the battle?" asked King Wyndham.
"Well it depends how you define winning," answered Longfield, one of the King's royal commanders.

In fact, the Humans are fighting a losing battle with the Trolls. Meanwhile the Ogres are up to something, which probably isn't good. Could one flying unicorn bring about peace in the Known World? No, obviously not.

But maybe a group of rebels have the answer. Or perhaps the answer lies with a young Pixie with one remarkable gift. Does the Elvish Oracle have the answer? Who knows? And, even if she did, would anyone understand her cryptic answers (we all know what Oracles are like!)

The Known World is in danger of being rent in twain, and twain-rending is never good!

Did I mention the dragon? No? Ah... well... there's also a dragon.

ISBN: 9781911409731 (epub, kindle) / ISBN: 9781911409632 (240pp paperback)

Visit bit.ly/TheMagicFix

As Ants to the Gods

Alex Burcher

If they found and destroyed the Scroll they would bring down all civilisation. Would the sacrifice of one man's life save humanity?

Five years after the Great Fire of Lundun, ex-dragoon Laqua is lured into helping the *Keepers of the Light*, a covert band fighting the equally clandestine *Cult of the Death of Hope*. The Cult would bring down the empire of the Moors and, indeed, all civilisation. An empire that has conquered most of Europe, where the language is Arabic and the flag of the falcate moon flies. Where alcohol is banned and hashish legal, prison is unknown and punishment by whip, knife or hook. A world in which the Industrial Revolution is already well advanced and steam engines chug. Where the Norse have settled the New World first. In Lundun, capital of the Tin Isles, the largest mosque looms over St Pauls Cathedral. And Samuel Peppin has given up his diaries to write bawdy poems.

Vital to defeating the Cult is an ancient secret Scroll, the final chapter of the sacred Script, its authenticity assured by the Seal. While the Cult would destroy it, the Keepers intend its dissemination to all. Until they have the means to do so, Laqua is charged with its safekeeping. He falls in with a dour eunuch, a functionary of the Court of the Amir in Qurtuba, and a perfidious, possibly drug-addled, heretic. And what part might a libidinous Norsewoman play? Ahead of him lie spying, fighting, loving, torture and tragedy … and the discovery of a hideous truth.

As Ants to the Gods is an alternate history adventure that challenges some of the orthodoxies and assumptions of Western culture. For adults only, certainly not for the faint-hearted or easily shocked, it is a ribald and irreverent exploration of a world that could have been.

ISBN: 9781911409724 (epub, kindle) / ISBN: 9781911409625 (520pp paperback)

Visit bit.ly/AsAntsToTheGods

About the author

Christopher G. Nuttall has been planning fantasy and sci-fi books since he learnt to read. Born and raised in Edinburgh, Chris created an alternate history website and eventually graduated to writing full-sized novels. Studying history independently allowed him to develop worlds that hung together and provided a base for storytelling. After graduating from university, Chris started writing full-time. As an indie author he has self-published a number of novels, but this is his twelfth fantasy to be published by Elsewhen Press. *The Truthful Lie* concludes the story of Isabella and Reginald in *The Unwritten Words*, set in the world of his bestselling *Bookworm* series. Chris is currently living in Edinburgh with his wife, muse, and critic Aisha and their two sons.

www.ingramcontent.com/pod-product-compliance
Lightning Source LLC
Chambersburg PA
CBHW062014190726
48285CB00001BA/281